PENGU

A WORLD OI

Nadine Gordimer was born and lives in South Africa. She has written seven collections of short stories and eight novels, of which *The Soft Voice of the Serpent*, *A Guest of Honour*, *Livingstone's Companions*, *The Conservationist*, *The Late Bourgeois World*, *Burger's Daughter*, *July's People*, *No Place Like: Selected Stories*, *A Soldier's Embrace* and her most recent novel, *A Sport of Nature*, have been published in Penguin. A further collection, *Six Feet of the Country*, containing stories from *A Soldier's Embrace* and *No Place Like*, has also been published in Penguin. Among the literary prizes she has received are the Booker Prize and the French international award, the Grand Aigle d'Or. She was awarded the Scottish Arts Council's Neil Gunn Fellowship for 1981.

A World of Strangers

NADINE GORDIMER

PENGUIN BOOKS

PENGUIN BOOKS

Published by the Penguin Group
27 Wrights Lane, London w8 5TZ, England
Viking Penguin Inc., 40 West 23rd Street, New York, New York 10010, USA
Penguin Books Australia Ltd, Ringwood, Victoria, Australia
Penguin Books Canada Ltd, 2801 John Street, Markham, Ontario, Canada L3R 1B4
Penguin Books (NZ) Ltd, 182–190 Wairau Road, Auckland 10, New Zealand

Penguin Books Ltd, Registered Offices: Harmondsworth, Middlesex, England

First published 1958
Reissued by Jonathan Cape Ltd 1976
Published in Penguin Books 1962
7 9 10 8

Made and printed in Great Britain by
Hazell Watson & Viney Limited
Member of BPCC plc
Aylesbury, Bucks, England
Set in Monotype Baskerville

'I want the strong air of the most profound night
to remove flowers and letters from the arch where you sleep,
and a black boy to announce to the gold-minded whites
the arrival of the reign of the ear of corn.'

FEDERICO GARCÍA LORCA

ACKNOWLEDGEMENTS

The quotation on page 5 comes from *Selected Poems* by Federico García Lorca translated by Stephen Spender and J. L. Gili (Hogarth Press, 1943). The lines of Rilke quoted on page 74 are taken from 'Autumn' in *Selected Poems of Rainer Maria Rilke*, translated by J. B. Leishman (Hogarth Press, 1941).

I HATE the faces of peasants.

I thought that the day the ship anchored at Mombasa, and I saw the Africans for the first time. The whole quayside was alive with them, their faces turned up momentarily from labour as we came in. In the quiet that followed the cessation of the ship's engines, I saw them clearly. Heavy, mild, and brutish faces, on which emotion settles momentarily, from the outside, like a fly on the face of an ox, and is flicked away as a fly is flicked away, by an involuntary twitch that is nothing more conscious than the reaction of a muscle. I hated them in England, those faces in country lanes, red and smiling at nothing. These down among the crates on the quay shone black instead of red under the sweat, that was all, and the bloodshot eyes were brown instead of that bright vacant blue, appropriately the colour of blankness, space.

What happens to faces like these if, finally, goaded and pricked as slow beasts must be before anger rises through their turgid patience, they are roused? I could not imagine. I only knew the sharp, jowled, curved, and jutted faces of those shaped by books and doubts and ambitions, which, in anger, take on the splendid horror of Notre-Dame gargoyles. And the only Africans I had ever met with before were a few students at Oxford, and two writers and a painter in London, and they belonged in the gargoyle class, rather magnificently carved by their struggles to get there.

While I was thinking this, I was sitting in the launch that was taking us from the ship to the shore (our ship was too large to draw right into dock) beside Mrs Turgell and her daughter Rina, responding pleasantly to their exclamations at the beauty of the palm-trees. 'The *greenness*! Can you *believe* it? It makes you thirsty!' Mrs Turgell was saying, sitting up very straight like an excited child. And for once her daughter was almost like her, twisting her long young neck this way and that, and crying 'Oh mummy! Do look!' 'Exactly like something out of Somerset Maugham!' said Mrs Turgell, turning to me with that mixture of gaiety and appeal – you felt she so fervently wanted you to experience what she was experiencing that, however romantic and idiotic it might be, she was irresistible. 'Can't you imagine degenerating most marvellously in one of those thatched huts, with a beautiful native girl, a Polynesian or something, with long black hair?' 'Mummy, you ass,' said the daughter, in matter-of-fact reproach, but her mother put out her hand over mine in my lap for a moment, laughing.

Mrs Turgell did not flirt with me although she knew and I knew that I liked her better than her daughter. After all, she liked herself better than her daughter; it was one of those small tacit agreements taken for granted between us in our shipboard friendship, then about a week old. I was not quite – that expression beloved of women – young enough to be her son, because she was probably forty and I was twenty-six, but I was only eight years older than her daughter. I saw them both in the ship's offices at Venice when we were queueing for our embarkation cards, and took a dislike to their familiar high English voices at once. By the time we touched Mombasa they were almost the only people on the ship with whom I had anything like a close acquaintance. I had made up my mind that they would not speak to anyone but the ship's officers and the few Italians on whom I heard them flaunt their theatrical Italian, but Mrs Turgell slipped on to the stool beside me at the little bar before lunch one day and fell at once into her amiable chatter, apparently quite ready to overlook the fact that she had recognized me as one of the 'stuffy English' to whom she belonged and about whom she was often amusing as well as disparaging.

We spent the day ashore in Mombasa together, Mrs Turgell, Rina, and I; or rather Stella (as Mrs Turgell insisted I call her) and I were together, alternately losing and finding Rina the way one progresses when in the company of an unleashed puppy. When we got out of the docks, I wanted to get a taxi to take us into the town, but Stella insisted that it would be more fun to walk and 'explore as we go'. ('Explore' was one of the bright schoolgirl words which abounded in Stella's conversation.) We had not gone far up a wide road spattered with shade, fallen flowers, and seed-pods from brilliant trees when Rina disappeared into some sort of warehouse, her badly-fitting green slacks flapping against her long legs, her cheap sandals, bought in Port Said, with pictures of palm-trees painted on them in red and green, slapping against her thin bare feet. She wore a boy's American shirt with a design of film-stars' faces hanging outside the pants, and it was by this garment that her mother, charmingly dressed in some sort of full dress that showed her small pretty figure and bared the delicate flesh of her shoulders and the top of her breasts, recognized her in the gloom of the warehouse.

We went in after the girl and found some other passengers from the ship, the consul and his mother and wife, standing about and prodding at bundles of elephant tusks, tusks of all sizes, hanging from the roof and piled on the floor. With the knowledgeable eagerness with which people love to impart information of which they themselves were ignorant until a few minutes before, Rina and the rest of the little group passed on to us, interrupting and correcting each other, what the attendant of the warehouse had just told them about the prices of elephant tusks. The consul, although he had never before been stationed in Africa – he was on his way to take up an appointment in the Belgian Congo – murmured about the ivory market with the matter-of-fact acceptance of one accustomed to the exotic. He had lived for years in the Balkans and in Turkey, I gathered. 'The poor little things,' said Rina, sliding her sandal over the short curve of a baby elephant's tusk; and I could see that she was going to be another of those English women who can love only animals: the weak, dumb, and dependent.

We all struggled out into the sun again together, an untidy group, undecided about our destination. The consul's wife said nothing but looked eloquently, and I guessed that she must have timidly expressed a wish aside to Rina in the dim warehouse, because Rina, slopping gawkily along, said,

'Let's find Kalindini Road. That's the place where the shops are where you can buy topaz. Mummy, I want a big oblong topaz for my little finger.' 'They're Indian jewellers, I believe,' said the consul's wife, politely, as if repeating something of no interest to herself. 'Oh and I'd like to find the sandal-makers,' said Stella; and the whole sight-seeing excursion threatened to fizzle out into one of those wearisome foreign shopping expeditions where the men trail around patiently behind the women.

The consul had joined the ship at Port Said. He had all the distinguishing physical characteristics of the ideal upper-middle-class Englishman which I had not. *My* appearance was such a thorough debunking of the wistful popular conception of what my sort of breeding and background ought to produce that it seemed deliberate, the gleeful contrivance of bored genes; though I didn't delude myself with the consolation that by this fact I had escaped the insular Britannic stamp, prime on my rump, as it were. I have brown eyes and brown hair which is not as straight as an Anglo-Saxon's should be, but my large features and too-big head set on my stocky body come straight out of Dickens and nowhere else. (Not one of Dickens's slim Copperfields, but a friend of one of the heroes, one of those staunch friends with large, intelligent dark eyes to make up for their unattractiveness, etc. This was pointed out to me at Oxford, but I confirm it for myself.) The consul was tall – inevitably – sharp-kneed, large-footed, and broad-shouldered, and he had a long patrician face with thick eyebrows over fine grey eyes which looked blue when he was looking at the sea or the sky. He had all his hair and it was straight and grey. He was a Celtic type and I suppose was once dark-haired. His mother was exactly like him (I let the situation rather than biological correctness decide precedent here), almost as tall, every bit as distinguished. They used each other's names all the time, like people in a play: 'Mother, would you like your tea now?' 'Yes, Hugh, I think so.' They never called the wife anything at all: 'Where is she?' 'Down in the cabin, I suppose.' Sometimes when the consul was forced, as he seemed to feel himself to be, to answer for her in her presence, he referred to her as 'my wife', giving a curiously legal ring to the designation, as a judge might speak of the defendant or the plaintiff. For the first few days, when we were passing through the Red Sea and lived in a spell of heat anyway, as if the world had stopped turning, so that recollection of whom we saw or what we did was dreamlike, she did not appear at all, so far as I knew. Heat or seasickness must have kept her to her cabin. The consul and his mother were alone at meals, and I played bridge with them several times in the air-conditioned card-room, where we sat around numbly like so much refrigerated food, and if our hands touched accidentally, recoiled at the fish-like contact of chilled flesh.

I had no idea of the existence of the wife until, on the first day on which we woke up in the Indian Ocean and the streaming, flapping, gusty life of the monsoon, I was attracted to a remote upper deck by the yapping of a dog, and found that there was indeed, not one dog, but three, housed in special kennels up there. All three were out of their kennels and were fawning in joy over a dumpy, lumpy little woman with tiny features buried in a big, round face. Bunches of curly brown hair, to which some sort of reddish dye gave a bright nimbus, made her face seem even bigger, and even I, who know nothing about the subtleties of women's make-up, could see that there was something very wrong with the way she had applied hers. Her florid cheeks had rounds of another tone of red overlaying them. It was an astonishingly innocent face, in all its coarse crudity. She introduced me to the dogs and squatted, bunched up, on the deck, her arms round the neck and her cheek against the ears of the biggest one, a brown retriever. Like Rina, I supposed, she must be one of those women who love only dogs; but somehow I felt that this was in a different way and for different reasons – the woman hung round that retriever's neck the first day I saw her the way a child communes in silent love with an animal when humans fail him. With her I should say it was not that she could not love anything other than animals, but that animals were all she had to love.

She certainly did look grotesquely out of place beside the consul and his mother. She always wore a great assortment of varied jewellery, as if in nervous confusion, not knowing which piece to choose, and that day in Mombasa, perhaps in honour of the jaunt ashore, she was even more recklessly adorned than usual. A tourist's Egyptian necklace made after the style of the huge fringed bead collars from Tutankhamen's tomb warred with a violently patterned dress, and there was a diamond fox-head with ruby eyes pinned on her bosom, and plastic cornflowers under the gay hair curling round her ear-lobes. In the Indian jeweller's she sidled timidly and excitedly up to her husband and his mother where they stood, very tall and cool and pastel, near the door. In her little plump beringed hand she held cupped, like a drop of rain-water faintly tinged with rust, a large topaz. The consul looked down at her, his hands crossed on the walking-stick held in front of his white tropical suit. His mother held her white parasol similarly at rest. 'Please to remember your *size*,' he said. His voice, like his eyes, was fixed somewhere above the frizz of the reddish head. His wife went back to the counter, carefully keeping her hand level. I don't know whether or not he bought her a topaz, in keeping with her stature or not, because, to my surprise and relief, Stella came up to me at that moment and whispered – 'Let's go. It's a pity to waste the morning haggling in here. I don't suppose they're genuine anyway.'

The shop was full of people from the ship now – they kept coming in, as, in passing, they saw fellow passengers already inside, and soon every woman was fired with the desire to own a topaz. Some were arguing over carats and price, and one man, proud of his ability to deal with 'the natives' of any country, was informing the jeweller that if an expert in Johannesburg pronounced the stones synthetic, he would sue the Indian jeweller. Rina, long hip jutting as she leaned against the counter, was giving her opinion of each purchase in her loudest, highest English voice, and swooping about from group to group. 'What?' she called, looking up over the huddled bargaining heads. 'No, I'm not coming. Mummy, you are frightfully mean! Can't I have even a weeny one? Look at this smoky little thing.' Her mother went over to her and they spoke in the low voices of controlled argument for a moment, but Stella joined me at the door, without her. 'Come. Let's be off,' she said, shortly, because she was angry. But her good manners and the pleasing façade of even temperament she had been taught as a girl immediately gave cover to irritation. She said lightly, 'I wonder what the story is behind the consul and that poor little creature?'

'Well, she is rather awful, isn't she? I mean you feel annoyed at his being so obviously ashamed of her, and at the same time you wouldn't really care to have a wife like that for yourself.'

'Oh she's vulgar, all right,' said Stella. 'But so are *they* in their way – don't you think? – Such official-looking impeccability, such diplomatic immunity from life itself! And that dragonish queenly old lady, with china tea in her veins and venom in her heart, I'm sure. Have you looked at their nostrils, those two? Positively curled back.'

I laughed. 'What's that significant of?'

'I'm always afraid of those nostrils,' she said wisely. Of course, Stella was just the sort of woman to believe in physiognomy and signs and portents, too.

'Oh I do think people are *fascinating*! Don't you?' She was instantly buoyant again at the thought; she paused as we walked, overcome with an urgency of eagerness. I had noticed in her these very real moments of excitement and relief, when as now, by the pronouncement afresh of some commonplace generality, she reaffirmed or rediscovered for herself some concept of life that was important to her and which she sometimes lost or feared to lose.

As I have said, there was something about this woman which made one feel surly if one did not respond, as it was so easy to do, to the mood generated by her enthusiasms, even if one did not happen to share the enthusiasms themselves. I don't think I find people 'fascinating' in quite the way she meant, but, just the same, we talked and laughed in a shared inconsequential lightheartedness all the way in the taxi that took us to Nyali Beach.

She was undressed before I was – I suppose she must have

had her swimming suit on under her dress – and by the time I came out from behind my clump of bushes, clutching the rolled-up bundle of my shirt and trousers, she was already in the pale turquoise, transparent sea. Although (I calculated) she would be of the generation of the Twenties, when girls 'did everything' perhaps even more determinedly than they do now, her demeanour in the water immediately set her apart from the generation of the girls I knew and with whom I had swum at home, or on holidays in Italy or France. She did not swim at all, but floated gently, tamely, and conversationally, close in-shore. She did not wear a bathing cap, and her short, pretty blonde hair, like the make-up on her pretty face, remained perfect. You could see that all her life her body had been carefully shielded from the sun, and in place of the tanned legs and arms and the yellowish-brown necks I was used to associating with women, all her flesh shone pale and pearly under the shallow water and against the swimming suit which was a darker tone of the water colour. It was a remarkably youthful and pretty body (I'm afraid forty seemed old to me, for a woman), though not like a girl's, softer than a young girl's, and I admired it, though oddly enough I didn't find I desired it. I felt sorry I didn't desire it; I supposed I was conditioned for ever to firm-fleshed girls with the limits of carefully-cultivated sunburn imposing a pattern counter to the pattern of their bodies.

I swam about a bit and then floated in the tepid calm with her for nearly an hour. After the dreary wet summer and the cold wet autumn at home – after a whole lifetime of dreary English winters and wet English springs – I was enchanted with the slack, warm beauty of the place. I seemed to feel an actual physical melting, as if some component of my blood that had remained insoluble for twenty-six years of English climate had suddenly, wonderfully, dissolved into free-flowing. I gazed in lazy physical joy at the lovely, smooth-patterned boles of the coconut palms, waving their far-off bouquets of green away above our heads, the water, and the white beach. I lifted an arm out of the water to feel the air, warm as the water. I dug my feet into the clean sand, so soft its substance was soft as the water. The last jagged crystal in my English blood melted away.

But Stella Turgell talked of Italy. Warmth and beauty and physical happiness meant Italy to her, though they might be experienced on a beach on the East Coast of Africa. She and her daughter had just spent nearly two months in Florence, and apparently Stella spent several months of each year somewhere in Italy – in Rome, Perugia, Venice, Garda, and, always, Florence. They did not seem to me to be really rich people, and I wondered what circumstances in their background gave them this freedom. Stella's passion for Italy was nineteenth-century, Byronic – the nearest I can possibly bring it to the present day is to say that when it came to Italy and all things Italian, she saw everything like one of those young girls in Forster's early novels about the English in Italy, girls who marry the libertine sons of dentists in places with names like Poggibonsi, or whose lives are changed irrevocably after being spectator to an Italian quarrel in an Italian square. The Italy of Moravia and the realist films did not exist for her. Her way of talking about Italy embarrassed me, even when we confined ourselves to discussing paintings and churches, though my mood that day when we were floating in the sea was such that nothing could irritate or embarrass me more than mildly.

As she talked I saw that her months in Italy were her life, so far as she was concerned; the rest of her time, spent, apparently, between her mother's home in Devon and her husband's farm in Northern Rhodesia, was impatiently and almost blindly lived through. Her only comment on the stay in Africa to which this voyage which we were sharing was carrying her, was to remark, closing her eyes and wrinkling her nose in pleasure at the breeze: 'Well, six weeks from now, we'll be on our way back. Not this way, of course. West Coast.'

'To Europe?'

'England. But not for long. By April I'll be back at Pensione Bandolini.'

I pictured her, endlessly, timelessly, coming down a hill road in Florence in the sunshine, a parasol open behind her head, pausing to smile at a bambino in the dust, waving her fluttering greeting and calling out in her clear English-voiced Italian to some peasant woman with black eyes, a black-downed lip, and 'character'. The road, the child, the peasant – all were unreal. . . . I said: 'Have you never lived in Africa?'

She said, without opening her eyes, 'Rina was born in Rhodesia. When she was very young, I did.'

I wanted to say – that impossible question, idiotic, irresistible when you are on your way to live in a new country: What is it like? But I was aware that the fact that I was going out to live in Africa, and the fact that she was bound to it in some way, was a bond about which we never spoke; was something she would see that we stepped over or around, conversationally – something accepted and therefore not worth discussing, was it not? – her manner always seemed to imply, passing on rapidly and easily to the enchanting things about us, or left behind in the Mediterranean.

There was a moment of silence, and then she went on, lightly, almost as if I had spoken after all, 'You must have an active and not a contemplative nature, to take Africa. My husband adores it. He rushes about the farm, completely absorbed from morning till night. The people are quite terrible. I shall never forget them. Their awful dinner parties. Awful food. Same people, same food, year after year, simply at this one's house this week, someone else's house the next. Nothing to talk of but crops, female complaints, servants. Ugly, ugly. Nothing but ugliness.'

Suddenly she opened her eyes and drew herself upright, rising out of the water, and, shining, eager, she brought out one of her paralysing generalities again: 'Beauty is *the* most important thing in life, don't you think so?'

When people come out with statements like that, I always feel that I do not know what they are talking about. I flounder before this bold snatching-up out of the half-sensed, dimly-realized things I have only now and then thought I might have touched for a moment. Is this great glittering flashy fish what it was that brushed my hand then and then, rarely? Is that all – this impossible great artefact? I recoil from it. If that's the case, I shan't let my perception wander down *there* again.

I was sure that whatever this woman meant by 'beauty', whatever the word was a cover for, *was* the most important thing in her life. But I could not answer for it for myself, certainly not yet, not then. I said something empty, non-committal, the kind of remark Americans put with glee into the mouths of the English in films. We came out of the water together, and parted to dress.

Just as we were walking back over the sand to where our taxi was waiting under the palms, we saw the long-legged figure of Rina, flying down a path through the bushes toward us. Some people from the ship who had hired a taxi to take a look around had dropped her at the beach. 'Here, darling,' said Stella, throwing her swimming suit to the girl. 'Hop in quickly. It's heavenly.' But Rina would not swim. Stella went back to her dressing-place to fetch a towel she had forgotten, and the girl said, nibbling at a leaf she had in her hand: 'I'm so glad mummy's had such a lovely morning.' I thought, what an odd, patronizing child she is; what queer creatures English girls' schools turn out. (Already I found myself thinking of England and English institutions objectively.)

The taxi took the three of us up to the beach hotel and waited while we had tepid gin slings and a poor lunch. 'Ugh!' Stella made a face, though she laughed: 'The moment you put your foot back here. Anything does.'

The warm gin made me feel benevolent. I even found myself bantering quite pleasantly with Rina. 'We should have found an Indian restaurant in the town,' she said. 'I'd have liked something hot and sharp to eat.'

We decided, anyway, not to risk the hotel coffee, but to go back to town and look for an Arab café. We did not find one, but trailing back in the direction of the docks, we passed a place that looked like an unsuccessful compromise between a continental café and a tea-shop. It was not quite open to the street and not quite enclosed. People sat, raised back from the street, and looked out from behind the briars and scrolls of a wrought iron shopfront which had been put up in place of the customary glass. The consul and his two women were sitting there, and they called down to us. We were burningly thirsty and we went in and sat at an adjjoining table. The consul's party were just finishing lunch, and their coffee looked terrible, so, rather foolishly, at half past two on an afternoon of great heat, I ordered John Collinses for us. The place smelled of grilled steak and the drinks were a long time coming. A big fan went slowly in the middle of the ceiling, cutting up and pushing round shoal after shoal of warm air; it was odd to feel the movement of air past one's face, entirely without the coolness associated with such movement. The place was almost empty and against the imitation log-cabin bar, a tall African waiter in a limp white robe and a red fez slept bolt upright. He wore fancy socks and a shabby version of the sort of pointed-toed patent dancing-shoes I had once seen in my father's cupboard. His was the sweaty monkey-face that I associate with the few new-born babies I've been unable to avoid seeing; the sweat made it interesting by creating planes and highlighting creases that gave it that same innocent ancientness. The consul, who was sitting back with his elbow hooked round one of the iron curlycues on his chair, saw me looking at the man and waved his hand; a hand that, in movement, always looked as if it were giving an order. 'There you are. Can you believe in the Mau Mau, here? We're only three hundred miles from Nairobi, this is Kenya. You couldn't credit it. Pangas and burnings. . . . And look at *that*. Wouldn't want to harm a fly. . . .' As if to prove the consul's point, a fly settled on the sleeping face and crawled up the left cheek from mouth to eye.

The amused bewilderment that must have shown rather stupidly on my face at that moment was not so much a sharing of the consul's incredulity at the sight of the waiter in the face of facts, as a sudden realization about myself. I had spent the day in Mombasa like Sinbad the Sailor, seeking with my northern blood the old voluptuous adventure of warm seas and idleness in the sun. What about all the books I had read before I left England, all those books about Africa I had been reading for the past three or more years?

The bluebooks, the leaflets, the surveys, the studies – the thick ones by professors of anthropology and sociology, the thin ones by economists and agronomists, the sensational ones by journalists? How far away was the scene of the Mau Mau situation in which my circle of friends and family had been so intensely interested, now that I was three hundred miles near to, instead of six thousand miles away from it?

I sat and drank my sweet drink and did not feel even the mildest self-reproach. In fact I felt rather pleased with myself, as if I had been absolved from one suspicion of priggishness, bookishness I had harboured against myself. I simply did not care at all. I had not made any attempt whatever to use the day; I hadn't presented the letter of introduction I'd been given to a prominent government official, I hadn't tried to see for myself anything of African labour conditions, housing, or political emergence. I began to feel overwhelmingly sleepy; I still found the big, wide, lax heat (like being involved in one of creation's enormous yawns) pleasurable, my veins widened, my pores opened to it. The two pretty women (I supposed one must admit that Rina was pretty too, if one considered the small head without its relation to that long body on which it was perched) looked very nearly female, instead of feminine, as if the food and liquor that relaxed their faces and the heat that made their hair cluster damply had melted away, along with the powder, that English cast of beauty – a real cast, in the concrete and not the figurative sense of the word – from which I have suffered all my life; yes, even as a child, even in the face of my mother.

We went back to the ship very content; I noticed that Rina sang softly to herself, like a child, when she felt at peace with the world. The launch was full, and I sat listening to the tired, giggling, or earnest voices, tense with the excitement of shopping, of our fellow passengers.

Once aboard, the Turgells and I retired to our cabins to sleep off the enervation of gin and sun. Before I lay down I saw for a moment in my porthole the round brilliant picture of the shore, a picture like those made up under glass on the tops of silver dressing-table utensils, out of butterfly wings. Glittering blue sky, glittering green palms, glittering blue water. When I stretched on the bunk, the little shelf of books beneath the porthole rose to eye-level. *The Peoples of South Africa*, *The Problems of South Africa*, *Report on South Africa*, *Heart of Africa*. I began to read the titles, the authors, the publishers' imprints, rhythmically and compulsively. Suddenly, I felt the warm turquoise water swinging below me as I kept myself afloat. Sand like the dust of crystals was pouring through my fingers, hairy coco-nuts like some giant's sex, swung far above my head, under the beautiful scimitar fronds of a soaring palm. Sinbad, Sinbad, Sinbad the Sailor.

I woke just after five o'clock and went up on deck. We were moving slowly out of the harbour, that smooth, silent retreat from the land while the ship is borne, not of its own volition, but under tow. Every time we left a port of call there was this strange moment, a moment of silence when here and there a hand lifted along the rail in a half-wave to the unknown figures standing on the shore, like a drooping flag stirring once in a current of air. Then the engines began beating, the ship turned in the strong wash of her own power, and we were no longer merely slipping out of human grasp, away, away, but heading on out to sea and our next objective, toward, toward. It was the time when we turned from the rail, sought each other's company, pulled the chairs up round the small deck-tables, and summoned the bar steward. Stella arrived, freshly dressed and scented, carrying the Italian grammar which she studied assiduously an hour a day, then the consul, in shorts and white stockings which transformed his distinction into something vaguely naval. Soon Mamma followed, with her stiff, Queen Mary gait and her writing materials – she had always just written, or was about to write, letters. Rina, still in those dreadful green trousers that hung down slack where she hadn't enough behind to fill them, came up with Miss Everard, the tall, handsome spinster of fifty who wore a man's watch, and in the evening, magnificent gauze saris. She had been something called 'household adviser' to some Indian prince who, despite Indian democracy and Nehru, seemed to have lived in all the splendour of the old days of independent princely states. She was going to live with her brother in one of the British Protectorates in Africa, and she, too, was a passionate Italophile, scattering her speech with *cara mia*'s. Carlo, the fat partner of the duo of Carlo and Nino, in charge of the little mosaic-decorated bar outside the dining-room, stood back to usher the two ladies before him out on to the deck, but Everard swept him along with them, shrieking at him in aggressively musical Italian over her shoulder. It seemed that all her talking, and she was a vast and enveloping talker, was done over her shoulder. In passing, as it were, she had always the final word. She sat down with us, made herself comfortable, talking away to Carlo all the time, and only interrupted herself to say to us in English, as if the suggestion were absurd: 'I'm not intruding?' Before we could protest, she had ordered drinks for us, in Italian, with many gestures of stirring, of adding a soupçon of something, of putting in plenty of ice, and more terse interjections in English: 'And you? Pink gin? An Americano? With or without bitters?'

Carlo, with his Hallowe'en pumpkin smile, his round amiable eyes, and those little feet in white pointed-toed shoes which supported him almost twenty-four hours a day on such missions, went off to his bar and came back with the specified variety of drinks, perfectly mixed, perfectly chilled, and accompanied by dishes of black and green olives. After the indifferent food, the heat, and the tepid, over-sweet drinks ashore, the sight and taste of his calm handiwork made one regard the big fat smiling man with almost sentimental relief – we were 'home', cherished, attended, indulged. I remarked to the consul, perhaps not-so-un-consciously paraphrasing Stella, that I thought luxury was one of the most important things in life. But he merely smiled, lifting his eyebrows in polite agreement with something he felt he had not heard aright, but which was not important enough to bear a repetition. Of course, he had not lived in England since long before the war; he knew nothing of the world in which I had grown up, where every small service you could afford to buy yourself was given you grudgingly, where, justly, no doubt, but drearily, nevertheless, you often had to retire with your host after dinner, not to the library for port and cigars, but to the kitchen for dish-washing.

The dense green coastline with the masts of coco-nut palms criss-crossed against the sky faded into distance and the radiance of a sunset that seemed to arise, like a halo, from, rather than be reflected in, the sea. But other coastlines, those of islands at all levels near and far in the distance, emerged before and sank away into light behind us, little coastlines with a pearly dip of beach, and the pinkish-mauve haze of pencilled boles, and the dark-green, almost blue, crowns of palm. Our table grew quite gay. The consul ordered another round of drinks and then I did. Rina went into competition with the consul, flipping olive pits into the water. Miss Everard began a long, animated discussion of the day ashore with me in French (she presumed I must speak *something*) to which I replied with equally obstinate animation in English. I absolutely refused to speak to Miss Everard in any language other than English; I had even managed to cultivate a questioning look in my eyes when she trotted out some old Latin tag.

The ship's first officer, a dapper Triestino, more like a Frenchman than Italian in appearance, strolled past and was invited to join us. He was an obvious admirer of Stella, and complimenting her graciously in Italian as he sat beside her, brought a happy blush to her bosom and neck, as if her body had never learned the cultivated decorum of her face. Even the consul's wife, coming bewilderedly and cautiously from the direction of her cabin, outrageously painted and in an 'afternoon' frock, fitted in somehow, and after changing her mind twice about her choice of a drink, settled beside me.

'He seems a lot better since we sailed,' she said to her husband, not noticing that she was interrupting. He shook two olive pits together in his hand and screwed up his face in her direction: 'What is it you say?' 'I said Flopsy's a lot better, dear.'

The consul said with rasping pity, 'My wife's cat appeared

to have some difficulty in digesting his luncheon fish, or whatever-it-was.'

It was clear that he intended the subject to be closed, so far as the general company was concerned, and so she turned to me and said, confidentially, 'It was not fish, it was mince. But not ordinary mince, some spice was in it.'

Was she Welsh, perhaps, I wondered? There was a stiltedness, an absence of elision in her speech which somehow was not English. Stella had suggested that she was an early indiscretion of the consul's, from Turkey, or perhaps the Middle East; an indiscretion with which he found himself saddled, in honour bound, for the rest of his life. Certainly there was something Levantine if not Eastern in her appearance.

The consul grew positively gallant with Stella – the nearest he could ever get toward being flirtatious – and the eyes of old Montecelli, or whatever the first officer's name was, swam bright and bulging as a pekinese's with smiling Mediterranean maleness. Everard (in English, astonishingly) told some really funny stories about her Indian prince and his household. Our laughter and our raised voices had the effect of isolating us rather enviably from the other passengers; they strolled past, or sat apart in their own little groups, like children who pretend not to know that there is a party in the next-door garden. How ridiculously much these trivial things matter in hotels and ships, how they reproduce in miniature the whole human situation, the haves and the have-nots, the chosen and the rejected, the prestige of the successful fight for the female, the singling out of their leader by the herd! All there, on the air-conditioned, safe, and sanitary liner, being worked out in the form of shuffle-board championships, the crossing-the-line ceremony, and the parties made up for the Captain's ball. Psychologists say that the activities of children at play are one long imaginative rehearsal for life; adults, too, never stop muttering the lines and reproducing the cues, even on holiday; even between performances. Though none of these people with whom I sat drinking were people whom I would choose as friends, I was surprised and a little inclined to sneer at myself to find that I enjoyed the warm feeling of being one of the group, of belonging. Long after most of the other passengers had gone down to dress for dinner, we continued to sit on, drinking and laughing and talking noisy nonsense. When at last we rose we were agreed, with rather gin-borne accord and enthusiasm, that we should gather after dinner and make something of a party, so far as we were concerned, of the decorous dancing to the ship's band which took place on those nights on which there was no cinema show.

'I think Hugh has an arrangement for bridge,' said the consul's wife, the only hesitant voice. On dance nights she always put on silver sandals, and then if she was asked to dance blushed a refusal, not liking to deprive other wives or single women of a partner. The consul did not attend dances with her.

But this time the consul, brown knees together, rising elegantly from his chair as Stella, Rina, and Everard rose, said, with a handsome narrowing of his deep eyes, 'Oh I think we might postpone the bridge, just this once.'

Stella, dragging Rina down the corridor which separated our cabins, blew me a mocking kiss as she disappeared, laughing.

I sat at the other end of the dining-room, far away from the Turgells and Miss Everard and the consul's family. While I ate I saw Everard sweep in in green and gold, resplendent as the howdah with the foam-rubber cushions she had described earlier, but I did not catch a glimpse of any of the others. After dinner, in the lounge, the consul beckoned me over to a collection of chairs round two or three small tables he had had prepared for our party. He wore a black tie, but politely ignored my rather rumpled blue suit, too short over the behind, as all my suits seem to be. Mamma was absent, playing bridge, and the wife sat with the expectant face of a girl at her first party and the dreadful clothes of a provincial mayoress at a reception. The band was playing some jaunty old fox-trot from a Fred Astaire film I dimly remembered having been taken to see once with some cousins in the school holidays. One or two couples were hopping mildly round as if they were climbing, counter to the slight tilt of the floor, first this way then that. Everard came in, signalled that she would be with us at once, hung over the backs of the chairs of a group of Italians, declaiming in high-pitched Italian, and then swept out again as if with a sudden recall to purpose. Like the other member of the weather couple, RAIN and SHINE, Rina swept in through the other door and made for us. She wore one of those chiffon dresses, vaguely flowered, vague in cut, vague in fit, which so many of my young female compatriots own, a dress about as becoming, though much less revealing of the lines of the body than a winding-sheet. Round her neck was a thin chain with some weakly blue stone pendent from it. Only the tips of her ears, unexpectedly showing under her brushed-back hair, and unexpectedly adorned with little gold gipsy rings, gave a hint of life.

'I must apologize for mummy,' she said, rather breathless, pausing at the back of the consul's wife's chair a moment before she sat down beside me, dropping a limp beaded bag in her thin lap. 'Fruit cup? How simply lovely.' She lifted the plastic stirrer out of my Pimm cup and licked it. 'She won't be up, I'm afraid. She's gone to bed.' She shrugged her shoulders and her face, as if to say, well, that's that. 'What's wrong with Stella?' I said, amazed.

'Is your mother not well?' The consul's wife leaned forward.

'I say! I am sorry!' said the consul.

'Oh no,' said the girl, with the air of someone in charge of a familiar crisis. 'She's all right. She's not ill. I've ordered a brandy for her. I'll dash down again directly and make her take a sedative. It's Africa,' she added, matter-of-fact. 'First day back in Africa, ashore today.'

'But I thought Stella enjoyed today,' I said. 'She *did* enjoy it.' I remembered the gaiety with which she had scuttled off to dress for the evening, blowing me a kiss from the corridor.

'Just Africa,' the child said wisely, almost bored. 'It's all right. I'll give her a sedative and she'll calm down and it'll be out of her system.' I realized that this old–young girl, this child–parent had made this journey with her mother many times since childhood. She was an old hand at – whatever it was that ailed her mother.

Rina danced with me, and then with the consul, and then excused herself, going serenely out to her charge and reappearing ten minutes later. 'Reading,' she said. 'I've given her her pill.' A little later, the girl disappeared again. This time she said to me on her return, 'Asleep.' There was a Paul Jones in progress and I saw that she was eager to be in it; I led her to the floor, lost her, and went back to my drink. She was obviously enjoying herself; she preferred a dance that was more of a boisterous game than a tête-à-tête contact between a man and a woman.

The evening was not exactly a success. Stella's withdrawal was a betrayal of the mood in which the party had been spontaneously arranged; if the excuse had been one of the conventional ones of sickness, a headache, the commonplace jollity might have survived quite well in spite of her absence, but the uncomfortable oddity of her reason for absence seemed to show up the nature of the jollity for what it was – an alcohol-hearty camaraderie between rather incompatible strangers. Everard brought over two more officers and an amiable, fat Italian girl, and the party became very much her own. The consul excused himself early and went off unrepentant in the direction of the card-room. I was suddenly angry to find myself left with the wife, the frizz-haired, pathetic bore, with her plump silver shoes crossed at the ankle, patiently. Rather abruptly, I left too, going to my cabin by way of the deck.

I lay on my bunk, bored and wakeful. I felt a sickening at them all. A spoilt woman who got ill from the idea that she had put her foot back in Africa again. So that was the reason for the life of romantic, genteel exile in Italy: inability to face the husband, marriage, reality, inability to face even the fact of this inability, so that husband, marriage, reality took the discreet disguise of 'Africa'. Poor devil of a husband, working his farm to foot the bill at the Pensione Bandolini. Even the daughter given the mock-Italian name, the label of escape, 'Rina', and taught to live her life on the move, because the mother could not bear to alight in the one place where she was, conventionally, bound to live.

And the other one, the diplomatic gentleman with his queenly dowager, dragging shamefully from country to country the suffering and insufferable 'mistake' he had made in one of them. Were these the sort of people Africa gets? Christ, poor continent!

Mombasa was our first port of call in Africa.

PART ONE

Chapter 1

My mother sometimes says, with the mixture of polite diffidence and embarrassed culpability with which understanding parents are apt to regard their adult children, that there must be something of my grandfathers in me. The one, my mother's father, was in the Indian Civil Service, and the other, who pre-dated him considerably, was killed in the Boer War. He was a colonel and a hero, and I discovered when I was quite young that my family was ashamed of him. When I was a child, the maternal grandfather was still alive, retired in Bournemouth, and they were ashamed of him, too. My father and mother were of the generation that, after the first World War, turned upon their parents and their heritage even more contemptuously than is usual with each succeeding generation. They felt themselves to be almost a new species. My mother refused to come out, with a presentation at Court and a party of her mother's family house in the Cotswolds; she went to London and took a job as secretary to one of the international peace organizations which flourished hopefully at the time. My father left Oxford before taking Greats and went to Berlin with a young German student to carry a Socialist flag in the Revolution. He married there, too, and so although he and my mother lived together for several years after they met in England, they were not able to marry until he had managed to divorce his first wife – she was a Pole, I think. I barely scraped into legitimacy by being born when my parents had been respectably married for five months. My father edited two or three short-lived literary reviews, translated German and French political writings and some poetry, and although he was in his late thirties at the time, managed to get to Spain, if not exactly into the war, with the Republicans in 1936. He came back safely, but died of kidney disease in 1938. All this time, and, indeed, all through my childhood, we were supported in conventional comfort by his sinecure as a director in the publishing house which was, and is, his mother's family business.

Our flat in Kensington and later our house in the Cotswolds near my maternal grandmother's house – once it had been part of the estate – were places much frequented by victims and their champions. The world of my childhood was the beginning of the world of victims we now know, and each of these victims, like an ox attended by a group of tick-birds, had his attendant champions who, as tick-birds both batten on their ox's misery and relieve him at the same time by eating the vermin on his skin, gave the victim succour and drew from him for themselves a special kind of nourishment. Do I sound sneering? I don't mean to be. But I suppose I got tired of them, as a child and an adolescent; tired of the German refugee professors, and the earnest Christians and passionate Jews who ran the committees to care for them and protest for them, tired of the poets who limped in from their stint in Spain, and the indignant intellectual volubility of the brilliant people who spoke for them; tired of the committee members for the relief of Chinese war orphans, and the organizers of protest meetings in support of Abyssinia, and the saintly or urbane Indians who came to address the English committees for a free India on the best way to defeat the British Raj.

One day, when I was still a small boy, I found the sword that had belonged with my grandfather's dress uniform and thought I would hang it up on the wall in the hall of our flat in London. I was busy assembling nails and hooks and hammer for the job when my mother came in with a friend. 'Darling, what on earth are you doing with that?' She pointed the toe of her shoe at the sword, lying on the carpet. 'It's grandfather's sword; I found it at Grannie's and she said I could have it. We can hang it up here. Won't it look lovely? And look, she gave me this, too – it's the citation about his bravery at Jagersfontein.' Perhaps the friend my mother had with her was the representative of some spirited minority or other – I can't remember who he was – but she obviously found it embarrassing, in a light sort of way (she was laughing, I know), to be confronted with a son who wanted to display his grandfather's citation for Boer War bravery in a home where Imperialism was deplored. 'Look at this,' she said to her companion, pulling a face in mock pompousness, and handing him the framed citation. And then to me, 'Toby, you don't want to hang that thing up there, really, darling . . .' I said to the man, eager to explain, 'Grandfather is buried at this place Jagersfontein. He killed a hell of a lot of Boers, though. He was a colonel.' The two grown-ups roared with laughter. Then my mother said firmly, 'Toby, I will not have that thing hanging here or anywhere. Not the sword. Not the citation. Positively not.'

Because her creed of living included a nervous and almost exaggerated respect for the feelings of her children, she took me aside later and quietly explained that to honour my grandfather's exploits in the Boer War was almost like celebrating a victory for Franco in Spain. She thought this comparison would be the most meaningful for me because of my father. It was, but not in the way she thought. She did not understand a child's uncomplicated personal loyalties. 'But grandfather fought on the English side, daddy was *against* Franco – how do you mean nearly the same?' My poor mother, if only she hadn't taken so seriously her self-imposed task of impressing upon a schoolboy the ethical difference, irrespective of personal ties, between the Wrong Side and the Right Side, she might have realized that my interest in my grandfather was nothing more than the inspiration of the boy's books that she considered suitable reading for me, in which great deeds were done and much face was gained in the name of dead ancestral heroes.

Anyway, the sword and the citation were packed away again, and the war came and there were more and more dispossessed and more and more committees. I was just old enough to get into the end of the war – I was in the Navy, but I never left my training-ship – and when I came back and went to Oxford and then joined my great-uncle, old Faunce (we have ridiculous names in our family; I was lucky to get away with Tobias), in the publishing firm, there was no shortage of injustices to champion, nor has there been, ever since. Of course, by then, I was old enough to take up my own stand in a house where it was considered sinful not to take a stand. I did often find that my interest in the sudden acceleration of the problems of human relationships now that man-ordained barriers of race, creed, class, and colour were breaking up, was as great as that of my mother and Faunce and their set. But I reserved to myself, even in that house, the right not to take a stand if I didn't feel like it. Not to shame myself into indignance if I didn't happen to give a damn. Was this just a rather childish defiance? Perhaps. But I assure you that there was something about Uncle Faunce, banging down his sherry glass beside the sheaf of letters and papers he had brought with him to Sunday lunch, and saying, 'People don't know the facts. We must start a newspaper campaign. Letters. Get Donald to do something for the *Statesman.* And what about Larry? I'll call a public meeting myself ...' that was inclined to cool the adrenalin of partisanship for any issue or person to stagnation in my blood by the time we had reached the stewed pears.

The atmosphere of ideological flux which I had breathed all my life sometimes seemed terrifyingly thin, a rare air in which one must gasp for the want of the oxygen of certainty, of an established way of life. Paradoxically, there had been bred into me a horror of the freedom that is freedom only to be free; I wanted to be free to cling to what I should break from, if I wished. I did not think that a man should have to lose himself, in Gide's sense, in order to find himself. Something in me clung strongly to the need for mediating powers – tradition, religion, perhaps; a world where you might, if you wished, grow up to do what was expected of you. My mother and father gave up a great many small, unworthy things that together, constituted a workable framework of living, but what did they have to offer in their place? Freedom; an empty international plain where a wind turns over torn newspapers printed in languages you don't understand.

So it was that at times like the Sunday I've just described, I found myself settling back into a cold, turgid solidity, not an opposition so much as an obstinacy, immovable, silent, and tight-lipped, that was, I was told, completely exasperating. At these times I assure you that I honestly could feel my responses battening down against the talk; I felt that what I really wanted was to enjoy what was left of the privileged life to which I and my kind have no particular right, and which exists, even in its present reduced condition, much as it was gained, by discrimination and exploitation. I felt, with a kind of irritated relief that I really belonged to that bad old good life which my parents helped push down into a dishonoured grave. At Oxford once, when I was talking like this, a rather drunk friend (I was rather drunk too) said that when I was in that sort of mood what I really inspired in others was a strong desire to kick me in my pompous backside; which pleased me very much.

Since India had been off their conscience, my family and their set had had an overwhelming supply of victims and their champions from Africa. First it was Seretse Khama, then Michael Scott, the Hereros, Nkrumah. Pamphlets about Dr Malan and the new Prime Minister of South Africa, Strijdom, about the Mau Mau, about Belgian colonial policy in the Congo, and self-government in Nigeria, piled up beside my mother's bath, where she liked to do this sort of reading. Journalists, foreign correspondents, and crusading parsons who had been to shake a Christian fist in the face of the godless white oppressors in South Africa, came to dine and tell their tales. All this had had the usual effect on me; had rather put me off Africa.

When Faunce began to talk of sending me to South Africa to relieve Arthur Hollward, who had been the agent there for our firm, Aden Parrot, for fifteen years or so, most of my friends, and my mother, were at once in a flurry of excitement. What an opportunity! Wouldn't I like to be briefed about the situation out there by a Negro doctor from Johannesburg who happened to be giving a series of lectures at a summer school in Kent? Wouldn't I collect data about the housing of Africans for a world convention on housing which would be held in Stockholm next year? Would I look into the situation of the Indian minority? Would I be sure to visit the African College at Lovedale? Would I be willing to send a weekly newsletter on the effects of racial segregation?

I told them all that I would be going to Africa as a publisher's agent, to visit bookshops and promote the sale of books. I didn't want to investigate anything; I didn't want to send newsletters home.

I had no intention of becoming what they saw me as, what they, in their own particular brand of salaciousness, envied me the opportunity to become – a *voyeur* of the world's ills and social perversions. I felt, as I had so often before, a hostility, irritation, and resentment that made me want to shout, ridiculously: I want to live! I want to see people who interest me and amuse me, black, white, or any colour. I want to take care of my own relationships with men and women who come into my life, and let the abstractions of race and politics go hang. I want to live! And to hell with you all!

I lay on the deck and my immediate surroundings made nonsense out of that over-dramatic statement. The sky was so blue that it looked as if it might crack, splinter with the shining intensity of its blueness – rip as the sea did, spilling out seething whiteness where the ship cut through. The sun was blinding as a mirror or a miracle. You could not look upon his face; it was too much pagan glory for a human. Below me was the lido deck, where the water of the swimming pool tilted solidly with the slow roll of the ship, like a slice of green jelly. The children screamed as they cast themselves into the water in their rubber rings. A delicious smell of soup came before my nose and was snatched away by the wind. The men lay like dogs, basking almost naked round the feet of the women. The women wore big hats and dark glasses like a disguise, and you could not tell whether or not they were looking at you. I was barefoot and in swimming-trunks and could feel the sun leaning steadily on my shoulders. I was hungry again (it was only an hour since breakfast) and full of the pleasant consciousness of the desire to stretch my arms and legs.

It was our last day aboard. Early next morning we were

to reach harbour in Durban. Miss Everard had asked for my address in Johannesburg because she wanted to send me a case of pineapples from her brother's estate. Half-an-hour before, I had had a last swim with Rina Turgell and was amazed to notice that, despite her black woollen swim-suit with the school badge, she had a really beautiful body. One could not believe this when one saw her flat-chested and dressed. Had it happened on the voyage?

The chief steward – the light of frenzied creation in his eyes – was busy making swans and dolphins of ice, and neo-classical women out of butter, for the farewell dinner that night.

Chapter 2

I SEEMED to have progressed merely from one unreality to another. Before me, as I sat at dinner, I saw a swan made of ice carried by.

I had been in Johannesburg three days, and was living in what I had discovered must be the biggest tourist hotel in the city. When I woke in the morning I had absolutely no idea where I was. The room was designed to give you no clue; it was as anonymous as a prison cell or a ward in a hospital. It was a hotel room, circa 195–, anywhere. The carpet was pale and thick. The curtains were pale and thick. The shiny pale yellow wood of the bedside table had the classic pattern of cigarette burns. (Are there perhaps factories that supply these articles of furniture ready burnt, just as fake antiques are said to be supplied with worm-holes?) In the dining-room, where there were gilded interior balconies which could not be reached because nothing led to them, and the concealed lighting produced the effect of a perpetual stage sun-set, English, Americans and unidentified foreigners sat with the stunned faces of wealthy travellers. The waiters were the usual weary, flat-footed Italians and Germans. Admittedly, the lift operators in their red-and-gold bell-hop outfits had black faces; but with them it seemed to be black-face in the vaudeville, rather than the pigmentation sense. In the marble foyer there were small show-cases of the kind you see at airports, displaying luxuries and curios; one showed a crystal bottle of perfume on a velvet altar, another an embroidered oriental coat, in another there were two crossed assegais before a shield covered with the skin of some animal, and a curious-looking gourd covered with coloured bead-work. A gilt card behind the glass announced that these last were obtainable at so-and-so's, the house for genuine native crafts and African curios. I would hand the key of my room to the receptionist, whose hair was like a small helmet of tarnished brass; she would rake the key toward her across the counter in a hand whose nails were so long that the hand seemed to stand over and trap objects in the manner of a spider, rather than pick them up. And so, I would go out into the city.

The sun had been shining, out there, every day since I arrived. Nothing remarkable about that, I suppose, in this country. The brightness seemed strange to me, not because I'd come from early winter in London, but because I'd just left the coloured twilight of the hotel. It was a surprise to find that morning and noon, a waxing and waning of the day, existed, after that dim timeless light. The slither of feet on concrete came up to meet me from the city pavement; I descended to it from the hotel steps, entered into it, moved off with it. At the corner, where I crossed the street, the traffic lights held back rows of big American cars – black, pomegranate-coloured, turquoise – impatient bicycles, creaking tramcars. Cries, bells, hammerings, shufflings, talk, roaring exhausts, and muttering engines – the sounds generic to a city surrounded me as the sound of the wind in leaves would indicate to me that I was in a forest. The air seemed to strike sparks off the corners of buildings in the sun; the shade was black and hard. There seemed to be a great many more white people than black. Women brushed me, smelling of expensive perfume. Parcels nudged me. A pregnant woman burgeoned toward me; a black man wearing a dust-coat and a cap with the name of a firm in celluloid letters across it swooped to pick up a cigarette someone had dropped, and put it behind his ear. He whistled piercingly as he went along. Three youths with the ends of their stiffly-oiled hair dyed brassy, like the gilded heads of cheap plaster busts, the dwindling silhouette of vast loose jacket and narrow trousers, and the fast soft gait of shoes with soles thick as rubber bathmats, passed with narrowed eyes, as if some purpose held them together. They appeared to be talking, but they were not; two were making with their lips the broken, bubbling half-syllables that babies make, a kind of babbled tune, not quite singing.

The buildings were brand new, taking up quite a lot of, if not quite scraping the sky, or gimcrack, balconies cut out of tin with a fretsaw, plaster plaque proclaiming 'Erected 1911' above a new shopfront obvious as a set of the latest false teeth. The clocks, whether set in the gilded cupolas of the nineteen hundreds, or the skin-thin marble of this year, didn't agree. The plaster mannequins leant toward the street behind concave glass, showing clothes from London and Vienna. There didn't seem to be any trees; but then I had only been in the place almost a matter of hours, and I'd seen scarcely anything beyond the streets between the hotel and Arthur Hollward's office.

Arthur's office (it would be mine, soon, when he went home to England) was less than three short blocks from the hotel and was on the ninth floor of a fairly new building. On the ground floor there were a bookshop, a chemist's, something called 'Adorable' I hadn't yet identified (probably some sort of woman's dress shop – the windows were entirely blanked out with yellow satin draping), a dry cleaner's depot, and a bar. The bar was called the Stratford and had lattice windows of beer-coloured glass with a tudor rose as a central motif. The rest of the façade of the building and the foyer had an anonymous, cinema-splendour; the lift doors – there were two of them – were bronze, the stairs were of veined stone, like a well-ripened cheese, the floor was an abstract mosaic and the whole of the wall opposite the lift was covered with sections of mirror, tinted blue, and secured by crystal knobs. An ante-room of God, if ever there was one. When the lifts came down, it was discovered that one was lined with dirt-streaked padding and had a splintered wooden floor – it was a goods lift – and the other had initials scratched all over its chipped enamel interior; the Gorgonzola stairway gave way, after the first floor, to narrow cement steps; the inner corridors, with their plumbing system running exposed along the greenish walls, were like the intestines of some cold-blooded animal.

Behind his plain varnished door, old Arthur had a small outer office where his typist sat, and where, in addition to her desk and two dingy chairs, there was a stand displaying the latest in the famous series of pocket-books put out by our firm. Arthur's own office led off this room, and the moment I stepped into it for the first time I felt the unremarkable assurance that the rabbit must feel on entering a burrow, or a fox an acrid den: it had the look and smell – new books and dust, typical as the smell of a chemist's – of the offices at Aden Parrot in London. Even the threat of Faunce's presence seemed to be there; perhaps old Arthur created this by what I can only describe as wholesome awe of Faunce. Arthur regarded Faunce as preposterous and delightful; which was like a child being led to give the right answer, for this was just what Faunce, goodness knows how long ago, decided to be. Of course, I'd known Arthur Hollward (or rather he'd known me), through the London office, since I was a schoolboy. He was one of those almost charmless people for whom contact with a person of the enormous charm of Faunce was a ducking in a vivid element which left, so to speak, a rosy tinge in the colourless lesser personality. By quoting Faunce, even by being roused to the warmth of appreciating him so much, Arthur had acquired a mild charm of his own.

Any member of our family had, for Arthur, the aura of Faunce, and he treated me with a mixture of the self-respecting deference of the old retainer to the young son of the house, and an avuncular good-humour, which, I think, was the attitude he imagined Faunce himself took with me. (As if Faunce would ever be bothered with a minor role such as that of kindly uncle!) Arthur was delighted to see me, obviously had been excited about my coming, and shook my hand and patted me about as if it were all he could do not to say, 'My! What a big boy you've grown.' We talked a little, about business and Faunce, and what was going on at Aden Parrot generally, and, as I had thought he would, Arthur said that his wife expected him to bring me home to dinner on that, my first night in Johannesburg. He introduced me to the typist, Miss McCann, who was one of those common little girls to whom anaemia gives a quenched look which may be mistaken for refinement, and who, appropriately, smelled of sickroom cologne. I should have to find some means of getting rid of her. He also introduced a young black man who came into the outer office with a small mail-pouch which he emptied on Miss McCann's desk – a young man whose clothes were all a little too large or too small for him; I couldn't help noticing his shoes, in particular – they stood away all round his heel and ankle. 'Oh, and this is Amon,' said Arthur. 'Amon, this is Mr Hood who's come from London to take my place while I'm away.' The youngster smiled sheepishly, not looking at me, and mumbled, 'Yes sir. Thank you, sir.' The typist was turning over the mail with an air of strong suspicion, as if she were sure to find something unpleasant, or amiss. She took out two slips of paper, signed them and handed them to the youngster. He went out without having looked at me.

The Hollwards' house was exactly the sort of house they would have had in England. Arthur laid the crazy paving himself and it was he who kept the standard roses tied to their supports; Mrs Hollward had refurnished the sitting-room in what she called 'modern' Swedish-style – low chairs covered in abstract design linen, lamps made out of Chianti bottles with raffia shades, a Van Gogh reproduction over the fireplace. Flower vases were in the form of hollow swans or fish; you stubbed out your cigarette in the gouged-out belly of a pottery rabbit. The whole managed to reproduce exactly the effect of the chintz-and-barbola-work scheme which it had evidently replaced.

Dinner was served by a thin, silent African woman with steel-rimmed spectacles, and several times, as dishes were carried back to the kitchen after we had been served, I heard Mrs Hollward instruct: 'Cover that up and put it in the refrigerator' or 'You can finish that'. After dinner, Arthur gave me a South African cognac, which wasn't bad, and talked some more about Faunce; Mrs Hollward listened with a sort of shy, polite glee, her pleasure in these anecdotes obviously increased rather than staled by their familiarity, as a child loves to hear its favourite fairy-tale over and over again.

The next night I found myself at a concert. When I left Arthur's office at five, I went into the Stratford bar, not because I really wanted a drink, but because it was to be part of my surroundings for some time; I was prompted by the mixture of dogged resignation and curiosity which sends one peering all over a ship on which one is to be living for a few weeks. This Stratford was the sort of place that looked dreary and might well come to look absolutely trustworthy and welcoming as one invested it with habit. I'd only have to be there having a few drinks with a charming girl just once, to feel attached to the general uninvitingness of the place. But when I came to think of it, there were no women there at all; and in a way, that was rather nice, too. I eavesdropped over my beer, and it seemed that most of the men there were lawyers or newspapermen. Then I wandered back to the hotel through the harassed scurry of the afternoon rush – people didn't seem to linger much in this city after work – and took a look at the scene in there.

The unvarying pinkish light shone on, as it had in the morning; in the great lounge, three cowed-looking café-musicians produced the musical equivalent of this light, while loud parties of flushed young men bought drinks for giggling girls unused to such splendour; older men, with faces arranged as carefully as their pale silk ties, rose to greet the heel-clicking entrance of elegant, disdainful girls who must be mannequins or actresses; and the tourist residents, whether English, American or Continental, looked curiously foreign among these others, who, if varied in class and purpose, were at least clearly on their own ground.

I took a look, and that was all; I went straight out into the street again. But it was hard, I found, to loiter in

Johannesburg. It was a warm evening – the sun dying in angry flashes between the buildings – and I looked for a pavement café, but couldn't find one. I looked into one or two other hotels, but they seemed much like my own. I found a park, and in it an art gallery – it was shut – but unless you are with a girl, or are a child, or are very old, somehow you can't sit about in a park.

Where now? I said to myself.

And I crossed a bridge over a railway cutting into the town again. Down to my left, along the town bank of the cutting, I saw a thick queue sheltered under a tin roof. I walked a little way to see what it was about. And I saw that it was a bus queue; the people in it had the tired, unimpatient faces of those who wait in the same place at the same time every day. They were all black.

As I made my way uptown past the butchers' shops and the dry cleaners' and the corner hotel bars, I realized that the fact that they were black had come to me last, and least importantly, I had registered it as an afterthought, in fact. Whereas, in Mombasa, that day, when the launch approached the shore, the first thing that had struck me was the blackness, the Africanness of the faces waiting there. Yet I knew at once what the difference was. Those were peasants; the vacant, brutish-faced peasant, if you like, or the fine, unspoiled natural man – depends how you see it. These faces in the Johannesburg bus queue bore all the marks of initiation into western civilization; they were tired by city noise, distasteful jobs, worries about money, desires for things they couldn't afford, their feet ached from standing and their heads ached from the drinking of the night before – much like those faces you used to see all over London in those endless queues during the war.

I had dinner in a third-rate restaurant with a fancy name, where the waiters were all Indian. The one who served me made a great show of busy zeal and produced my steak and limp, pale chips with a flourish, but the restaurant was almost empty, and the others stood around the walls, flicking their waiters' napkins like horses switching at flies with their tails.

Then I began to walk again, with the vague intent of finding a cinema showing something I hadn't seen in London; but I happened to walk past a hall where, in a crowd that spread out into the street, an enormous photograph announced an orchestral concert with a famous violinist as soloist. I had heard him four or five times at home, and I don't suppose I should have gone out of my way to get in to hear him again, but somebody waved a ticket under my nose – a single ticket – and I bought it from him. While I took the money from my pocket, half a dozen people closed in hopefully round us in case the deal fell through and the ticket was still for sale. Anyway, it was mine, and I was a duly qualified member of the throng in a big, ugly foyer. Inside, the hall (I discovered that it was the city hall itself) was ugly, too. But the audience was not – ugly, I mean; there were some beautiful women there, and everyone had an air of ease, well- even if not always becomingly dressed, well-fed, and unruffled. There was a fair sprinkling of the sort of faces you see at concerts everywhere: the serious devotees, old men with crests of white hair, old ladies in shawls or oriental turbans, students who sat with downcast eyes over the score as if they were praying, pretty girls with strange hair styles and stranger clothes. I sat and listened in an atmosphere of perfume and silky furs; beringed hands and bleached hair; pomade and the lingering, after-dinner cigar smell in fine cloth. In the interval, the usual talk flew about: brass weak, pace a little too fast, violinist himself *absolutely* divine, violinist not so good as last year in Salzburg, violinist still the *only* interpreter of Mozart, violinist *passé* now, only good enough for South Africa – the same talk, with different place-names, that you hear at any concert in London.

When the concert was over, I streamed out with these glossy-looking people, and found my way between their cars and back to the hotel. In the lounge, the pink light still shone on what were either the same people I'd seen there at sundowner time, or others exactly like them. Except the tourists. They had gone to bed. One of them had left a pamphlet at the empty table at which I sat while I waited for a cup of coffee. AFRICA IN ALL ITS SAVAGE GLORY. ONLY HOURS AWAY. LUXURY SAFARI CARS PICK YOU UP AT YOUR JOHANNESBURG HOTEL, TAKE YOU TO THE KRUGER PARK – THE SAME DAY, YOU SEE LIONS, BUCK, HIPPO. AFTER A REFRESHING NIGHT'S SLEEP IN CAMP WITH ALL COMFORTS, YOU'RE OFF AGAIN, TO SEE ELEPHANT, GIRAFFE, AND MANY OTHER WILD ANIMALS IN THEIR NATURAL STATE, LIVING THE LAW OF THE JUNGLE. The next page told, in similar terms, of the native war dances to be seen twice monthly at a Mine compound near Johannesburg. On the next, a picture of a beautiful black girl with an enchanting smile, dressed in a beaded tribal costume, but with plump bared breasts, advertised THE UNSPOILT CHARM OF ZULULAND. I felt as if I were reading of another country, from seas away. But then the country of the tourist pamphlet always is another country, an embarrassing abstraction of the desirable that, thank God, does not exist on this planet, where there are always ants and bad smells and empty Coca-Cola bottles to keep the grubby finger-print of reality upon the beautiful.

Was I in Africa? I went to bed in that hotel room where even the drop of the loosed button from my shirt was muffled in a conspiracy of stuffs to keep the atmosphere anonymous.

I told Arthur that I must find somewhere else to live – a small flat perhaps. 'Ah well,' he said with a smile of indulgent sympathy, 'good things can't last for ever.'

'No.'

'I thought it would be nice for you to start off here with a flourish, though.'

'Oh, it was.'

I was afraid that he was about to recommend an alternative, a more modest edition of the hotel, a smaller version of that package of fluorescence and stale air.

'There's a particularly nice place in Parktown, I believe – private hotel where a lot of people out from home stay.'

(No, he'd decided that what I needed as a more permanent base after my flutter in the Plaza-Ritz, or whatever it was called, was a genteel English boarding-house.) 'I'll speak to Jessie about it; I think she knows someone who lives there.'

'Oh, thank you, Arthur, but I think I'll definitely try for a flat of some kind. As a matter of fact, I may be on the track of one. I mean, one of the people I was given a letter of introduction to has more or less promised to see what he can do –' I embarrassed myself by the glib lie.

'Now that's sensible,' said Arthur, pleased to think that I must be making use of Faunce's illustrious connexions. 'Much better idea to have a little *pied à terre* of your own. And if there's someone to pull strings for you, well and good.'

I believe there's some sort of propaganda dictum to the effect that a lie, spoken with conviction enough, becomes true. Anyway, the influence of a personal lie is a curious thing; mine had the effect of sending me to read slowly through the sixpenny notebook of addresses I hadn't opened since I sailed from England. I didn't know what I was looking for; certainly not for someone who could pull strings. It was almost with reluctance that I went through the meaningless names and addresses scribbled down in my own and other people's handwriting, in London and in the Cotswolds, in cars and restaurants, the houses of friends, and at Aden Parrot. What had I said at the time that they were being written? Oh yes, please do. Of course, I'll look them up. I'm sure it'll be a great help to me. Yes, I'd like to get to know them. Signor A. Pozzi, 177 Barston Place, Riviera Road. And in parenthesis '(Arnolfo and Betty)', Arthur Coutts, Inanda Club, Sandown (ask for Ex. 53), Max and Doreen Brown, Cleantry Court, Isipingo Street. Hildegarde Cegg, 42–7831. David Marshall, c/o Broadcast House. And then my mother's and Faunce's list: 'worth-while' people. A writer, who'd brought out, under our imprint, the miscegenation novel now as regular a South African export as gold or fruit. A newspaper editor. A university professor. An ex-chairman of the Institute of Race Relations. A priest who was something to do with the Penal Reform League. A woman doctor who was superintendent of a hospital for Africans. Reverend This, Doctor That. An Indian who was secretary to some congress or other; an African leader. An M.P.

Squashed in at the bottom of the page was a name I remembered my mother hesitating over. She had discussed with Faunce whether it was worth-while my bothering to look up this woman; she *had* been a rather pleasant girl when they knew her in her youth, but she had married this tycoon, this man who was supposed to be second only to Ernest Oppenheimer in importance in the gold-mining industry and she didn't seem to have *done* anything since. Wouldn't I be likely to be bored stiff by that sort of family? Then Faunce had said, well, he might be amused in a way; it might be interesting for him to get a look at these people – and so my mother wrote it in, after all: Marion (and Hamish) Alexander, The High House, Illovo. The telephone number was written so small, I could hardly make it out; my mother had thought it unlikely that I should use it.

I decided on the Alexanders, Hamish and Marion Alexander, of The High House. A voice that I had already learned to distinguish as an African's answered the telephone. Mrs Alexander was out; I left my name and the telephone number of the hotel. And somehow I felt satisfied with the gesture. If the Alexanders didn't telephone me back, I didn't ever have to bother about them again.

While I was at dinner, that night, I was called to the telephone. I walked through the dining-room with that swift, furtive air which characterizes people summoned to private business from public rooms; everyone ignored me as steadfastly as I did them. (All kinds of living have their codes, and how quickly one conforms to the particular one in which one finds oneself, no matter how ridiculous it may be.) I lifted the hotel telephone receiver, still warm from someone else's ear, and there was my mother's voice; a product of the same school, brought into tune, so to speak, by the same fork. 'Mr Hood? Toby? – This is Marion Alexander.'

'Yes, Toby Hood. Hullo, Mrs Alexander.'

'I couldn't believe it! I thought the servant had got the

name wrong! The last time I saw you, you were still at school, before the war. ... How and why are you here? And how wonderful!'

She asked me to Sunday lunch. A black Buick driven by an African chauffeur came to fetch me at the hotel at twelve o'clock. I tried to talk to him as we drove, but he answered in a reluctant, pompous, off-hand manner, using Americanisms in not quite their right sense. I think he thought I was very badly dressed.

We left the city – which is without life on Sunday; even the cinemas are closed – and crossed the new Queen Elizabeth bridge. I twisted my head to look back and I must say that, from there, it all looked rather fine; the rectangular buildings, bone and sand and stone colour, pale as objects picked up on a beach, made a frieze of clean, hard shapes against a sky that was all space. If there had been a river under the bridge, this might have been a beautiful city – but there was no water, there were the sheds, tracks, and steel tangle of a railway junction. We passed mean little houses clinging to the fringe of the city, then the University – grey buildings, green trees, and red earth sloping down the hill – and then suburb after suburb of pleasant houses, neat, tame, and comfortable, as such houses are anywhere, but surrounded, overshadowed, overlaid, almost, by trees and flowers of unusual and heavy beauty. The further we drove, the bigger the gardens were; at last we turned off the tar on to a sand road. The car rode softly; the trees nearly met, overhead; in a clearing, I saw the watery shine of a horse's rump. On a rough stone gateway, white-painted iron letters spelt THE HIGH HOUSE. The drive was lined with round-limbed, feathery trees; hydrangeas grew in green cumulus, billowing beneath them. I saw a tennis court, a swimming-pool with a rustic changehouse, lawns green without texture, a lily-pond, a bank of irises, and then the house, built on a green mound. A large house, of course, rather like a bloated cottage, with a steep thatched roof curling up over dormer windows, thick white chimneys, and a balcony and abutting porch extending it on the two sides I could see.

The car dropped me at the front door, which was open,

and while I waited for someone to answer my knock, I could see in and also was aware of the vibration of voices on the other side of the big bay window on my right. The entrance hall led away down a few broad shallow steps to the left; I got the impression of a long, mushroom-coloured room there, with gleams of copper and gilt, flowers and glass. In the hall there was a marquetry table under a huge mirror with a mother-of-pearl inlaid frame. Further back, the first steps of a white staircase spread in a dais; carpet seemed to grow up the stairs, padding the rim of each step like pink moss. An African appeared soundlessly; I followed him soundlessly (I found later that the entire ground floor of the house was covered with that carpeting the colour of a mushroom's gills) past the mirror that reflected three new golf balls and a very old golf glove, sweated and dried to the shape of the wearer's hand, on the table below it, and through a large living-room full of sofas and chairs covered in women's dress colours, that led to a veranda. If you could call it that; a superior sort of veranda. The entire wall of the room was open to it, and it was got up like something out of a film, with a bar, a barbecue fireplace, *chaises longues*, glass and wrought-iron tables, mauve Venetian glass lanterns and queer trailing plants.

A burst of laughter was interrupted by my appearance; five people looked up, and a thick-set man with a bald, sunburned head struggled from his chair and came over to greet me. 'You'll be Toby Hood,' he said. 'Come and have a drink. Marion's not back yet.' He seemed to think that his own identity, that of Hamish Alexander, was self-evident, and he began to introduce me to the others. 'Archie Baxter' – a thin, youngish man with the good looks of the distinguished drinker in the whisky advertisements. 'Kit Baxter', an equally good-looking young woman, also with a commercial finish about her; they were the kind of couple whose clothes – in this instance, riding clothes – might have been donated by some firm in return for having them worn to advantage, and in the right company. 'And this is Margaret Gerling and her big sister, Cecil Rowe.' At this they laughed, and looked alike, the two pretty girls who were also in riding clothes. It seemed a bit ridiculous to stretch myself out, almost supine, the moment I walked into a stranger's house, and so I sat on the foot-rest of one of the long chairs, between Mrs Baxter and what I now saw was the elder of the two sisters, Cecil Rowe. Baxter, who was over at the little bar, said, 'Won't you try one of my Martinis?' and Mrs Baxter pushed a tray of olives and nuts along a low table, within my reach.

Once I had a drink and was seated, they took up their chatter again; Hamish Alexander had the totally impersonal welcome and perpetual smile of the man who has many guests, most of them not invited by himself. The women were animated and talkative, especially Margaret Gerling and Mrs Baxter. All three had short, bright fashionable hair, not blonde and yet not brown, the blue eyes, the sunburned necks and brilliant finger-nails, the high actressy voices and oddly inarticulate vocabulary – vogue words, smart clichés, innuendo, and slang – of young upper-class Englishwomen. Nice girls, I should say. Gay, quite witty, and decorative. A shade more sophisticated, a shade less intelligent, a shade more sexy than Rina Turgell. I laughed at their stories – mostly riding stories, against themselves – that were not very good but were well told, along with the others. I contributed a story, not a riding one, but also against myself. A number of other guests came, and the elaborate outdoor room began to fill up.

There were middle-aged couples, the wives looking far younger than they could have been, in cotton dresses which displayed a lot of well-preserved flesh. But they were good-looking women who smelled luxurious. The men wore the clothes of whatever sport they had just left off playing, or, pasty and wattled, sat, stranded, in a well-pressed get-up of flannels, silk shirts, and scarves that covered the ruin of the hardened arteries, the damaged liver, or the enlarged heart that lay heavily in the breast. One of these last sat next to me, eventually; and I felt myself moved to a kind of disgusted pity, as I always am by the sight of one of these old bulls of finance, still sniffing the sawdust, with the broken shafts of money-tussles, overwork, overeating, over-drinking stuck fast in their thick necks. There was a thin, tall man with thick white hair – the sort of man who plays a fast game of tennis at sixty, and marries a twenty-five-year-old at seventy. He had just been on a crocodile-shooting safari in Northern Rhodesia, and he talked about it in a loud, natural, overbearing voice that had the effect of breaking up minor conversations by the sheer contrast of its absolute confidence in the interest of what it was saying.

'Is it true that you must get them between the eyes, John?' asked Mrs Baxter.

'I don't know about that, but I don't mind telling you, they've got to be pretty damn well dead before you can count on 'em to *be* dead,' he said. 'You think you've got them, and then they just knife off through the water and you never find them again. We must've shot a dozen for every one we got aboard. But what beasts they are; you feel you're doing 'em a favour by killing them. And when the boys slit 'em open –' he put his hand – with one of those expensive watches that tell the time, date, and phases of the moon, on the wrist – over his face, hiding it to the wiry, tangled black eyebrows.

Hamish Alexander, who obviously enjoyed him, sat forward grinning, his strong, patchy yellow teeth oddly matching the gingerish bristles on his red neck. 'I've heard about that,' he said gleefully. 'I've heard people ...'

'Hamish, hearing about it couldn't give you the least idea. ... The whole boat, I mean. It stank like a – a,' his mouth pursed itself but stopped in time.

'– Charnel-house,' said Kit Baxter, sweetly.

Everyone laughed. 'Tactful Kit,' said Baxter.

John leant over and kissed Kit on her round, smooth brow. 'And how good *she* smells –' There was more laughter. 'But honestly, I don't mind telling you, though you know how dignified and all that my behaviour usually is –'

'Did you dress for dinner every night, John?' someone called.

' '– I wanted to jump off that boat and swim ashore. Honest to God, nothing would have kept me on that boat but crocodiles still in the water!'

Lifting her glass, against which the rows of bracelets on her wrist slid tinkling, in a call for attention, one of the women said, 'I remember once going out to the whaling station at Durban. – Why, of course, *you* were there too, Peggy; and Ivan – That was a smell to beat all smells; a real eighty-per-cent proof distillation of disgusting fishiness, oiliness, oh, I don't know what.'

'My dear Eve,' said the man John, 'I'm sorry, but we just can't have evasions in this, this – '

'Context,' said Kit.

'This context – '

Kit seemed sure she could say it better for him: 'You must call a stink a stink.'

In the shrieks of laughter that followed, the hostess, Marion Alexander, arrived, and with a general greeting to her guests, came straight over to where I had risen from my chair.

'It's Toby!' and she kissed me. 'I'm so glad you're here. I hope they've been looking after you. I had a match this morning, so you must forgive my rudeness. There, I've put my lipstick on you. No, a little lower. That's it.' She took my arm, and then repeated her apologies, in a clear, singing voice, for the benefit of everyone: 'Please forgive me – I didn't think I'd be the last luncheon guest, I *did* believe I'd be home by half past twelve.' I thought she looked extraordinary: she wore a white linen dress and a panama hat with a band round it. For the first few moments I did not realize that this was the outfit that women wear when they play bowls, and wondered why she should choose to look like a horribly ageing schoolgirl. I did not remember her, though on the telephone she had said that she remembered seeing me just before the war, when I was already a schoolboy, but I could see that she must once have been a pretty woman, and was much older than my mother. Or maybe it was just that she had grown older badly, and self-consciously. Underneath that hat, her face was painted whiter and pinker than it could ever have been when she was young; yet no doubt that was how she imagined she had looked, and so was what she chose to fake. She went to change, and Kit

Baxter, with the pleading air of asking for a treat, jumped up and followed her, saying, 'I want to come and talk to you, Marion!'

While they were gone, the last three guests arrived, and with them the Alexanders' son, Douglas. He had come from golf; and the two new male guests were in riding clothes. Along with the old bulls, I was the only male guest not fresh from conquest of field or ball. The two latest were youthfully apoplectic, blond, with small, flat, lobeless ears, short noses, and bloodshot blue eyes. Every feature of their faces looked interchangeable; they burst in crying, 'Hullo! Hullo! Hullo there, you people,' like a comedy duo. They were, in fact, a duo: identical twins; looking at them was disturbing, like looking at someone after you've had a blow in the eye, and you keep seeing the outline of head, gestures, and talking mouth, duplicated. But they had with them a stunning American girl, thin as a Borzoi, in what looked to me like black tights (anyway, they were women's trousers that didn't hang down at the seat) and a thing like a man's striped shirt that enveloped her but got caught on the two little shaking peaks of small breasts as she moved. She was very fair, without a hint of yellowness, and her hair was drawn back and held by a strand of the hair itself, twisted round it. Her face was very young and made up to look pale and downy, and her expression was as old as the hills. As she was introduced to the company, she flickered a kind of lizard-look over everyone, then put her long cigarette holder back in her mouth, like a dour man with a pipe. I got the impression that Tim and Tom (or whatever their names were) hardly knew her; that women caught on to their ruddy hide like burrs on wool. They were off again almost as soon as they came, waving away Archie Baxter: 'No, no, old boy, before we have any of your stuff, we must have a swim. Have we time for a swim before lunch?' 'Course we've got time. Always time in Hamish's house, isn't there?'

They went off over the grass to the pool, and in a few minutes we could see them, hugging their arms round themselves on the edge, waving, then exploding the surface of the water, shouting at each other in their identical voices, as if someone were holding a conversation with himself out loud.

I felt inkstained and rather stale inside my hairy old suit, and, with my third drink disappearing, contented in this. Almost everyone had had a number of drinks by now (Hamish did not stir from his chair, and Archie Baxter managed the little bar, with the help of two Africans in white suits and gloves who passed endlessly into the house and out again, bearing soda and ice and cigarettes, and carrying away dirty glasses and ashtrays) and this, added to the anticipation of lunch, raised the pitch of the company. Mrs Alexander and Kit Baxter had returned. Mrs Alexander went about her guests with the warmth of a hostess who enjoys people and knows how to bring them together in a paper-lantern glow. She flattered, she exaggerated, you could see that, but the effect was to make one more agreeable; with the result that the whole conglomerate – guests, alcohol, gossip, and, later, enjoyable food – *was* agreeable. This is quite a different sort of success from that of the hostess who brings people of ideas together. This, in fact, was making something out of nothing very much.

The twins, freshly doused and towelled, came up and clamoured round the bar, with their American and Kit Baxter and the two sisters Cecil and Margaret. They spoke actor's English, with exaggerated stresses. They showed off, I felt, rather than flirted, with the women. Marion Alexander kept taking me by the arm and presenting me to people: 'Have you talked to this boy? I do wish you would, before I get a chance to, so that you can tell me if he's altogether too bright for me. He's Althea Thomas's boy – Aden Parrot, the publishers, such a brainy family.'

'This is a very special day for me. This boy's the son of my friend Althea Thomas, and Graham Hood. – I was devoted to them.' She made it sound as if my mother and father were a cause; and perhaps, to her, they were: the embodiment of the causes of the Thirties, to which she remembered herself responding for a time, just as she had taken to cloche hats a year or two earlier. Anyway, the name of my father cheerfully meant nothing to these people, just as, I suppose, the names of his more illustrious contemporaries – a Spender or a Toller – would have meant nothing. But I could see that Marion Alexander's insistence on my parentage suggested to some of the sharper women that mine must be a family that featured in the *Tatler*. Some of those who were English accepted me with the airy freemasonry of those who know the privileges and disadvantages, for whatever they are worth, of their own order. Those who were not English all seemed to take travel in Britain and Europe as much for granted as a journey in a suburban train, and talked to me of most Continental countries as if they assumed my familiarity with these places was as easy as their own. One flew from here to there; hired a car; met one's daughter in Switzerland; one's husband flew in from Rome; sister met one in Vienna; fjords and alps, casinos and cruises, palazzos and espadrilles. . . .

One of the black men in a white suit came out and beat a gong through all this.

As the people rose to trail in to lunch, conversations took a final turn: the last word was said on English furniture, on someone's wedding the week before, on the values in real estate in Johannesburg, on the merits of a new golf course being laid out by someone named Jock, and the cannon bones of a horse named Tom Piper.

On the way to the dining-room, I had a ridiculous encounter with the American girl, who happened to be the last of the women shepherded before me. She turned her head and said in a low, dead, American voice, 'I hear you're a gread wrider?' 'No, no, just a publisher,' I said, embarrassed, because I wasn't really even that, yet. At which she burst out laughing – a bold, full laugh, surprising in contrast to her speaking voice – and said: 'I guess I've got the wrong purson.' But she offered no explanation, and the conversation promptly died. It was only later, when I was studying her where she sat, across the table from me, beside Douglas Alexander and one of the twins, that I suddenly realized that what she had said was not 'writer' but 'rider'. I had an agitated impulse to lean across the glasses and silver and the Italian bread basket and explain; but it was obviously no good. Explain that I was neither writer nor rider? I was the wrong person, anyway. She'd accepted the fact, that was that. Bored and indifferent to their company, she belonged and could belong only to the twins, part of their cutting a dash. Yet she ate and drank steadily without the lipstick coming off her beautiful mouth; which seemed to me wonderful: the casual mark of a special kind of girl, not quite real, whom I would never get; perhaps would never try or really want to get.

Douglas Alexander, as the children of self-assured, temperamentally vigorous parents often are, was a rather blank youngster, with the look of a perpetual listener on his face; as if, since childhood, he had been taking in conversations to which he was not expected to make a contribution, and long habit had vitiated his desire to do so, although he was not longer disqualified by being under age. He certainly did not behave like any sort of popular concept of a gold-mining millionaire's son that I could think of; all the time that he was keeping up an apparently lame and stilted conversation (about New York, I gathered) with the American beauty, his eyes kept gliding out of their polite focus on her and looking sharply to the other side, as if there were something there attracting his urgent attention. On the girl's left, the one twin jounced and twisted, waving his glass about, bumping her frequently with shoulder or elbow, as he chattered to his neighbour and audience. Every now and then he would notice her, and with the impersonal, momentary, instinctive recall to sex with which a dog will briefly lick, once or twice, another dog, would pass his hand down her arm or pat her hair.

I was at Hamish Alexander's end of the table, with Kit Baxter on my left and Cecil Rowe on my right. Mrs Baxter had a voice of great conscious charm, that she used, with purpose and efficiency, as if it were some piece of high fidelity equipment rather than the final, faulty evolution of those grunts and cries with which man first tried to give expression to the awful teeming of his brain. She was carrying on an exchange of banter and flattery with old Hamish, who was too far away for conversation to be comfortable.

While her head was turned from me, the long fingers of her smooth hand with its uniform of red nails and rings felt blindly up and down the mother-of-pearl handle of a small knife, quite near me, carrying on some secret life of its own. Hamish Alexander's red face, with the simple, short, plump-featured, retroussé profile of a child and the teary grin of his blue eyes, was cocked toward her along the table; but someone suddenly passed a question to him about uranium deposits, and immediately his face not only came to itself, but took on the close, guarded reasonableness, the poker-face frankness, of a man asked about something important and not to be disclosed. He gave himself the second or two of a peculiarly Scotch clearing of his throat, and then he began a long, blunt, bland, confidential red herring, with the words: 'Now it's not as simple as all that . . . As far back as nineteen forty-one –'

Kit Baxter turned to me with perfectly convincing and certainly assumed delight. 'I've been waiting to talk to you!' she said. I grinned at her disbelievingly. 'I hope you haven't written a book,' I said, 'because I'm afraid I haven't much influence with Aden Parrot, in spite of what Mrs Alexander may have told you.'

'Heavens, no, Kit couldn't write anything. You're quite safe there. It's just that Marion tells me you're likely to be in this country quite a while, and she and I thought you might like to come down to the farm some time – see something of the country. Not that it's beautiful – though it is, to me, in a way – but it's characteristic.'

'What farm?'

'Hamish's. The Alexander stud farm, in the Karoo.'

'Oh, I see. I didn't know about it. What does he breed?'

'Horses. Hamish started it more for fun than anything else. But now it's turning into a big thing. Archie and I have been there since the beginning of the year.'

'You and your husband live there?'

'Hamish asked us to go down and take over, more or less permanently.' She phrased it in order to make it clear that her husband's appointment as manager of the Alexanders' stud farm was a matter of friendship and patronage, rather than an ordinary job.

'And how do you like that?' I said.

She laughed, and the skin crinkled prettily round her painted eyes. 'You don't think I'm the type for the farmer's wife! But you're wrong you know, quite wrong. I'm not a city person at all, really, I'm an absolute bumpkin in towns. I've always led a country life at home, and I *hate* London – Archie and I lived there for two years after the war and I couldn't wait to get out of it. Our time in Johannesburg has really only been bearable because of Hamish and Marion – they're such fantastic darlings, and we've been able to come out and ride whenever we like, and they've whisked us off down to the farm whenever we could get away' – a dish held in a white-gloved hand that showed an inch of matt-black skin between cuff and sleeve, came between us – '(Won't you have some more mousse? Marion's cook makes the best mousse you've ever tasted.) – It's absolutely in the bundu, of course, forty-three miles from Neksburg and that's not much to speak of, itself, I may say. I can't describe these Karoo villages as "villages", unless the person I'm talking to has seen them. They're nothing at all like *our* idea of a village. Don't start thinking of cottage gardens, mossy churchyards, and the rest of it.... Just think of dust and stones, that's all, dust and stones, and a flybitten "hotel" with a couple of big shiny cars belonging to commercial travellers outside – also covered in dust.'

'And the farm – also dust and stones?'

'Oh no,' she said; and I realized – not without comfort, for the delicious lunch and the wines had, as usual, awakened in me a great respect for life lived in the exquisite orderliness of wealth – that nothing in Hamish Alexander's empire would be dust and stones.

'There's water on the farm, of course; all sorts of pumps and gadgets huffing and puffing to keep it irrigated. And there are huge trees round the house, cypress and pepper trees – it should be quite charming when we've got it fixed up more or less the way we want it. I hope that by the time *you* come there'll be a second bathroom built on, and the painting will be done.' She said this with the complacent, determined air of a woman who is making a house over to conform as closely as possible to the setting for herself that she always carries in her mind. Uproot her again tomorrow and she will begin again at once to attempt to make the next shell of habitation conform to this master setting. In this primitive cause those waxy, inutile, decorated hands would work as tirelessly and instinctively as any animal's claws making ready the nest; and in the nest would be – she herself. It was a perversion of the nesting instinct that you see often in sophisticated women; the drive remains, crazily fixed, while the purpose for which it was rooted in human nature has been lost, truly forgotten.

'I work a lot with the young horses,' she was saying. 'Archie's time is taken up with the administrative side, mostly. But I play around, helping to break them in, making a fuss of them, generally acting Mama. They're fantastic darlings! Adorable! The dogs are quite unhappy sometimes, they're so jealous, you know, Cecil,' she said to the other girl.

'Are they?' the girl said, raising her eyebrows while she ate.

'Two funny old sealyhams,' Kit Baxter confessed to me, as if I were sure to be disgusted at the idea, 'quite moth-eaten and lazy and not very bright, I know; and a Siamese whose eyes are much too light. But they adore me, I say it quite immodestly, they adore me. Kit's own regiment, that's what I call them, Kit's own.'

It was impossible to think of anything to say to this forlorn piece of whimsy. It was one of those thin places in conversation through which one suddenly sees something one isn't meant to see. Cecil Rowe saved me by catching my eye with the friendly opening of a smile struggling against the disadvantage of a mouthful of braised pigeon and rice. You would never have caught the exquisite American out in a smile like that; I warmed to it, all the same. When the girl could speak, she said, 'I was so hungry I was quite drunk. I had to eat quickly to give myself some ballast.'

Kit Baxter and I laughed with her. 'People here certainly

do eat a substantial lunch,' I said, 'but you've all had such an energetic morning, I suppose you must.'

'Restaurateurs wouldn't agree with you,' said Kit. 'They complain that people in Johannesburg hardly eat at all, in the European sense. A meal is always simply a necessary prelude to be got over in good time for some other entertainment, not an evening's pleasure in itself.'

'Do you find South Africans eat more than we do?' I said to Cecil Rowe.

'How would I know? I'm not English,' she said.

I was surprised; she looked and dressed like any upper-middle-class English girl, and what was more, she did not have the flat, unmistakable South African speech that I had heard all about me in the town, and that I had noticed at once in the Alexanders' son, Douglas, and the crocodile-hunting John, for example.

'Then you're an Afrikaner,' I said, taking care to pronounce the word of identification correctly, like a naturalist coming upon a species of which he has heard, but never before encountered.

'No, no,' she said, laughing and indignant, 'I'm not. I'm not that.'

'Of *course* you're English,' said Kit. 'Your *parents* are English. You happen to be born here. Just as you might have been born in India, or Egypt – that's all.'

'I've never met a publisher before,' said the girl. 'Have you, Kit? I've somehow never *thought* about publishers – you know, I mean, you read a book and it's the author who counts, the publisher's simply a name on the jacket. It's difficult to think of the publisher as a person sitting beside you at lunch.'

'Rightly so, too,' I said, 'when the person is really only a sort of publisher's office boy.'

'But aren't you a son or something of the people who own the publisher's?'

'Nephew.'

'Well, there you are.'

'I'm being trained from the Ground Up. And I haven't got very far.'

'How far?'

'Trade relations. I've come to South Africa as the agent for our firm.'

She nodded her head, thinking a moment. 'Didn't you bring out that book there's been such a fuss about?'

My mind skimmed over the last three or four Aden Parrot titles that had filled the correspondence columns of the papers with protagonist letters. 'You mean *God's Creatures*? The anti-vivisection one?'

She looked faraway, shook her head, 'M-mh. Nobody would know about that here.'

'The one about institutional personality – children in orphanages?'

Her frown rejected this as outlandish. '*You* know, the book about the natives, the one that was banned –'

'Oh, you mean *White Cain, Black Abel* – no, unfortunately, that wasn't ours.' The book, brought out about six months ago by Aden Parrot's closest rival, had sold over fifty thousand copies. It was written by a missionary who lived for six years in the Native Reserves, and was a passionate attack, from the standpoint of a deeply religious man, on the failure of Christianity to influence the policy of white people toward black in South Africa. 'What did you think of it? Did you read it?'

She cut herself a slice of Bel Paese and said, 'Oh I thought it was jolly good,' as if she were talking of a novel that had served to pass an evening. 'I *must* have a cigarette. D'you mind?'

All up and down the table, people were smoking; the meal was at an end, and we all got up and went into the room I had caught a glimpse of from the front door. There was coffee and also old brandy and liqueurs, and the smell, like the smell of fine leather, of cigars; a warm fug of well-being filled the room, in which, in my slightly hazy state, I saw that every sort of efficient indulgence lay about, like in those rooms conjured up by Genii for people in fairy stories who always seem to wish for the same sort of thing, as if, given the chance, nobody really knows anything else to wish for: there were silver or limoges cigarette lighters on every other table, as well as the little coloured match-books on which were printed 'Hamish' or 'Marion', silver dishes of thin mints and huge chocolates, jade boxes and lacquer boxes and silver boxes filled with cigarettes, silver gadgets to guillotine the cigars, even amethyst, rose, and green sugar crystals to sweeten the coffee.

Most of the guests were drawn to look at Marion Alexander's new 'find' – a picture she had evidently just bought. 'Come and tell me what you think of this,' she said, with the faintest emphasis, as if I didn't need any more, on the last word. It was a small and rather dingy Courbet, deeply set in a frame the colour and texture of dried mud. 'Interesting,' I murmured politely. 'They're not easily come by, I imagine.' 'Here!' she said. 'Can you believe it? I found it here, in Johannesburg!' I attempted to look impressed, although I couldn't imagine why anyone should want to find such a thing anywhere. 'How do you spell the name?' a woman asked me, quietly studying the picture. I spelled it. The woman nodded slowly. 'I love it, Marion, I think it's the most exciting thing you've bought yet!' said someone else.

'Well I can tell you I couldn't believe it when my little man told me there was a Courbet to be bought in Johannesburg,' Mrs Alexander said for the third or fourth time. I managed to drift out of the group of admirers, back to a chair. '... of course, I still think *that's* a wonderful thing,' I heard, and saw one of the bulls straddling his heavy body on two thin legs before an enormous oil that must surely have been painted with the offices of the Union Castle shipping company in mind – it showed a great duck-bosomed mail-ship, tricked out with pennants, in what I recognized as Table Bay, with Cape Town and Table Mountain behind it. Now that I noticed, there was quite a variety of pictures in the room; most of them were in the Table Bay *genre*; the *genre* of the room, generally: not a discomforting brush-stroke in any of them. I decided that I didn't mind; I didn't mind any more than I did my mother's collection of charcoal drawings, woodcuts, lithographs, pastels, oils, *collages*, mosaics, and wire-and-cardboard compositions that she had bought from unknown, unsung, and unhung prophets of art over the last thirty years.

Cecil Rowe wandered over and sat on a low chair beside me. Her legs, unsexed by gaberdine jodhpurs, rolled apart and she looked down at them, stirring her toes. 'Well, how do you like it here so far?' she said, managing not to yawn. 'Think our policemen wonderful? No? That's fine – nobody does.'

'You know, the thing one never remembers is how much the same things are likely to be, rather than how different,' I said.

'How's that?' With her face in repose, I noticed that, although she was too young to have lines, I could see the pull, beneath the skin, of the muscle that always exerted the same tension when she smiled; her mouth, too, though pretty enough in its fresh paint in contrast to the patchy look of the worn make-up on her cheeks and chin, had about it when she talked the practised mobility of having expressed much, and not all of it pleasant.

'Well, when you arrive in a new country, you generally find yourself living in a hotel, and hotels tend to follow the same pattern everywhere, and then, at the beginning at least, you meet people to whom you've been given an introduction by friends at home – and so you meet the same sort of people everywhere, too.'

'You mean this', she lifted her chin to indicate the room and the guests, 'is the same as being in England.'

'It could be. It doesn't necessarily follow that I should be a guest in this house, if it were in England' – I did not like to say that it would be most unlikely – 'but the point is that this house could be *there*. You and your sister and Mrs Baxter – pretty girls who are nice to lunch with, who go to each other's parties, and live, eat, and sleep horses,' I was laughing, but she listened seriously, 'you might be in any English county.'

'I'm a butcher's daughter,' she said. 'My sister Margaret and I. It's funny, all the big butchers here seem to keep horses. Two or three wealthy butchers in this town have fine stables. Of course I don't mean the sort who stand behind the counter in a striped apron! Wholesale butchers, who control prices and whatnot. We start riding when we're small and go to the kind of school where riding's the thing, and then we grow up among riding people. As you said – they do what riding people do anywhere else, same old thing: hunt, and go to hunt balls and so on. Know other sporty people and belong to country clubs.' She pulled a face. 'That's how we end up looking, speaking, dressing, even behaving like a class we don't belong to in a country we don't live in. – It's sort of the wrong way round, isn't it?'

'Oh come, now. Why shouldn't people ride simply because they like to?'

'But they don't,' she said, grumpily, in the tone of telling me something she knew quite well that I knew. 'That's the trouble. They can't.'

'Well, I used to, sometimes, when I found myself near horses.'

'Oh you. *Exactly*. You could. You're not the kind who can't ride, and you're not the kind who has to.'

She said it with the air of paying me an enormous, terse, reluctant compliment.

'I take back what I said about you being found in an English county,' I said. 'You're not a bit like any of the young county ladies I've ever known.'

'I don't think you know any, anyway.'

And then she was carried off by the inevitable conversational scene-shifter whose reputation for popularity seems to rest on the confidence with which he interrupts everyone.

Chapter 3

I FOUND somewhere to live; a flat, ugly but cheap, in the steep suburb of boarding-houses and flat buildings that was more an extension of the city than a suburb. At the corner, trams lurched down or struggled up, screeching. The street was one of those newly old streets that I saw all over Johannesburg – a place without a memory; twenty-year-old houses seemed to be considered not worth repair, and blocks of flats ten years old had sunk into their own shoddiness in a way that everyone seemed satisfied was commensurate with their age. The building itself smelled of frying and the stairs were of uneven depth, so that you kept putting your foot down and missing the step that wasn't where you expected it to be; this much remained of my impressions after I'd been to look over the place. There was a fair-sized room with a small balcony that had been glassed-in to make it a room-and-a-half, and a pitch-dark bathroom in which, coming to it out of the sun of the street, I could make out nothing; but I supposed what the estate agents called the 'usual offices' would prove to be there.

I found that flat through, of all people, John Hamilton, the crocodile hunter, who was going into town after that Sunday lunch at the Alexanders' and gave me a lift back to the hotel. He drove as if his car were a missile it was his pleasure to guide through the streets, and he talked all the time. When he was held up by the traffic lights, he looked about him with restless interest, commenting on whatever caught his eye – a new car: 'That's a lovely job for you! The Stud, see it? I wonder how good the lock is in this model . . .' – an African in a beige fedora, and a suit of exaggerated cut, carrying a rolled umbrella and escorting an elaborately dressed black woman with the haunches of a brewer's dray-horse: 'Look at that pair! God these natives are dead keen on clothes! Dressed to kill!' Then, as he let the clutch out, and the car sprang ahead, he released again the main stream of his talk. He was a great enthusiast about his country, and all that it offered in the way of physical challenge; there was hardly a mountain he hadn't climbed, a piece of coast or trout stream he hadn't fished, an animal he hadn't stalked. He told me about abalone diving near Cape Town, angling for giant barracuda off the East African coast, riding a pony through the passes of Basutoland, and outwitting wily guinea-fowl in the Bushveld. Also about the things he had only looked at: the flowers in Namaqualand in the spring, the wild beasts in the game reserves, the great rivers and deserts from the Cape to the Congo. He regarded Africa as he might a woman who gave him great pleasure; an attitude unexpected and unaffected.

I asked him if he'd been to Hamish Alexander's farm in the Karoo.

'No,' he said. 'Nothing much to tempt me there. Poor old Archie's having a go at it now, of course. Or rather Kit is, as usual.'

I said that Kit Baxter had seemed very enthusiastic about the farm.

'Kit's a great girl,' he said. 'That girl's always trying to make something of Archie. Unfortunately, there's nothing much to work on,' he indicated Archie. 'I hate to see a person wasting their energies. All you can say about Archie, he's a good-looking chap, always has been and always will be; prop him up in a lounge or bar and he'll look right. You know those ventriloquists who have marvellous dolls, and the ventriloquist's the stooge, and the clever things come out of the mouth of the doll? – Well, that's Kit and Archie. Whatever he seems to think or do, it's Kit pulling the strings and thinking for him. Now this whole last year she's been around the Alexanders, Marion loves her to death, Hamish loves her to death, they can't move without the Baxters. Next thing, Kit's got them believing Archie's a great horse breeder, got them believing they love Archie, and she's all set on the Karoo farm, making something of Archie again. – You did say the Plaza, didn't you?'

'Unfortunately, yes.'

'I hear it's not too bad,' he said with the careless air of disposing of someone else's expense account.

'Our agent here booked me in. But I must get out of the place within the next few days; I can't afford it, anyway. I must start hunting for a flat or a room somewhere, tomorrow.'

'I'll give you a note to someone who'll fix you up,' he said practically and sympathetically, and when he stopped the car at the hotel, he lifted his lean body and fished a card out of his pocket. He wrote on it quickly. 'Barlow's a good chap. I'm sure he'll find something for you. – No trouble; I'm glad you mentioned it. Good-bye, boy; we'll bump into you again some time.' And with the alert look of a man who is always expected somewhere, he drove off.

Once I'd got the flat, I felt I ought to telephone and thank him, perhaps ask him to have a drink with me. On the other hand, his unhesitating offer of help was so casual, that my imposing myself on him with thanks might provide, for him, the only burdensome thing about his gesture.

I felt mildly elated at the idea of the flat. I still hadn't caught up with a sense of my own reality, here in this country; perhaps once I'd got my personal squalor around me, I should be convinced of my validity. I remembered how comfortingly that used to happen at school: you would go back after the holidays, and for the first day, in the bare, institutional cubicle, you didn't seem to exist at all; then the books unpacked, the pullover and shoes lying about, the picture of the lolling-tongued dog stuck up on the wall, the smell of the raincoat behind the door – these would combine in sudden assurance of your identity and its firm place in the life of school. I should have to buy a divan, I supposed, and a table and chairs. Then, the next week, when Arthur was gone, I'd take the easy-chair out of the office; oh, and a rug, I'd have to get a rug. . .

I woke up very early one morning at the hotel and kept thinking about all this, quite idiotically. In fact, I'd been wakened early several mornings that week by the sound of hurrying footsteps and voices that didn't bother to keep low. The first couple of times, though I was awake, I couldn't muster the weak weightlessness of my still sleeping body and get up to see what was going on, but on this morning I did. Behind the curtain that smelled of dust and clung to me with static electricity, I struggled with the catch of the window and pushed it wide; down below in the grey street, black men were on their way to work. They coughed, shouted, and chattered in their ringing Bantu languages. I could not see the sun, but light ran like water along the steel shopfronts opposite and a gob of spit shone in the gutter. No one else was about.

Arthur dragged me round the bookshops those first few weeks. Like all the booksellers I've ever come across, these were either cheerful businessmen who sold books like so many pounds of cheese, or scornful intellectuals whose lips were perpetually curled in contempt for their customers' tastes. I lunched with one of these last. At his suggestion we went to a coffee bar, where we ordered Parma ham and Camembert with our espresso; after a long time, during which he told me how he had educated public taste in Johannesburg, and greeted, with a curious lift of the hand that was more like a dismissal, the number of good-looking young women who swept in and out of the crowded little place, a harassed Indian brought us goulash and apple strudel. Near us two greenfaced Italians argued and, with their black eyes, gave the passing girls a merciless anatomical appraisal. Outside on the pavement a squawking, gibbering band of filthy black children, ragged and snot-encrusted, sang the theme sob-song from a popular film. People fumbled for pennies to throw, and the brats scuttled like cockroaches to retrieve them. My friend the bookseller apologized for the bad service and explained that the place had only recently been opened and was rather too popular for the time being. 'It's pathetic,' he said. 'They've got so little to hold them together, they'll rush to any new rallying point you offer them like dogs tearing after a bitch. Specially if they can pretend they're somewhere else; Italy, for example,' he waved a hand at the abstract mosaics, the black, bitter brew in our cups. 'Anyway it does give one the illusion one's in a civilized country,' he added, for himself.

That was the first time I encountered what I was soon to recognize as a familiar attitude among South Africans; an unexpressed desire to dissociate themselves from their milieu, a wish to make it clear that they were not taken in, even by themselves. It was a complex attitude, too, and it took many forms and affected many different kinds of people. On second thoughts, I had met with it even before that: the girl at the Alexanders', the rider, had, in a way, shown the same uneasy desire.

Arthur left; I moved into the flat; a warm, gritty wind swept people, dogs, papers, together in the streets. The membranes of my nose felt stiff and dry and I cut myself when I shaved every morning. A skin of ochre dust had grown over the tree-trunks and fences of the sand road that led to Hamish Alexander's house, when I went there again, to a cocktail party in honour of the Baxters. Then the rain came, and lasted three days; a hard, noisy rain that scrubbed behind the city's ears. Everything was flattened, drenched, and exhilarated; it was summer.

Of the people I had met at the Alexanders' before, only the twins, Margaret Gerling and one or two of the middle-aged married couples were at the Baxters' party. There were a great many people, all standing up, with that air of impending crisis that characterizes cocktail parties. If you sat down, you were confronted with the debris of a lower level: half-drunk glasses, abandoned cigarettes, mislaid handbags, and canapés that had found their way into ashtrays or to the floor. I came away with an invitation to 'drinks and supper' next Saturday (from the beautiful wife of a steel man), an invitation to a first night party after the opening of a play (from what I gathered was the leading lady, a triumphantly ugly red-head with a fine memory for dirty stories and a talent for telling them) and a request to lunch sometime, at a Services Club, with the local equivalent of a Harley Street physician. Marion Alexander said why didn't I come out and ride with the young people? And Margaret Gerling, in blue with a string of pearls, smiled across the room.

The office was going smoothly, now that the over-anxious Arthur was no longer hovering, but the flat was proving an unexpected nuisance. There were so many things I hadn't thought of, when I'd calculated what I'd have to buy when I moved in. Towels, for example, and bed linen. Adaptors for electric plugs; the bedside radio and the second-hand lamp I'd bought myself couldn't be used with their existing fittings. I had been out of the office one afternoon looking for these things in the shops, when I returned to find a woman waiting to see me.

'The lady-dee tel-i-phoned you twice this morning, Mr Hood,' said the typist, in her limp, sing-song incurious voice. I stood there nodding a polite greeting, holding my parcels with the awkwardness of the male unused to shopping.

'Will you open the door for me, please, Miss McCann? – If you'll just let me dump these things,' I added, to the caller.

'Of course.' As I was going through the inner door to my office, I remembered: 'I *did* ring the number left for me, but when I got through, a voice said Legal Aid Society, or something like that, so I thought the number must be wrong, and hung up.'

The voice came through the open door: 'That was right. I was telephoning from the Legal Aid Bureau.'

I had put down my parcels, placed Arthur's brass hand on some loose papers lying on the desk. 'Please come in,' I said, going to the door again.

She was a short, dark woman, young, with the neat head of a tidy bird. She entered and sat down with the confidence of habit; few people I had known could enter a room like that unless they were going to sell you advertising space or insurance.

'I hope you won't mind my walking in without an appointment, Mr Hood,' she said. 'But you're close by my office and I thought I might as well come on my way home and see if I could talk to you for a few minutes – it's always so much better than trying to explain over the telephone, anyway.'

'Of course. Besides, to tell you the truth, I don't have any appointments. So few people seem to need to see me.'

She was at ease already; the confession, with its implications of amateurishness, put me at ease.

'I'm Anna Louw,' she said, and although I'd been in the country less than a month, the name, the pronunciation of which told me it was Afrikaans, already produced in me a slight shift of attitude; mentally, I changed balance. I had experienced the same thing, in myself and others, when we met with German visitors to England, after the war. 'I'm a lawyer and I work for the Legal Aid Bureau, which you may know handles the legal troubles of people who can't afford to go to law through the usual channels.'

'I've been in Johannesburg only a month –'

'Well, of course, then, how could you know? Anyway, as you can imagine, most of the people we help are Africans.

Not only are they poor, they're also the most ignorant of their rights.'

I said, half-jokingly, 'I've been led to believe they haven't many to be ignorant about.'

She seemed to consider this carefully a moment before she said, 'Those that they have we try to help them know and keep.'

I suddenly felt embarrassed and inadequate; Faunce or my mother would have known so well what to say to this woman; they would not have missed this opportunity to align themselves on the side of the angels. Since all I could do was mumble sympathetic approval, I kept a dull-witted silence. Perhaps she mistook it for impatience, for she went on at once with the imperturbability of the professional interviewer: 'I've come to see you about Amon Mofokeng.'

'Amon?' The flickering figure of the young black man who was always seen coming or going on errands and trips to the post office, suddenly jumped into a third dimension. He had another name, another life. 'What has Amon done?'

A smile broke the considering calm of her face. She had a square jaw – all her face was too broad for its size – and her white teeth were pretty against the pale gums that very dark people sometimes have. 'He hasn't done anything. He's got a mother, living in Jagersfontein location. Or at least, she was living there. She's been evicted, along with the other residents, and re-settled in a new native township. The only trouble is, she had freehold, a house of her own in the old location, and in the new place there is no freehold. The old story – I'm sure you've read about similar things before you came here.'

I nodded. I offered her a cigarette, but she put up her hand saying, 'Only after six,' and I withdrew the packet and took one for myself.

'We are going to use Amon Mofokeng's mother as a test case,' she said, bringing her black brows together over the bridge of her nose: one of those short, jutting noses with an abrupt bulge, turning slightly up, at the tip. 'We are going to ask the local authority to show cause why the owner of confiscated freehold property should be satisfied to receive leasehold property in compensation. We've chosen Amon's mother because she seems to have been the oldest freehold householder in Jagersfontein – she lived there for twenty-two years.'

'Where is this location?' I asked.

'Not in Johannesburg,' she said. 'It's part of a town named Jagersfontein on the West Rand – the gold-mines to the west of Johannesburg. They've started mining uranium there near Jagersfontein now, too, and the town's been going ahead furiously. Hence this move to give the Africans the boot; to push them further out of the way of the town.'

'You know, I believe my grandfather may be buried there,' I said. 'He fell in the Boer War at a place called Jagersfontein.'

She smiled, as if, like me, she had suddenly remembered the framed citation, my mother's foot pointed at the sword: Darling what on earth are you doing with that? 'It could be,' she said. 'There are several Jagersfonteins, but this would be a likely one for a Boer War grave.

'Well, as I say, we're going to use the old Mofokeng woman as a test case, and we need her son to help us for a day or two – the old lady's a bit bewildered about this business and she wants to have him around as moral support, to interpret for her and get dates straight and so on. I want to ask you to give him the necessary time off from work.'

'But of course,' I said. 'He could've asked me himself, for that matter. He can go off whenever he's needed.'

'That's very nice of you, Mr Hood. I think he didn't want to ask in case you thought it was just another one of the grandmother tales, and refused.'

'Grandmother tales?'

'You know – I've had a letter saying my grandmother's sick, and I must go home....' She stood up to take her leave.

I said, conversationally, 'I must say, Amon is about the last person I'd imagine as a *cause célèbre.*'

'It's not quite that' she said.

'I mean I haven't felt much interest in him, as a person; he's simply a part of the office set-up.'

'Of course' she said. But I felt sure she misunderstood me; surely that very non-committal politeness stemmed from a sense of moral superiority; she would be one of those for whom every utterance was a move to a black square or a white square.

'He reminds me of someone in our London office – only, of course, *he* happens to be an old chap of sixty-eight or nine, he's got too old for his job in the dispatch room, and he's gone full circle back to a kind of working second childhood, making tea and licking stamps. But he's like Amon; doing his work, but scarcely *there* at all. So it's difficult to believe that he's *there* anywhere else, either. You couldn't imagine meeting Johnson in a pub, having his pint of beer, for example.'

'Well, you certainly won't meet Amon in a bar!' She spoke gently, with her head a little on one side.

'I'm coming down too' I said, as she walked to the door. 'Let me collect my parcels and we'll continue this in the lift.'

'Isn't it finished?' she said, laughing.

She stood waiting for me; she had no hat, no gloves, none of the usual paraphernalia that women usually have to grapple with before they are ready to go out into the street, and so, oddly, the roles were reversed, and she stood as I was used to standing, while I loaded myself with packets and boxes. Miss McCann had the cover on her typewriter and was setting off with soap and towel for the cloakroom down the corridor. I asked her to lock up, and said good-bye. ' – Where's Amon?' I asked.

'He's run down to the Post Office with that registered letter for Better Books in Cape Town.'

But in the lift we talked of other things. 'I've just got myself a flat,' I told the neat dark head and little, tough face beside my elbow. The drop of the lift gave her that apprehensive, listening air that I often notice in people in lifts. I thought, irrelevantly, but with pleasure at being reminded of something I'd forgotten so long, of a Rilke poem I had once regarded as something awful and comforting:

And night by night, down into solitude
the heavy earth falls far from every star.
We are all falling. This hand's falling too –
all have this falling-sickness none withstands.
And yet there's always One whose gentle hands
this universal falling can't fall through.

When we got outside, the street was full of men and women hurrying with the bent backs of city people, hurrying against the crowded bus, the brief evening of leisure. It was the time to seek the delay of a pub. I wondered whether I should ask her to have a drink with me; I felt in myself the restlessness, the inclination to let myself be carried away by cheap music, the shoddy titillation of dim corners, the swimming, fish-eye view of the world after a few drinks, that usually presages in me that other and deeper hunger, for love; so I pass from being too easily pleased to the greatest of all dissatisfactions.

She said 'If your car's a long way, I can take you to it. Mine's just on the corner.'

'Thanks, but I have no car. I'm going to the bus.'

'Oh, then I'll give you a lift; it's easy for me.'

I decided that her company would be better than nothing; even if she annoyed me a little, she was pleasant. 'Thank you very much. I wasn't looking forward to bashing my way through the bus with this lot. But if you're not in a great rush, won't you come and have a drink first?'

We went, of course, into the Stratford; we were standing almost at the door, in any case. We went into the bar lounge – bars are for men only, all over South Africa – and sat at one of the yellow wooden tables with the scratched glass tops. The chairs had plastic-covered seats but the tall backs were stoutly Tudor and pressed hard between your shoulder-blades. Henry VIII in a muffin hat and a beard that looked superimposed on his face, like the beards small boys scribble on the faces of women on advertisement hoardings, stared at a gilt plaster lion that was the symbol of a South African brewery. Rings of wet shone up from the table.

She had two brandies and I drank gin, and we talked about flats – she had lived in three or four, and now had a cottage in the grounds of someone's house – and about her Legal Aid Bureau. She told me some amusing stories about divorce cases she had handled for the Bureau, and I found myself telling her something of the lighter side of my mother's and Faunce's preoccupation with the world's wrongs. I told her how Faunce had invited an ex-prisoner to dinner who entertained us by teaching us how to pick a lock, and how, another time, my mother had dashed all over London to get chickens killed according to Muslim ritual, in order to provide appropriate food for some Indian guests, only to find that the guests were Hindus and didn't eat meat anyway.

'It's so easy to be ridiculous when you're trying to identify yourself with the other person.'

'Of course,' she said, smiling reminiscently. 'But it's a risk you have to take, sometimes.'

'Oh, there are ways and ways. Thing is, not to presume too much on your own understanding; never meet the other one more than half-way.'

She continued to smile attentively, looking down into her glass; she was clearly the kind of person who often disagreed, but seldom argued: the sort of person who lets one run on.

My case for reserve against presumption began to take on some of the eager bombast I was decrying. I was aware of this, but, because she gave me the space of her attention in which to go on and make a fool of myself, somehow I could not stop. What did stop me instantly, what took my mind from what I was saying as surely as if a nerve had been cut between my brain and my tongue, was a snatch of voice that I knew. 'We could do some mud-slinging, too,': the phrase came to me clearly out of all the criss-crossed sibilants, laughs, and exclamations of the room. Who had spoken? In this town where I was a stranger, how could I know a voice? While I went on talking, my attention went all about the room, over the faces and the glasses and the cigarette smoke. And there was Cecil Rowe.

I hadn't even noticed, that day at Hamish Alexander's

what sort of voice the girl had. She was sitting, half-turned away from me, at a table with two men; they must have come in after we had, but people were going and coming all the time, and her entry must have been screened from us. She looked, too, quite different from the way she had looked at the Alexanders'. Even her hair was a different colour. She wore a very small black hat in a straight line on her forehead, and a black dress that showed her collar-bones. From where I sat, her face had the poster-like vividness of a woman who is heavily made-up. She was talking and gesturing animatedly, conscious of success with her companions.

She did not see me, but when Anna Louw and I rose to go, and had to walk past her half-turned back as we went out, she turned and stopped me, looking up. She had just taken a sip of her drink, and her mouth was parted. 'Well,' she said, 'And how are you?' The commonplace greeting was spoken like a challenge; as if I were someone from whom she had last parted in some extreme situation: drunk, angry, or in love.

'Why, well, as you see . . .' I said, foolishly. She did look different. Standing a foot or two from her upturned face, I saw that her eyes were orientalized with blue shading and black lines, her hair showed her ears and lay in short, silvery feathers against the velvet of her hat, the shape of her mouth had somehow been altered by lipstick. I noticed that just in front of her right ear she had a raised mole; it had been covered with the warm-looking extra skin provided by an opaque make-up, but it showed itself just the same. So, oddly enough, beneath all this, the woman showed herself too. She looked very attractive; knowing, greedy, unsentimental. I wondered which of the men, the thick fair one with the tight-filled skin, or the thinner one, also fair, was her husband. She did not introduce me, and so, although I was about to do so, I did not introduce Anna Louw, either, and, with a smile, walked on. But *she* remained turned in her chair and included Anna Louw in the smiling movement that said good-bye. When I saw her looking at Anna Louw, I remembered how, a month ago, I had thought that I would only have to be in the Stratford once, with a girl, in order to feel attached to the place. Cecil Rowe was that kind of girl. Sitting there among the men in their office suits and the briefcases laid by the Tudor chairs, she was as much the charm of the queer, public yet furtive life of town as a shepherdess, all ribboned crooks and roses, is of a pastoral idyll.

Even Anna Louw's car bore the signs of a woman who was accustomed to look after herself; in the dashboard cubby-hole there was a road map, a first-aid kit, and a card of fuse wire.

She said: 'What's your time?' And when I told her, five past six, 'Would you give me my cigarettes – they're in there somewhere.' I gave her one of mine, and she drew the first breath of it deep in as she drove, so that her small, compact body seemed to grow. 'That's the great thing about denying oneself something – the pleasure of having it again at last,' I said.

'Oh this first cigarette!' she said. 'The whole day seems to melt away.'

'I think perhaps that's why people make these rules for themselves; the emotional equivalent of dumping thousands of tons of coffee in the sea, in order to keep the price up.'

'That's a nice idea,' she said. 'It's much nicer than saying that you do it for your liver, if it's drink, or your lungs, if it's cigarettes.'

'But I believe it's true; mostly the health reason is the least of it. And it's the sort of subterfuge titillation that only arises out of plenty. The Africans you deal with – I'm sure they don't have to break a diet in order to appreciate a good meal, or go on the wagon for a week to make a drink taste wonderful. It's only people like us, who are sated with comfits of one kind and another, who have to go in for these dodges.'

'Poverty without boredom.'

'Yes.'

She smoked concentratedly for a moment before she took the cigarette out of her mouth and said, with her customary mildness (as if she had added up a line of figures and found an error), 'I think there's something wrong there. Poor people' – I wondered if she deliberately broadened the reference – 'can't afford things; and that makes anything you want seem marvellous. Wouldn't a cigarette seem just as wonderful to a man who couldn't afford to buy himself one all day, as it does to me, who have kept myself from one all day on purpose? – You see?'

'Ah, but his has been a real situation of want – yours is play.'

'He doesn't *want* to want; I do?'

'That's it.'

She laughed and shifted expressively in her seat: 'Oh, my friend, you don't know a thing about how I feel about smoking.'

A minute later she went on, 'But I think, so far as other things are concerned, there's something in what you say. I often think how it is that Africans don't have as many made-up troubles as my white friends. – You know the sort of troubles that people have, women particularly, women with not much to do. – Anyway, it's nonsense to generalize.'

'Do you know a lot of Africans?'

'I told you, most of our clients are Africans.'

'That's not what I meant.'

'Oh yes,' she said, 'I know some. Quite a few.'

I offered her another cigarette, and there was the business of lighting it and throwing the match out the window.

'Why don't you want to talk about it?'

She said, for time, as people do, 'What. Oh, it's not that I don't want to talk about anything. But you must understand that you are in a country where there are all sorts of different ways of talking about or rather dealing with this thing. One of the ways is not to talk about it at all. Not to deal with it at all. Finished. That's possible, you know; you'll find out.'

'I have. I've seen it. And apparently functioning perfectly,' I said. Archie Baxter poured the drinks, the twins dived into the Reckitts-coloured pool, someone blew a cloud of cigar smoke through which a Courbet landscape appeared as a mirage. Uranium, cannon bones, Kit's own regiment. 'I'm afraid I wasn't shocked at all. It was pleasant. It was like being anywhere else, only perhaps more comfortable.'

'There you are' she said, as if I were a child who had followed so far in a difficult lesson. In turn, I thought I recognized sweet reasonableness, that wide-eyed dissembler at Faunce's dinner-table; but, in all fairness, I had to admit that she *did* seem quite bluntly to agree. 'There you are. And there are the other ways. . . . You're a person I don't know, someone from whom I've asked a favour for a client. Isn't it better for me to leave it at that, rather than force upon you a consideration of my particular way? Force you into hostility, perhaps, because yours may be another?'

'But you must know that I haven't a way. I've only just got here.'

She looked at me quickly, as she drove. 'You will have, soon, and that adds up to the same embarrassment. Anyway, you must have arrived with some idea, all ready. Even if it's one that's impossible now you're here.'

I thought how steadily she spoke. The people whom I knew, I myself, seemed always to speak in rushes and checks, as if nothing ran clear in us, but struggled past uncertainties, squeezed thinly through doubts, and kept bursting the banks of conviction. She had an intonation and a rhythm of speech that was foreign to English, too, but was not the nagging sing-song of Miss McCann, the sing-song that seemed to me to be the dialect of Johannesburg.

I said, 'It's like love, or God; and I thought that here everyone would be discussing it over coffee cups, the way we do Russian foreign policy or expense accounts.'

Chapter 4

THE car had come to a standstill under the jacarandas in my street; we sat in a natural silence for a moment or two. There ought to be some punctuation mark specially to indicate such pauses, like the sign that indicates a rest in music. 'Where are you?' she asked. 'Oh, just over there, the one with the pillars.'

She started up the car again. 'I'll turn round and get right outside the door.' 'No, don't please, this is fine.'

'Do you find it very dull here?' she said, as she handed my parcels to me through the window.

'Well, I don't know. I don't seem to have any definite sort of life, yet. There are very few cities in the world that can stand up to being taken neat.'

'We always feel so apologetic about it,' she smiled. 'You get used to hearing people from England and Europe telling you that there's *nothing* here – rolling their eyes and throwing up their hands. . . . You don't know exactly what they mean, but you feel they're right.'

'What *do* they mean, d'you suppose?' The gathering darkness was like blotting-paper into which one shape ran into another; only her hands, resting on the steering wheel, and her face, showed in the car, and the street-lamps made pastel corollas for their luminous pistils out of the black mass of the trees.

'I used to think it was because everything in town life here relates to another world – the plays are the plays of Europe, the cabaret jokes are those of London or New York. . . . You know what I mean? Johannesburg seems to have no *genre* of its own . . . ?' She put her hand on the window in appeal. 'That's what people feel. Partly. But now I think there's something else. Loneliness; of a special kind. Our loneliness. The lack of a common human identity. The loneliness of a powerful minority.'

'I was told that no one walks in the streets here, at night,' I said. She said candidly, 'It's not so much that we're in danger, but that we're so terribly afraid.' We both laughed. 'You're not,' I said, convincedly. 'Oh yes I am,' she said. 'Afraid of the dark.' A lighted balcony sprang out from the flat building opposite and a man walked out on to it, holding a bottle of beer and a glass. He knocked the cap off the bottle against the railing, and when he had poured the beer into the glass, stood looking out into the evening like a horse put out to grass after a day's carting. From somewhere in the block of houses and shoddy flat buildings a voice screamed to the children playing below: 'For the last time,

I say . . .' An African servant woman came out of an alley fluidly as a cat; she went barefoot along the pavement, clutching a newspaper parcel, and then suddenly threw back her head and gave a great shouting laugh of greeting to someone we couldn't see.

The woman in the car and I had the reluctance to part company of two people with no particular commitments who have suddenly got on quite well together. There was no tension of attraction between us; no reason why either should pretend the demands of other, more private plans. Like most young men, I took for granted the aimless freedom to decide simply from one moment to the next what I would do. Even at home in England, the evenings were foreign ports through which I, a sailor off a ship of unknown destination, wandered, not very curious, not very expectant, yet always, somewhere below my rational self, aware that round some corner, one day, would be the face or the street-fight that would do as my destiny.

I was interested in what Anna Louw had to say, but not sufficiently interested in her as a woman for it to occur to me to wonder why she should seem to be fellow to this kind of freedom. I merely took it for granted that she was.

'Why don't we go and have some dinner?' I said. I had been standing on the pavement for ten minutes or more, still holding the parcels, and with no sign of going in to my flat.

Out of the dark, her voice was friendly, matter-of-fact, without intimacy, but without coquetry, too. 'I would have liked to ask you to bacon and eggs at my cottage, but the fact is, I'm supposed to go to a party.

'Why don't you come?' The words were spoken as the outcome of a decision.

'Could I?'

I saw her smile slowly in the dark. 'If you'd like to, of course you can.'

'Well . . . ?'

She waited for me to answer myself. 'I must dash up to the flat and dump these things. I need a wash.'

'I'll wait,' she said.

When I was across the road she leaned out of the car and called, softly, decorously: 'Don't change, you know. It's not a *party* . . .'

As I met myself in the thin ice of the bathroom mirror – even with the light on, there were corners in that bathroom that remained sunk in darkness, and there was always the feeling that if the brittle, peeling reflector broke, the image would fall into the steamy dark – I saw that my hair was dirty and in need of a cut. That morning I had managed to nick the lobe of my ear, and there was a little black crust of blood sealing the place. Nicotine had stained striations on my lower teeth. I saw another face: the painted, stylized, woman's face of Cecil Rowe, so pretty above the hollow collar-bones. It occurred to me as the face of another species than myself; I sometimes had this feeling about women, and it excited me. A wry form of romanticism, I suppose; if I could not believe them better, purer, gentler beings, I liked to see them, in a flash, now and again, as some charming creature in a tank or a cage.

I wondered what Anna Louw was thinking of while she waited for me down below in the car, with the crickets shrilling steadily through the lurching drunken quarrel of radios that came from the flat windows. When we drove off again, she seemed to have withdrawn a little, as if perhaps she doubted the impulse that had made her invite me to accompany her.

I tried to be as pleasant and easy as I could, in order to reassure her, like a dog showing, with sidlings and submissive flattened ears, that he will behave if he is taken along on a walk. Presently she parked the car under a street-light, and in its harsh wash, she looked tired as she said, 'This will be a mixture of people. It's not always a success.'

I felt that she almost wanted me to say, let's not go, let's drive away, go somewhere else. 'You don't have to worry. I'll find some way of letting everyone know that you hardly know me, that you've brought me along out of the kindness of your heart.'

She shook her head and laughed; the laugh turned into a weary yawn. She had the flatness of a person who has had several drinks rather too long ago, and is in need of several more, or a meal. I misunderstood her, but she could not bring herself to explain.

The house was a very small bungalow and it was filled with people; from the gate, shadows moving against the reddish, curtained light of the windows, and the deep vibration of voices and movement gave it the charged air of a house in full use. There fell upon us the subdued moment of entry; and then we tramped in over the worn boards of a narrow passage (the front door was off the latch) and a large, beautiful woman in a tight black dress that made it a struggle for her to walk, and a bright pink shawl whose fringe hung over the drink she kept upright in her hand, opened her eyes wide, lifted her eyebrows and, clasping Anna, held her away in what was apparently speechless joy at seeing her. From the way Anna kissed her hurriedly and cut in at once with her own greetings and introduction, I realized, before the woman got anything out, that she was not overcome, but simply unable to speak because she was a stutterer. At last, as if a hand had suddenly let go of her throat, she said in a rich torrent, 'S – so glad to have you, Mr Hood. Come in and I'll see if I can find something for you to drink – it's glasses that are the problem, I'm afraid. I tried to phone you and ask you to bring some, Anna –' And she drew us into a small, full room where a portrait of herself looked over the heads of fifteen or twenty people, some of whom were black men or some other dark-skinned race. Her eyebrows lifted again, her lips parted agonizingly as she prepared to call people's attention to me and introduce me, putting a long, strong hand, the hand folded like a lily in the painting, on my arm, but again Anna came gracefully to her rescue: 'Sylvia, darling, don't bother, I'll get Mr Hood circulating.' 'You'll f – give,' the woman turned to me in an apology that went mute. 'Of course,' I nodded and smiled, trying not to exaggerate these signs of goodwill the way one does for the deaf. She gasped something to Anna about the food; and then left us, swept her queenly way through the guests, and disappeared, in what I gathered was the direction of the kitchen.

A woman waved a glass at Anna across the room, from here and there, voices greeted her; we passed a little group deep and oblivious in some argument as cows in a stream, passed a slender tense man who smiled at Anna on bad baby teeth, in an aside from his tête-à-tête with a tall redhead, and made our way to a table crowded with bottles. It was true, there were no clean glasses – but we found two – the kind that have once contained cheese spread, and have a flower motif painted on the outside – that were at least empty.

A party has something in common with a battlefield in that, if you are in it, of it, you do not see it; your tête-à-tête or the little group in which you drink and talk is the party. But if you are a stranger, recognizing no one, drawn into no private context of friendship, there is a time, at the beginning of the evening, when you see the composition of the party as the armchair strategist sees the battle: steadily, formally, and whole.

As the stiff gin stole about my body, like a torch opening up a dark house, I saw the pattern of that room with an almost omniscient eye. Those other faces, dark faces, other hands, dark hands, emerging from the same old coatsleeves, made a difference. The pattern had the tangled fascination of an Oriental rug my mother once had, where, if you looked, the scrolls and flowers that you expected to see were also found to be people, animals, jokes, and legends; things that, in real life, are not found together, cheek by jowl in the space of one experience. Nothing very remarkable was happening in the room; three Africans were talking to each other, a conspicuously well-dressed Indian was explaining something surprising to a white man and woman (you could see the serious, eager incredulity on their faces), the scrum of white people near the door still kept head-down over the ball of their discussion, there was the usual couple – a white one – who have made of the party a place to be alone together, and the only African woman there – as far as I could see – sat ignored, smiling into a tumbler of wine. All these people lived together in one country, anyway; all their lines were entangled by propinquity.

Yet to have them in one room together, in the voluntary context of a party – to have them there because they wished to be there – did have, even for me, after one month in their country, the quality of the remarkable: the ordinary social pattern seemed as intricate and ambiguous in its composition as the Oriental rug.

A man broke away from the group of Africans and came up to get himself a drink; he had the sauntering, abstracted air of the man who always knows where the drinks are kept; 'The brandy run out?' he said to me. It was the first word a black man spoke to me that wasn't between master and servant. I moved away from the table so that he could look. 'See if Sylvia can raise another bottle,' he mumbled, and turned to the door through which she had gone earlier. Then he saw Anna. 'I knew you'd be somewhere here!' he said, grinning. He was a tall, thin man, with a long waist and a small round head. He was the pleasant, light colour of polished wood and his hair was like wool embroidery. His eyes were far away, burnt-out; he had a small, delicately-made nose, from whose characteristically flattened tip the nostrils curled back, and the gathered-together bones of his face gave prominence to his large mouth. When he smiled, charmingly, at Anna, he showed a battleground of gaps and fine broken teeth. 'It seems people just can't do without either of us, that's all,' said Anna, smiling. 'How've you been?'

'Oh, not bad, not bad.'

'This is Mr Hood, Steven – I don't think you told me your other name, did you?' she added, to me.

'Toby. Like the jugs.'

The other man laughed. 'That's a good name. That should have been the name for me.'

'Toby Hood, just from England – Steven Sitole.' We shook hands. He went through the formula absently: how-do-you-do, pleased-to-meet-you. 'How's your drink, Mr Hood?'

'Not good,' I said, for my glass was empty.

'Let me fix it for you,' he said, with expansive party amiability. 'And yours too, Anna.'

'No, Steven, you're a bad influence. I must set myself a time limit. Not more than one drink an hour.'

'She's quite a one for time limits, isn't she?' I said.

Steven was tipping gin into my glass. 'Is she?'

Indicating Steven, she said to me: 'We only meet at parties, and they're inclined to be timeless.'

He laughed at her admiringly, as if he had certain expectations of her, and she always came up to them. He was familiar and at ease with her, but the familiarity and ease were those of a foreigner: a Frenchman, Italian, or German not sure whether the English woman whom he has met is a fair sample of all the English women whom he will never know, or an exception under no circumstances to be regarded as representative.

His purpose, which was the bottle of brandy, was not to be deflected, and once he had given me my drink, he excused himself. Anna introduced me to the young man with the redhead – an Englishman – and then we drifted over to the earnest group near the door, which, in its turn, had taken in the Indian, Jimmy Naidoo, and his wife, who sat – on something so low and small that it was hidden by the draperies of her yellow sari – ample and vague in outline as a piece of municipal statuary whose sculptor has not dared attempt the feet. All the rest stood, and she looked up into the talk with an attentive and well-brought-up air, a sallow face with the sleepless look of deeply-ringed eyes. The other woman in the group was an Englishwoman with a Modigliani neck rising white and splendid to a slightly receding chin and a thick streaky coil of blonde hair that rested like a heavy hand on her nape; white arms and hands long and perfect, as if the mould in which they had been cast had just been gently cracked from them, were crossed over a flattened and exhausted-looking body in a green velvet dress. She had the ghost of a voice, and she had once been a painter; they were talking about painting. 'If I could paint,' said a grey-haired man who screwed up his eyes and bared his lower teeth in attack when he talked, '– especially if I painted in this country – I'd revive literary painting. There are too many landscape painters here.

They don't know how to deal with man, so they leave him out.'

'Or if they do put him in, they use only the picturesque aspect – they treat a face or a figure as if it were a tree,' said a young man who seemed to have struggled with his clothes and lost – the sleeves of his brown shirt hung over his wrists, but the collar was too small and had popped open under a very big woollen tie.

'What do you have in mind when you say literary painting?'

'"When did you last see your father,"' whispered the Englishwoman, who had been introduced to me as Dorothea Welz.

'And why not?' said the grey-haired man. 'What's wrong with pictures that tell a story?'

'Fine for backache pills,' said Naidoo, beaming.

'I think he means what I call *problem* pictures,' someone else said. 'A scene that poses a certain situation.'

'That's what he *said*. That's what literary painting is.'

'– a white child playing with an expensive toy under the eye of an African in one of those fancy maid's uniforms, and in the street outside the garden you see some tsotsis sauntering past – '

'Oh Christ!'

'. . . much abstract painting is, in fact, literary painting, the expression of ideas, what else can you call it?'

'. . . those nubile Zulu maidens, all boot-polish breasts and flashing teeth.'

'When are you going to paint again, Dorothea?' said the untidy young man, as if he were in the habit of questioning everybody about everything.

'Why should I?' she said, as if she really hoped for an answer.

Steven Sitole appeared beside me. 'What's Gerard Sekoto turning out these days?' someone turned to ask him. He shrugged, grinned irresponsibly. 'I wouldn't know. Do you know what's happened to him?' he asked me.

'Who's that?' I said.

'I don't think he's known in England,' Anna put in.

'Oh but he must be,' said the grey-haired man, 'Isn't he hung somewhere important, the Tate?'

'Musée National d'Art Moderne bought something,' whispered Dorothea, 'not London.' Those hands and arms looked as if they had never before been out of long white gloves.

The party formed, broke apart and reformed, like a shoal of fish; Steven was the one that darts about, in and out the body of the shoal at different points; the hostess, Sylvia, burst into the room at intervals, as a wave washes out the formation of a shoal, breaking up a conversation, dragging someone off to talk to someone else, begging another to help her with some kitchen mystery, and withdrew again, as a wave recedes over the bodies of fish, and they gently float back into their order of suspension in calm water.

With the third or fourth drink, I met the two Africans with whom Steven had been talking when we came in. They had long unpronounceable names, but they were also called Sam and Peter. Sam was short, hardly as tall as Anna Louw, and had the little man's neatness – well-shined shoes, a blue suit with a waistcoat, a red bow tie – and the astonishing, beaming face of the picture-book piccanin, the little Black Sambo face. I thought at once how awful it must be for him to know that he bore this face – large, shining brown eyes with curly lashes, the huge happy smile on white teeth, the large round head, uneven and top-heavy, like a tender gourd. It was as if an Englishman should find that he looked exactly like Lord Fauntleroy. Peter was boyish-looking, with a prominent Adam's apple, a pimply skin, and tiny ears that seemed to participate when he talked, and lay flat back against his head when he laughed, like a pleased animal's. He kept putting dance records, from a pile on the floor, on the superior sort of gramophone – part of an intricate high fidelity system with which the room was wired – to which nobody listened. Sam smiled at me over the soup; Anna had brought round a tray of cups of good hot borscht, cups so hot we had to hold them from hand to hand. Peter took one experimental swallow of the sweet-sour, earthy-scented brew and then left his cup behind the records. But Sam and I drank ours with relish. 'It's a Russian dish, isn't it?' Out of that small body, he had a deep, strong voice: 'Tell me, Mr Hood, do you know what Kvas is, perhaps?'

'*Kvas?* How do you spell it?'

We both laughed. 'Kvas,' he said. 'I'm just reading a book where somebody drinks it – she has a sudden longing to drink it. You know how it is, you want to know what this taste is she's thinking about.'

'A pity it wasn't borscht, now,' I said. Sylvia came up to us with her beautiful raised brows: 'A-all right? You've had some s-soup?' We showed our cups. 'It was delicious,' said Sam. 'But you haven't had a potato? You *must* have potatoes!' She rushed off, magnificently hampered by her dress, to fetch a dish of boiled potatoes. We had no soup left but we each took one.

'Always have potatoes with kvas,' I said to Sam. 'Always,' he said.

'Y-you've been reading Anna Karenina!' she got out, triumphantly. 'I remember, I remember! What's her name? The girl Levin marries – she drinks kvas.'

'Wants to drink it,' said Sam, opening up in a smile of pure enjoyment.

'He has – not me,' I said.

She put her hand on the little man's arm. 'Ah,' she said, with a deep, exaggerated breath that expressed the enthusiasm she would never get out in words, 'isn't that a m—' the m hung in the air for seconds. 'Miracle,' said Sam excitedly. 'That's what that book is; God, I think about it all the time I'm not reading it.' 'I hadn't read it for f-fifteen years, and then, only last year, when I was in hospital –' They went into an enthusiasts' huddle.

Some people had plates of food, by now, and there seemed to have been a lavish re-issue of red wine. They wandered in and out of what I had thought was the door to the kitchen, helping themselves. I took my empty soup-cup, and Sam's, and went the same way. The redhead, carrying a full plate and a glass of wine and a roll, called out 'Oops – mind me.' We were caught in each other's smiles for a moment, foolishly, like a cobweb. Seeing that she was rather drunk, I realized that I must be the same. But the hot soup gave me the illusion of a temporary check; weighted me down. I went soberly enough through the door and found it led into a passage, where an old man with misted glasses and the face of an embryo chicken said in a strong Eastern European accent, 'Is my vife still dere?'

'Which one's your wife?' I said, as I might have said to a lost child, which one's your mummy?

'Dorosea,' he said impatiently. 'Don't you know Dorosea?'

'I've just met a tall woman in a green dress.'

'Dat's right. Dat's right,' he said with relief, walking with me into a room fumigated with the stink of ripe cheese rising from a marmite on a Victorian marble-topped washstand that had been painted white. He wheezed a chuckle. 'To tell you za trus, I fell asleep, ya know. I fell asleep in Sylvia's room, there at the back. Honestly, I had no idea whether it's ten o'clock, three o'clock, one o'clock. Vot's de soup?'

'Have some.' I felt happily solicitous toward this pixie, strayed out of a Barrie play. He got his soup, and I helped myself to a plateful of risotto – like most arty women of her type, this Sylvia cooked very well, but overdid the garlic in the salad and on the hot bread – and we went back to the party together. He went up to the tall woman with the Bloomsbury elegance, and she looked down and spoke to him with the half-attention of connubial familiarity.

The record planged and faded; was lifted off and replaced with a tango. Suddenly, Steven Sitole and the little old man's wife, Dorothea, were dancing. She was as tall as he was, and they danced perfectly: like professionals, giving an exhibition, unaware of and uninterested in each other, his drunken face in a courteous trance, as if transfixed by the graceful and precise pattern through which his feet were guiding him, her abashed and broken, wilted body recalled to discipline. She danced as she spoke: as if everything were over, for her. Presently he returned her to her coffee.

At some point during the evening, Anna Louw had done something to her make-up and acquired – I suppose from the hostess – a shawl of red silk over the business-like dress she had been wearing when she walked into my office five or six hours earlier. I danced with her; she had the air of distinctness that a sober person has in a room where everyone else's aura is quickened and blurred by euphoria – as if their souls were in motion while hers was still. 'Good party,' I said.

'I'm glad.'

I felt sorry I'd wished her someone else in the bar in the town.

Steven Sitole had been standing over the solitary African girl, one arm on the wall behind her, his back screening her from the room, in the other hand, the glass that was never empty. Yet this show of attention had the perfunctoriness of a joke; it reminded me, somehow, of the absent-minded attentions of the twin to the American beauty at Marion Alexander's lunch.

'Steven's a charmer,' I said.

She glanced at him a moment, but said nothing. 'Have you had a chance to talk to Sam, Sam Mofokenzazi?'

'Not really. That's the little one?'

'He writes well – I think. I don't mean his job – he's a journalist on a paper for Africans that's published in English. His own stuff, stories and so on. And he writes music.'

'And Sitole? What's he do?'

'Insurance agent. He used to be a newspaper man, too. He spent a year in England after the war.'

'Is that the important thing about him?'

'Yes.' She looked at me in my innocence. 'That's rather like returning from that bourne whence no traveller returns. Africans can't pop in and out of Africa.'

The African girl had been persuaded, giggling, away from the wall, and now she sat awkwardly on a table, among the bottles, disposing her head and her hands in the manner of someone who is about to sing. The gramophone was stopped. In the hastily assembled silence (a voice cried out: What's happened to the music, damn it? – a group of talkers were shushed, Sylvia crept grandly about refilling glasses with wine) she assumed a professional coquetry. She sang a popular torch song, in the innocent, sensual voice that I have always enjoyed in American Negro singers, the pagan voice in which sex is not suggestive and guilty, but overt and fine. She tried to imitate the vocal titillations of white singers she must have heard on records, but the strange shrill of her high notes and the gentleness of her low notes escaped artifice: all the warm, continuous gamut of sensuality was there, from the mother's breast to the lover's bed. Delight was like a sudden, simple happiness in the room; the catalyst that I have sometimes seen come upon the isolated units of an audience at a concert. She sang on; another torch song – a piece of wild, ritualistic swing that sent the young Peter off dancing to himself in a corner, panting and jerking – even a sentimental ballad in Yiddish, and then songs in her own tongue and others that sounded the same to me. Sometimes, from across the room, Sam and Peter would come in like the toll of two big bells, or the low accent of the big bass. Sylvia, who had tiptoed up beside Anna Louw, whispered, 'Thank God she *sings*, at least. Their women never utter. One simply c-can't have them.'

'How did she get here?' I asked, since it was obviously not by invitation. 'The way I did?'

Anna laughed, 'Steven must have brought her. Quite a triumph; she's very popular. She's Betty Ntolo. She sings with their best band.'

When her songs were over, the African girl was danced round once by the untidy young man who had talked about painting, and then returned to the chair in which she had been sitting all evening. Once she was not performing, an insurmountable naïveté cast her, so to speak, underfoot; it was impossible to rescue her from it, because the moment anyone, with a polite word or an invitation to dance, made an attempt, they threatened to go down with her in the threshing ineptness of her giggling unresponse. I danced with her, for three or four interminable minutes. I had gone up to her to tell her how much I liked her songs, but once I had said this, and she had giggled as if she were going to bring out something paralysingly funny, and then said the single word: 'Yes,' I was aware that I couldn't simply walk away, and couldn't carry the conversation one monosyllable further. So I asked her to dance, a request to which she could, and did, respond by getting to her feet, tittering, and saying nothing.

She had a pretty, golden-brown face powdered dull, and a sooty beauty-spot was drawn next to her left eye; her ears, like Peter's, were smaller and neater than any adult ears I had ever seen, and in them hung large gilt hoops. She wore a kind of turban of black chiffon that covered her hair, and was secured with gilt-nobbed hatpins. Every now and then, as she followed me, her pink tongue came out to touch her top lip and looked pleasing against her white teeth. She had large, round, prominent eyes, bovine and rather yellowed. They were quite blank; as if, here, she was frightened to think.

The top half of her body was slight and her waist small, but she was weighted down with great solid hams, monumental calves, and feet that made trumpery out of the high-heeled sandals strapped round them.

I said to her, 'I hear you sing with a band.'

'Yes.' Like a child trapped in the kindly interrogation of a well-meaning uncle.

'What's the band called?'

She answered something unintelligible; her brown hand with its meaningless armour of red-painted nails was cold with pride and misery.

'I'm sorry, I didn't quite catch it.' I bent my head to her.

Like many singers, who successfully manage half a dozen languages in as many songs, she was not so good when she spoke. 'The Township Ten,' she said, with a strong accent.

The Indians were going; the wife stood at the door with a camel-hair coat over her sari, patient and bored, while the husband made his conscientious round of farewells. Anna was dancing with the Englishman with the baby teeth, and the redhead, suddenly before me, blew a cloud of smoke between her face and mine. When I had led the African girl to a chair, I went back to the redhead. 'About time,' she said.

'You've been much occupied.'

As we danced, she leant her head back to talk and her two breasts touched my chest firmly and distinctly, buttonholing me.

'Stanley's a bloody leech,' she said. 'You drunk?'

'No.'

'So'm I. Let's have some wine.'

We went, clumsily arm-about, like two boxers after a fight, to the drinks. 'How'd you like to have a picture like that of yourself in your room, Sam?' Steven Sitole was saying. 'Oh I know it's revolting to have oneself staring at oneself all the time,' said Sylvia, hiding her face in her glass of wine. When she suddenly spoke fluently, it was as if some other self were speaking up inside her. 'Oh, I don't know,' said Sam, admiring a foreign custom. 'I think, for a woman, it's rather nice.' 'A rep-proach to me, a reproach to i-idiotic vanity – did I ever look like that? Or d-do I only think n-now that I did? Now that I can blame the difference on baggy eyes and wrinkles and a jacket crown on a tooth?'

I am bad at caressing women publicly; I looked foolishly encumbered by the redhead, and I knew it, and so all the pleasure was gone from the contact with her tall, warm body. We dropped apart and she went to Stanley, murmuring up to him in relief at the escape. I drank somebody's glass of wine and looked from Sylvia to her portrait. 'When was it done?' 'Oh don't be so bloody t-tactless!' There was laughter. The portrait looked right into your eyes, the way she herself did; but she must have been much more self-centred then: the face looked aware of the feather curving down from the hat, the shadows exchanged by the black hair and the wine-coloured dress. It was a portrait of a woman thinking about herself. 'A Spanish or Italian beauty,' I said.

'Why is that always considered the compliment?' Sylvia asked the company. 'I'm a Jewess; couldn't one say I used to be a beautiful one?'

'Berenice, then,' I said, looking at her. 'That's exactly it. The beautiful queen.' Talk and laughter and argument swept another way. I could not follow it because of a pressing need; I wandered through the house but did not come upon the bathroom, so I went out into the dark garden, beyond the light of the windows. The physical relief, the fresh night air after the close room, and slow, pleasant turning of the wine in my head brought me to peace with myself. I staggered a little, but I was at home on this earth. A shape like my own brushed past the shrubs, and I was joined by someone. It was Steven Sitole. 'What are you doing here?' he said, as we stood companionably. I laughed. 'Same as you.'

He found this very funny. '– I'm selling books, I'm connected with a publishing firm.'

He took out a packet of cigarettes and we strolled down to the gate, smoking. 'I used to be a journalist,' he said. 'I know, Anna Louw told me. What made you give it up?' 'Various things,' he said, in the vague, jaunty tone, mysterious and important, that I recognized as the tone of the man whom many jobs give up. 'I had other things on the go. I couldn't manage everything at once.' 'So what do you do now?' Anna had told me, but I had forgotten already. 'Insurance. Much more money in it.' 'You mean the usual sort of thing, life policies and so on.' 'That's right,' he laughed pleasantly. 'Fire, funeral, accident, loss – all that stuff. Of course, we're not like you people, mostly we insure against things we're sure will happen, funerals mainly. Yes, I exploit the poor simple native, and in return he gets a lovely funeral – what do you say, a slap-up do.'

'Did you really like England?'

'I shouldn't ever have come back here.' He stumbled and I caught his arm. The darkness accepted him; his face and hands were gone in it; he sat down on the grass. 'If you'd stayed,' I said, searching for the right kind of meaningless reassurance, 'if you'd stayed, you would have longed to come back.'

'Man, there's nothing in Africa I want,' he said, grinning, and I became aware of his face again, though I could not see anything but his teeth; that smooth, polished-wood face with the withdrawn eyes, the delicate nose, the gathering-up of planes toward the mouth. Suppose he had been born to the old Africa, before the Arab and the white man came, suppose he had had a tribe, and a place in that tribe, and had known that his life was to hunt and fight and reproduce and live in the shelter of fear of the old gods – would that have been what he wanted? I thought of him in the room from where the blur of music and voices sounded, lean and gangling and befuddled, with a glass of brandy in his pink-palmed hand with the too-long nails. The idea was sad and ridiculous. And then I thought of myself, and what I wanted: a house lived in, a place made, a way of life created for me by my fathers, a destiny I could accept without choice or question. That was not sad and ridiculous. The wine closed over my head, and, sunk in myself, I fiercely and dismayedly resisted the idea; that could not be sad and ridiculous. It was what I wanted and could not get.

'Let's go,' he said. I turned, in agreement, toward the house.

'Let's go and drink. I'll take you to a place. You're an Englishman, I can take you. Show you round. "Can I show you around?" Do the honours.' The phrase pleased him and he repeated it, shaking his head and making a clicking sound of approval.

'I came with Anna Louw. How can I?'

'Woman'll get herself home,' he said. He stood up, threw his cigarette into the hedge, and a dog, scavenging along the gutter in the deserted street, stiffened into hostility and began to bark at him. He cursed it amiably. 'They always bark at us. You don't have to teach them, they know. People like Sylvia don't know what to do to stop them. Hers is locked up, so he won't embarrass her.'

When we got inside again, he seemed to forget his suggestion. He got into a political argument with Sam, Dorothea Welz, and the Englishman, Stanley, against whom the redhead leaned, silent. I danced, dazedly, with Sylvia, and, her tongue loosened by wine, we talked about London and Aden Parrot paper-backs. Anna Louw came up and said, 'Darling, I have to be in court at nine tomorrow and I haven't even finished preparing my stuff.' 'Anna!' Sylvia was concerned. 'Honestly, I must go. But you don't have to come,' she said to me. 'Don't you come because of me.

Someone else will always take you home.' I protested my willingness to go, but she knew I didn't want to. I thanked her, tried to tell her across the restlessness of the room that I would telephone her to do so properly, but she slipped out with the considerateness of one who does not want to break up a party. Old Welz went with her: Dorothea had rushed up, when she saw Anna leaving, and begged: 'For heaven's sake, take poor Egon with you, will you, Anna? He's had a long day and he's quite dead.' 'Thank God.' The little man put his arm round Anna. 'It's enough. Let's go. Sylvia, Sylvia, thenk you. You are a woman of qvality. Look how you last; the others,' his chin jerked in the direction of the redhead, 'they droop, their paint runs. ...' 'Oh, go *on*, Egon, do,' said Dorothea. 'As soon as I've proved myself unquestionably right, I'll follow. ...' Steven had dropped out of the argument and was singing, a soft, two-part Bantu song, with Sam. Sam waved his hand gently, to keep Steven in time. Steven's cigarette held its shape in ash, burnt down in his forgotten fingers. 'Come on; again,' Sam coaxed. When Sitole saw me, he stopped the song abruptly and the ash fell on his shoe. 'Let's go and drink. I'll take you,' he grinned.

'In what?'

'Your car.'

'I haven't got a car,' I said. Peter had just put on a particularly loud record, and he was trying to persuade the African woman to sing again.

'No car.' Steven put a hand down on Sam's shoulder and laughed. 'He hasn't got a car.'

'Don't all white men have cars?' said Sam, with obedient good humour, giving his line.

'Once upon a time,' said Steven, 'dear children, there was a man who didn't have a car. All right. We'll use Sam's.'

'Steve, I have to go straight home.'

'He's married,' said Steven, in a high voice, 'Sam's a married man. Ah, go on, Sam.'

A few minutes later, when I was talking to someone else, he came up and said: 'Sam wants to go now, Mr Hood.' I excused myself and went with Steven back to the table where Sam was. 'Sam'll drop us off where we're going,' said Steven. We had one more drink, and then left, with Peter and the woman singer. We went almost unnoticed, for the party had suddenly blazed up again, as a dead fire will when a handful of crumpled letters catches the last spark. I know that I kissed Sylvia, and her cheek smelled of powder, and the others shook hands with her. The stray dog was still in the street, and he circled the car with a stiff tail, gurgling threateningly.

Sam's little Morris was new and went with the smoothness of a car that is taken care of, though it was heavily loaded. I sat in front, beside him, and Steven, Peter, and the woman were pressed into the back. It was nearly one o'clock in the morning and all life was withdrawn from the streets in the white suburbs through which we drove, and the town. We followed tram-car tracks, we skirted the sharp corners of darker, meaner streets; the car took me along as the world whirls and turns through space: I had neither recognition nor volition in its progress. The street-lights ended. We went down, into the dark. There were shapes, darker against the darkness; there was the moon, half-grown, spreading a thin, luminous paint on planes that reflected her. A graveyard of broken cars and broken porcelain; an old horse sleeping, tethered, on a bare patch; mute shops patched about with signs you could not read; small, closed houses whose windows were barred with tin strips against the street; a solitary man stooping to pick up something the day had left; a sudden hysterical gabble behind a rickety fence, where a fowl had started up. Sam stopped the car. 'You're sure this is what you want, Steven,' he said. Steven laughed and answered in their own language. He struggled out of the back, and I got out. We said goodnight. Sam seemed uncertain about leaving us there; he stood looking at us for a moment, and then he revved the engine rather longer than was necessary before he drove away.

The street had the comforting, out-dated sinisterness of a back-alley habitation, deserted and late at night. I have grown up to a world whose bogeys are bombs and the horrors of atomic radiation; in people like me there is a certain nostalgia about the personal, palpable threat of flesh-and-blood robbers and assassins, those bogeys of the past, long out-shadowed in evil. I felt a mild and pleasant excitement, adjunct to my drunkenness. Steven went along with the happy ease of a man who could have found his way in his sleep; he was at home in a dark and lonely street. He sang softly, under his breath, in his own language; so softly, he might have been breathing music. There was a little street-light, rheumy and high up, on the corner, and he took the top of my arm in his thin, hard hand and guided me to the right. There was some light here and there, behind windows – as if the dark had worn thin. And one door, leading right out on to the pavement, was open. From it, light the colour of orangeade made a geometrical shape of brightness in the dark. 'No good,' murmured Steven, and turned me sharply round again. 'What's wrong?' 'If the door's open, the place is shut; that's wrong.' At the corner once more, I saw him grinning at me affectionately under the pale splash of the street-lamp: 'I'm looking after you, Mr Hood.' We felt we understood each other very well, in the manner that drunks do; just as they may equally suddenly feel curdled with long-borne grievances against each other, and may be compelled to fight.

'Here.' We turned into an unlit yard, with two rows of rooms or cottages – each row seemed to be under one continuous roof, but there were four or five doors in the length of each. They were shut against the night as if they were deserted and empty, but our feet were sucked by mud round a tap that snivelled and drizzled, and there was a strong smell of rotting vegetables, and the general sourness of a much-used place. Beyond and slightly behind the end wall of the right-hand row, there was a small detached building with some kind of lean-to porch attached – a creeper grew over it like a fishnet draped to dry. Steven pushed me up three broken steps and knocked on the door. The knock gave back its own sound; but in a moment the door opened the width of a face and a voice spoke, sleepily it seemed to me, and then changed its tone with recognition when Steven murmured. Of course I could not understand what was said.

But we went in, past a woman's face with a woollen scarf wrapped round the head, under the candle she held against the wall. I remember noticing that it was the swollen-looking face of a stupid woman. We went through a cave of a room where something smallish, probably a child, was asleep on an iron bed, and the candle caught, in passing, a bunch of paper roses and a primus stove, and then into a larger room with walls painted olive green half-way up like the waiting room in a station, and an electric bulb with a celluloid shade hanging over a table where four or five men did not look up. There was also another group, sitting on a bed, and they stubbed out their laughter, almost with relief, as if it had gone on too long beyond the merit of what had occasioned it, as we came in, and started talking in what, even in a language I didn't understand, I could recognize as the interrogatory tone of a change of subject. Everyone was drinking, but there were no bottles in sight. On the walls, a huge Coca-Cola calendar – a girl on a beach, in bathing costume and accompanied by a tiny radio and a carrier of Coca-Cola – hung with the look of inevitability of a holy picture given its niche. It was the barest room I had ever been in in my life; it depended entirely on humans.

Most of the men seemed to know Steven. If they happened to catch his eye they nodded; one or two said something. A man in American-looking trousers and a pastel shirt with a bow tie got up. Steven asked him a question; he answered; Steven nodded. The man went out of the door – not the door by which we had entered, but another next to the chimney that had no fireplace beneath it, and in a moment came back with two tumblers. 'Have you got two dollars?' said Steven, taking a half-crown out of his pocket. I gave him a pound; 'Ten bob'll do,' he said, as he took it. He paid for the drinks and for a moment, as the change was counted out, I saw, very close, the face of the man who had brought them; a broad face, smooth and the colour of olive oil, almost Chinese-looking, with a very large straight mouth whose width was accentuated by a pitch-black moustache that followed the outline of the upper lip closely, and even went down, parenthetically, round the two sides.

'You drink brandy and coke?' said Steven.

Room was made for us at the table; a man in the grease-stiff cap of a garage attendant lifted his head from his arms and regarded me as if he believed he were seeing me with some inner sight, the drunk's sight. Steven had taken his drink at a gulp. He said, patronizingly, 'I should have taken you to one of the Vrededorp places, where other whites come, and you wouldn't be noticed.' 'Who comes?' I said; I was feeling the conspicuous unimportance that a child feels in a room full of words he doesn't understand. 'Not many like you,' Steven laughed, narrowing his nostrils and lifting his chin as if he were telling me something highly complimentary. 'White bums and down-and-outs.' Then he called across my head to the group talking on the bed; a young man in one of those cheap knit shirts with a picture stamped on the chest, took up the exchange, which was laughing, scornful, and animated. I had the feeling it might be about me. Perhaps it was. I didn't care. You always think people are talking about you when they use a foreign language.

Two men left; their hands were pushed into their pockets in the manner of those whose pockets are empty. Like the room, this shebeen in which they had taken their pleasure, they were bared. They had nothing but themselves. Cheque-books, those little purses women have, foam-rubber cushions, the deathly moonlight of fluorescent strips; these things came to my mind confusedly, mockery and salvation. I felt very drunk; all the room was retreating from me, draining away like water down a plug-hole, with a roaring gurgle that I didn't understand. Steven's voice, right in my ear because it was English, was saying, 'I was good at darts in England. I used to walk into the pub and take anybody on. They used to call me Lucky. Imagine that. Why d'you think they called me Lucky?'

'You must call me Toby,' I said, feeling it was urgent.

'Did they call me Lucky because they call you Toby?' said Steven, finishing another brandy. I pictured, with the dreamy pleasure of casting together the here and there, the tall black mascot in the London pub. I seemed to feel, myself, the spurious superstitious power of the other race; if you sleep with a Jewess (Negress, Chinese) you will never want any other kind again, gipsies read the future – and Queequeg, I saw Queequeg like those pictures I'd seen of American cigar-store Indians. I said something to Steven about Queequeg but he'd never heard of Moby Dick. He said, 'We like to read the Russians. You'll see, Africans want to read Dostoyevsky, man, they read lots of Dostoyevsky.'

I said, '*You* read that somewhere, Steven.'

There was a shout of laughter from the group in the corner.

He laughed in ready guilt. 'Anyway, a few do. They read Dostoyevsky because they want to feel miserable, to glory in another misery. I follow the racing page,' he added swaggeringly. But even he didn't believe in himself, as a man of the world. 'The comics,' he said, putting on a serious, considering face, 'and the comics.

'Trouble with me,' he went on, 'I don't want to feel miserable, I don't want any glory out of it. Sam and Peter and all those others, yap-yap all the time, chewing over the same old thing, this they've taken from us, that they've denied our children, pass laws, injustice – agh, I'm sick of it. Sick of feeling half a man. I don't want to be bothered with black men's troubles. You know that, Toby? These –' and he circled the noisy room with a movement of his slim black hand with the too-long fingernails and a signet-ring in which a piece of red glass winked, exasperated and distasteful.

'A private life,' I said. 'That's what you want.' He caught my arm. 'That's it,' he said. 'That's it,' while I nodded with the reiteration of a discovery. There it was, the truth. The drowned, battered out, howled down, disgraced truth. This young man with the brown face given a blueish, powdered look by drink and fatigue, with the ruined teeth and the flecks of matter at the outer corners of his stranger's eyes – this young man and I, two strangers, had just cornered it in a small hour of the night like an animal almost believed to be exterminated entirely. We were drunk, yes, but we had it there. It was ours, a mouse of a truth, alive. Created by drink or not, I had had few such moments in my life, even in my own country, among my own friends. We did not understand each other; we wanted the same thing.

When Steven suddenly stood up, sending an empty glass rolling down the table, I stood up too, because the need for abrupt departure was what I myself felt: when you are brought to face yourself, the moment must be broken, as you must turn away if you look into your own eyes in a mirror. But the woman with the woollen scarf round her head was standing in the doorway, the one through which we had not come, and she was saying something terse to the man with the pastel shirt and the Chinese-smooth face. Whatever it was that she said drew the whole room to its feet in crisis. Steven yelled 'Come on, man' crazily and dragged me, knocking into shoulders, backs, past someone who was shaking and heaving at the unconscious man with the greasy cap, into the cowering dark room through which we had entered when we came. He jumped up on what must have been the head of the bed I had noticed – the springs squeaked and he almost overbalanced – and fumbled at the window. 'Christ Almighty,' he was saying, 'Christ Almighty.' It was a sash window and at last it gave stiffly, then helter-skelter. 'Steven, are you mad?' 'It's the police, my dear Mr Hood.' He stood grinning at me for a second. 'Do you want to go back to town in the Black Maria? Get on.' The top half of the window had joined the bottom, so we had to climb out of the upper half. Steven balanced on the sill and then went over; I heard a thud outside. I was alone in the strange little hovel-room a moment. The outline on the bed; it was still there – was it a child, or a bundle of clothes? It was too dark to see. The smell of the room came to me; the stuffiness of sleep, a dankness, like a shed with an earth floor, and something else, a sweet, fecund smell of coal-smoke and fermentation. And then I fell out into the night, and landed, surprisingly, quite well, with only one hand to steady myself on the ground, in an alley. Steven hissed at me and I flattened, giggling, against the wall. We heard shouts and the heavy running of police boots. The shuddering, rubbery bump of a fast car stopping. Overhead, two stars had the burnt-out look of fireworks the second before they die away. The sky was steeped to a clear, transient green, a becoming rather than a colour. We shinned – very noisily, it seemed to me – over a wall into a yard much like the one where the shebeen was. A thin white dog barked and snarled and wagged its tail. 'Kaffir dog,' said Steven, ignoring it. We passed a row of rooms, went out into the street, and then calmly walked into the fenced 'garden' – there was a peach-tree, and a path outlined with bricks – of a house on the opposite side of that street. As we passed beneath the windows on the side, a voice called out. Steven answered cheerfully; and the voice came back, charmed. There was no fence at the back of the house; there was the piece of ground with the horse tethered on it that I had noticed before.

The green was gone. The sky was all light now, but not the light of day. 'Best thing I can do with you –' Steven was overcome by a fit of uncontrollable yawning. There was the virago shriek of a police car, behind us, to the left of us, we did not know where. This time I did not need any example from Steven. With one impulse we scrambled over a curling galvanized iron fence and found ourselves on the roof of a low shed among pumpkins put out to ripen. Steven put a pumpkin under his head, as you might use a plump quilted cushion for a sofa nap. We lay there panting and laughing in swaggering, schoolboy triumph.

All at once, it was morning.

PART TWO

Chapter 5

THAT day had a second morning. Steven had found a taxi-driver friend to take me home, and I got into bed in my flat about five o'clock, just as the yelling, whistling, and clanging of a new day was beginning in the roof-top servants' quarters of the buildings all around me. But I slept. These mercilessly cheerful sounds were whisked away from me instantly and I sank from gibbering, gabbling level to level of nightmare until, like a stone, I lay at the sea-bed of sleep. I never read or listen to accounts of other people's dreams and I have an unbroken vow never to recount my own, so I will not describe what I saw and experienced on the way; I will only say that when I woke, as I did with knife-stroke abruptness when the flat boy came in to clean, I seemed to have awakened from months-long sleep and heavy dreams. I had landed on a corrugated iron roof among the pumpkins; all that went before that – the ship plying south in warmer and warmer seas, the hotel, the parties and faces, the Stratford and Arthur Hollward's office – seemed as exaggerated, high-coloured, and hallucinatory as the room in Sophiatown where I had been drunk with Steven. I felt as if I had just arrived in Johannesburg. I knew, in my bones, without opening my eyes to the room, where I was, that morning. Sick, shaky, insatiably thirsty, and with the restless aching in my hands and feet that I always get with a hangover, I was aware of the place as one would silently accept a familiar presence on a morning too hideous for speech or sign.

I went to the office at noon, and shut myself in; twice I sent Amon out, first to get me aspirins, then a bottle of lime juice – I had read somewhere that the quickest way to rid your bloodstream of alcohol is to wash it away with innocuous liquids. The second time, as he was leaving the room, he hesitated at the door and tramped slowly back to my desk. 'I wish to tell you, thank you, sir, for the permission to go off,' he said.

'What's that?' I wished he would not mumble; one always had to go over twice whatever he had to say.

As he began again, I suddenly remembered. 'Oh, that's all right. Just try and let us know the day before you're needed, eh, Amon.'

The day climbed to the full power of its summer heat in the early afternoon; when I went to the window, seeking ease and air, an unbearable brightness flashed off everything metal and there was a tarry smell from the melting street. I opened letters from my mother and Faunce but did not get so far as to read them.

When at four o'clock I gave up and decided to go home, I walked out of the building and straight into Cecil Rowe. For a moment I had a wild hope that she would not see me, that somehow the cruel street that, after the cool and dim lift, almost put my eyes out with glare, would blind her to me. All around me, the melting make-up on the women's faces gave them the swimming look of a mirage, the men were flushed and shiny or greenish and greasy, as if the heat were a fever alternately producing flushes and chills. A few street Africans had gone into immobility, caps over eyes, against whatever poles or shopfronts offered support. I stopped and turned to the fat newspaper seller who, brisk with purpose in all weathers, had just dumped his pile of evening papers on the kerb. But she was there, at my side. She said, 'Why are you always around this part of the world?'

I couldn't find change to pay for my paper. While I dredged into my trouser pocket, I felt, feebly, that I couldn't defend myself against her. Again she was dressed with showy simplicity, a cosmetic emanation – not merely the perfume she had used, but the impregnation of skin, hair, and clothes with the incense of the rites of female self-worship – came headily from her. 'I've only met you here once before.'

'Yes. Yesterday,' she said, as if this called for an explanation. 'So it was.' I really could not believe that it was only twenty-four hours since I had encountered her in the bar.

She laughed. 'You *are* vague,' she said, then, mimicking my startled air: 'Yes, it was yesterday.'

'My office is here, in this building.'

She craned her neck, smooth with powder under the tight necklace that the flesh swelled against as she talked. 'Up here? Above Adorable? Well I'm darned!'

'What is Adorable – I've been wondering ever since I've been here.'

She opened her handbag, as if compelled to get my fumbling over with. 'Here' – she gave me three pennies for the paper seller. 'It's Paul's place – the hairdresser. My hairdresser; that's where I've come from now.'

She wore one of those wide hats that every now and then hid her face entirely; from what I could see of her hair it looked different again; brighter, gilded. It seemed to me stupid and tiring to be expected to find an approach to a woman who changed herself every day.

She was looking at me curiously, with a faint rise of interest. 'You look awful,' she said. 'What's happened to you since yesterday?'

'I feel grim,' I said, with a smile.

'This bloody heat *is* grim,' she said. 'I'm going to go home and lie in a cold bath. Thank goodness I don't have to do any social drinking today.'

There was a pause; one of those imperceptible moments of hanging-fire when the direction a conversation is to take is silently decided.

Almost reluctantly, I was the one to speak. Yet the instant in which she saw that I was about to do so, her eyes gave the faint blink of encouragement and part responsibility.

'I was trying to decide which one was your husband.'

She said, 'They're two idiots who make film advertisements.'

'And you act in them.'

She pulled a face. 'Not yet. I've been fiddling about, doing a bit of modelling lately. As you see.' She indicated herself with sudden naturalness, as if she were in carnival dress.

'You look charming,' I said, dutifully.

'Thank you.

'So you see', she spoke again, quickly, 'that was why I

didn't introduce you when you came up to the table yesterday.'

I remembered, out of the hazy immediate past, how animated and eager she had seemed with her companions. 'You appeared to be enjoying yourself very much.'

'Oh, my *dear*' – an echo of that same social manner sounded in her defensive voice – 'Enjoying myself! And you thought one of them was my husband – what a mood of self-deception you were in!'

'Oh well,' I said wearily, 'anyway, I'm forgiven, you're forgiven –'

'Forgiven?' she said shrewdly, happily, '*I'm* forgiven? What for – ?'

I was confused. 'Not introducing,' I said, and she knew that I meant, 'For enjoying yourself so much.'

So I found myself in the Stratford bar again, and this time I had what I had wanted; I was with the girl, Cecil Rowe. But this carelessly-aimed largesse from whatever pile of favours has been stored up in the name of my existence, was flung at me on the wrong day. I was tired and the idea of a drink filled me with nausea; but it was more than that; the girl I had coveted jealously yesterday, the girl I had met at the dream-feast in the Caliph's house above the gold-mines, the fair lady to my urban knight, pinning her colours on a briefcase – she belonged to the unreality through which I had fallen. It was odd to find her here at all; it was an effort to confirm her existence in, and therefore her sober kinship with, the city that I was aware of when I wakened in my flat that morning.

I sat with her in the bar on the hard Tudor chairs under the sign of the plaster lion and the picture of Henry the Eighth, without a trace of the triumph and pleasure I had imagined, but male opportunism, with the farsightedness of instinct, saw to it for me, in spite of myself, that I behaved just as I would have if that triumph and pleasure had been alive in me.

As we sat down, she said, with a careless air of wanting to get it over with, 'About the husband; I have no husband, idiot or not. I'm divorced.' And as we both laughed, she added: 'I never know whether to tell people or let them find out. If I say nothing, they say something that embarrasses them, sooner or later, and if I come out with it, it always sounds like an *announcement*.' She was rather forlornly lively (perhaps my own subconscious inert state affected her) and she clutched a young Englishwoman's bright social manner about her as if it were a disgusting old coat that she'd love to throw away. Now and then, when I was talking and she was listening, she would lapse, quite unconsciously, I was sure, into perfect mimicry of the part she was dressed for – the languid object that is the mannequin, showing herself off like a diamond whose facets must be turned in the light. She told me that she lived in a flat with her three-year-old child; the modelling work was something quite new to her, it seemed to be fun; she would like to go to Rome and be a model there. There was a girl who'd done quite well – but she was dark and had an angry tom cat's face. That was the fashionable face to have, just now, she assured me. When we parted, she said, 'Why don't you come out to Alexanders' on Saturday and ride?' I said I might; unable to project myself into the imagined scene as to the milieu of the moon.

I wanted to see Steven Sitole again, quickly. I had no idea where to find him, so next day I telephoned Sam at the magazine offices where I had been told he worked. His big voice sounded surprised, then obliging: 'Oh, Mr Hood – were you all right the other night?' 'Of course. Fine.' 'Well, I'm glad to hear that. I was a bit nervous about letting you go off with old Steven.'

He couldn't tell me, right off, where I could telephone Steven, and a third person, someone in the office, was drawn into the conversation. '– Eddie, where's Steven operate from these days? What? No, man, the phone number. Where can you get hold of him?' Back into the telephone, he said, 'You can try him at this number, Mr Hood. He's not there all the time, but they'll take messages for him. It's a printer's; 31–6489 – got it?' I thanked him and said I hoped I'd see him again some time. He laughed embarrasedly and said, 'I wonder if we will,' as if it were not a simple matter that would be likely to be brought about without any particular effort on our part.

Steven was in when I telephoned the printer's. 'Wha-at? Oh, that's O.K. And me too, I'm O.K.,' he said, when I thanked him for taking me with him the other evening. 'The taxi was magnificent,' I said. 'Got me in well before the milk.' 'Wh-at?' he said again. 'The what? Oh, old Dhlamini. Good. Good.' He was one of those people who, over the telephone, always sound as if they are not listening. Some small tension of novelty and excitement that had drawn tight in the recollection of the unexpectedness of the night I had spent with him, gave way; for him, the incident was part of unremarkable experience to which my presence had perhaps given a mild fillip. I said guardedly, because I meant it, as I had said merely as a piece of meaningless politeness to Sam, I hoped I should see him again some time. But he said, 'Sure thing. Whenever you say?' 'Could we have lunch together, Friday, perhaps?' He laughed at me in a leisurely fashion. 'But where can we go together for lunch, man?' Of course, I hadn't thought; he couldn't go into any restaurant or tea-room in town. 'What about one of your places?' I said. 'Would I be allowed in one of them?' Now he roared with laughter. 'You haven't seen them,' he said. 'You wouldn't suggest it if you'd seen them.' 'All right, all right. Where do we eat?' 'I could come over to your place if you make it Saturday instead of Friday,' he suggested. 'Jolly good. We'll knock up some lunch at the flat. What time? Half past twelve-ish? I usually leave the office about eleven on Saturday mornings.' As I agreed, I suddenly remembered the half-promise to go riding at the Alexanders'; and dismissed it. I told Steven where the flat was, and we hung up.

I also telephoned Anna Louw before the weekend. She said, 'I hear you went with Steven to Sophiatown. Where'd he take you?'

'I don't know, exactly,' I said, stiffly.

'That shebeen-lizard,' she said mildly.

'You know, I like him. He's unexpected, I suppose, that's it.'

'What had you expected?' she asked with patient interest. With *her* you felt that your most halting utterance was given full attention. This scrutiny of the clichés of perfunctory communication, the hit-or-miss of words inadequate either to express or conceal, embarrassed me. Like most people, I do not mean half of what I say, and I cannot say half of what I mean; and I do not care to be made self-conscious of this. Much that is to be communicated is not stated; but she was the kind of person who accepts nothing until there has been the struggle to body it forth in words.

'I don't know, really,' I said, confused by pressure and irritated by my confusion. Confusion brought a momentary blankness, a blotting out, and I thrust forward the image of this blankness itself for answer, and it served: 'I hadn't expected anything, I didn't know what I could expect. I hadn't thought about it.' But of course, that wasn't right, it wasn't true; what I had done, in fact, was purposely *not* to think about the only expectations I could have had from my second-hand information; I had shrunk from the idea of meeting an earnest, bespectacled black man who would talk, over the tea-cup balanced on his knee, of the latest piece of discriminatory law against his people – Uncle Faunce's black man, my mother's black man. A man who would bore me and bring to the surface ponderous emotions of self-righteousness and guilt. I suppose any real, live black man would have seemed unexpected to me after this cipher. Certainly a young man who took me drinking with him.

On Saturday morning I bought some cooked ham and salami (there was beer in the flat) and set it out on the table when I got home; it had the forlorn look of food that has been processed rather than cooked. Then I opened a bottle of beer and sat down by the open window with my unopened *Observer* and *Sunday Times*, that followed me to Johannesburg by airmail, only a week late. The noises of the suburban street came up to me sociably; I found that I heard not just voices, shouting children, barking dogs, but the fading screech, as it went away up the street, of the tricycle belonging to a particular small boy, the shrill hysteria of the collie dog forever patrolling the fence of the house hard pressed between two flat buildings, half a block away, and the laughter of the two Italian immigrant children from the building next door. Between half past twelve and one, I looked out a few times to show Steven, if he should come round the corner, where he was bound for, but there was nothing but the relaxed Saturday life of the street – different, I imagine, from the week-day life which I was seldom there to see: cars disgorging working couples piled with their weekend food supplies, men carrying bottles of brandy and cases of soda and Coca-Cola out of the boots, small boys in the shabby khaki or violently jazzy American shirts that South African children wear, kicking and straggling their way to the municipal swimming bath, with their bathing trunks pulled on their sunburned bullet heads of spiky fair hair. I read on and finished the bottle of beer and then found it was two o'clock. The street was almost empty now, everyone was indoors, at lunch; Isaac, the flat boy, had begun his Saturday afternoon washing of one of the tenants' cars, and was sloshing buckets of water over a blowsy chromium beauty now several years out of date and badly in need of decarbonizing. Steven didn't come; and at last I sat down and ate. I found I was so hungry I could have eaten all the meat, but I thought he might still turn up. He didn't come. At three o'clock the young couple from the flat above mine emerged in clean tennis shorts and drove away in their little car, business-like and preoccupied as they were when they went off to their offices in the mornings. Gradually the street was almost cleared of cars; Isaac gathered his group of sophists from the aimless and the delivery men cycling by, and, as he flapped his chamois about the big car, delivered an off-hand oration to them where they squatted on the kerb. A sentimental song skirled out of a high window, was snatched back out of the air by the turn of a knob somewhere, and replaced by the mad chatter of race-course commentary, like a quarrel between parrots. And on all this, round all this, a splendid afternoon shone, clear and brilliant, dwarfing the thin smoke of boiler-room chimneys and the small dirty breath of car exhausts.

I felt a little flat and foolish, as one does when a guest fails to present himself. If Steven had had a telephone, and if I had known where to find him at his home, I should have phoned and said 'What the hell has happened to you?' and perhaps not minded at all that he hadn't come. But he had no telephone and I had no idea where he lived. A whole complex of streets like this one, and beyond that a place half-imagined (tin huts, sacking over doorways in a newspaper picture), half-remembered (between mean houses, narrow darkness crowded with the sleeping presence of too many people, pumpkins on the roof, and an old nag sleeping): all this seemed to blot out the possibility of communication between us.

I might just as well have gone to the Alexanders' after all; the afternoon, too beautiful to be contained by the suburban street, suggested this. But it was too late to do anything about it, anyway. I dragged the chair I had taken from the office out on to the little cement box that was my balcony, and sat there with my feet up, reading and dozing; all up the street there were men doing the same, like canaries hung out to get the sun. The Alexanders, on their side of the town, did not claim me. Steven, away on his, had not claimed me, either. Up on the roof of the flat building opposite, two African nursemaids in the dishabille of dirty woollen headscarfs instead of workday white caps, and three or four flat boys still in their cleaners' dress of cotton shorts and tunic, danced and yelled to the scratchy, repetitive music of one record, played on a portable gramophone. In amorphous, anonymous suburbia I lay low; not a stranger, but a man who, for the moment, belongs to himself.

It was true that a black man and a white man, though acquainted, were unlikely to run into each other again by chance in Johannesburg. The routine of their lives might run parallel most of the time, but it was astonishing how effective were the arrangements for preventing a crossing. But I did see Steven Sitole again, simply because I knew Anna Louw; had it not been for this, perhaps we should unremarkably have lost sight of each other at once.

I was kept busy about the affairs of Aden Parrot all the

next week; I even had to take work home to the flat in the evenings. During the day, I was mostly out of Johannesburg, visiting booksellers in the small towns strung along the path of the gold mines of the Witwatersrand. It was the East Rand I went to that week, I remember, and I went by train, because Faunce was still hedging about letting me have a car, though it was clear enough that in a country with poor public transport, I must have one. I was struck at once by the queerness of the landscape; man-made to a startling degree – as if the people had been presented with an upland plateau and left to finish it, to create a background of natural features instead of to fit in with one – and at the same time curiously empty, as if truly abandoned to man. Between the factories that thinned out from the perimeter of one town, almost meeting the last industrial outpost of the next, there was a horizon of strange hills. Some of them were made of soft white sand, like the sand of the desert or the sea, piled up in colossal castles. Others looked like volcanoes on whose sides the rolling yellow larva had petrified; fissures stained rust-coloured, and eroded formations like the giant roots of trees, marked their bases. There were others, cream, white, buff-coloured, and yellow, and worn into rippling corrugations by the wind, built up in horizontal ridges, like the tombs of ancient kings. Where coal mines had been, black mountains of coal dust glittered dully.

There were no valleys between these hills for they were simply set down, on the flat veld. Patches of tough green grass and short waving grasses showed, but mostly the growth was weird, wet and thin; a few cows would stand in the reeds of an indefinite swampy patch where the ooze shone mother-of-pearl, like oil; a rectangular lake out of which pipes humped had sheets of violet and pink, like a crude water-colour. In some places there was no earth but a bare, grey scum that had dried and cracked open. And there was black earth, round a disused coal mine, where somone had once thrown away a peach pip, and it had grown into a tree, making out of the coal dirt some hard, hairy green peaches.

There were trees; eucalyptus trees, confined to plantations

that formed grey geometrical shapes in which, as you passed, you caught a glimpse of white, peeling branches like the flash of flesh. A few spindly outcasts, eucalyptus and wattle, got some sort of living in tortured angles against the steep sides of the yellow hills.

It was a man-made place in quite a different sense from that of a city. (Quite a different sense from that of the midlands in England, too, or the Welsh coal-country.) If it had not been for the hills, the horizon would have been a matter of the limitations of the human eye. Men themselves had made their own spatial boundaries, themselves had created the natural features of hills, water, and woods. What they had made, in the emptiness, was the symbol rather than the thing itself. The cyanide dumps were not hills, the dams of chemically-treated water pumped from underground were not lakes, the plantations were not woods: but they suggested them, they stood for them. And like all true fantasies, this one had been created subconsciously. The people who had made this landscape had merely been concerned to dump above ground, out of the way, the waste matter that was incidental to the recovery of gold.

The towns themselves were quite another matter. They were conscious creations, all right. They were ugly, cheap, and jazzily dreary, got up in civic 'beautifying' efforts on the taste level of a housemaid's Sunday-best. The main street invariably led in one end of the town and out the other, and on the way were the lines of shops, offering, in coloured neon, fish-and-chips and furniture on terms and building-loans and gents' outfitting, grinning brides and kiddies in the photographer's, dingy bars in the brewers' chain of hotels, a cinema with Cinemascope and, of course, the town hall with the municipal coat-of-arms picked out in pansies between fat palms like pineapples. One of these places had coloured lights on fancy wire frames arched across the street at twenty-foot intervals; at the end of the diminishing vista, you could just see the headgear of the nearest mine-shaft. In each town I visited the local booksellers – there was a newsagents' chain, like the brewers' chain, running through them all, and usually one other independent shop – and talked shop to them as best I could before getting to the business of taking their orders for new Aden Parrot books. Most of them were nice chaps, who stuck doggedly to what they knew they could sell, and were as nervous about ordering a new author as the proprietor of a grocery shop might be of offering his customers an unfamiliar kind of cheese; they reminded me of the comfortable pipe-smokers who kept the local bookseller and stationer's in the English seaside towns of my childhood.

I had felt that I owed Anna Louw some sort of entertainment or hospitality, and so I had asked her to come to a cinema with me on the Friday night. When I got back to Johannesburg from my last day's journeying about the East Rand, I felt too tired to bother with her instructions about buses and routes (she had asked me to dinner) and took a taxi to where she lived. The address was north of the town, on the way to the Alexanders', in the pocket of a half-developed suburb that lay surrounded by, but neglected by contrast with, other suburbs. There she had a cottage in the grounds of a larger house; a kind of paste-board cottage that had been formed out of a reversal of the onion-peeling process: first there had been one room and a bathroom, week-end shelter for a casual guest from the big house, then someone had added a kitchen, and so a more stable existence was possible there, then a veranda, and, finally, the veranda had been closed-in and subdivided to make a small, cellular house. The first thing I noticed was the lowness of all the doors and ceilings; I had to dip my head to step into the softly-coloured complexity of Anna's house. It was like stooping to look into a nest or a cave, a hidden, personal place that exists unperturbed under the unnoticing eye of the passing world.

Two or three people were sitting about the small living-room; the windows were open wide, and I had a sense of the light running out, moving from the room like a tide. 'Hullo, Mr Hood,' said little Sam, welcomingly. Anna introduced me to a dumpy, grey-haired woman in slacks, who kept saying, in a strong Hollands accent, 'I got do go, now, my deer, eh? I got do go now.' Steven was there. He got up from the divan under the windows, where he had been sitting, and backed away in invitation to me to sit down. He shook hands. 'Hallo, how are you? This is a very comfortable place.' He was grinning, with his glass dangling in his hand, held by the rim. Glasses and a porcelain vase shone once, as the ebb in passing sometimes turns over bright objects to gleam for a moment out of the mud.

'I can't make out what I'm pouring,' said Anna, and switched on a lamp.

'Doesn't matter, perhaps it'll turn out something interesting,' said Steven. They all stirred in the sudden warm light; started a little in themselves as shadows jumped out at once at angles from the objects in the room. 'No!' said the Hollander, standing up and shaking her thick body inside her slacks; I saw that her coarse hair was streaked with its original yellow, like the nicotine stains on the fingers of heavy smokers. 'I must go, Anna!'

Anna hurried back to the circle of the lamplight after seeing her off. 'Toby! Now please pour yourself a drink!' 'Got one,' I held it up. She was carefully dressed, in red, and she looked suddenly pretty in the vivid way of dark women. Perhaps because she was at home, she seemed to have relaxed, too, that measured seriousness of manner that I associated with her. 'I'm sorry!' she said. 'She's not a bad old thing at all.'

'What's the matter?'

'Oh it was before you came. You wouldn't notice it so much.' She turned to the others, apologetic, but confident that they would share her amusement at the same time.

'Going, going, never gone,' said Steven, putting down his glass and waving his hands.

'I think she's a nice lady,' said little Sam. 'Nothing wrong with her.'

'She came in – she occasionally comes in just about this time, or after supper, for coffee with me – but when she saw Sam and Steven she kept saying, all the time, I must go, I must go.'

'But she didn't!' said Steven.

Anna asked me how I'd got there, and then we got talking

about the car I needed, and what kind it should be, and where I should get it. The subject of cars is paraffin on the fire of talk among most men, and Steven and Sam lit up at once in passionate discussion. Sam said that I should get a new small British or Continental car that would be cheap to run. Steven plumped for a good second-hand job, a big powerful American car, a model of a reliable year, that, once overhauled, would go like new. 'What's a good of a car without power? What d'you want a machine without power for? May as well walk,' he cried flamboyantly to Sam. 'Steven, man,' said Sam, planting himself before him to get a hearing, 'a second-hand car spends more time in the garage than on the road.'

'You find a good American car,' said Steven to me, over his head.

We all began to talk at once: 'Listen to me . . . look here . . . so long as it goes, I don't. . . .'

Steven burst through. 'I've got a friend who works in the biggest garage in town. You know the Ford people? You know the Chev people? He's worked with their crack mechanics for years. He can buy and sell them, ten times over. You get your second-hand car and don't you worry. I'll get him to do over the whole engine for you. It'll cost you half. Maybe even nothing. You leave it to me.'

They had come in to see Anna on their way home from work. We all walked out to Sam's little car to see them off, and I said to Steven, 'What happened to you that Saturday, anyway?' He smiled charmingly, utterly culpable and self-reproachful: 'I'm awfully sorry about that, Mr Hood, really I'm sorry. I suddenly had to go off to Klerksdorp. I asked some chap to let you know, but you know what these people are. . . . I want you to come to my place to a party tomorrow night. Yes, there's a big party on tomorrow and I want you to come. You'll both come. We'll fix it tomorrow.'

They went off, waving and talking. I had the feeling there was no party; or there was not going to be one until a few minutes ago.

'Silly ass,' said Anna, as we entered the house again. She picked up a couple of official-looking letters from the table where the lamp was. 'He bought a woman's watch and a camera from some place in town, and he hasn't paid for them. Now he's being sued. Don't know what I'm supposed to do about it. It's hardly a thing for legal aid.'

I smiled. 'Hardly.'

'Of course, Sam always thinks I can fix everything.' She sighed and sat down, gazing accusingly at the lamp.

'I should think he's pretty well right.' This confirmation of the confidence she inspired seemed to distress her; as if, for a moment, she saw a diminution of herself in the habit of capable response which was expected of her.

'What's Steven's excuse?' I asked, curious.

'The girl ran away with the watch, and the camera had a faulty lens, anyway – so he felt it was justice all round if he didn't finish his payments.'

We both laughed, but there was an edge of irritation to her amusement.

'It's part of the Robin Hood code that a lot of them like to think they live by, just now. It's an elastic code that can be stretched to cover even gangsters with a moral justification of some kind. And, of course, it's romantic. There's terribly little that's romantic in location life. That part of it I understand very well. In the Karroo dorp where I grew up there was nothing romantic, either.'

'I don't know whether I understand what "romantic" means to you,' I said.

'Well, what does it usually mean? – Something foreign, something outside your familiar life? That's what I mean, anyway. Even if it's only an unfamiliar way of looking at your own life, another interpretation of it. Then you're not just a black man doing down a white man, you're robbing the rich to give to the poor.'

In the kitchen she did everything unhurriedly but practisedly. When she lifted the lid of a pot, there was the comforting vegetable scent of a home-made soup, and there were two thick pats of fillet lying on a board, ready for grilling. I hung about, talking to her, getting in the way rather than helping, as you do in a kitchen when you don't know where things are kept. 'I'm glad to hear that you're not too down on Steven's romantic view of life – although I'm not sure, yet, that I agree about it being romantic.'

'It's romantic, all right,' said Anna, sending tomatoes seething into a hot pan, 'and I am down on it. I understand the need to be romantic in some way, but I'm down on this way. It's a waste of energy. You won't catch Steven working with Congress or any other African movement, for that matter. He never defied, either – I'm talking about the defiance campaign, the passive resistance movement of a year or two back. The only defiance he's interested in is not paying his bills, or buying drink. He's got this picture of himself as the embittered, devil-may-care African, and believe me, he's making a career of it. He doesn't care a damn about his people; he's only concerned with his own misfortune in being born one of them.' The sizzling of the tomatoes in butter spat angrily around her.

'Why should Steven *have* to be involved in these movements and congresses and what-not?' I said. 'I must admit, the whole idea would fill me with distaste. I'd run a mile at the thought.'

Over the tomatoes, she smiled the private smile of the old hand: the stoker when the ship's passenger marvels at the fact that anyone can work in such heat, the foundryman when someone says, 'How do you stand the noise?' 'Somebody's got to do it. Why should you expect somebody else to do it for you? Nobody really wants to.'

'Ah now, that's not so. I've always thought that there are two kinds of people, people with public lives, and people with private lives. The people with public lives are concerned with a collective fate, the private livers with an individual one. But – roughly, since the Kaiser's war, I suppose – the private livers have become hunted people. Hunted and defamed. You must join. You must be Communist or Anti-Communist, Nationalist or Kaffirboetie' – she smiled at my pronunciation – 'you must protest, defy, non-cooperate. And all these things you *must* do; you can't leave it all in the infinitely more capable hands of the public livers.'

She turned from the stove with her answer all ready, but then paused a moment, filling in the pause by gesturing for me to pass her the soup bowls, and said, as if she had suddenly discarded her argument, 'Yes, there's less and less chance to live your own life. That's true. The pressure's too strong.'

'From outside, as well as within, that's my point,' I said, obstinately, not wishing to claim common ground where I did not think there was any. 'The public life people have always responded to pressure from within – their own conscience, sense of responsibility toward others, ambition, and so on; but the private livers, in whom these things are latent, weak, or differently directed, could go on simply going their own ways, unless the pressure from outside became too strong. Well, now it's just bloody irresistible. It isn't enough that a chap like Steven has all the bother of being a black man in this country, on top of it he's expected to give up to political action whatever small part of his life he can call his own.'

I followed Anna into the living-room, where she carried the soup. 'He wants the results of that political action, doesn't he?' she called, over her shoulder. 'He wants to be free of the pass laws and the colour bar and the whole caboodle? – Well, let him fight for it.' She laughed, indignant in spite of herself.

All the old, wild reluctant boredom with which I had borne with this sort of talk all my life was charged, this time, with something more personal; a nervous excitement, a touchiness. I felt the necessity to get the better of her; to punish her, almost, 'My dear Anna, you're so wrong, too. The private liver, the selfish man, the shirker, as you think him – he's a rebel. He's a rebel against rebellion. On the side, he's got a private revolution of his own; it's waged for himself, but quite a lot of other people may benefit. I think that about Steven. He won't troop along with your Congress, or get himself arrested in the public library, but, in spite of everything the white man does to knock the spirit out of him, he remains very much alive – getting drunk, getting in debt, running his insurance racket. Learning all the shady tricks, so that, in the end, he can beat dear old white civilization at its own games. He's muscling in; who's to say he won't get there first? While the Congress chaps are pounding fiercely on the front door, he's slipped in through a back window. But, most important of all, he's alive, isn't he? He's alive, in defiance of everything that would attempt to make him half-alive. I don't suppose he's been well fed, but he looks wiry, his schooling hasn't been anything much, but it seems to me he's got himself an education that works, all the same, well-paid jobs are closed to him, so he's invented one for himself. And when the Congress chaps get in at last, perhaps they'll find him there, waiting.' I laughed.

'Oh my God! What a horrible idea.' She pressed her napkin against her mouth and drew in her shoulders.

I was perversely triumphant. I added, with some arrogance 'Well, don't underestimate the Sitoles of this world, anyway. They're like history; their progress is inexorable. Let that be a consolation to you when your Congresses and protests don't seem to be getting very far.'

When we had finished our dinner and she was out of the room, getting her coat, I wandered about, looking at books and objects that I had been noticing since I had arrived. The books were what I would have expected to find, political books on Russia, China, and India, all the books I had ever read about Africa, and a great many more besides, some old Left Book Club editions, a couple of books of reproductions of paintings, and no poetry or novels at all, so far as I could see, except a paper-back mystery. But some of the objects were unusual, and, to me, highly interesting. There was a huge, benign African mask of black wood, and a small, evil one with a grey ruff of what I guessed must be monkey fur, there was a beautiful hide drum, and a clay pot blackened with stove polish and studded with red lucky beans; there was a little brass Shiva, and a Chinese marriage fish hanging from a nail on the wall. All these things were brought together in intimacy in the small space, and each retained, absolutely unmodified by the presence of the others, the look of authority of its place in the life from which it had been taken. I have noticed this before in objects which have been created for utility or ritual: even out of the context of their use, they never take on the banal look of ornaments. I had just picked up a snapshot of Anna, standing beside a smiling Indian woman, and herself wearing Indian dress, when she came back into the room.

'A sari suits you very well. Have you been in India?'

She shook her head. 'I was married to an Indian. He gave me this, too; isn't it beautiful?' She showed me the white Kashmir shawl she was wearing. I admired it and we talked about it for a few minutes, while she went round locking up the cottage.

In the car, she said, 'Were you surprised about my marriage?'

'Well, yes. I suppose I was.'

'But of course, it doesn't seem so very extraordinary to English people.'

'No.'

'Not the way it is here.' She added, in her matter-of-fact voice, the voice of the conscientious committee member drawing the attention of the meeting to something she does not want them to overlook: 'It was before the Mixed Marriages Act, of course.'

I suddenly choked with the desire to laugh; I couldn't help it, it came spluttering out. 'I can't think of a marriage in terms of legislation. That's all I mean.' Did she think of anything in any other terms?

'Was it very difficult, being married like that in this country?' I asked, as I might have asked about the cultivation of some plant in her garden.

She hesitated a moment. 'A bit. Didn't seem so then; seems so now.'

She changed gear with a typical, neat, considerate movement. And I had a sudden sense of loneliness, her loneliness, that appeared unsummoned behind her flat, commonplace talk like a face at the window of a locked house.

Chapter 6

STEVEN, in a graduate gown, was at the centre; the party spun round him, slowly at first, then whipped up by the black skirts and flailing sleeves that flew from the mast of his energy. When I arrived at the house in Sophiatown (Sam had come all the way to fetch me, because Anna Louw was not coming to the party) there were a dozen or so young men standing about against the walls of the room. Some leaned on each other's shoulders, and a cigarette was passed up and down for each to take a draw. They murmured among themselves now and then, laughed suddenly, or dreamed, as loiterers do. Steven swept among them a few times, clutching the arm of one enthusiastically, bending his head for an explosive, confidential joke with another. They were dressed in anything they could find, it seemed: one, in a laundry-creased white shirt and new flannel trousers with a fancy belt, hung on a friend in a sweater almost completely unravelled and tattered brown pants whose turn-ups, stiff with motor-oil, were held round his bare legs by bicycle clips. They wore loose, hairy tweed jackets, suit-jackets that might have been filched off a scarecrow, filthy old caps, fancy gilt tie-pins, torn laceless sandshoes, impeccably brushed suède shoes. Their faces had the glazed look of youths who have spent their lives in the streets, watching; watching the earth-mover eating out the vacant plot, the fire-engine screaming by, or the drunk, weaving along the gutter.

On a few benches and old dining-chairs, there were some women in haphazard cheap-jack finery and one or two men in business suits and glasses. The room itself was as empty of objects as the shebeen had been; and in it, everyone simply stood or sat, without awkwardness, and without any tension of expectation. More poeple kept coming in all the time; Steven seemed to make sorties beyond the door and return triumphantly each time, gathering new arrivals. Sam was his lieutenant, speeding and skidding about him with twinkling importance. A piano was pushed in; its strings jarred and jangled and died away. Steven was in conference, his arms spreading his gown about two other men; he dashed out, dashed in, grinned at me, raised his brows at someone else. A yellow boy with girl's hands and a huge, pitch-black man with the weight of his body resting on the tight belt of his pants brought brandy round in coloured lemonade glasses. It was offered to me, and to all the others who, like me, sat on the benches or hard chairs. A second serving came in, this time in cups. But it did not get as far as the chaps hanging round the wall, and they did not seem to expect it; only watched. Talk rose, as the volume of people displaced the silence. They kept sauntering in, girls hand in hand, with the little breasts and big haunches that I noticed in very young African women, pretty tarts with faces broad with pleasure, powder showing dull mauve like the bloom on a black grape, on their skin, thin young men whose shoulders hunched-in their chests, gangling young men with the benign look of the very tall; pale, yellow fat faces, bony, reddish-skinned faces, shining black faces. They spoke to each other in the monosyllabic, subdued way of an audience, and threw in a few words of dated American-English, as if that were the fashionable thing to do. 'Doing all right there, Dan?' 'Sure, boy. How's it with you, these days?' 'Hullo, baby –' 'You in good shape, honey?'

There was a little breeze of notes on a saxophone; it died down. A clarinet gave a brief howl. Somewhere behind the press of people, the big bass began to pant. Music grew in the room like a new form of life unfolding, like the atmosphere changing in a rising wind. Musical instruments appeared from underfoot; people who had been talking took to another tongue through the object they plucked or blew. Feet moved, heads swayed; there was no audience, no performers – everyone breathed music as they breathed air. Sam was clinched with the piano in some joyous struggle both knew. A yellow youth in a black beret charmed his saxophone like a snake, with its own weaving voice. The bass thumped along for dear life under the enchanted hand of a man with the bearded, black delicate face of an Assyrian king. A fat boy with a pock-marked face jumped with rubber knees into a little clearing; girls began to swing this way and that from their partners' hands, like springs coiling and uncoiling.

I had seen jazz-crazy youths and girls at home in England, in a frenzy of dance-hall jive. I had seen them writhing, the identity drained out of their vacant faces, like chopped-off bits of some obscene animal that, dismembered and scattered, continue to jig on out of nervous impulse. But the jazz in this room was not a frenzy. It was a fulfilment, a passion of jazz. Here they danced for joy. They danced out of wholeness, as children roll screaming down a grass bank. Now and then a special couple would make space for themselves, and gather the whole swirling vigour of the room into their performance. They laughed and shouted to the others who danced around them, corollary to their rhythm; comments and challenges flew back.

One of the men in business suits came up to me and said confidentially, 'I suppose this must all seem rather crude.'

'Crude?'

He waved a hand at the room, that buffeted him where he stood, so that he had the stance of a man on a ship in a high sea.

'My friend,' I said, 'you don't know what our parties are like.' And it was true that that very first night I was struck by the strange innocence of their dancing. In all its wild and orgiastic shake and shamble, there was never a suggestion that it was a parody of or a substitute for sex. There was none of the dreamy concupiscence that hangs, the aura of a lean, wolfish sex-hunger, about the scarcely moving couples in a white night-club. For these people, the music and the dancing were not a dream and an escape, but an assertion. Once or twice I took one of the young women in their bright nylon blouses and danced, but it was more than my own lack of skill and half-hearted experience of dancing as a rather embarrassing social necessity that made me feel almost as if I were maimed in that press of dancing people. It was more than my stiff, shy, and unwilling limbs. What was needed was – at a deeper level – something akin to the feeling I had had when I was swimming with Stella Turgell at Mombasa, the feeling that the age-old crystals of the North were melting away in my blood. The men and women about me had had little to drink, they had none of the trappings of food and ease without which the people among whom I had lived are unable to whip up any sort of mood of celebration; yet it was there, spontaneously. Their joy was something wonderful and formidable, a weapon I didn't have. And, moving feebly among them, I felt the attraction of this capacity for joy as one might look upon someone performing a beautiful physical skill which one has lost, or perhaps never had. Lopped off, gone, generations ago; drained off with the pigment fading out of our skin. I understood, for the first time, the fear, the sense of loss there can be under a white skin. I suppose it was the point of no return for me, as it is for so many others: from there, you either hate what you have not got, or are fascinated by it. For myself, I was drawn to the light of a fire at which I had never been warmed, a feast to which I had not been invited.

I looked at Steven, dancing proudly as a strutting cock before a little round-eyed, painted black girl, calling out remarks that kept admiring eyes turned on him, and I thought of him playing darts in an East End pub. Why should he want that grey, fog-sodden world with its dreary pastimes scaled down to dwindling energies? Yet he did. He was drawn to it just as I was drawn to the abundant life that blazed so carelessly in the room about me. When black men lose that abundance, sink it, as they long to, in the vast vitiation of our world, both the hate and the fascination will be gone, and we will be as indifferent to them as we are to each other.

Like Alice plunging after the White Rabbit, I went with Steven into the townships, the shebeens, the rooms and houses of his friends. I do not want to suggest by this a descent into an underworld, but another world, to which the conditions of the Johannesburg I worked and lived in did not pertain. First, the scale of proportion was reversed: in the city, and in my suburban street, the buildings rose above, the gardens made a space round the people – we lived, as city people do, in the shelter of the city, in a context that, while overshadowing, also provides the dignity of concealment: figures in the street pass out of sight under trees and shadows, living passes out of sight behind walls and fences. By contrast, an African township looked like something that had been razed almost to the ground. The mass of houses and shacks were so low and crowded together that the people seemed to be swarming over them, as if they had just invaded a deserted settlement. Every time I went to a township I was aware of this sudden drop in the horizon of buildings and rise of humans; nothing concealed, nothing sheltered – in any but the most obvious sense – any moment of the people's lives. A blinding light of reality never left them. And they lived, all the time, in all the layers of society at once: pimps, gangsters, errand boys, washwomen, schoolteachers, boxers, musicians and undertakers, labourers and patent medicine men – these were neighbours, and shared a tap, a yard, even a lavatory.

So convincing was Steven's confidence in himself and his friends that when Faunce advanced me the money to buy a car, I bought a second-hand Chevrolet and took it to Steven's mechanic friend to be overhauled. He lived in Alexandra Township, an abandoned-looking place outside the northern boundaries of Johannesburg, a kind of vast, smoking rubbish-pile picked over by voracious humanity. All the people who lived there worked in Johannesburg, but the town did not own the place, nor was it responsible for it. It had the aged look of all slums – even the earth, the red dirt roads, seemed worn down to their knobbly shins, and there was nothing, no brick, post, or piece of tin that was new and had not been battered in and out of the shape of a succession of uses – but, in fact, like everything else in Johannesburg, it was, in terms of human habitations, young, fresh, hardly begun; perhaps thirty or forty years old. From the beginning, it must have been a proliferation of dirt and decay, the pretty Shangri-la legend in reverse – the place where rot blooms.

A stream that flowed thick, blue-grey dirty wash-water ran by the house of Steven's friend. Children played and screamed in it, and when they came to stand round the car, the scales of scum coated their legs like a disease. Although we went there three or four times (I had to leave the car with this man Alfred for some days) I was never asked to go into his house. It was a brick shack with a dead tree leaning over it; from the tree hung bits of rope and an old tyre on which the children swung, and the yard was a surrealist sculptor's garden of old motor car parts – a yellow bumper, a rusted hood, and other unidentified shapes. While Alfred, a fat, shy man who fingered his nose tenderly while he talked, and Steven who, I am sure, knew nothing about cars, but could not bear to be nothing but a looker-on, lay wriggling along on their shoulder-muscles under the car, the children and I watched each other. When they had tired of giggling about me, they went back to their own absorbing aimlessness. Among them an idiot, a kind of baboon-girl of about fourteen, hunch-backed, grotesquely steatopygous, grunted and squealed in subhuman frustration at their teasing. Two plump, easy-eyed women gossiped and, with a quick hand at the right moment, kept setting to rights a fat baby with bead anklets who kept tumbling down the steps of a home-made clay veranda on the shack opposite. A donkey-cart selling wood screeched and tottered by; people bounced over the rutted road on bicycles, women, endless women, yelled, threw buckets of slop into the road, laughed and thumped at tubs of washing. And the monster was as unremarkable as the fat baby.

Sam's house was in another township, a rather better one. The core of most of the houses was brick, even if the usual extensions of tin and hessian had accreted round them. I went there with Steven one night for supper, and when we walked through the yard-smell of ammonia and wood-smoke, to which I was by then accustomed, with the strange, conglomerate night-cry of the township about us, and the dim lights and the sudden, intimate voices of the houses that shared the yard, close to us, and through the door that opened abruptly from two uneven concrete steps, I was bewildered. I might have stepped into a room 'done over' by some young couple in a Chelsea flat. Green felt deadened the floor underfoot. There was a piano, piled with music. A record player in what all cabinet makers outside Sweden consider to be Swedish style. A divan with cushions. A red lamp. All along one wall, a bookcase made of painted planks and bricks. At the window, a green venetian blind dropped its multiple lids on the township. Sam's wife, Ella, pretty and shy, served a roast lamb and potato dinner with a bottle of wine, and afterwards the four of us listened to a Beethoven quartet and then to Sam, playing some songs of his own composition.

Steven wanted to go to a shebeen when we left. It was run by a man who was part Indian, part African, part white, and a Basuto woman with the proportions of a whale who called me 'master' in the intimate obsequiousness of a house servant who knows the family too well. Steven knew everybody there, flirted with the shrill coloured tarts who, drunk, reminded me of pantomime dames, and had about himself generally an air of sophistication and relief. He stood beside me, at last, twisting his cheap signet ring with the bit of red glass in it fondly, as if its shoddiness pleased him. 'A place like Sam's is all right,' he said, 'but it costs too much.'

'His wife's got quite a well-paid job, too, I gather, so I suppose they can manage,' I said. I had already got over the bewilderment of the difference between what was well-paid for blacks and what was well-paid for whites; just as one becomes accustomed to translating values from one's own currency to that of a foreign country in which one has lived for a little time. And I had learned to accept too, without embarrassment, the fact that I, with my not-very-generous salary, and my flat all to myself, was a rich man when I was in the townships.

'I don't mean just money. The effort and trouble. Keep up a place like that in a location. All the dirt, the easy-going, all round you. Imagine the way the neighbours look at you; you're like a zoo! All the old women want to come and peer in the door to see what people do in such a house.' Like most exhibitionistic people, Steven was a good mimic.

I laughed. 'Still, it's an achievement to manage to live that way, in a location.'

'Ah,' said Steven, 'that's it. It's a showplace.' He assumed a high falsetto, parody of some white woman's voice he must have heard somewhere: '". . . an oasis of culture, my dear!" Is it a king's house, a millionaire's house? Man, it's just an ordinary way to live.'

I saw what he meant. If living decently, following a modest taste for civilized things, meant living eccentrically or remarkably, one might prefer to refuse the right masquerading as a privilege.

'Why should I guard like a cave of jewels,' he said, changing his sharp-eyed fake ring from one finger to another, 'a nice little house that any other man can have anywhere he likes in a street full of such houses?' And he grinned at me with that careless aplomb, shrugging his shoulders and looking down his nose at himself, that gave him such an air, and always, wherever we went in the townships, drew the young bloods about him to hear what he would say next.

He was, without question, the most 'popular' person I have ever known. I put the word popular between the quotes of the suspect, because to me it connotes a man who gets the most votes in a presidential election at a golf club, and I don't mean that sort of popularity. Perhaps 'loved' would be a better word. But he wasn't exactly loved, either; he was too impersonal and elusive for that. I think they gloried in him, those hangers-on – they gloried in his white man's ways produced unselfconsciously in their company, like a parlour trick that looks easy enough for anyone to learn. Looking always as if they'd just sheepishly awakened from a sleep with their clothes on, they sought something: was it the gum they pushed ceaselessly from one side of their mouths to the other, like the Americans do? Would the latest slang, in English, do it? Or the sports shirt with the pink and black collar? They did not know; they had not found out yet. But Steven had; they could see it, there he was. He had not gone under beneath his correspondence college B.A. the way black men did, becoming crushed and solemn with education, and the fit and cut of that aspect of the white man's

Johannesburg that dazzled them most hung on him as comfortably as his well-tailored jacket.

Feckless, aimless, like creatures flopping in the sand in evolution from water to land, they saw his slippery-footed ease between the black man's element and the white. He was something new, and they worshipped the new, which lack of possessions made them believe must always be the better. He was a new kind of man, not a white man, but not quite a black man, either: a kind of flash – flash-in-the-pan – produced by the surface of the two societies in friction.

It never seemed odd or extraordinary to me that Steven himself, free of so many rooms, houses, shacks, and shebeens, had no particular place to live, during the time I knew him. He once told me that he had no idea how many times he had moved, in his lifetime; he had lost count. He had been born in a location in one of the Reef gold-mining towns, and except for his year in England, he had been moving from one township to another, from one room to another, ever since.

I could not imagine what sort of place would have been right as home, to Steven.

Chapter 7

IT was on a Sunday morning, after a party to celebrate the first of Steven's moves since I had known him, that I went to see Cecil Rowe. The party was a warming- and naming-party for a house in a rakishly dingy part of Sophiatown where Steven had taken a room, in the company of his other bachelor cronies. It seemed to me highly unlikely that they were really living there, for there was little evidence of furniture or clothes – in fact, the place had the stunned and stripped look of a house that has been moved out of, rather than into – but it was blessed with jazz and brandy (someone even brought along a birthday cake) and it was duly named The House of Fame. ('What's it famous for?' I asked, and Steven said, 'Me, of course.') The party ended about one on the peculiar note of promise of African parties, with all the men drifting off cheerfully into the dark to other assignations. I gave one or two of the lesser hangers-on lifts to various parts of the township, whose steep streets were still alive with strollers, tsotsis, lovers, quarrels, people singing, and drunks, and drove back to the shut-down quiet of the white town. My steps rang up the stairwell of the flats, and I had a sudden wave of homesickness that took the form of a vivid sense of a corner off Ebury Street, just below a little garden with wall-flowers smelling sweet and cold at night, where I used to go, one spring, to the flat of a girl with whom I was in love.

In the morning this mood of alienation persisted slightly – like most homesicknesses, it was for what I should have liked to have had, rather than what I really had left behind – and I thought I would go to church. There were bells ringing tangledly through the clear air while I bathed and shaved carefully and put on a blue suit. I walked vaguely in the direction where I remembered having seen a small Anglican church, and found myself there in less than ten minutes. Little girls with curled hair, dangling handbags, hung about their mothers; there was a strong smell of brilliantine in the group outside the church, and a strong smell of floor-wax inside. It was a cottagey-looking building and the priest was to match; he seemed embarrassed by the prayers he offered, and doubtful about the intercession of his blessing. He took as his text 'Without me ye can do nothing' and he advocated Christ as if he were suggesting a course of vitamin pills; the congregation listened politely. The whole service was very Low, and I decided that I would try the Cathedral in town, next time.

But at least when I came out I was prepared to accept the fact that this place in which I found myself was not the blue-grey Cotswold village, calm as a shadow, where, of my family, only my grandmother and I sometimes sat in church in the empty pew that had once belonged to our family; and I respected the flat statement of the sunlight, hitting everything full on, and the chipped façade of the corner Greek shop opposite the church, and the two Africans sitting with their feet in the gutter, drinking lemonade and carrying on a conversation that could have been heard three blocks away, and the pretty plump Jewish girls swinging down the road in their Sunday shorts, and the shoddy suburban houses, ready for the knockout of the demolition gang after only twenty or thirty years – respected the place for being itself.

It was then that I noticed the street-name and realized that I must be quite near where Cecil Rowe had told me she had a flat. On an impulse I let the steep gradient push me down the hill like a hand in my back, and, half way down, there it was – a building that was newer and more pretentious-looking, if not better than the one in which I lived. In the front, there were wind-torn rubber plants in bright pots, and a mosaic mural in the foyer representing a Zulu girl, a water-pot, and a beehive hut against a lot of saw-tooth greenery; but, as I thought, the open corridors behind, which led to the flats, were the usual grimly functional thoroughfares, full of drifts of soot and dirty fluff, empty milk bottles and garbage bins.

The Rowe girl's flat was on the ground floor. I rang and rang and was just about to turn away, when I heard the soft slap of bare feet coming down a passage and someone struggled with the lock, giving muffled exclamations of exasperation, and at last flung the door open.

'My God, I thought it was the Salvation Army,' she said. 'Hullo, it's you – come in. Where've you sprung from?'

'I've been to church, it's just near here.'

She looked at me as if I were joking; then her expression changed to one of curiously feminine curiosity, that expression women get when they think you may be about to give away some aspect of yourself you really had not intended to let slip. 'Church? You don't mean to say you go to church?' She sounded most disbelieving.

'Yes of course I do. At home I go quite regularly.'

She burst out laughing; embarrassed, gleeful laughter, as if she'd discovered that I wore corsets. 'Well, I'm surprised at *you*,' she said. 'I mean, you're such an intellectual and all that.'

I can't explain why, but I was somehow touched and reassured, in myself, by her out-of-date, six-thousand mile distant, colonial notion of an 'intellectual' as a free-thinking, Darwinian rationalist. It pleased me to think that to her, God was simply old-fashioned; it was better than to suspect, as I sometimes did of myself, that God was merely fashionable again.

'Come *in*,' she said, and certainly she was not dressed for lingering conversation in the doorway. She trailed before me into the living-room, in a splendidly feminine but grubby dressing-gown, and settled herself on a hard chair at the table, her bare feet hooked behind the bar of the chair, and her hand going out at once for a cigarette. (I imagined how it was with just that gesture that she would grope for a cigarette the moment she woke up in the morning.) It was over a month since I had seen her, and if she had appeared in a different guise each time I had encountered her before, these were nothing to the change in her now. I suppose no man ever realizes how much of what he knows as a woman's face is make-up; I know that my sister has often hooted in derision when I have remarked on some girl's wonderful skin (You could take an inch off with a palette knife, my poor simpleton!) or the colour of another's hair (It costs pounds to keep it like that!). This waxy, sunburned face with the pale lips and the sooty smudges round the eyes was older and softer than the other versions of it I had seen, there were imperfections of the skin, and habits of expression which grew out of the prevailing states of feeling in her life that I did not know, had made their fine grooves. Yet I recognized this face instantly; it was the one that had attracted me, all the time, beneath the others.

'I drank a lot of vodka last night,' she said. 'Have you ever tried it? It's true it doesn't give you a hangover, but I feel as if my blood had evaporated, like a bottle of methylated spirits left uncorked. Do you know any Poles? There are a lot of Poles here, now. Perhaps, you've met the Bolnadoskys – Freddie and Basha, a lovely blonde? We were in their party and of course Poles can drink any amount of anything.'

'How's the modelling been going? Not off to Italy yet?'

'Oh that.' I might have been referring to something out of her remote past. 'I've been riding morning noon and night, training for the show. You knew that Colin and Billy asked me to jump Xantippe? I came third with her, two faults, in the Open.'

I remembered that Colin and Billy were the names of the twins I had met at the Alexanders', but I was not sure about Xantippe. She saw this and said, 'You've heard of Xantippe, of course?'

'What a shrew.'

She frowned. 'Nonsense, people are jealous of her. Once she knows you won't stand any cheek, she's the most obedient horse in the world.'

'I *was* talking nonsense. What about Xantippe?'

'Well, she's the most famous horse in this country, like Foxhunter in England – surely you've heard of him?'

We had some coffee, brought in by a pretty, giggling African girl who wore a lot of jewellery, and Cecil said, 'Oh Eveline, you are a pet,' and talked on about the horse show in which she had taken part.

'So your modelling career is completely shelved,' I said, at last.

She answered quickly, as if the subject bored her: 'I'm really not the type to sit about posing indoors.'

'It's all very horsey, at the moment, eh?'

She jerked her chin on to her hand and blew a great smoke-screen between herself and her coffee-cup. 'That's the kind of life I was born to.' I was delighted to see how she looked every inch the hard-riding, hard-drinking bitch, just as, in the Stratford, she had unconsciously assumed the spectacular narcissism of the mannequin.

I planted my feet stolidly before me and said, 'That's not what you told me. You said you were a butcher's daughter, that just because your father had a few horses you'd drifted into a way of life that went with a class and a country you didn't belong to.'

She was unperturbed. 'I must have been mad. Drunk, more likely.'

Our talk picked up, slipped into naturalness, and we began to enjoy ourselves. Later the front-door bell rang again, and this time it really was the Salvation Army. She begged sixpence from me for the collection, and when she came back into the room she was suddenly stricken with a kind of helpless consciousness of her dishabille, and stood there running her hands through her hair and lifting the corners of her eyes with her fingers on her temples. 'I should get dressed, I must get dressed,' she kept saying. She held her dressing-gown tightly, exclaiming over its stains as if they had appeared since I'd come, and curling her toes as if she were ashamed of her bare feet. I knew she felt me looking at her, but I could not stop. Then she went away, and when she came back, bathed and dressed, she was the conventionally pretty, unremarkable girl I had met that first day at the Alexanders'.

Each spoke out of the train of thought with which he had been preoccupied while we were in separate rooms. 'What made you come, after all this time?' she said, fastening a bracelet on her wrist, and shaking her arm, as a dog settles into the feel of its collar. 'I saw the name of your street. Where's your child – it's a girl, isn't it?' 'A boy. Spending the week-end with the grandparents,' she said, absently.

'Don't you care for him at all?'

'Don't be ridiculous! I adore him.'

From where she sat, with her beautiful, thin-ankled legs crossed, on the sofa, she regarded her living-room with the same kind of critical helplessness she had shown toward herself, before she was dressed. It was an unsatisfactory room. A florist's bouquet was dead in its vase. (I wondered who had sent it, and why.) The modern print on the cushions and the curtains that blew limply at the balcony door was a design of masks and faces in yellow and black, cross-eyed and mean, like Hallow-e'en pumpkin cutouts. There were two table lamps of black porcelain with irregular-shaped holes in their torsos, as if someone had dreamed of Henry Moore in an art china shop, and a large print of a vase of magnolias, all watery sheen and pastel light, like a reflection in a flattering mirror. It seemed to be a room of many attempts, all of which had petered out into each other.

'– It's not much of a reason,' she said, broodingly, raking a cigarette out of a tarnished silver cigarette box. She was referring to my remark about having come to the flat because I had recognized the name of the street. 'Ugh, these must be at least three months old.'

I got up to give her one of my cigarettes. She continued to look at me inquiringly.

'I don't know. I was homesick. I've been tied up. Anyway, you've been very busy yourself.'

'Well, you're not busy today, I gather,' she commented. I had been there an hour already.

'I say! Am I keeping you from something – I'm sorry!'

She laughed. 'I'm as free as a bird. All I have to do is to be at Hamish and Marion's for lunch. What about you?'

'I can't simply turn up there again,' I said.

'Nonsense; people turn up there all the time. It's what they like.'

I said with a sudden rush of desire to talk about myself: 'I've had some curious experiences lately.'

She said, with interest and mild envy, 'Really? Tell me, whom do you know, anyway? Who are these mysterious friends with whom you occupy yourself?'

'I've been into the townships quite a few times; they're extraordinary, you know.'

'Where? What townships?' It was clear that she had no idea what I was talking about.

'The African townships – Sophiatown and so on.'

'Oh, I know,' her voice at once took on the tone of the old Londoner being told by the visitor that the Tower is well worth a visit. 'Everyone who comes here gets all het up about the locations. They *are* simply too awful. Marion helps to run a crèche out in one of them, you know; Alexandra, or one of the others, I'm not sure.'

'Last night I went to a house-warming party, in Sophiatown –'

She tucked her legs up on the sofa and sat back, intrigued, smiling. 'Oh no! A "house-warming", if you don't mind!'

The impulse to talk closed away as suddenly as it had opened. 'It was quite a party,' I said lamely, and smiled.

'You should see Eveline sometimes, when she's got up in her best. She's got one old white dress of mine that she looks marvellous in. She spends every penny of her wages on clothes, and honestly, she looks a lot smarter than many white women, when she really puts her mind to it.'

I said, 'By the way, how's Kit and the Karoo?' and, with a quick turn of interest, she began: 'I must tell you. Hamish has just been down there for two weeks . . .' and launched into a long mischievous gossip about the Baxters.

I bought a great bunch of lilies and roses from an Indian vendor on the corner of a street, on the way to the Alexanders', without much hope that this gift of flowers with which Marion Alexander's own garden was in any case filled, would soften the obvious fact that I had turned up at The High House again chiefly to seek the company of one of the more regular guests. But I need not have worried; like those publishers of paper-back novelettes who must keep a long list of titles in print, the Alexanders wanted to keep their guest list full and varied, and welcomed the presence of casual if presentable hangers-on like myself, who would and could never offer reciprocal hospitality. There was the usual luxurious lunch, this time, as it was high summer, served in the garden beside the pool – a kind of Watteau picnic, with iced strawberries trickling maraschino into bowls of cream, and a great deal of pale wine that the women left lying about in their glasses on the grass. There were the usual amiable people, with plenty to say about nothing in particular, in whose company the fear, joy, strangeness, and muddle of life seemed mastered by a few catch phrases, like a tiger confined in a cricket-cage. Shadow lay on the grass lightly as the lace of thin foam on a calm sea. Every now and then the pool gave an enormous bright wink in the sun, and the laughter and voices seemed suddenly louder.

I borrowed a pair of trunks and swam, and later I borrowed some jodhpurs, so that I could ride out with Cecil, who wanted to show off to me on her horse – or rather, one of the Alexanders' horses. She watched me indulgently, as if she were torn between wishing me to make an ass of myself, and bridling at the idea that anyone might suggest, by a word or a look, that that was what I was doing. In fact, she wished me to succeed and to fail, which excited me in that underworld of unspoken, sometimes unrealized, exchanges in which people retreat from or advance toward each other. But in the overt world of the Alexanders' paddock, it left me unconcerned, for as I have never been a sportsman of any kind, I truly have – out of indifference – that contentment in the activity for its own sake which sportsmen grit their ambitious teeth and try to assume. Cecil put the horse through its paces in a little dressage (this was not the famous Xantippe that she was riding) and jumped him a few times; she rode very well, of course, though a trifle grimly, I thought, as if she were only aware, through all the movements that led up to it, of the successful conclusion of each thing she and the horse did. A few of the guests had strolled along to the paddock to watch, and they murmured approval and commented to each other; the twins, who had just arrived, woffled cries of pleasure in conditioned reflex each time she landed on the other side of an obstacle: 'Oh, good girl! Well done, sweetie!' Yet she came out of the manège subdued and even sulky, like a jockey who, after a race, finds his feet on the ground and himself no part of the yelling crowd.

For myself, I was finding a particular lulled and sentient ease in the nature of my presence in the Alexanders' garden that day; even the borrowed clothes contributed to the feeling that I was gratuitously dipping into the pleasures of a life for which I had to take no responsibility, pleasures for which I would not have to settle, even with myself. Pleasures, indeed, for which I perhaps would not have cared to have to settle.

I saw Cecil several times during the following week. I took her to a play that I don't think she liked very much, and, on another night, to a new restaurant she knew about. Whenever I went to fetch her she was stunningly dressed and looking beautiful, and it was easy for me to escort her as if I were taking a lovely and entertaining exhibit about, minding that doors did not catch her dress nor the wind her hair; I was not troubled by her at all. Each time, as the door banged to, the flat was left behind her like a discarded chrysalis, and, as her little boy was always in bed by the time I came, all I saw of him was, once, a crayon picture of a sun with a smile and a creature with two legs as long as a late afternoon shadow, that was lying on the passage floor. When she had had a few drinks, Cecil unfailingly became gay, just as you can depend upon a cat to strike up a purr after milk, and we were both in that stage of acquaintance when to each the other's small stock of stories and anecdotes is new, so that each seems to the other a fund of wit and charm.

Steven telephoned me, but I did not have a chance to see him; he turned up at the office one lunch-time with an Indian, to ask me to come to a boxing match. Steven's elegance always amazed me; I could not imagine how those trousers creased to a fine line, those well-brushed suède shoes, that smoothly-hanging tie, could come out of the permanent makeshift of the sort of place he lived in. It made me ruefully conscious of the fact that I, by contrast, reflected only too truthfully the state of my flat; sometimes my shirt was none too clean, because I had forgotten to make up my bundle for the wash-woman, there were buttons missing on the sleeves of my suit, and so long as the holes in my socks were where they could not be seen once my shoes were on, I continued to wear them.

'You are becoming rather elusive,' said Steven. 'I suppose it's the car. This is Dick Chaputra, you've heard of him, of course.'

'It's time to forget it, if you have,' the Indian said, looking pleased.

I wondered at the odd variety of things I was supposed to have heard of in Johannesburg. We shook hands and Chaputra immediately took a piece of the dried meat that people in South Africa call biltong out of his pocket and, having offered it round, began to eat it, looking pleased with himself all the time.

Chaputra took the chair I gave him, but Steven, as usual, preferred to wander about the office while we talked, inspecting everything with his amiable and inquiring gaze, and perching where he felt like it. 'Dick's just been to India,' he said, as if it were an unaccountable whim for anyone to have indulged.

'How'd he like it?'

The Indian's grin tightened on the thong of leathery meat, loosened another tidbit. 'Awful,' he said, with his mouth full. 'Boy, I wouldn't live there for anything. D'you know, in Bombay, you see hundreds of people sleeping in the streets? It's a fact. That's where they live, just sleeping outside in the streets every night.'

'Worse than natives,' said Steven, opening his mouth, curling his tongue back to probe the socket of a tooth, and widening his nostrils. He chuckled to himself.

The Indian spoke English with the typical South African accent and intonation; if I looked away from his plump dark face, his satin-bright eyes, the white teeth, and thick, fly-away black hair that gave him that combination of Orientalism and aggressively Western boyishness that many Indians outside of India seem to have, I might have been listening to the voice of any of the white South African youths who passed me in the street every day. I asked him how long ago his family had come from India.

'My grandfather was born there,' he said. 'I never saw the old man. But I'm telling you, you can have India, for me.'

As we could not go out anywhere to lunch together, I thought I would have sandwiches sent up to the office. I went into the outer office to ask Miss McCann, who would be going out to lunch in a few minutes, to order them for me from the usual place.

'Two ham and two cheese?'

This was what I had most days, when I did not go out. 'No, of course that's not enough. Mixed sandwiches, for three.'

She said nothing, and kept her eyes on the pencil in her hand, as if she were waiting for me to go. When I was back in the office, I remembered some personal letters for the post, and rang for her. We were talking, and I had forgotten what I had rung for, when she appeared. She stood in the open doorway and did not speak. I said, 'Yes, Miss McCann?' She said, after a moment, 'You rang for me, Mr Hood.' There seemed to me to be something ridiculous about our exchange; then I realized that it was because instead of coming into the room, she was standing in the doorway like that.

'Oh yes,' I said, remembering. 'If you'd just put these in with the mail' – and I held the letters out to her. She stood for a moment without moving, and in a flash I understood, and then said, motioning with the letters, 'Here they are.' I stood holding them out to her like a lettuce offered to coax a rabbit, and slowly she came, looking not at me nor at anyone else. But as she took them, I stopped her. 'Just a minute – this one's to go airmail, and this, but ask about this one, perhaps it could go by ordinary mail, find out how long that would take –' And so I kept her for perhaps two minutes, in that room, unable to get out. Steven struck up an exaggeratedly careless and swaggering chatter, displaying familiarity with my ways, and, as Miss McCann took the letters and walked out, was saying, in a lordly, weary manner, 'Where's the beer hidden today Toby? – Toby always has a bottle or two tucked away somewhere –'

The door closed finally and precisely behind her, first the handle rose, then the latch clicked into place. My heart was thumping and I was suddenly irritated with Steven, for behaving as badly as the girl. Yet, after all, his only alternative was the negative rudeness of ignoring her; I understood, now, that he dared not show the common politeness of greeting her, as any man might expect to say 'Good afternoon' to any woman.

It was true that I did have a couple of bottles of beer in the cupboard, which I kept there to drink when I had lunch in the office, on the principle, which even I didn't believe, that it was a refreshing thing to do in summer. We drank it, tepid as it was, from some glasses I found put away unwashed in a cupboard (Amon was having one of his days off, to attend to the affair of his mother and Jagersfontein location) and, at last, the sandwiches came. The Indian looked all round the room, smiling, while he ate, and asked me direct, brisk questions about the business of Aden Parrot in South Africa, rather as if he had been called in to give an estimate of the firm's assets. This was all done with the airy politeness of commercial habit; although he was probably a year or two older than I was, he even called me 'sir'. When he left the room for a few minutes, the door had scarcely shut behind him when Steven said with the air of an impresario, 'D'you know who he is? D'you remember that series of robberies in Hillbrow? You were here already, I'm sure you were. The big case where one of the witnesses disappeared? D'you remember? – Well, that's his crowd. He's Lucky Chaputra. That's why he went off to India, to lie low. They didn't have anything on him, but they knew the whole outfit was his. Couldn't pin him down on a thing.'

'What's he busy with now?' I said.

'Resting,' said Steven. 'He's got plenty of dough. Boy, if he were a white man he'd be a mining magnate or something. He's cleverer than a cage of monkeys. He's got a white man who plays for him on the stock exchange – yes, he's made money like nobody's business, out of gold shares. But he's a restless boy, doesn't know what to do with himself.'

Chaputra came back into the room again, chuckled, and said, 'Nobody saw me' – he had slipped into the men's room in the building, which was, of course, meant only for white men. He shook hands and thanked me in his gauche South African accent: 'Gee, that was a nice lunch, man. Thanks, Mr Hood.' I felt as if I had given a schoolboy a treat.

'You should see his Cadillac,' Steven waved his long arms in ecstasy. Then murmured to me as they went out: 'I know it's not the car, with you, I suppose you're busy with some woman. Well, that's how it is with all of us at some time or other.'

'I'm sorry about tonight, I should've liked to have seen the fight. What about next week. Are you doing anything Monday night?'

Immediately he lapsed into important vagueness, a device that, I had noticed before, he used to cover up the fact that for him, next week was too far off to have any reality. 'Well, you see, I don't know, I may have to go away on business for a few days. . . .'

'Business! What business have you to do outside Johannesburg?'

He made a graceful, swaggering exit, roaring with laughter that made the lie and the evasion inoffensive, and praised me out of all proportion for my mild perspicacity.

That afternoon, before she left the office for the day, Miss McCann, smelling strongly of lavender water from a fresh application, appeared in my office accompanied by a fair, red-faced young man to whom I had nodded once or twice before when he had come to see her. He could easily have been her brother, an earlier-born member of the family, who had got more than his fair share of the vigour which had given out before her conception, but as he walked in behind her, I realized what should have been obvious to me before: he was her young man. I thought they must have come to make an announcement of some sort – perhaps that they were getting married and put on a grin of suitable expectancy, which was met with a stony, puffed-up stare from the young man, and was not met at all by Miss McCann, who kept her eyes on the tray full of old pencils and empty ball pens before me.

Embarrassment settled like dust upon the room.

'I know I have to give you two weeks' notice,' said the girl in her faint voice, 'but I would like you to let me go. I mean, without waiting.'

The young man moved up a little closer behind her, looking straight at me. He had that look about his mouth which suggested that he was saying, silently, things to himself that would encounter some break in the impulse between brain and tongue, and would never come out, except as some kind of shameful, strangled cry.

I said, 'I see. When would you like to leave?'

'I want to finish now, tonight.'

I said, trying to keep the balance of my indifference from exaggeration, 'Have you worked out your pay, with holiday pay, and so on?'

She whispered, with a hint of tears to come, 'Yes.'

I had a sudden thought of how ugly she would be if she cried; perhaps her face, so nondescript now, would wash away altogether. I pitied the stocky, resentful young man.

She handed me a slip of paper on which she had neatly typed the sum. I made out a cheque, and there was no sound in the room but the slither of the pen and the young man's breathing. She took the cheque and went out, the young man trooping behind her, like a bull that has been led into the ring and out again, without using the blind urges in his breast. Before he closed the door he turned and paused a second, a pause that was directed at me. I said, 'Yes?' but, as I had thought, the impulse that stirred in him was too muddled, too little understood to find words or action. They were gone.

For minutes I felt a tingling braggadocio, I wanted to feel that, truly, I had insulted and menaced the girl. I walked up and down the small room in a kind of nervous turmoil that some other, confusedly detached part of myself watched with excitement, as a scientist might observe in himself the phenomena of the fever which at last he is able to record subjectively. Why didn't I dismiss without a second thought the idiotic girl and the whole stupid incident? It was an incident which, in the given set of circumstances and with the given participants, was so completely predictable that it was nothing but a cliché. On the face of it, I should have been bored by the whole thing. But the fact was that, once in it, it was not boring, it was not to be experienced as a standard social situation, because, once in it, all the unguessed-at things that underlie one's predictable reactions leap up and take over; one cannot take them into account before, because they can only be touched off by certain situations – if those situations do not happen to arise around one, one could go through one's life innocent and ignorant of their potential existence.

How was I, how was anyone to know it was like this? This evil embarrassment, a thing like a spell, like the moment in a dream when you wish urgently to speak and nothing comes out of your open mouth, that had suddenly sucked all the normality out of a room in which I sat between two men and a drab girl whose maximum assertion in life would not exceed the making of a crocheted tea-cosy. How could we, all of us in that room, have generated it? The skunk-odour of the spirit, down into which my head had been thrust and out of which I had now come up smarting-eyed and gasping, there's a snoutful of it for you, my boy. And it was all so stupid and petty. A nobody of a girl thinks she's too good to come into a room where a white man is sharing lunch with two black men. That's all. Yet there I was, in a strange thrill of irritation, contemptuous of the girl, longing to punch the young white man on the nose, impatient and angry with the black man. Like a savage! I kept saying to myself. Like a savage! And I did not know whether I meant Steven (I kept having a consciously cruel picture of him, dressed up – I thought – as he imagines a gentleman to dress, a fatuous cinema-smirk of worldliness on his black face) or the inarticulate, red-faced suitor of Miss McCann, or myself, in my state of unaccustomed belligerent excitement.

There is no distraction in the world to equal the pursuit of a woman, as men great and small have been demonstrating since Antony, and, as I had an arrangement to meet Cecil in the Stratford at six, my conscious preoccupation with the thought of her, as I made preparations to leave the office and join her, soon thrust down the incident beneath the lid of the past day. To hell with black men and white men and, indeed, all men. Oh the delightful, narrowing orbit of the evening, with the first whisky dissolving into peace and expectancy inside, the ice bobbing in the glass, and the woman, who, after so much thought, so much speculation, so much concentration of recollection in absence, really cannot be seen any more, so that you could not describe her face or the dress she is wearing, even if you had to – the total presence of the woman, imagined and real, all in one, beside you.

As the lift fell through the layers of the building, the thought came to me, almost from outside, that perhaps I wouldn't talk to Cecil about what had happened; it was quite honestly a relief to think I didn't have to, without going into any reasons with myself. I had, I supposed, an Eastern equation of women with pleasure; I fiercely resisted any impingement on this preserve.

Cecil would not have to go through the tests which Miss McCann had failed. There was no need to know how she would have met them.

She was sitting at the same table at which we had already sat several times before. She watched me come in with the down-turned smile that was always like a challenge putting you on your mettle for you did not quite know what. She said, 'Where is Chibuluma?'

'Why?'

'I've been listening to that couple over there. They're having a wonderful quarrel. She wants him to take a job at this place, and he says even though he doesn't like "the flicks" he likes to know that in Johannesburg there are forty "flicks" for him to choose from if he does want to go.'

'I think it's right up in Northern Rhodesia somewhere.'

'Just let me listen another minute. When I was a child, I could never eat at all in a hotel dining-room, I was so busy listening to other people. They say you never hear any good of yourself, but think of the things you hear about other people.'

Chapter 8

My relationship with Cecil moved with queer inconsequence. We dropped apart for days and met again. This did not slow, or change, or damp what was happening between us. She was very much a stranger to me, I realized; much different from the two or three women with whom I had had affairs at Oxford, and the girl in London with whom I had been in love. If any of those women had had a background and childhood entirely dissimilar to mine (and this was true of the Ebury street girl, certainly) at least we were both part of the old, old pattern of an ancient country, and our bones shared with its stones an ancestral memory. If we did not know what we were, we knew what we had been, and this continuity was unbroken by the trauma of the birth of several generations in a new civilization.

Like many people who are young now, Cecil apparently had been brought up into a life that did not have much meaning for her; the only difference was that she believed unquestioningly that meaningful ways of life existed, unchanged. For her, the trouble was that when she tried to follow one or the other, it was like reading from a formula from which one of the ingredients has always been left out. She seemed to have no doubts about the worthwhileness of the things she attempted, whether she wanted to be a mannequin in Rome or a champion show jumper; but like a bloodhound that has had no nose bred into it, she was guessing at the trail, and ran helter-skelter, looking back inquiringly all the time, uncertain if she were going the right way about her pursuit, and in the right style. Nothing came naturally to her.

She hardly ever spoke of her marriage, except in the most casual fashion, not, I think, because the fact of its failure was too important and painful to her, but because she was ashamed that she thought of it so little. It was like one of those dresses that she said had 'never been a success', that I once found stuffed in the back of a cupboard to which she had sent me to look for a thermos flask. She lived in today, this minute, and if the past or the future caught at her, struggled helplessly in moods that, watching her, you could give a name to, but that she herself did not relate to the circumstances of her life. She had the blues: so she shifted her feelings from the particular to the general.

One Sunday afternoon we were riding together down the valley below Alexanders', when we came upon a deserted house. It was during early November, when in Johannesburg an extraordinary theatrical light lay every afternoon between the sky and the city. The summer rains, sucked down so quickly that the earth was ringing hard again a day after storms and torrents, had produced a sudden, astonishing, deep-green luxuriance of foliage; all the trees, fir, gum, acacia and willow, sugar bush and poplar, had taken on full plumage. Between the black-blue greenness, like an optical illusion of bloom created by the damp air, there were huge purple smudges and pale mauve blurs – the jacaranda trees in flower, and behind them, over them, the sky, heavy with unshed rain, blue and purple with charged atmosphere, exchanged with the trees the colour of storm.

The air was cool and massive and the horses went slowly up the neglected drive under more jacarandas. As always on Sundays, there was drumming and far-off singing somewhere down among the trees, where groups of Africans who were servants in the nearby suburbs were having a prayer-meeting; and Cecil was telling me a long anecdote about the first wife of John Hamilton, the Alexanders' crocodile-hunting friend (he was at Alexanders' that day), with the peculiar relish women have for the iniquities of their own sex. The horses stopped of their own accord on the overgrown terrace where last year's leaves rotted, and she said, gaily, as if in answer to a suggestion, 'Come on, then – let's go in.' We hooked the reins on to an iron spike that must once have held the pole of an awning, and tramped over the flagstones. We peered in at the windows, rattled the front door, and Cecil said, 'Oh look!' and ran to pick a yellow rose from the bushes that had thrown a defence of barbed entanglements across the terrace steps. They scratched across her boots. Though it was not more than ten years old, and, from the condition of the paint, could not have been empty longer than six months, the place had the air of a ruin that all things that are the work of men have about them the instant men desert them.

'Oh, I want to get in!' she said, rattling at the french doors that led on to the terrace. I looked up and around. Someone had begun to make alterations to the upper story of the house, but had never finished; there were builders' planks and ropes about, and raw brickwork gaped where half a gable had been taken away. We struggled and laughed while I tried to lift her to test a likely-looking window, with a broken pane, but it was round the side of the house where there was no terrace to shorten the distance from window to ground, and she couldn't reach the latch. We became idiotically determined to get in. 'Wait a minute! What if we brought Danny round and you got on his back?' 'No, let's try the kitchen first.' At this, she turned and ran ahead of me through the yard and shook at the kitchen door; it was fast, and she left it at once, in the manner of someone merely satisfying another that he will have to resort to her plan, and ran up the three steps to the next door and took its handle firmly in both hands. But as she touched it, it gave way. She looked round at me, astonished and smiling. And we trooped in. It was the scullery door, and from it we went into the kitchen. 'Natives must have broken in,' she said. There was a chaos of emptiness and smashed glass; the cupboards had been wrenched open, the light fittings lay spintered like hoar frost upon the floor: the moment when it had been ransacked seemed to grip it still. In the passage and the living-rooms, mice-pills were all about the floor, and everywhere, through all the empty rooms, drifts of silvery down, blown in from the catkins in the garden, lifted and sank in the draught of our passing.

'This must have been a nice room,' she said, placing herself at the french doors and looking out through the dirty glass from the context of some imaginary setting. Outside, we saw one of the horses snort, but could not hear it. She wandered from room to room, touching the dead wires that hung, wrenched loose, from the wall, the empty sockets and brackets. 'The telephone must have been here.' 'This was for a lamp, I suppose.' Sadness settled on her movements; wondering, she took my hand and clung to it without noticing me. Was she thinking of places she had left somewhere in her disregarded life, lights she had touched on, a pattern of rooms her feet had come to know as a blind man knows? Perhaps it was not as simple as that; the disquiet of the emptiness seemed to take a sounding in her; she was aware of depth and silence, communications the telephone could not carry, a need of assurance the electric light could not bring.

She had a strong fear of herself, as many active people do. I sensed this fear, and, excited by it, began to kiss her. She let me kiss and caress her with a kind of amazement; she was like one of those people who, called up by a conjuror from an audience and told, do this, do that, produces something unimaginable – a bunch of roses, a cage of mice, a Japanese flag. Her open eyes were watching me, her mouth did not participate with the practised pleasure-giving I had found there before. Only the nipples, those unflattering and indiscriminate responders who really never learn to know the hand of a lover from any other stimulus, automatically touched out at the palm of my hand through the stuff of her clothes. 'For Christ's sake!' she said suddenly, recalled to herself. 'Not here.' Social caution, her only and familiar arbiter, restored her to a sense of her own known world. The fit of the blues was gone; I had provided her with a situation that she could deal with.

Someone who loved her would have done much more. But she did not know what she needed, and accepted, without knowledge of failed expectation, my preoccupation with the taste of nicotine and lipstick in her mouth.

As we rode back along the valley, a pile of livid light from the hidden sun showed along the grassy ridges. A black man wearing an old white sheet robe and carrying a long stick with a piece of blue cloth tied to it, passed us on his way to join the worshippers we could just see, going in a stooping, leaping, yelling procession round a drummer, where a knot of acacias made a meeting-place. He was singing under his breath, and he murmured 'Afternoon, baas.'

When we got back to the Alexanders', Cecil remarked, with the confidence of an order where dirt and chaos went with one side, and beauty and power went with the other, 'We really ought to get hold of the agents for that empty house. All the out-of-work natives for miles around must be sleeping there. You should just see it, Marion.'

The first time I made love to her was one night in her living-room, after we had been to dinner at the house of some friends of hers. What a lack of spontaneity there is about the first act of love between two people who seem familiar enough with each other on other levels of association!

In the dark each apprehends in the other a secret creature who never appeared across the dinner table, or bought a newspaper in the street, or leaned forward to make a point in a political discussion. I could imagine that becoming aware of a life after death might be something like that: all the accepted manifestations of the awareness of being, stilled, like an engine cut off, and then, out of a new element of silence, another way of being. She groped, at last, for the table beside the divan: 'Can you find me a cigarette?' 'Let me find the lamp first.' 'No, no, don't turn it on. Here's the box.' We sat up in the dark with the divan cover pulled round us, smoking, like people come to shelter after a disaster of some sort – shipwreck or storm. I dressed and left not long after midnight; people who had been visiting one of the flats along the corridor were making their farewells and we emerged from the building together – they were a grey-faced bald man with strong hair curling out of his nose and ears, as if it had turned and grown down into instead of out of that cranium, and one of those heavy women who, despite large bosoms, corsets, and jewellery, when they reach middle age suddenly look like men. The moment the last good-bye had left their lips they sank into the grimness that is one kind of familiarity. They came along behind me like jailers, and the slam of our car doors, theirs and mine, as we drove off, was the final locking-up of the night.

But, the next time, I went to bed with Cecil in her warm, crumpled bed that smelled of perfume and cigarette smoke. She argued about the light, but I wanted to see her face, to know what she was feeling. (Who knows what women feel, in their queer, gratuitous moment?) She looked, in the light, like she had that Sunday morning, in her dressing-gown. Pride, bewilderment, vanity, greed, want, and determination were not smoothed out by the banality of make-up; her eyes were faintly bloodshot from sun, smoke, and gin, and the shape of her smile, drawn in knowingly at one corner, was there, marked for ever on her face, even when her mouth was in repose. At the back of her neck, the real smell of her hair came out from under the chemical scents of the processes it was subjected to in that be-curtained shop below my office – the real smell of blonde pigment, waxy and acid, which I always notice at once, perhaps because I am dark.

'I didn't want you to see my stomach,' she said. 'I can't bear to look at it myself.'

'Why, what's supposed to be wrong with it?'

She rolled over face-down with her elbows tight to her sides and said resentfully, 'Haven't you ever seen a woman who's had a child? It ruins the skin of your stomach. It looks like crinkle paper.'

But whatever the human climate to which she had been exposed in her life had done to weather her face, her body was entirely itself, sure and beautiful. She was a loving woman in bed, clever and full of tender enthusiasm: Now just wait, she would say, just wait a minute ... as if her caresses were carefully prepared surprises that must not be discovered before the right moment. The narrow bed, intended for a single sleeper, kept her close to me as I wanted, all night; there was no inch away to which she could move, even if she had wanted to. Her whole body burned with a steady warmth of energy, even while she slept, and only her buttocks and her breasts were cool, the way some people's hands are always cool.

I got up to leave very early in the morning, so that I should be out of the flat before the servant came in. I was coming back down the passage from the bathroom when I saw, standing in the open doorway of the second bedroom, in the colourless light that comes in before dawn, a little boy. He was barefoot, and in mis-buttoned pyjamas, and he was holding his pillow. He was quite awake, but perhaps not sure where he had awakened: in some grown-up part of the night he did not know. But even as he watched me the light began to golden, and he must have known it was morning. He did not speak and he did not move while I passed his room and disappeared through the next doorway. Cecil turned at the sound of me dressing, moved her mouth as if she were tasting, and put out her hand to me. I said: 'Your child met me in the passage. What will he make of that.'

'Don't have to worry about him,' she murmured. 'He won't say anything.' When I was ready to go, she suddenly woke up properly and called me back to kiss her and reproached me for trying to slip away without saying 'a proper good morning'.

There was no one in the passage when I left, and the door of the second bedroom was shut.

Chapter 9

I WONDER why it is that the life of poverty is regarded as more real than any other life. In books and films, the slice of life traditionally is cut from the lower crust; in almost all of us with full bellies, whose personal struggles are above the sustenance level, there is a nervous, even a respectful feeling that life may be elsewhere. The poor man has got it; he staggers beneath its violent weight, of course; one wouldn't wish to be in his shoes – but he has it.

I thought about this idea a lot, at this time, when I was so often in the townships with Steven, and sometimes stayed for a night at Sam's two-roomed house, sleeping on the divan in his living-room. I thought about it, but I never came to any firm conclusion. What do we mean by real life? That which is closest to the basic trinity, shared by all creatures: survival, food, reproduction? Then we indulge in romantic fallacy, stemming from some atavistic guilt, because, in life, reality is not an absolute, but consists of one set of conditions or another. To regard total pre-occupation with survival, food, and reproduction as the criterion of reality is to ignore other needs that men have created for themselves, and which, in combination with the basic ones, make men's reality. In a society where laws take care of a man's survival among his fellows, his part in commerce and industry ensures that he will eat as a matter of course, and his reproductive function is secured by the special mating system of marriage, the greatest reality of his life may consist in his meeting the growth of the financial empire which his brain and energy have created. The greatest reality, for the scientist, must lie in his patient onslaught on the opposition of the formula he can't get right; for an artist, in accepting that no one, at present, will accept his particular vision. That is 'real life'; for each man, the demands of his own condition.

I decided that possibly life in the townships seemed more 'real' simply because there were fewer distractions, far fewer vicarious means for spending passion, or boredom. To each human being there, the demands of his or her own condition came baldly. The reality was nearer the surface. There was nothing for the frustrated man to do but grumble in the street; there was nothing for the deserted girl to do but sit on the step and wait for her bastard to be born; there was nothing to be done with the drunk but let him lie in the yard until he'd got over it. Among the people I met with Cecil, frustrated men threw themselves into golf and horse-racing, girls who had had broken love affairs went off to Europe, drunks were called alcoholics, and underwent expensive cures. That was all. That was the only difference.

But was it? With so much to comfort and distract them, don't people perhaps learn, at last, to feel a little less? And doesn't that make life that much less 'real'? – But, again, this sounded convincing, but seemed disproved in actual fact. For the people who frequented The High House (and also myself, my friends and acquaintances in England) made a great deal of their feelings, nervous breakdowns and other long-drawn-out miseries followed on their misadventures, and they knew that life very easily comes to a standstill; but the men and women of the townships, after brief and public mourning, wiped their noses with the backs of their hands, as it were, and did the next thing, knowing that nothing could interrupt life. There was the woman who lived in one of the houses that shared a yard with Sam's house. One day she stopped us as we were entering the yard, and spoke to Sam. She was a cheerful, dirty slut with the usual pretty, milk-and-pee smelling baby falling over her feet, and Ella had often complained about her. When she had gone back to her house, Sam said to me, 'D'you know anybody, any friend of yours in Sandown? That woman's looking for a backyard room somewhere. She's got people she washes for there, and she'd like a room nearby.'

'What about her house?'

'Her husband's disappeared. Perhaps some of your friends have got a servant's room they don't use.'

Then, one night, there was a murder close by The House of Fame. Steven was hurrying home to one of his own drinking-and-talking sessions which I and a number of the hangers-on had not waited to begin (it was quite common for Steven to invite you to his room and then fail to be there when you arrived), and he came upon the dying man, lying in the street. He had pulled him up on to the steps of the nearest house, but: 'He'd had it. Gone,' Steven told us when he came in. 'I'm sorry I'm so darned late, Toby, I've been fixing up insurance for an old Indian who owns a string of bug-houses' – this was what the township cinemas were commonly called – 'and, you know – he's the sort of old chap who every time he wants to tell you something, no matter what, he's got to begin right at the beginning of his life and lead up to it.' He grinned, said, 'Mind,' and pushed aside the legs of the people who were sitting on his bed, so that he could put his smart tan leather briefcase under the bed. He straightened up and peered down at the side of his jacket, twitching at the sleeve. 'There's nothing on my suit, is there?' One of the young men, who had never owned such a suit, jumped up to examine it, hitting at the cloth and saying, in Suto, that there was nothing to worry about. And it was true that there was a only a little red township dust on the suit, that dust that seemed more the powder of decaying buildings than the surface of the earth. But there was a smear of blood on one of Steven's shirt-cuffs, like bright rust. 'He's made a bit of a mess of me,' he said, and sighed. 'Never mind, poor chap couldn't help it.'

'It was a gang, eh?' someone said.

Steven nodded. 'I should think he had it coming to him. It was a knife job, no chances. It must have happened about ten minutes before I came along, that's all. They'd cleared off. People in the house there didn't hear anything. When I saw he was finished, I just said, here you are, and skipped out as quick as I could.' He was sitting down, now, and a glass of brandy dangled in his hands between his knees, in his characteristic fashion. He wrinkled his nose, not at the dead man, but at death. 'A short life and a happy one,' he said, and drank.

When I woke up in the morning in Sam's house, I did have the strong, vivid feeling that life and death were breathing on me, hot and cold. No doubt in my own flat in a white suburb, or in the Alexanders' house among the paddocks and the swimming pools and the jacarandas, you were surrounded by living and dying, too. But there, you were not aware of it outside the personal aspects. In the townships, on a Saturday night, there was only an hour or two, between the late end of the long night and the early beginning of the day, when groans and laughter and fires were out. For the rest of the time, the whole cycle of living made a continuous and simultaneous assault on your senses. 'There's never a moment's peace and quiet,' Sam would say, standing in his little room with his old typewriter in his hands, as if in the space of those four thin walls there might be some corner of acoustical freak where he could put himself down and not hear the men shouting in the street, a procession of some sort, perhaps a school or a funeral parade, children quarrelling, a baby crying, a woman singing at a washtub, and the rusty bray and slam of the door of the communal lavatory in the yard as people trooped in and out of it. And in my flat, Steven would wander restlessly from the balcony to the living-room, saying, uneasily, 'Man, I'm used to Sophiatown, there's always something going on.'

I would walk with Sam in the early evening out on to the waste ground near his house. It was a promontory of ashes and clinker, picked bald, by urchins and the old, even of the rubbish that was dumped there, and it looked back over most of the township. At that time, the day seems to relent, even the dreariest things take on disguising qualities in the soft light. The ashheap took on the dignity of loneliness; we might have been standing on the crater of a burnt-out volcano, the substance beneath our feet gave no life to anything, animal or vegetable, it was a ghost of the fecund earth. Behind, and down below, everything teemed, rotted and flourished. There were no street-lights, and in the night that seemed to well up like dark water round the low, close confusion of shacks and houses – while, higher up, where we were, the day lingered in a pink mist – cooking fires showed like the flame of a match cupped in the hand. Sam said to me once, in the rather awkwardly jocular manner which he almost always used when speaking English, probably because it had been the way in which he first had managed to bridge the gaps of unease between himself and his first white acquaintances – 'I suppose when you get back, this will seem like an ugly dream.'

But he was wrong, and it was hard for me to explain to him why, without having him attribute, on my part, too much to the romance of foreignness and poverty, the picturesque quality of other people's dirt. He had his inner eye fixed quietly and steadily on his and his people's destiny as decent bourgeois, his curse fell equally upon the roistering wretchedness of life in the townships, and his own childhood, when, as he described to me one evening up on that same ash-heap, he had herded tribal cattle in the Northern Transvaal. I sometimes thought, when I suddenly became aware of him through some expression on his face or something he said, how except when he was playing jazz, there was not one moment when his being was not quietly revolving on this purpose. His manner was a mixture of anxiousness and sad determination. He was full of dogged hope, a person whose life was pinned to a future. Just as Steven was hopeless, a person committed entirely to the present. Sam said of him, sadly: 'Steven is just a white man in a black man's skin, that's the trouble'; which, taking into account the context of Sam's affection and concern for Steven, was another way of saying what Anna Louw had said when she complained that Steven cared damn all for the African people. The only difference was, Anna saw Steven's attitude as loss to his people, Sam saw it as a loss to Steven himself. Yet it was Steven who had some affection for the life down there, below the ash-heap, it was Steven who lived it as the reality of the present to which he was born – the only sure destiny any man has.

It was this aspect of township life, Steven's aspect, if you like, that would make it impossible for me ever to look back upon it, from another country, as 'an ugly dream'. It was no beauty, God knows, but it was no dream, either. It would not vanish from the mind's eye; I should be able to believe in its existence even when I was somewhere else.

The first time I stepped out of Sam's house on a Sunday morning, after spending the night there, the men and women stared at me, looked at me quizzically, and passed sniggering remarks – a white man who slept in the house of Africans was unheard-of, and under the greatest suspicion; a concupiscent grin informed the face of an old man, and he moved aside for me, saying 'Morning, baas', for what could I have come for but sex?; and even when I was well known as an unexplained visitor at Sam's house, and I took his little daughter by the hand down the road to buy her an orange from the row of vendors' tin huts and home-made stalls and wares spread out on sacking on the ground, known as the 'shops', I was never anything but a stranger. But, as a stranger, I found in these places and among these people something I had never found at home. There were summer nights in Sophiatown, where Steven lived, when no one seemed to go to bed at all. The worse smells were made harmless by the warm, sour smell of beer. Urchins gambled under the street-lights that, spaced sparsely, attracted into their yellow light people as well as moths. There was singing and strolling; now and then one of the big American cars that the gangsters use would tear scrunching over the stones, down the street, setting long tongues of dust uncurling. The girls clicked in their throats with quick annoyance and screamed defiance in defence of their dirtied dresses. There was giggling and flirting. Some were primped and got up in high-heeled shoes, some were barefoot, dressed in a torn series of ragged garments, one overlaying the holes of another, and the last, inevitably, in spite of everything, worn through at the vital places, breasts and backside. On such a night, suddenly, a procession would burst round the corner, swaying, rocking, moving by a musical peristalsis: men and women and children, led by a saxophone and tin whistles, a rehearsal for a wedding due to take place next day. They sang and chanted, a sound to lift stones.

The life of the townships, at such moments, seemed to feed a side of my nature that had been starved; it did for me what Italy or Greece had done for other Englishmen, in other times. It did not change me; it released me and made me more myself.

Chapter 10

'YOU don't have to worry about him, he won't say anything,' Cecil had said of her child, when he saw me walking down the passage of her flat in the early hours of the morning. She was more than half asleep, and her tongue was unguarded when she spoke. Whatever that casual truth implied, I found, after the first automatic twinge of jealousy, that it was powerless to affect me. I had another life, outside the parenthesis of the time I spent with her; she, too, had hers. Each tacitly forwent inquiry into that of the other, because each suspected that the discovery of his own life by the other would make the parenthetic shared relationship impossible. I heard her say, to some people with whom we were having coffee after a cinema, 'Toby does a lot of work among the natives.' Later, when we were alone, I asked her, 'What made you tell the Howards that I do a lot of "work" among natives?' 'Well, don't you?' she said, yawning. 'I never have,' I said. She let it drop; she assumed that anyone who had anything to do with Africans was concerned with charity or uplift, and that was that – she wasn't going to quibble over what she satisfied herself could only be a matter of definition. And I, I left it at that, too. I had had my little flirt with danger by questioning her at all; thankfully, I hadn't had to take it any further.

For I knew that if I told Cecil that my closest friends in Johannesburg were black men, and that I ate with them and slept in their houses, I would lose her. That was the fact of the matter. And I was damned if I was going to lose her. There was a good chance that her sophistication would save her from the classic reaction of horror and revulsion, but her strong instinct for the conventionally unconventional mores of the wealthy 'smart' set would have labelled me queer (not in the accepted, fashionable sense) and ruled me out. I knew that it was natural and unremarkable that I should sleep at Sam's, in the township, on Sunday night, and in Cecil's bed on Monday, since it is natural and unremarkable for a man to have friends and a woman to love. What did it matter that, because she did not know that it was natural and unremarkable, she was not told about it. The facts of my having been there, at Sam's, and being here, at Cecil's, existed whether accepted or not. So, unaware, in her own life, Cecil demonstrated the truth she would have denied with every drop of blood in her body, had she been confronted with it openly.

For herself, she was often secretive and vague about her movements. She was hiding, I thought, not something, but nothing; she did not want me to know how she spent her days, because she herself suspected the style and rightness of what she did, and in imagination, she transferred her own judgement of herself, to me. She wanted no confirmation of this from outside. In fact, she wanted assurance that she was *not* as she suspected herself to be; and anyone who could have presented her to herself, strongly enough, as something other, could have made her into that other. She saw almost nothing of her family, even of her younger sister Margaret, whose clean pretty face was troubled by none of the ambiguities that had endeared her elder sister's to me, and she spent more time than she always admitted with her great friend Rosamund Bell. The Bell woman was divorced, too, and had been left in possession of a splendid establishment so well-stocked with servants, children, and animals that it did not seem there could ever have been room for the husband who had provided all this. For women of a certain economic level, living on alimony seemed quite a profession in Johannesburg; it was taken for granted by many that, once having been married, they were entitled to be provided for, for life, in idleness. Another woman whom I met sometimes at the Alexanders', a lively and charming woman, had been living for ten years with a man whom she admitted she could not afford to marry, because she would then lose the income of her ex-husband's alimony – she and her lover used it to finance their trips to Europe. Like these women, Cecil lived on alimony, too, but either she was a bad manager, or the alimony was not as generous as theirs, for she grumbled continually about lack of money. It was true that though she had (what seemed to me to be, anyway) luxurious clothes, the flat was poorly stocked and shabby; the glass shelf in the bathroom was crowded with perfumes and elaborate cosmetics for the bath, but the towels were threadbare and too few, and, although there was always plenty of whisky and a bottle or two of good wine in the cupboard, she would make a great, despairing to-do, every now and then, in the kitchen, because too much butter had been used, or the maid, Eveline, had ordered a particular kind of fruit for the child, before the season of plenty had brought the price down. I remember a fuss about peaches. 'Why can't he eat bananas? Why must a child have fancies for peaches at sixpence each? Bananas are nourishing and I don't want to hear any more nonsense about peaches, d'you hear? Honestly, Eveline, you seem to think I'm made of money.'

The servant, Eveline, laughed, and shouted to the little boy, Keith, in her loud, affectionate voice, 'Come on, Cookie, let's go up to the vegetable place. Mommy says we must eat bananas, bananas.' The child trailed along beside her, hanging from her hand, while she laughed and swung the basket, and called to friends and delivery men as she went. Standing beside me on the balcony, Cecil watched them crossly. The boy turned and waved, fingers moving stiffly from the knuckle, a baby's wave. She waved back. 'If only he didn't look exactly like me,' she said, in irritation. 'Why shouldn't he?' I asked, but she was serious. 'You don't know how horrible it is to reproduce yourself, like that. Every time he looks at me, and I see that face. . . .' It was as if all the distrust she had of herself was projected into the way she saw the little boy.

'Women are strange,' I smiled at her. 'I should have thought it would have pleased you.' What I was really thinking was that surely she would prefer the child to resemble her, rather than his father, from whom she was divorced, and for whom she felt, at best, indifference.

The servant, Eveline, shielded Cecil from the irritation of the child, and the child from Cecil's irritation. Cecil was always saying, with the air and vocabulary of wild exaggeration that was the *lingua franca* of her friends, 'I simply couldn't live without my Eveline.' She had no idea, of course, that this was literally true. Not only did the warm, vulgar, coquettish, affectionate creature keep 'Cookie' trailing at her heels all day long; all that was irresponsibly, greedily life-loving in her own nature leapt to identify itself with and abet Cecil in Cecil's passionate diversions. Eveline, who herself wore a fashionable wedding ring although she had no husband, would drop her work and carry off Cecil's earrings to the kitchen for a polish, while Cecil was dressing to go out. Cecil, feverishly engrossed in her hair, her face, or the look of a dress, often padded about in her stockings until the very second before the front door closed behind her, because Eveline had seen, at the last moment, that Cecil's shoes could not be worn unless they were cleaned first. Cecil bribed, wheedled, and quarrelled with Eveline, to get her to stay in and look after the child on those days or nights when her time off clashed with some engagement Cecil wanted to keep. She appealed to her in desperation a dozen times a day: *don't* call me to the telephone, please, Eveline, d'you hear – tell them I'm out, whoever it is, take a message, anything; *please* take Keith out for a walk and don't come back till five – I've got to get some sleep; oh, Eveline, be a good girl and see if you can find something for us to eat, won't you, we don't feel like going out, after all. 'Eveline adores Keith,' she would say; as if that, too, she had delegated to hands more willing and capable than her own. I didn't think Eveline did; but she didn't mind the child, she took his presence around her ankles as the most natural thing in the world, and that, I imagine, is what a child needs more than 'adoration'. Cecil regarded Eveline as a first-rate servant, and took this, as I have noticed people who have a good servant tend to, as some kind of oblique compliment to herself: as if she herself deserved or inspired Eveline's first-rateness. In fact, the woman was her friend and protector, and, breezily unconscious of this role, stood between her and the realities of her existence.

When I met Cecil at the Stratford after one of her visits to the hairdresser, or she came frowning out into the sun on horseback at Alexanders', all dash and style, it was difficult to believe that the effect had been produced in that flat, with the rumpled drawers, the bills lying about, and the urgent appeals to the untidy kitchen. But, like Steven, whom she would never meet, her appearance was contrived in indifference to and independence of her background. This was not the only point of resemblance between them. Like Steven, she kept up a fiction of importance; she would suddenly suggest that we should change our plans for a particular day because on that day she had committed herself to some (unspecified) arrangement, a mysterious 'something she couldn't very well get out of'. Once or twice she announced that it was a damned nuisance, but she'd had a week-end invitation she couldn't refuse. Sometimes the mere mention of these engagements was enough to fulfil whatever their purpose was, and she forgot about them, at other times she did disappear for an evening or a week-end. On one of these occasions, when I had gone with Sylvia Danziger, Anna, and a man who was a friend of theirs from Capetown, to a cinema, I looked over the balcony and saw Cecil moving out of the foyer with John Hamilton, Rosamund Bell, and another man who came quite often to Alexanders'. They were in evening dress, so I supposed they must be going on to a nightclub. Why she should think it necessary to make a secret of an evening spent with these people, I did not know. Did she think I should be jealous? But that was ridiculous; it was not as if she were going out with some new man she'd found for herself: these people were all old friends.

In their different ways, and in their one country where they pursued them, both Cecil and Steven were people who had not found commitment. Theirs was a strange freedom; the freedom of the loose end. They made the hour shine; but now and then they leapt up in half-real, half-mock panic and fled – perhaps, at that very moment, something better was waiting, somewhere else?

I respected this; for hadn't I, for *my* reasons, felt myself a stranger, uncommitted, in my own world in England; and wasn't that the reason why, in this African country, I had come to feel curiously at home, a stranger among people who were strangers to each other?

Chapter 11

IN the few houses in Johannesburg where people of different colours met, you were likely to meet the same people time after time. Many of them had little in common but their indifference to the different colours of their skins; there was not room to seek your own kind in no man's land: the space of a few rooms between the black encampment and the white.

I got asked to these houses because it was known that I had made black as well as white friends since I had come to Johannesburg. It was not easy for people who did not want to keep their lives and hospitality exclusive to one race, to find new blood; most of these people found that they had two sets of white friends and acquaintances, those who could be invited along with coloured people, and those, sometimes very close friends, who could not.

But of course it was natural that a particular phenomenon should arise, and this was just beginning to happen, while I was in Johannesburg that summer. On the one side, there was the great mass of whites for whom the colour bar was not a piece of man-devised legislation, but a real and eternal barrier; on the other, there were the people who, through social conscience, or (like myself) impatience with restrictive distinctions which they, personally, found meaningless, mixed with coloured people. It was inevitable, with all the books and newspaper reports being written about South Africa, that the forbidden fraternization should become, in a sense, fashionable, and attract certain white people who might never, otherwise, have overcome their prejudices against or indifference to the races on the periphery of their lives. They were often people who had failed to secure attention in other ways; by identifying themselves with Africans, they were able to feel the limelight on their faces for the first time, even if it was only a refraction of that brilliance which was falling on black faces. They 'discovered' African painters, theatre groups, dancers and crafts; they collaborated with Africans in all sorts of arty ventures in which their own shaky talents were disguised by the novelty, the importance of the fact that their material was genuine African. It began to be fashionable (in a very small, *avant-garde* way, I may say; on a par, perhaps, with the personal exploration of the effects of mescalin, in other countries) to have at least one African friend. A pet-African, whose name you could drop casually: 'Tom Kwaza was telling me at our house the other day . . .'

Sam had been taken up by one of these people, an amateur composer, with whom he was 'collaborating' in the writing of a one-act 'African' opera, and, through him, I found myself at the composer's house. There was a mixture of people, gathered for drinks; some of the old guard, who had always moved indiscriminately between black and white worlds – Dorothea Welz, a jolly priest in a dishevelled cassock – two young University lecturers who were married, the correspondent of an English newspaper, and an unidentified pretty girl, Sam, Steven, his friend Peter, and a young coloured man from the Cape. The hostess moved about in a state of suppressed high excitement, offering sausages and cold potato chips; she hung beggar-like at the edgc of every conversation, with her plate and her entreating smile. The host raced from glass to glass, chivvying people to drink faster, filling up for those who had. Theirs was the desperate hospitality of people who are unsure of themselves. They communicated their ill-ease to the guests; at first it seemed that this was going to be an evening of stunted conversation: Dorothea Welz smoked, Sam sat on the edge of his chair, ready to raise himself a few inches, politely, every time the hostess approached with her plate, Steven sat back looking down under arched brows at his shoes, with the expression of a man who is thinking his own thoughts and doesn't care who knows it. But if the hospitality was overdone, it was, literally, intoxicating. We all passed swiftly from sluggish reserve to the slightly theatrical confidential mood common to drinking parties. The newspaperman told the lecturer's wife: 'What enchanting feet you have. I noticed them the moment you came in. If I were your husband I would give you rings to wear on your toes. Perfectly beautiful little feet.' And, in her fancy sandals, she curled her toes with pleasure: 'Bells on my toes, don't you mean?'

In a huddle with Dorothea and the host, the priest – on one beer – listened open-mouthed and laughing, protesting, 'Lovely! lovely!' to the young coloured from the Cape, who was giving an imitation of coloured speakers at a political meeting. Peter, the university lecturer, and I were part of an exchange that centred on the newspaperman's pretty girl, Sam, and Steven. Her particular style was that while she looked and dressed like a conventionally fashionable young woman, and had the sophisticated, consciously charming and slightly deferential manner with men that such women practise, she carried this into situations where such women would never be found. She was the progressive young woman in disguise, like the poet in the clerk's neat suit. The disguise was so successful that Steven was clearly taken in; she seemed to him to be the one kind of white woman whom he would never meet, the private ornament of the white man's house which represented to the white man the purity of his race and the height of his privilege. She and Steven got on particularly well together, but there was an edge of haughtiness to Steven's voice, an extra-careless twist to his banter that suggested that he could not really bring himself to believe that she regarded him, as she treated him, like any other man.

There was a general sort of disagreement about the respective merits of newspapers, which somehow became an exchange of personal spelling idiosyncrasies, and, in turn, became a discussion about languages, and accents. We had all (except the priest) had so much to drink that all our talk veered to the personal. As the discussion sub-divided into smaller conversations, I heard the girl say to Steven, 'Now take the way you speak. You speak English much more like an Indian than an African.'

Sam giggled and said to Steven and the girl, 'It would be a good idea to have a competition, you know. Like they have competitions for the beauty queens with the best legs, and the rest of them is covered up. We should all stand behind a screen and talk and get someone to guess what we are.'

'It'll be interesting to see what kind of English comes out of Africa, eventually,' the girl said, with her easy manner of deep interest. 'Don't you think it may be almost a new language, as it is in America?'

'That may be,' said Steven condescendingly. 'That may very well be, eh, Sam? We are talking it already,' and as the others laughed, added, 'But seriously, in Sophiatown the tsotsis have got a language of their own, a mixture of English, Afrikaans, Zulu, anything. Perhaps we should all learn to talk it.'

The girl picked up her drink and leaned forward. 'That must be a kind of local Cockney, eh?'

'Perhaps we should all understand each other,' persisted Steven, sniggering and drinking down the rest of his brandy.

'D'you remember Esperanto?'

'It's still going strong, I imagine.'

The hostess, now so delighted with her party that she was recklessly swallowing drinks at the pace she had imposed on her guests, said out of her stock of bold phrases: 'It won't be the whites who'll decide what language is going to be spoken here it'll be you fellows.'

The conversation became even freer and more confidential; cigarettes smouldered on the floor, someone stepped on someone else's drink; the old phrases began to come up, in the old, frank, confessional tones: 'The trouble with the whites is. . . .' 'At least the Afrikaner says to you straight out, look here Kaffir.' 'I've always wanted to know what Africans really think about mixed marriage.' 'And what's the good of the Liberals opening party membership to us Africans if we haven't got votes?' 'How do you really feel. . . .' 'What do you honestly think. . . .' The young coloured was railing against coloureds who wouldn't identify themselves with the Africans and Indians. Sam was saying urgently: 'Don't you believe there isn't still time. Don't you believe it.'

'For God's sake,' said Steven, accepting another brandy, 'must we always talk about it?' 'By all means,' said the pretty girl, spreading out her hands as if to draw the company closer, 'Let's talk about anything you like. Hundreds of things I always want to talk about.' 'You see,' Peter suddenly contributed, giggling, 'we always think *you* want to talk about it.'

'And *we* always think you want to!' said the lecturer.

'There it sits,' said Sam excitedly, 'the uninvited guest, wherever you go –'

'Hey, we should write a song about that,' the host looked in proudly upon the conversation.

'Can't we talk about something else?'

The hostess looked at us all, fondly. There were almost tears in her eyes. She felt so released, accepted, that she said, arch and wordly, to Sam and Steven: 'I'm going to see if our black brothers in the kitchen can't rustle up some tinned soup for us.'

The female member of the university couple had appeared on the arm of my chair: 'May I perch next to you?' and when I had persuaded her to take the chair instead, I turned back to the company just as the newspaperman's pretty girl was asking, 'Cigarette, anybody? Has anyone got a cigarette for me?' Mine were finished. So were the university lecturer's. While we fumbled, the girl sat forward, expectantly, her lovely grey eyes exaggerating her need, in response to the audience. I suppose if a woman is beautiful and greatly appealing, it is almost impossible for her *not* to use the virtuosity of her charm, sometimes simply for the careless pleasure of using it, as an acrobat might turn a masterly somersault at home on his own lawn, or a peacock shake out his splendid tail when there was no hen about to be impressed. She was dressed up – as it were – in the look of a woman cajoling a favour from a lover; there it was, that look she could do so easily, in a minute, anywhere.

Sam said, 'Here, Steven, you've got some cigarettes –' And Steven raised his eyebrows in inquiry, already twisting in his chair to get at his pocket. 'Sure thing, somewhere here.' He found the paper pack, and talking, dividing his attention, opened the torn top; there was one cigarette in it. The girl, following what he was saying, held out her hand in a charming mock supplication and relief. And then I saw, quite distinctly, an exact moment, between one word and the next, when Steven's mind cut out from what he was saying – he saw the girl, saw the feathers of her charm all spread out in complacent display – and then cut back to the sound of his own voice again. He went on talking without a pause, and while he did so, he carefully took the single cigarette out of the crumpled pack, tapped it on the table to settle the tobacco, and put it in his mouth. Peter, the lecturer, Sam, the lecturer's wife, myself, and the girl with her hand still held out before her, watched his hand go out to the cigarette lighter on the table, pick it up, and light the cigarette, pinching in his nostrils with the first draw.

No one said, 'Hey, what's the idea? What about that cigarette?' No one laughed. No one acknowledged, made of the incident a moment's absentmindedness on the part of a man who had had rather a lot to drink. We exempted him, and so gave away what he and all black men must always suspect of the company of white men: he was not like us, after all; after all, he was black.

The girl's hand came slowly back to her; she covered it with her other one, in her lap. And she too, went on talking, smiling, asking questions with an air of intense interest, confessing her own opinions self-critically and with laughter. A little later, when I had drifted into another group and out again, I heard her say, detaining the host with a dove-like inclination of her head, 'Sweetie, do you think you've got a filter tip in the house for me?'

At this time, I didn't really want to go and see Anna Louw. Once I was in her company, I was always glad of it, and couldn't understand my reluctance; yet no sooner was I away again than I was conscious of a childish relief, and an impatience to get back to my preoccupation with other people.

I was a bit ashamed that it seemed to work out that the times when I sought her out coincided with the times when I couldn't be with Cecil, or when Steven had gone to ground on one of his enthusiastic mysteries, which, these days, were likely to be involved with Lucky Chaputra. In the first few minutes, I always felt that I had a left-out air about me that was unmistakable to Anna; my ring of phrase had echoes of the people with whom I had been spending most of my time, my manner carried still the impression of theirs.

I drove out to see her one afternoon after I had left the office; she was in the tiny part of the garden which was considered hers, and while she dug a thin little Indian girl flitted about her, calling out in a soft twanging voice nasal as a mosquito's. I heard them across the garden, before they saw me; peaceful sounds, the singing whine of the child and the slow, reasonable answers of the woman, monosyllabic but somehow satisfying in sound, as Anna's Afrikaans accent tended to make them. I had encountered the child there before, several times – 'She's Hassim's little sister,' Anna had told me. Hassim was Anna's divorced husband, whom I had never met, and whom I don't think she ever saw.

The child ran away into the house when she saw me coming, but slowly, as a background to the talk between Anna and me, I was aware of her approaching, step by step, hanging back and yet coming on. I called 'Hullo, Urmila!' but she was behind a bush; and only when I turned my attention back to Anna, and forgot about the child, did she take up her game where she had been interrupted.

I had thought I should have to make some excuses for not having come before (the real excuses were the only plausible ones, but though they might tacitly be accepted, they must not be spoken aloud) but, as always, I had forgotten that if Anna spoke little, she was also the easiest person in the world to talk to. All she said was, 'How're you getting on, Toby?' and I lay down on the grass while she went on pressing down the soil round the seedlings she was planting, and I told her about the incident of Steven and the cigarette. That was how it was, in her company. I'd wonder what on earth I'd find to say, and then something I didn't even know I'd been brooding about would come out of my mouth as simply as a remark about the weather.

She threw no new light upon the incident. 'He's an odd customer,' she said mildly, when I had finished. Yet the very matter-of-factness of her acceptance had the effect of bringing the incident into perspective; a perspective, I realized with surprise, that was not mine. It was the perspective of the frontier, the black-and-white society between white and black, and I was only a visitor there, however much I had made myself at home. Anna was a real frontiersman who had left the known world behind and set up her camp in the wilderness; the skirmishes of that new place were part of the condition of life, for her.

I rolled on to my back and watched the leaves run together in the magnetism of gathering darkness. Anna went on methodically, digging and planting, making little grunting sighs of effort as she moved round the bed of earth. She had the absorption in her activity of people who are used to doing things alone. For a moment, I had the feeling of not being there; I was aware, as one seldom is in the company of another, of her being, in depth, beyond the surface at which her life had touched upon mine. I asked her, suddenly:

'What made you marry Hassim Bhayat?'

She shuffled round – she was sitting on her haunches – and

picked up a seedling held in its little fist of earth. It was an inquiring gesture.

'Was it because he was an Indian?'

She was still holding up the seedling, and though her back was to the fading light, and I could not see her face clearly, I sensed her following my face. She said, 'I was in love with him. But what's the good of saying, I would have loved him whatever he'd been. He *was* an Indian. That was part of what made him what he was. A woman who falls in love with a rich man will tell you she'd love him just as much if he was a lorry driver. Of course she wouldn't. His money, the things he's done with it and it's done to him – they're part of what he's like and what she's fallen in love with. Of course, that doesn't mean to say she couldn't fall in love, another time, with a lorry driver –' She turned away and put the plant into the place prepared for it.

'You don't think there was something of a gesture in it? Nothing like that?'

'No,' she said, with slow conviction. 'But it's terribly hard to keep a marriage like ours personal; it starts off like an ordinary marriage but then everything else, outside it, forces on it the onus of a test case. If you quarrel, you can't simply be a man and wife who don't get on, immediately you're the proof that mixed marriages don't work. You've no idea how this influences you, in time. You get terribly nervous; honestly. You begin to question yourself, all the time: do I disagree about this only because I'm white? Does this depress Hassim only because he's an Indian, or would a white man feel the same –' The Indian child called out something, and Anna answered her. 'It's a good thing we didn't have any children,' she said. I didn't answer, because I thought perhaps she was hardly aware that she had spoken. 'It's a good thing, after all.' And now her voice broke through her thoughts, so to speak, 'I used to say, it's too bad if it's hard for the children; you just have to make them understand that they're only misfits in a worn-out society that doesn't count, that, in reality, they're the new people in the world that's coming, the decent one where colour doesn't matter. D'you think that's true?'

'I don't see why not.'

She laughed. 'It's not true *yet*. It's a hell of a life to impose on a half-and-half child in the meantime; waiting for a kingdom of heaven that probably won't come to earth in its lifetime. It'll come. But it's too big, too far off – you can't measure an historical process against the life of a kid. That's what I think now, anyway.'

'It has to start somewhere, of course.'

'Yes,' she said. 'But not with a child of mine.'

I got up, and realized how damp with coming night the grass had become; my shirt was cold against my back. 'Anna, I'm glad to find you're a coward about something. You've always impressed me as being brave as a lion.' She gave a little Afrikaans exclamation of derision, and laughed.

The Indian child had switched on all the lights in the cottage. From the darkening garden, warm light coloured by the objects on which it shone in the rooms, where all the curtains were open, seemed to swell up and fill the house's shape like breath in a coloured balloon. We put the garden tools away together, and went up to the house. Anna, in a sudden mood of animation unusual for her, was telling me about the stuffed lion that stood in the hotel in the Karoo village where she had lived as a child. 'Have you ever heard of the Cape Mountain lion? Well, it's supposed to have been extinct since heaven knows when. This one was shot round about 1865, and somehow or other they've preserved it all this time. An Englishman killed it and sent it to England and had it stuffed, and it was in some club in London for years. When I was a kid, it was in the lounge of the old Neksburg hotel, right next to the cigarette machine. It doesn't look much like a real lion, to me; more like one of those funny-looking beasts made in stone, what d'you call them – chimera, is it?'

'Is it still there now? I think that's the name of the place I've been invited to over Christmas – Neksburg, yes I'm sure.'

Anna gave a long, whistling exclamation: 'Christmas in Neksburg, you don't know what you're in for!' She seemed much amused.

'Well, it's not actually *in* Neksburg itself, it's a stud farm belonging to some people I know, here – the Alexanders. People called Baxter run it for them, and there's some idea about a house party – I don't know if't'll come to anything.'

'Ah, that's a different sort of Neksburg,' said Anna, smiling. 'The Chamber of Mines Alexander? *Very* posh. It must be one of the thousand morgen efforts around there. Swimming pools and heaven knows what.'

'But Neksburg *is* the village you come from?' I asked. 'Isn't it odd? I have the feeling we've had this sort of conversation before.'

'We have,' she said. 'You remember? The first time I met you. I mentioned that Jagersfontein Location case, and you said, Jagersfontein – my grandfather was killed at Jagersfontein!'

'And we've never been to look for his grave,' I said.

She waved her muddy hands in distaste. 'Ach, it was probably my grandfather who killed him. Leave these old wars alone.' She went off to the little bathroom to wash.

'How much longer is that Jagersfontein case going to drag on, anyway,' I called. 'Amon was off again last Friday, it seems to have been going on for months.'

'He was off *when*?'

'Friday.'

'The case was dropped a month ago.'

'Grandmother tale, eh?'

Anna came in, hair tidied, inspecting her nails. 'You fix him,' she said, toughly. 'Ah, how beautiful, Urmila! Toby, see what she's done?' The child had decorated the table with garlands of those brass-coloured dwarf marigolds that smell rank. I stayed to supper and smoked all through the meal to kill the weedy reek, since I knew not only Urmila but Anna would be offended if I removed my garland. After supper Urmila brought a book and stood, leaning on Anna's chair, while Anna read her a chapter. The book was *Peter Pan*, and I wondered what Urmila made of even such an unconventional English nursery as the Darlings'. But I had the feeling, watching the child's dark, ugly face, with the nervous lips along which her fingers wandered all the time, as if to read reassurance, and the dark eyes whose expressionlessness never altered, that it was not the story she listened to or wanted, but the fact of being read to. Anna put her to bed herself, and I heard the child murmuring and laughing to her.

When Anna came back into the room, she said, crossly, 'They make the poor child so *timid*. I don't know what she'll be fit for –'

'A good Muslim wife,' I suggested. 'Maybe,' said Anna. 'Maybe,' and sighed.

'At least we were brought up to be able to look after ourselves,' she said. 'Didn't always end up doing it the way the old people had imagined, but still. When I was her age I was at boarding-school in Bloemfontein, and I used to go there by train on my own.' Sometimes she showed a sturdy, obstinate pride in the ways of the family she had, I gathered from what I knew of her, broken with irrevocably. We sat drinking brandy-and-soda and talked about her childhood. Her family owned a tea-room in the Karroo village of Neksburg, '*Tee-en-koffie-kamer*,' she told me. 'On the main road that runs through the dorp to Cape Town. It's for tourists mainly, but since my uncle made it bigger in 1935, it's also been a gathering-place for the local youngsters on Saturdays, and a place where natives come in to buy a bottle of milk, or bread, or cigarettes. Someone told me that the latest improvement is that natives are not allowed to come in at the front door of the shop. My cousin Toy – he's running it now with one of my brothers – has another door, in the lane off the street, for natives. I haven't been home since before I married Hassim, so I haven't seen it for myself. We used to live behind the shop. There's a yard, with an iron pergola which has rotted away in the grip of a big old grapevine – the iron's embedded in the thick stem of the vine – and behind that's our house. An old house, too, with thick stone walls, a flat roof, and shutters – at least it was, until they built a wooden veranda on to it, and painted the wood orange. My grandmother had tubs with ferns in them put in the yard; that's where we used to play, with the children of our coloured servants, who were also supposed to look after us. The whole village is along that main street, the baker, the butcher, the two general stores, another café, run by a Greek, the estate agent's, the lawyer's, the old hotel and the new hotel, and, of course, an enormous garage. That went up about ten years ago. It's the only modern building in Neksburg and it really hits you in the eye, all shiny, with a huge plate-glass window, and the chromium petrol pumps, and a couple of the local coloureds got up in blue uniforms. That and the travellers' big cars outside the new hotel – they're completely unlike anything else in Neksburg, but their out-of-placeness is part of the place – d'you know what I mean?'

'. . . dust and stones, and a fly-bitten hotel with a couple of shiny cars. . . .' – Anna's was the Neksburg Kit Baxter had talked about months ago, that first day at the Alexanders'.

'Right opposite our tea-room there are five pepper trees.' Anna was picking her way among the significant things of a child's life. 'I remember beginning to look at those pepper trees. You know how, to a certain stage, you don't really look at things? Well, up till then, the pepper trees had been the same as the tea-room and the yard and the house. – I forgot to tell you that on the walls of the tea-room, we had coloured photographs of the members of the family, particularly the children. We went to Bloemfontein specially to have them taken; I mean, if a baby was born, it was taken on its first birthday, and so on. There was a picture of me and my two younger brothers on the wall just above the paraffin refrigerator. I used to look at it for hours, in fact I looked at it every time I walked into the shop, because I believed that that must be the way I *really* looked, not the way I was when I saw myself in the mirror. In the picture my lips were bright red and my hair had touches of yellow. There was a big picture of my cousin Johannes's fiancée, with a rose in *her* long yellow curls – she really did have them – and her hand raised to her neck to show the ring on her finger. And there was an even bigger one of another little cousin, the beauty of the family, and my age, with a mauve crinoline. Well, I don't remember when exactly it was, how old I was, but I distinctly remember a clear division of time when I suddenly knew for sure that the pepper trees, always outside there, always to be seen, were one thing, and our *tee-kamer*, with the smirking photographs that didn't look like us, and the mirrors with the holders filled with dust-covered crinkle paper flowers, and the radiogram that shook when it sang, were another. It was in the season when the pepper trees were – in fruit, would you call it? – when the little pink beads were ripe, and mixed up with the pale greyish leaves, so that the trees looked soft. From then on, whenever I came back from school for the holidays, I found that the things I didn't mind about Neksburg were the things my brothers and cousins were impatient and ashamed of, and the things they admired and welcomed were the things I was ashamed of. More than anything, I was ashamed of the coloured photographs. I cried over them, once, down in the culvert where the stream was, near the cemetery. *They* were ashamed when they saw someone carrying a goat tied on his back while he rode a bicycle.'

I would never have guessed that Anna's revolt should have begun as a revolt of taste. I asked her when she had begun to be interested in politics.

'When I was working in Bloemfontein and then Johannesburg. You see, my family didn't think it anything unusual for me to want to go to work in a city. They thought I wanted smart clothes and dances and plenty of boy friends. When I got myself articled to a lawyer, they didn't take that too seriously. They let me go without a murmur. So long as I went to church on Sundays, that was all right.

'You know, long after I was a member of the Party and a trade union official, my father knew nothing about any of it, he wouldn't listen to anything about it. He was convinced that I had a nice office job in the big city, and that all I was waiting for was to come home holding hands with some nice Dirkie or Koosie, ready to hang a new picture of myself on the *tee-kamer* wall.'

'And when did they finally find out?'

'An uncle told them. There are Louws everywhere, all fifty-second cousins, and nosy as hell. I was running a union of coloured women, sweetworkers.'

'What happened?'

She got up and refilled our glasses. When she was settled again, she said, 'Oh, I got off quite lucky. They dropped me. They wanted to forget about me, quickly. I think they really did believe that I was crazy; they could be less ashamed of me, that way, it would then be something I couldn't really help. My mother used to come and see me now and then, but I had never been very close to her. I would rather have seen my father; no chance of that, though. She's dead. She died when I passed my final law exam, just before I married Hassim. The old man's still in Neksburg. They're strange people, really. There's very little dignity left in them; they're passionate Nationalists, of course, in the narrowest, most superannuated sense, they hate the English, they hate the blacks, they're terrified of them all. In fact they hate and fear everything and everyone except themselves – what a miserable way to exist. And yet, d'you know, they're directly descended from the Voortrekkers – one would expect them to have more guts. The Voortrekkers may have been bigotted, but they had guts.'

'Well, you're the answer,' I said, 'you're the one who's made the trek, this generation.'

She said, in her measured, downright manner, 'In a way, I understand my family's reluctance to own me, their own flesh and blood, reminding them of everything they're afraid of. And have you ever noticed how dark I am? I'm like a blooming Spaniard. Huguenot blood, they say. Probably true, too, we've got La Valles and Dupreez on my mother's side. But more likely some old boy's flutter with a black girl in the old days, as well.'

We talked on past midnight. The child called out once, from the bedroom, and Anna went to her. In the few minutes she was gone, I became aware of the night outside, that suddenly blew up and flung itself in a squall of wind and scratching leaves, at the window. I went to the bathroom and saw there, as everywhere in the little house, the serene order of Anna's mind; the tidy rows of toilet bottles, the fine soap, the clean thick towels.

When she came back to the living-room, a heavy, sparse fall of rain on the roof muted some remark she made, and I got up to go.

She stood, holding her arms in protection against some imagined chill from the sound of the rain. She looked very small and stocky, and tiredness, the burned-out animation of so much talk, marked deeply under her eyes. 'Wait till this goes over,' she said. We both had had quite a lot to drink, and a mood of confidential timelessness had settled around us, intensified by the rain, which, too, took a shift in rhythm and settled to a soft, steady, enclosing sound.

She told me about the visit to Russia in 1950 that had disillusioned her once and for all about Communism, and after which she had broken with the Party in revulsion. Unlike most ex-Communists I knew in London, Anna had not remained in that state of spiritual convalescence which was as far as they seemed able to recover from loss of faith – but she shared with those who would never be able to put themselves together again, a dogmatism of manner, as old military men never again walk quite like other men. Although she no longer had to believe unquestioningly, she could not shed the air of being always right.

Still later, she said, suddenly, 'When you go to Neksburg you must go and see the lion.'

We had been talking about Faunce and my father, but the remark did not seem irrelevant. After a moment, I said, 'Probably I won't go at all.'

She sat back, buried in the big chair and looked at me steadily, with the smiling concentration of vision slowed by brandy, as if she were a star whose light took a million years to reach me. 'D'you like those people?' she asked. There was genuine curiosity, not implied criticism, in the question.

'Some of them.'

She nodded in agreement. 'The one in the Stratford Bar. She's lovely-looking.'

I said, 'None of the people I know here seem to know each other.'

'What are they like?'

I told her about the people at The High House, colouring the picture a little, at once feeling disloyal and at the same time mildly, enjoyably revengeful, as if I'd just discovered I'd been taken in by them. They were as unfamiliar to her as people of another country; I don't suppose she would have wanted to know them, anyway, but it was another reminder to me of the boundaries she had left, and probably could never re-enter. Her face, chin lifted to pull at a cigarette, or bent, with the shadows streaking down it, over the glass cupped in her hands, was the face of burned boats, blown bridges; one of those faces you suddenly see, by a trick of the light, in the rock formation of the side of a mountain. I felt suddenly afraid of her, I put out my hand and touched, with the touch of fear, the thing I fled from. I had no desire for her but I kissed her. The rain had stopped as if to listen; the whole night was still. She did not shut her eyes for an instant; every time I opened mine, she was looking at me, as if she were waiting for something to be over, to have done. She went on talking while she took my hand, turned it palm up, then down, then pressed the nails, one by one: 'You think you'll keep free, with one foot here and another there, and a look in somewhere else, but even you, even a stranger like you, Toby – you won't keep it up.' She stood up and wiped the windowsill dry of the rain that lay on it in a scatter of magnifying lenses, thick and glassy. We were both standing about the room as if the night were breaking up. I thought of Cecil with a flash of longing, but she was like one of those women you imagine before you have ever had a woman. I made love to Anna at last, slowly because I had had so much to drink, and pleasure came to me as if wrung from my grasp. When our excitement was over the rain began again as if it had never stopped.

I suppose there's no use trying to explain oneself, so far as one's feelings about women are concerned. The whole mysterious business may be influenced by, even spoiled by one's idea of what one should feel, what one's code is, but the fact remains that old Adam has a code of his own that sometimes makes nonsense of the imposed one. You do something cheap, goatish, or foolish, and it feels right. That's all. And if you feel right and comfortable, reason – all the reasons why you shouldn't – cannot discomfit you. My extension of conversation with Anna (that's no polite euphemism – that was exactly what it seemed to be, the moment it was past) had the effect of deepening my interest in Cecil. For weeks, there was a gentle madness for me in the mention of her name; her faults entranced me, an inch of darker colour grown out at the roots of her hair touched me, her laugh, in the next room, astonished me, like a secret called aloud. A season of love seized me; and it was Christmas, Christmas in midsummer.

PART THREE

Chapter 12

A CHRISTMAS party at The High House seemed to have no beginning and no end. When I picked up Cecil and took her out there for lunch on Christmas Eve – this was to celebrate the arrival, from the Karroo, of the Baxters, whom Marion had talked out of Kit's idea of a house party in Neksburg – the pool was full of young men and girls, and roars of whisky-released laughter came up from the shade of the veranda, where Hamish Alexander sat in white bowling flannels and brown suède shoes, drum-bellied, bristling with good humour, surrounded by the older guests. When we left in the afternoon, some had gone but others were newly-arrived. Then there was to be a dinner-party in the evening, to which neither Cecil nor I were going. She had to take her child to a children's party at her parents'; I was going to a celebration arranged by Steven. She was to spend Christmas Day with her family too, and I had plans of my own to fulfil. So I did not see her again until Boxing Day, when we had been invited to go to Alexanders' again, and arrived at midday to find the party in its third day, the pool still lively as the seal enclosure at a zoo, the veranda still dispensing laughter from the bar.

It seemed hotter than it had ever been, all summer, so far, in Johannesburg. Sun and wine and beer and whisky made the atmosphere of a fiesta; it was not Christmas, to me, but I liked it. Outside my flat, piccanins shuffled and jerked their backsides to tin whistles and a banging on old tins. While the shops were open, a weary, sweating concourse streamed the streets, thick as a trail of ants following the scent of sugar; then, except for cinema crowds, the city was left to the drunks. Church bells jangled and, on the balconies of flats, the hot sun turned on the baubles of Christmas trees in tubs. Black men who delivered clinking cases from the bottle store wore paper hats. If the place was not gay, at least it had let itself go. At Alexanders', presents, flowers, glasses, and food covered luxury with abundance; even the garden, in the swell of midsummer sap, was heaped with so much colour, so pollen-thick, so vibrant with bees, criss-crossed by birds, so heavy with peaches and plums whose delicious over-ripeness smelled headier even than the perfumes of the women, that the very texture of the air was plenty. The cornucopia jammed down over your head. Cecil flashed and turned in this atmosphere, a creature in its own element: she seemed to me to exist, and rightly so, for no other purpose than to laugh, her eyes brilliant with alcohol, her lap full of presents, among flowers and drunken bees.

My Christmas Eve with Steven started at about ten o'clock at a club run by Indians some miles out of Johannesburg. Lucky Chaputra had insisted that we come, Steven said, but when we left the club, shortly before midnight, Lucky still had not turned up himself, though we had been well looked after, no doubt on his instructions. The club was one of those places one could never find again; I drove to it blindly, turning when Steven told me, following landmarks invisible to me, down dirt-tracks and through dongas, over the dark veld. Steven chattered all the time, and sometimes could not bear to spoil a story by interrupting it with a direction, so that, a minute or two late, he would suddenly call out, sensing something unfamiliar about our progress: 'Wait a minute! Stop, man! We've missed the turning.'

There was a concert on at the club when we got there. The programme went very slowly, because after every few items the audience, Muslim and Hindu men, drifted out to their cars. They would drift into the hall again in ten or fifteen minutes, each time a little more vociferous and critical in their calls for the entertainment to recommence. The reason was that the club – which had, like other country clubs, a swimming pool and tennis courts – could not, of course, get a licence to serve liquor. The members drank in their cars, fast and neat.

Steven and I, the only white man and the only African there, were hustled into an anteroom lit by a candle, where, first, the fat, pale organizer of the show, an anxious man named Jayasingh, and a thin business man named Mia and, as the evening went on, a number of other club personages, gave us Haig and water. When the others ate dry triangular sandwiches of the kind served at wedding receptions, we got plates of hot vermicelli with cinnamon and sugar. As usual, there were not enough glasses to go round, and we politely drank up quickly so that the others could get a drink in before it was time to get back into the hall. In this anteroom there was no furniture except an iron bed empty of a mattress and a table. There was a plaster figurine among the whisky bottles on the mantelpiece; I went over to look at it, and Mia, solicitously kind, rushed up with the candle: 'Ghandiji' he cried, 'I'll show you.' The plaster figure wore a tiny pair of wire spectacles. The candle lit up, too, on the wall, two or three group photographs of Indian business men with striped suits and important expressions.

In the hall we sat on the floor on spring mattresses. 'Indian-style,' my neighbours kept telling me, with an air of novelty. 'He sings in Hindustani and I only understand a bit of Gujerati,' someone complained, while the band-leader, a wild, mournful-looking boy whom I would sooner have expected to see giving a performance supine on a bed of nails, sobbed and wailed, exactly like all those other young men who drive adolescents to an adoring frenzy. Presently a girl, with face and body of the most tender grace and beauty, came out to a slurring roar of appreciation. She wore a sari and there were bells round the ankles of her bare feet; the men called and hailed while she danced and rolled her eyes in a rhumba. 'Lola, Lola, lovely my dear,' Mia kept saying. And to me: 'Those pigs can't shut up. Isn't she very good?' I admired her and asked if she ever did any real Indian dancing. Immediately Mia and a number of others began a fervent conversation in which the word 'classical' kept recurring like the date of some great discovery, a battle recalled, or a noble name remembered. Classical, classical. After one or two more intervals in the anteroom, it began to go up like a call of despair, a cry in the wilderness – each one of them loved only classical, classical, what did Indians in this country know of classical? Poor sweating Jayasingh, pathetic as only a harassed fat man can be, became offended: his show, the best artists at the greatest expense, did not please. We all went out into the garden with him, like a deputation, and Mia, in an official tone ('My dear, dear Mr Jayasingh . . .'), and Steven and I with appreciative agreeing noises, tried to reassure him. I don't think he was reassured, though perhaps he was mollified. A few minutes later, Mia had him in a corner again, while the show went on, and presently we were smuggled out of the hall during the performance of a band number, and, with Mia, Jayasingh, and one or two more, were closeted in the anteroom.

This time the Indian girl was there. I have never seen anything more beautiful. She had never been in India, and she spoke English with a strong South African accent, but she had an ancestral beauty, she had in flesh the round stone breasts and little round waist of women in Tenth Century Indian sculpture; I had once cut out a photograph of such an image, *Vriksaka*, the Tree Goddess. The live girl sat on an empty whisky-case, hardly touched by the thick yellow light of the smoking candle, hardly seen, and sang the way a bird sings on a telephone wire. People kept pushing into the room. Some were pushed out again. Those in the room talked admiringly, encouraged more than they listened, but I felt they really were moved by the idea of her singing. She sang traditional Indian songs as long as we wanted her to, which was as long as the important members dared keep her from the general audience, and then she went from among us, listening with attentiveness to the long compliments, slipping inoffensively from the pawings of those who would detain her, ducking her head swiftly beneath the hands, faces, the despairing, longing cries: 'Classical . . . classical. . . .' She was made to please: I had not seen a creature like her before.

Driving back to town, I talked about her to Steven, and soon we slipped from the particular to women in general, and then, inevitably, to the particular again, while Steven told me of his conquests in London. It was an old subject, one we'd come to time and again in the confidential small hours in the townships. It seemed to be a point of honour for a black man who'd made something of himself to boast of how, in his small beginnings as waiter, bell-boy, or some such conveniently-placed menial, he had been coveted by a white woman. Some of the stories rang true, and some of them didn't. But everybody had one to tell. I suppose that in the country I was living in, in the city I was living in, such tales were sensational, anarchic, and meant far more; but I must say that to me, as a stranger and an outsider, they were simply part of the old sex myth I have mentioned before – the wistful projection of joy not to be had at home.

We finished up the night at the House of Fame, where Steven was no longer living, but of which he was still master of ceremonies. In the township, singing people, arm-in-arm, filled the streets. The girls, yelling and shaking as they careered along, wore paper dough-boy hats inscribed 'Hiya Babe' or 'I'm No Angel'. The dingy houses, where old people tried to sleep and the smallest children were in bed, showed no life. But there must have been some, like the House of Fame, where people made their own music and danced and talked. From the hidden yards came voices with the particular, chanting quality of beer-drink frenzy. The shebeens were open for a roaring trade – we went into one to look for a friend of Steven's – and there were more police about than I had known before. 'A lot of broken heads and stabbings before Christmas is over,' said Steven, grinning and shaking his head. 'The Prince of Peace seems to skip us.'

On Christmas Day I went to church with Sam's wife, Ella, and their little girl. The child was dressed in a stiff frilly frock and she wore the gilt locket I had brought as a Christmas present for her. We went to the Anglican church in the location where they had their house, and only Ella accepted my going as an ordinary thing to do; Sam was delighted that I should want to go with Ella, but in the manner of someone who approves a piece of intrepid sight-seeing.

I was glad to be with a friend, instead of among the polite strangers who filled their cosy church near my flat with an incense of brilliantine. In this church in the township the priest was a tubby, untidy Englishman, tonsured by baldness. The church was built of ugly, purplish brick and smelled of the soap with which the congregants had washed, and of the smoke with which their clothing was impregnated from their cooking fires. A choir of small boys and another of women sang with the unearthly voices of Africans: voices that seem to have a register of their own. After one look round at me, the congregants accepted my presence with scarcely a whispered conversation, though I don't think it likely that a white layman had ever been in their church before. After the service I saw that the priest wanted to come up and speak to me, but I pretended not to see, and we left quickly. I don't suppose any church will ever suit me so well as our church at home, where once my grandfathers gathered their families about them in their own pew; so much for me, as a worshipper.

Christmas dinner was at Sam's. There was a chicken and everyone who was invited brought something for the table – there was a tinned pudding, a cream-cake, some sausages, nuts, and sweets. It was more like a picnic than anything else, in spite of the stifling little room in which we were confined; the hot, bright day, everyone wandering about the room picking up what they pleased to eat, the pestering flies, the nearness of voices and raspberry squeakers blown in the street outside. I had brought bon-bons and a couple of bottles of wine, and, inevitably, Sam ended up at his piano. Everyone there fell into song as easily as other people drift into conversation; carols, traditional songs, and jazz hummed and thrummed and soared from them. As I drove away in the afternoon, I was stopped by police and told to report to the charge office because I had no permit to be in the location; I was lucky – it was the first time I had been caught, and I had been in the townships innumerable times without a permit.

I got home to the flat and found it nearly as hot as the crowded room I had just left, and, a little before six, I half-undressed, lay on my bed, and fell asleep. When I woke, it was not, as I thought, early evening, but morning. So it was that I seemed to go straight from the township to the High House; sleep was a blank moment that scarcely separated the rutted township track that I had learned to ride like a roller-coaster, from the smooth driveway – a tunnel of feathery green and flowers – where the car drew soundlessly toward the fountain of voices rising beside the Alexanders' house.

I had picked up Cecil at her flat. Her little boy hung round the doorway as she prepared to leave. 'Are you going in the car?' 'Are you going to swim?' he kept asking me.

'Why not bring him along?'

She signed an impatient warning. 'No, no. He's going out later. He'll be fetched after lunch.'

In the car, she grumbled about the time she had spent with her family, but before we reached the Alexanders' she had sighed, stretched, fidgeted, lit a cigarette in pleased relaxation. She lifted her arm and put her hand round the nape of my neck, pinching my ear. One of her ways of making love was to lick my ear, like a dog, and I supposed she wanted to remind me. I slid my left hand into the warmth behind her bare knee, just to remind her. She laughed and demanded: 'And where did you decide to go, after all?' At once, it seemed absolutely necessary to belong along with her, I did not want to be even the remove of a surprised or baffled look from her. I mentioned the name of a bookseller and his wife of whom she had heard me speak before.

'What was it like?'

'All right.'

'Couldn't have been as bad as my collection of old crows.'

She sat on the grass beside the pool, opening the presents that had been kept for her from the day before. There was a piece of jewellery from Hamish and Marion that she unwrapped with a deep sigh of achievement; while she exclaimed and hugged them, while she cried to Kit and others with perfect surprise, I had the feeling that she had been almost sure she would get the ring, had made sure she would get it. Coloured and tinselled packages lay, burst open, all round her. Perfume, cosmetics, smoking gadgets, satin, and nylon; John Hamilton picked out a giant pencil that looked like bamboo and had a fur tassel, and began autographing the legs of the women sunbathing; Kit went through the loot with expert fingers; one of the Peever twins came over, hale and dripping, smelling of wet hair and the chlorine of the pool, and kissed Cecil in a scatter of water. 'Sweetie! My one and only! Happy Chrissie!' Donald Alexander had a girl at last, a soft little girl of twenty or so, who slithered away into the pool with a splash when John tried to write on her brown thigh. Archie Baxter called encouragement; in swimming trunks he exposed a stricken-looking body and dwindling legs, like a splendidly-furred dog shorn of its pelt. Kit seemed guardedly snappy with him; perhaps the strain of a three-day party made the front of the handsome, amusing couple wear thin. She had made as good a job of herself as usual and was bright as a cinema façade where the name of the next 'attraction' has just been newly put up in lights. John Hamilton was paying her a good deal of attention. His was a practical kind of court: 'Look here, Kit, d'you know what you want to do? You want to get one of your boys to blow through that pipe, a bicycle pump'd do it . . .' he said, advising her with the air of wanting to get down and do it himself, about the maintenance of the filter plant just installed for the swimming pool she'd had built at the farm.

I'd been given a silk shirt (from Marion), an expensive bottle of after-shave lotion (from the Baxters), and, from Cecil, one of those sumptuous-looking picture books that publishers bring out specially for Christmas, and which go vaguely under the name of 'art'. I'd never worn a silk shirt, never put scented stuff on my face, would probably never open the book again after that day. I lay idly in a big chair, talking now and then, listening; listening, sometimes with my eyes closed, to the slap and plunge of people in the water, and the talk of the Christmas Handicap that had been run the previous Saturday. There was a woman with blued white hair, the upper half of whose body swelled splendidly as a caryatid's; she had an affected, absent way of talking – 'Absolutely glamorous' was her standard comment. But the moment someone mentioned racing, I heard her voice change, her languor drop, and she spoke shrewdly, intelligently, and imaginatively; I opened my eyes because I couldn't believe my ears – and even after only a minute in the shelter of the explosive dark of my eyelids, the garden and the people sprang up with strong variety and brightness, a deep texture of colour and shadow through which I seemed to look down. I went into the pool before lunch, floating in a stream of pleasant sensations, a current that touched only the nerve-endings; the lave of cool water, the astringent prickle of mid-day sun, the smell of plums and hot grass, and the perfume on the skin of a woman as she rose out of the water a moment, beside me.

I succumbed completely to such moods. This one took me on the instant, enclosing as a bubble, and I did not compare or relate it to what had gone before; an Orpheus, I passed from one world to another – but neither was real to me. For in each, what sign was there that the other existed?

Cecil and I left about five o'clock and drove home in gathering silence. The summer sun was at a level to strike us right in the eyes, an impaling glare you couldn't escape. Cecil was like a bird suddenly quenched by the blanket thrown over its cage; all her gaiety went out under the sense of the holiday over. The ebb of animation from drinks and the atmosphere of playful admiration with which she and her friends surrounded each other, left her stranded. The idea of the New Year, only a week away, seemed to depress her. 'I'll be twenty-nine,' she said. She wondered what the year would be like; I said, meaning to reassure her, like any other year. She hardly spoke again.

I realized that I was incapable of generating the kind of atmosphere that we had just left, and which, like some drug without which an addict cannot live, though it brought her to the doldrums in which she was now, was also the only thing likely to float her clear again. I fell silent, too. And she sat like a child for whom the end of the party is the end of the world; that was how she lived, from one treat to the next, free of a job, free of her child, free of all the every-day ballast that, I suppose, makes life possible for most people.

Her flat smelled stale from being shut up through the heat of the day. She treated me with the absent, dependent, grateful manner of the convalescent who wakes and is glad to find someone sitting at the bedside. When we had opened the windows and the balcony doors, we simply sat about, for a while, talking desultorily and looking through a couple of the American picture magazines to which she subscribed and which usually lay about unopened. The building, the whole street, were not so much quiet as abandoned, with the gone-dead feeling of places awaiting the return of holiday-makers. She came and sat beside me and leaned against me, kicking off her shoes and putting her feet up on the stained table where I and my predecessors had rested their glasses. It was one of those hours when you feel that you will never be hungry again, nor want to make love again.

I got interested in an article that whipped familiarly through the Stone Age with a character named Prehistoric Jones, the prototype man-in-a-grey-flannel-suit, and Cecil decided to go off and have a bath.

I didn't realize how long she'd been gone – she must have been soaking for more than twenty minutes, the sun had dropped and the air seemed to breathe again – when she suddenly appeared at the doorway wrapped in her bath-towel and looking stunned, as if she could not believe what had alarmed her. 'Come and listen,' she said. 'Quickly.'

She took my hand tightly and led me to the bathroom. 'Listen.' She jerked my hand to be still. There was nothing, for a moment, except the drizzle of a tap, but when I made to speak she stopped me urgently. Then I heard the panting of a dog, somewhere on the other side of the wall, in the street. But as I identified the sound it grew, it was the panting of something else. What? It grew in volume, it quickened, it harshly filled and emptied some unimaginable cavern of a breast, while Cecil, dripping wet, stared at the wall in horror. Then, as she turned to warn me of the anguish of what was to come, it came: the last roaring pant, a breath taken in hell, burst into a vast, wailing sobbing, the terrible sorrow of a man. A man! I jumped up and opened the window, and she leapt up behind me to see me do what she had been afraid to do for herself. I looked. The street seemed empty, commonplace, peaceful. Some broken paper streamers, yellow and pink, lay in the road. A bicycle was propped against a tree. And then we saw him sitting with his head on his arms, in the gutter, just below us. He was a tall Zulu – the stretched lobes of his ears hung loose where he had once worn fancy disks in them – and he had on only a pair of trousers.

'It's William!' said Cecil, with an hysterical laugh of relief, as if the identification of the man as the familiar servant who cleaned the flats on her floor automatically put an end to the horror.

But as she spoke, the man got up, his back to us, and began to pace back and forth across the road, and in his splendid chest the hideous panting began again, working up to a gasping climax, and ended in the raucous and frightful sobbing that left him crouching in the gutter with his head bowed on his hands. 'William!' Cecil called. 'William!' – the voice of authority and reproof that never failed to bring him to the kitchen door. We saw his face, looking directly at us as he began to pace and pant again; saw that he did not see us, or anything.

'William! William!'

Cecil was shaking as if she had just been struck in the face. 'What's the matter with him?' she begged me. 'What's wrong with him?' She felt the threat of a disaster she had never heard of, the dread of the discovery of some human sorrow unknown to her, hidden as the New Year, something that was neither death, poverty, or divorce.

She thought of sorrow, I thought of madness. It seemed to me he must have gone crazy. I wanted to go out and try to talk to him, but she would not let me go without her, she flung on her clothes grimly and made me wait for her. 'You don't want to go. You watch through the window.' 'No, no.' Her hands could hardly put her clothing together.

She stood beside me on the pavement, looking down at the man, her one trembling hand with the nails scarlet against her temple, holding back her hair. We called his name, but the man did not know we were there. We clattered up the ringing iron of the back stairs to the roof, where the servants lived, and fetched one of the other flat boys. He was a small, bow-legged Basuto, who smoked a pipe as crooked as his legs. He stood looking at the man in the gutter, admiring his extremity. 'He been smoking. *Dagga* make him like that.'

'Speak to him, go on, speak to him,' ordered Cecil angrily; she might have been telling him to scrub the floor.

The little man didn't move. 'I don't touch him,' he said. 'He know nothing, nothing. Sometime three day he won't know nothing.' He enjoyed giving information.

'*Dagga!* But he's in agony!' Cecil covered her face, up to the eyes, with both hands.

It was true that the man in the gutter *knew nothing*; could not seem to find his way back to himself. His was an unspeakable anguish of alienation, lostness, the howling of the wolf of the soul in a waste. The ghastly ritual went on: tearing anxiety of pacing and panting, climax of sobs, then panting again.

Cecil took her hands from her face, and I saw that the palm of one was indented with the marks of her teeth.

She went into the flat and made some strong black coffee. When I approached him with a cup he flung himself away like a wild beast for whom food, in the hand of a man, is overlaid with the scent of fear.

Cecil never took her eyes off him; when he panted, her hand flew to her breast, when he sobbed, her mouth twitched. 'Should we send for the police?'

'They'll arrest him.'

'Get a doctor?'

It did not seem possible that any human being could reach him, where he was.

'Why did he do it?' she kept saying.

A few Africans had wandered down from the building, drawn by the spectacle. They talked and pointed, standing back, the way they might at a zoo. 'That's his Christmas,' said a tall man with speckless black-and-white shoes, a Stetson, and a happy way of chewing a match. Christmas. The word was echoed in agreement, indulgently. When they had seen the whole thing through two or three times, they went back up the stairs, or strolled off up the street talking in their own language and detaining each other with the sort of gestures described in the air that people use when they are capping each other's anecdotes.

We went inside, too, and in the living room, which did not face on the street, you could not hear the man. But Cecil kept going to stand in the bathroom, where you could. She sat on the edge of the bath and shushed me as if she must hear what there was to hear; the tap dripped and the steam parted to liquid runnels on the tiles while the frenzied travail sounded on, bestial and wretchedly human at the same time, a monstrous serenade from some medieval hell. It was all the cries we do not cry, all the howls we do not howl, all the bloody furies in our hearts that are never, must never be, let loose. Even I was afraid, hearing it; not of the man, but of a stir of recognition in myself. We sat in a kind of shameful fascination, and did not look at each other. She was tight-lipped, her long hands were clenched on themselves, the spikes of both blood-red thumbnails folded back on the fists.

The sobs died; whistled away like a wind in a broken, empty place. There was a roaring cry that brought tears to attention in Cecil's eyes, turned fiercely to me. Then the sound of a man running, running up the street, running away with the grit of the street powdering beneath his power. At the bathroom window, we saw him, past the leaning bicycle, past the stragglers, up the hill where the curve of the street lifted him behind the foreground of the jacarandas.

It was a gentle evening, as it so often is after a grillingly hot day in Johannesburg. Scraps of pastel floated about the sky, between the buildings, the trees and the chimneys of the street. Cecil went into the kitchen to get some ice and there I found her, her head against the grey dish towels that hung on a nail.

'Are you crying?'

'No.'

'What's wrong?'

She turned and she still had the look she had had when she couldn't stop listening to the *dagga*-crazy man. 'I don't know what I'm going to do.'

'How d'you mean? What about?'

'This year.' She stood in the kitchen as if it were a ruin. But the cheap alarum ticked and the engine of the refrigerator broke into a run; it was as I had always remembered it.

'What do you want to do?'

She said, 'What have I got to show? Twenty-nine. Not enough money to live decently. What on earth can I do with myself? The whole – thing – frittered away.' She pushed the child's tricycle aside with her foot, and began to run the hot tap over the ice-container. The cubes tumbled into the sink, and above the clatter she said savagely, 'Hamish's is a terrible place, your whole life could go there, like one of the lunch parties.'

She began to talk of what she would do if she had money, if she didn't have the child, if she lived in Europe. For the first time since I'd known her, I heard the South African accent come out in a phrase, in a word, beneath the carefully acquired upper-class English stereotype of her voice. I didn't have the heart to tell her that she would find the same parties, the same rich indulgent friends, the same thoroughbred horses, everywhere.

'His Christmas!' she said, suddenly. She was sitting on the divan beside me and I felt a convulsion move her body, like the shudder a dog gives before it is sick. 'What other country is there where you'd have a thing like that on your doorstep? What a Christmas for anybody! Nothing but a beast! How can you live with savages around you!'

I said to her, 'But you cried. You made coffee for him.'

'No,' she said. 'No. They said it was his Christmas. What would make anyone choose that Christmas?' Like evidence, she began to gather up the presents, with their coloured and tinsel wrappings, their ribbons and sprigs of holly and extravagantly affectionate cards, that we had brought from Alexanders' and piled on the table when we came in.

Chapter 13

OFTEN, in the letters written to me from England, I would come across the phrase 'the life out there': the people I knew read of strikes, of beer-hall riots, and arrests for treason, they saw pictures of smiling black babies dressed in beads, of tall buildings, of politicians whose defiantly open mouths might be prophesying doom or development. Out of all that, I suppose they rounded off some sort of sphere to contain me, vague to them but *of course* certain to be perfectly clear to me.

They would have understood a city of many different ways of life, all intermingled, but would they have understood the awful triumphant separateness of the place I was living in? Could I tell them how pleasant it was to be lulled and indulged at The High House? Could I explain the freedom I felt where I had no legal right to be, in that place of segregation, a location? I supposed that to have a 'life out there', a real life in Johannesburg, you'd have to belong in one or the other, for keeps. You couldn't really reconcile one with the other, the way people were, the way the laws were, and make a whole. The only way to do that was to do what Anna Louw had done – make for the frontier between the two, that hard and lonely place as yet sparsely populated.

In any case, I had no particular wish to explain myself, or the irreconcilables of the way I was living, to anybody, even myself. All my life I had lived among people who found it necessary to explain. If they hadn't given me any tradition but doubt and self-examination, then I had chosen to prefer to trust to instinct. In Johannesburg, at least, it had proved a fairly lively way to live.

Steven's gusto renewed itself as naturally as the sun rose every morning. Living by his wits kept them skinning-sharp; his whole life was an endless outwitting of authority. Sometimes he was a child playing cops and robbers; sometimes he was a lawyer cunningly, constantly, watchful for loopholes in a case that built up more formidably every day. He would slip into my office with his well-brushed suède shoes and his well-cut suit hanging fashionably loose, looking down his nose as he smiled, the way he had seen film-stars do.

'Well, who've you been talking into something now?'

Suddenly he'd sit down opposite me, throwing aside the pose, grinning his battered, broken-toothed grin.

'The trouble with you, Toby' – 'the trouble with you' was one of Steven's favourite openings – 'is that you've lost faith in the power of the human voice. You only believe things when you see them written down. It's much better not to have things on paper, for other people to keep after they've gone out of your head.'

'No simple wisdom this morning please.'

'Don't worry, man, I'm off. You remember that fellow from Tzaneen, Bobby, the short one?'

'I don't, but that doesn't matter; what about him?'

'He's a good guy. He's got a job with old Jake, in the printing shop, but he hasn't got a permit to work in Jo'burg. I'm gonna fix it for him now.'

He knew a fellow. This time a fellow who was a clerk in the immigration office. But always a fellow somewhere; a fellow who laid bets on horses for him; a fellow who bought brandy for him; a fellow who got him an exemption pass, so that he didn't have to carry a wallet-full of identity papers and tax receipts about with him. The more restrictions grew up around him and his kind – and there seemed to be fresh ones every month – the quicker he found a way round them. Much of his vitality and resource and time went into this; sometimes I wondered how long one could keep up this sort of thing – how would he live as he grew older? – but mostly I enjoyed the flair with which he did it. Nothing could keep Steven out. In the locations often there was the charged atmosphere, smouldering, smothered, and sour, like the porridge turning to beer in the pots, of a vast energy turned in upon itself. But he wriggled and cheated and broke through.

At least once a week he would drag me off on some fantastic jaunt, or suddenly bring me into the company of new people, all apparently old friends of his. We went to Lucky Chaputra's splendid wedding, in February, and to a conference of witch-doctors – pompous, prosperous men in blue suits with well-rounded waistcoats. He arranged a special performance of Indian dancing for me, and didn't tell me about it until we were at the door of the house in Vrededorp where the girl I'd seen before was waiting for us; then he laughed and swaggered and made boastful light of the surprise. 'You're really impressed with that baby, I think, Toby,' he murmured, looking at me sideways. He would have pimped for me, but he was never in the least dependent on me for anything; that first night in the shebeen when we were drunk together he had got the moment he wanted from me; he didn't want anything else, or less.

Often I thought how well he and Cecil would have got on together, if they could have known each other. Their flaring enthusiasms, their unchannelled energy, their obstinately passionate aimlessness – each would have matched, out-topped the other.

William cleaned the floor around Cecil's feet unnoticed; the New Year went on as unremarkably as William's return to working anonymity; he had disappeared for three days, the day the turn of the hill hid him, but once he was back everything was as before. Cecil was going to ride Hamish's prize mare in the big Show that is held in Johannesburg at Easter, and the muscles of her forearms were quite steely with the determination of her training. She went off to Kit Baxter at the Karroo farm for a week, and when I went to Hamish's for a swim, on the Saturday morning, I found that old John Hamilton had fetched the little boy Keith and coy Eveline, the nanny, from the flat, and was giving the child a swimming lesson. I felt guilty because I hadn't thought to do it; I might have taken the boy to the zoo, or something, while Cecil was away, but really, she did so little for him that there was nothing much to compensate him for in his mother's absence. He turned and frowned away from the glare of the water, and, in the moment, he was terribly like her. Suddenly I wished her back, very strongly; I was aware not of her laughing, talking, active social presence, but of her silent, sentient self that was inarticulate – her hand, smelling of cigarette smoke, early in the morning, the exact displacement of her weight as she flopped into the car beside me.

I continued to think about all this while John and I lay in the sun – an amber sun, with all the white heat turned to the other side of the world – and he talked with his usual ease and lack of demand.

'You've got to come along with me. We can't have you going off back to England one of these days without having seen the best guinea-fowl shooting in the country. Man, you'll love it. A couple of gallons of red wine, plenty to eat, and you walk twenty miles or so a day. You feel great, I can tell you. No trouble, no dirty work – I always see we have good boys to keep the camp going, and clean the birds and all that. I wouldn't take you on the first shoot, though, if there hasn't been a good ground frost yet it's the very devil, you get yourself covered in ticks. Then, if you go too late, say August, there's too much grass down, no cover for the birds and they're off, the moment you sight them. You haven't a snowball's to get anywhere near. God, that's maddening! You know what I mean, Toby?'

I answered with the appropriate, laconic show of response which is simply a series of polite noises hiding inattention, and that, I have to admit since living out of England, is done particularly and inoffensively well by Englishmen. Foreigners attribute the manner to that other famous English trait, a predilection for understatement, and so save themselves the implication of boredom. In any case, I was not bored by John Hamilton; I simply wasn't listening to him.

Marion Alexander came out across the lawn dressed for town, from where she had just come. Like many women who aren't young any more, when she was high-heeled and pulled in here and there and wore an elaborate hat and all the glittering, distracting surface of jewellery, veils, furs that such women employ, she looked, from a distance, almost beautiful. A quick look rapidly taking in all the adornments of beauty suggested a beautiful woman, and so, for a moment, you saw one. Then, as she came nearer, the components fell apart; there was a thick neck under the pearls, the legs were spindly, there were ropes of veins on the backs of the beringed hands.

'Have you had everything you want, darlings?' she called, and again, as she came up to us, 'Has Jonas been looking after you?'

'The lot,' said John, gesturing to the tray of used cups on the grass, and the table with glasses and a jug of orange juice.

'We could do with something a little stronger than that,' said Marion in reproof of the absent servant, Jonas. The Alexanders took it for granted that their guests needed a constant stream of refreshment, that the only way they could be expected to continue functioning as guests was by something approximating to the system whereby failing patients are kept alive by a night-and-day saline drip into their veins. Jonas was called and told to bring whisky and gin and all the things that went with them. Marion kissed Cecil's child, marvelling over him as she did over everything: 'Isn't that the most enchanting . . .' she said to us as she settled carefully to rest in one of the low garden chairs. 'That is the *most* adorable thing.'

'D'you know,' John agreed, 'he's got absolutely no fear of the water at all? He's ready to slip out of your hand and drown himself the moment you get him in.'

'He's *exactly* Cecil, isn't he?' said Marion, conjuring up for us a picture of touching maternal charm, Cecil and her son. 'Just exactly her spirit, her way of going at things, and her smile – too amazing, the smile.'

They built up this picture which I did not recognize; though I suppose, on appearances, it was recognizable. It did not exist, but it could *seem* to exist, as people or objects can be brought into relationship with each other in a faked photograph. I felt suddenly jealous and wanted to assert my own familiarity with Cecil by exposing the fake, denigrating her. It was on the tip of my tongue to say, womanishly, 'It's a pity she dislikes the boy so much.'

Marion was going to Europe in a week or two – 'You must look after Hamish,' she said to John and me; she said it to everyone, in that absent affectation of simplicity and childishness that the sprightly elderly rich love to adopt. She talked enthusiastically about how she would be seeing my mother; I could see her, telephoning my mother from a suite at Claridge's, talking about me as she talked about Cecil. And my mother, slightly appalled, trying to recognize me; my mother, at lunch with Marion, looking at Marion's clothes and diamonds, listening to her chatter, puzzled and even a little hurt (my mother always dutifully took the shortcomings of her children on herself) that I should choose to spend my time in South Africa with people *like that.* Then she would decide not to invite Marion to dinner after all – she was not young and pretty enough for Faunce to overlook her uselessness, nor was she clever enough for Faunce to forgive her age.

Soon Hamish Alexander came home – we had dressed, and moved with Marion up to the veranda by then. He gave us the formula of greeting and interest that always rolled off his tongue; Had we had a swim (or a ride)? Was the water not too warm, too cold (according to the season)? Had we had a drink? We would stay for lunch, of course. For himself, he never did any of the things he expected his guests to have done, except, of course, eat and drink. With all people who were not mining men or financiers, he kept a don't-bother-your-head-about-it attitude toward discussions about finance, and what he called 'precious metals'. When he was talking with his own kind about these things, he always gave his opinions the backing of the editorial or royal 'we' – it was never what *he* thought – as if he reported for another self, a corporate self, left behind in the great building in the city which housed the head offices of his company.

Politics sometimes gathered a little group of men into a huddle at The High House – the women there never contributed except for the rare passing interruption of some piercing and paralysing generality – but Hamish did not encourage the talk. In fact, he seemed to have some special sensory awareness of it, and he would call across, almost warningly, 'What's that you say? I don't think people quite realize the particular difficulty –' as if he resented the mere useless airing of views of men who had no knowledge behind-the-scenes. Perhaps all this was a device to protect his leisure; anyway, I know that a big strike of African mine-workers on the Rhodesian Copperbelt, that sent him up there to confer with people from the Oppenheimer group, was simply 'this Rhodesian nuisance' that absented him from a big theatre party arranged by Marion, and uranium – the discovery of which had been confirmed in some of the worked-out gold mines of his group – was practically a dirty word in the house, or a sacred one – it took some daring to bring it out, at any rate.

The few times I had heard politics talked at The High House, it had hardly seemed to be concerned with the same country or spoken by people in the same situation as the talk I heard in Sophiatown or in houses where black and white people met. The people at Alexanders' were almost entirely preoccupied with the struggle between the Afrikaner and the Englishman; that is, the Nationalists and themselves. To the other people I knew, the squabbling of the two white peoples was simply picayune; dwarfed by the towering bout between black and white. When an important Nationalist recanted and turned on his old Party colleagues, making speeches of high emotion calling for unity (between English- and Afrikaans-speaking whites) instead of a divided people, there was an air of triumph about politics at The High House; in fact, for the first time, politics came out of the corner and was generally talked. They discussed a possible refurbishing of their United Party as they might have considered doing up a perfectly livable room they hadn't used much lately, or reconditioning a plant that hadn't been in production for a while.

In Anna Louw's house, where the event wasn't mentioned until I brought it up myself, Sam said, 'United people? What's the paper mean? United against us?' And Sylvia Danziger, who was there too, went off into a peal of stuttering laughter.

Cecil did well at the show, but not quite well enough to keep her in the triumphant euphoria in which she was most attractive. I went along to see her compete, twice; when she came out, needle-straight above Hamish's prancing mare, I felt again in a flash the moment when I had noticed her first in the Stratford Bar, months before: she had the exciting, self-absorbed remoteness of a woman whom one does not know. But my attention wandered from the spectacle of one rider after another, uniformly the same, urging their horses to the same performance round the same course; beyond the creak of saddle-leather, a band bumbled somewhere nearby, flags stirred limply, prize cows lowed over in the agricultural section, and, farther away still, there was the vast snore of city traffic, rising and falling and twining. I found Cecil sitting beside me, grim under the black velvet cap, smelling of horse sweat. I gave her a cigarette and her hand was trembling. When someone did worse than she had done, she had difficulty in keeping her flushed face impassive, and looked swiftly sideways at Hamish and Kit. When someone did better than she had, she looked at no one, and fidgeted with the cloth of her breeches stretched tight over her knees. The day she won an event, we all had lunch together at the members' restaurant; Hamish hardly ever went to places that did not carry some sort of privilege. It was a poor lunch, but there was plenty of champagne and a great crowd of well-dressed people in an atmosphere of perfume and cigar-smoke. I was astonished, when I looked up across the heads, to see Anna Louw looking at me. She had a hat on (I had never seen her wear a hat before) and she was smiling, like a child smiling from the top of the big wheel. When Hamish's party was on its way out, and I had left the others to go and get Marion's coat for her from the counter where such things were handed for safe keeping, I found myself near enough Anna to go and speak to her. She was alone; waiting for her escort, I supposed.

'Keeping a tag on you,' she said, smiling with pleasure.

'How was I to know you, in that hat?'

John Hamilton, who was also in Hamish's party, came up as he left the umpteenth group of friends he had paused to talk to as he lagged behind the rest of our party. He had had a lot to drink and his down-to-earth debonair manner, a cross between Father Christmas in a department store and man-about-town, was in spate. 'Toby, there's no dragging you away from the girls. Come on now, who's this delightful young lady you've been keeping to yourself. – He's a dark horse, my dear, always keeps the good things to himself. – Why don't you bring her along to Hamish's eh? Proper Don Juan and pretty darned selfish about it. D'you ride, my dear? Well, what does it matter, you can just sit and look charming. . . .' He drifted on again, greeting people everywhere along the tables.

'Bubbly drinks at lunch have a hideous effect on people,' I said, awkwardly. 'I think he's rather a nice man,' said Anna. 'Oh he is, he is.' I felt rebuked.

'Did you have a good lunch?' I asked. She and I had never had a conversation like this before.

'Asparagus, turkey, ice-cream and chocolate sauce,' she announced. I felt she was laughing at me. I should have liked to have taken off that hat of hers.

'You sound as if you enjoyed it.'

'Toby, man, there's something fascinating about people like this, you know.'

'You don't really think so.'

'Oh yes. It's natural to be like them. If you're a whole person, perfectly adapted to your own functions, like a fish in the sea or a lion in the jungle, you don't give a damn for anybody else. There's something queer about people like me, haven't you noticed it? We want to change things because we haven't got the divine selfishness of really healthy beings. We're not *enough* to ourselves.'

They were waiting, the faces of Hamish's party, searching for me impatiently across the crowd. Cecil had her little whip authoritatively between her two hands, the winner's smile, not directed towards anyone, but meant for herself, lifted her head. John Hamilton beckoned with a high wave like a man casting a lasso.

One night in July, in late winter, the 'opera' that Sam had written and composed in collaboration with a white man was given in the dreary hall of a Bantu social centre.

The new kind of fashionable audience had come to see it; the people who had 'discovered' the Africans artistically and were making the most of the distinction. And, automatically, since, as I've said before, the range of mixed society was so limited, they had drawn in people who had always worked with and had friends among Africans – even one famous man, who had championed the African cause in Europe and America.

The opera was really more of a musical play than an opera, and yet too much like an opera to be a musical play; it just missed being either. It was also more of a white man's idea of what a black man would write, and a black man's idea of what a white man would expect him to write, than the fusion of a black man's and a white man's worlds of imagination. It missed being Sam's work, and it missed being the other man's too – for what that might have been worth. There were one or two good moments in it – especially in the music – but its general impression was that of one of those old-fashioned gipsy operettas that, so feebly wild and gay, never come alive, and it seemed to me to have about as much Africa in it as Ruritania ever resembled any Balkan country that's ever been on a map. Of course, there was a mixed audience of black and white men and women, and that, in Johannesburg, gave us all a strange, embarrassed pleasure; you couldn't help noticing it.

It's not supposed to rain in the Transvaal in winter but it was raining when we left the hall, and the winter wind of Johannesburg, the wind of high places, slapped at your face like a wet towel. Steven was with a few friends – Peter was there that night, and a shy little hospital nurse; Betty Ntolo, the singer, resplendent and giggling; and the man who owned the car that had brought them all, a fat man with a fat man's deep voice, Elias Shomang.

We stood, pressed back against the shelter of the hall's entrance with the rest of the audience, chattering, a glitter of eyes catching the mirror-light of the downpour, shoulders tightened against the cold, the planes of many faces, Indian, African, Caucasian, pleasantly contrasting. I could not help thinking that we seemed less sheep-like than most crowds just let out from an entertainment; I suppose it was the novelty, for although in Johannesburg I'd been in crowds composed of white men, and crowds composed of black, I'd never seen more than a roomful of both mingled. I asked Steven and the others to come to my flat for a drink on their way home. People kept making sudden dashes, driven before the wind, to their cars, and soon we found our opportunity and rushed out, too.

Our two cars reached the building where I lived at almost the same moment, and we clattered up the stairs and into my flat together in the mild relief and excitement of getting in out of the cold. Steven had no coat and his jacket had been pretty thoroughly wetted even in the short exposure to and from Elias's car, so he took it off and hung it over a magazine rack before the electric fire, to dry. He hadn't liked the opera at all. He and I argued while we poured the gin and brandy, and gave each person one of the hollow ice cubes – they were thin shapes of ice with water inside them – that, for some curious reason, probably old age, were the best my refrigerator could do.

'What's the good of a thing like that, to Sam. He can do much better on his own; what does he want that chap Brunner for? I get so wild when I see him panting after these whites, holding out his hand, let's be pals, thanks for the chance to work with you – and all they want to do is pick his brains and pinch his music. It makes me sick, man, I tell you.' Steven dismissed the whole evening.

'Right, it wasn't much good. But you can't say that Sam doesn't get anything out of it, he's had the chance to see the thing performed, and that's something. Without Brunner it wouldn't have happened.'

'Brunner!' said Steven. He broke a match between his teeth.

'Of course, he's a bit of a bloody fool; but what does that matter. Look here, Steve, Sam's got good ideas and some of his music's wonderful, but he doesn't know anything about the conventions of the stage, you know what I mean? He doesn't know how to combine his ideas into a whole, he doesn't even know how to get people on and off a stage. He doesn't know what the limitations of a stage are. How could he? How many plays has he seen in his life?'

'A few,' said Steven. 'Quite a few.'

I knew that even to Steven, who had been to England, the definition of a formal stage presentation was loose; he might count revues and even a concert or two as being part of Sam's experience.

'A very few. Twice since I've been in Johannesburg I've read that the cast of some theatrical company was going to give a performance for Africans in some location township, or in the University Hall. Has Sam ever been inside a theatre?'

Steven was mimicking: 'The Africans were an absolutely *marvellous* audience. Quite the *best* audience we've ever had. D'you know that they actually picked up points that white audiences missed?' – This was the standard comment of white companies when interviewed by the Press after a performance before a black audience, even if they had presented Anouilh to a hall full of black schoolchildren.

'Has Sam ever been inside a theatre?'

'No, of course not, how could he. But he's listened to hundreds of records. He's got opera, he's got *Macbeth,* and *Romeo and Juliet* acted by the Old Vic, he's got American musicals, that play *Under Milk Wood* – oh, dozens. I don't think Mr Brunner can teach him anything.'

'Don't be a damn fool. Anybody can teach him something. Anybody who's been able to see plays and hear operas.'

Steven looked patronizingly superior. 'He's a fool', he insisted, 'to let them pick his brains. And he even says thank you, Baas, for it.'

The others sat around politely, sipping their drinks almost surreptitiously, as if they were frightened to disturb us. Betty Ntolo giggled with embarrassment at the sight of Steven, talking as he did about white men in a white man's house; she was never at ease in the company of even one white person. But I think she wanted to show the little nurse, who was one of Steven's latest admirers – Steven is the only man I have ever known who *really* never had to pursue women, but had them come after him – that she was a familiar, used to him and his ways. 'I think that girl, the well-built one, the one who played the sister – she's rather good,' said Elias Shomang, settled back more comfortably in his chair now; he had been sitting, with the belly-burdened awkwardness of a heavy man, on the edge. And the talk became more general. 'I know her,' said Peter. 'She used to sing with an outfit I know, but she's gone all posh.'

'She's certainly ample,' I said.

Steven couldn't seem to stop worrying at me that evening; he said, treating the women present – as he always did when it suited him – as if they were not there, 'I can't understand it, Toby seems to find all our women too fat. What's this English taste for starved women?' We all laughed, but he went on, 'I've never been able to interest him in a nice African girl yet.' Everyone laughed again, and I gave him some nonsense in answer; yet he was not looking at me, he had turned away to someone else, and I understood that he meant what he said, it was a cover for some reservation he had about me, some vague resentment at the fact that I had not been attracted by any African woman. He, I knew, did not suspect me of any trace of colour-prejudice; he attributed my lack of response to something far more wounding, because valid in the world outside colour – he believed that African women were simply not my physical concomitants. It was a slight to him; hypothetically, he had shown me some woman he had possessed and I had detracted from his possession by finding her unbeautiful.

Just then, there was a ring at the door, but it didn't surprise any of us very much, although the time was nearly midnight, because it was quite likely that some other friend who had been at the opera had decided to drop in. I got up and went to the door with my glass in my hand. The caretaker of the flats was standing there; she wore her fur coat, a long-haired animal with tawny stripes that made a chevron down her bosom, and her huge, regularly-painted face confronted me like a target in a shooting game. She was one of those people, quite common in Johannesburg, who don't seem to be Afrikaans-speaking, but don't really speak

English either. She whined like an Australian, she dropped aitches like a Cockney – it would take an expert in phonetics to convey what she made do with for communication.

She must have drawn breath as she heard the door open, for she said at once, from the top of her chest and the back of her distended nostrils, 'Mr Hood, 'ev yoo brought natives into the bullding. I'v hed complaints yoo been bringing natives in the bullding, end jis now Mr Jarvis seen yoo coming in the front door with natives.'

I said, 'Yes, Mrs Jarvis?' standing there with the glass in my hand as if I were about to propose a toast.

She came past me into the hall and closed the door; I guessed that she was not fully dressed beneath her fur coat, she held it tightly round her all the time. 'I wanna tell yoo, Mr Hood, whatever yoo been used to, this is'n a location, yoo can't 'ev natives. If yoo bringing natives, yoo'll 'ev to go.' Her breath was quite expelled. She looked past me as if she could not bring herself to look at me. She was a very clean, over-dressed, over-painted woman, and now, just as always when she passed you on the stairs, she smelled of cigarettes and toilet soap.

'I can have whom I please in my own flat so long as I pay the rent.'

Through the open door into my room, she saw Peter and the nurse sitting on the divan and the jacket hanging before the radiator; Elias Shomang was hidden by the door, but Steven in shirtsleeves crossed with a bottle of soda-water, doing some imitation that made them all laugh.

Mrs Jarvis lost control of herself. Her hand left her coat and I saw an expanse of lace covering a vast flushed mound of flesh. 'Yoo can't bring kaffirs in my bullding,' she screamed. 'Sitting there like this is a bloody backyard location, I mean to say, the other tenants is got a right to 'ev yoo thrown out. Kaffir women coming here, behaving like scum, living with decent people. Wha'd'yoo think, sitting here with kaffirs. . . .'

Through the door, I saw that nobody in the room spoke, nobody looked at anybody else; the woman's voice took them like a seizure. It seemed to swell up and fill the flat, and I shouted back at her, my throat bursting, 'This is my flat, d'you hear, you've no right to walk in here.' But she went on and on: 'Mr Hood! Mr Hood! Yoo got no right. I shoulda listened to what I been told. What would Mr McKay say, in his bullding, I got my job to think . . . place full of kaffirs. I know. I been told. Yoo coming home five o'clock in the morning in a kaffir taxi. Yoo unnerstend, Mr Hood. . . .'

Steven said suddenly, standing in his shirtsleeves in the doorway between my room and the entrance, 'You have no right, Toby, look in your lease and you'll see.' His voice was passionless and removed; I heard it like the voice of someone not present, a voice in one's brain. His brown, pale-palmed hands rested delicately on the door-frame, he stood lightly, and his eyes were glitteringly bright.

The woman turned and went out the front door.

I still had my glass in my hand; I had never put it down – it had happened as quickly and unmomentously as that. Shomang was murmuring regret, like a guest who has broken an ashtray. The nurse sat staring down at her lap; she looked as if a hand must descend on her shoulder any minute. We were all a little incoherent, shaken, cocky. Peter, that sleepy boy, who lived like a snake in the charmer's basket, only coming to life with music, said again and again, excitedly, 'Bloody white bitches! Bloody white bitches!'

'Is it true about the lease?' I said to Steven.

'Of course. Haven't you got it?'

'Somewhere. I've never read it.'

'Read it and see. No natives unless they're in the capacity of servants.'

'It certainly makes social life a little difficult,' said Shomang cordially, in his stilted African English. At that we all laughed. Betty Ntolo, hanging on Steven's shoulder, put her hand over her mouth as if to stifle the sound of us all. Steven shook her off, kindly, 'A quick one and then we better get going.'

'To hell with her,' I said, bringing over the brandy.

'She's the kind to go for the police,' he said, 'Wheeeeee.

Bang-bang. Open up. Flying Squad here, sir. We got a report you're selling drink to natives in your flat. . . .' He did an imitation that combined the absurdities of gangster films with the absurdities that he had noted in his own experience.

'We should have gone to Ma Ramosa's.'

'We can still go.'

'Ach, one doesn't feel like it.' Elias Shomang was not a shebeen frequenter.

It was still raining hard, and I lent Steven my greatcoat; it was too short for him, and shabbier than anything he would have owned, but he seemed pleased to wear it. 'It'll get spoiled in the rain,' he protested, but he did not take it off.

'You know damn well it couldn't look any worse than it does already.'

'Whatever you've left in the pockets is mine, eh, Toby.'

They all trooped out after him, and in the dark passage I couldn't see him, I could only hear him call, about the coat, 'I'll bring it in to the office on Monday.'

'Yes, yes. O.K. Anytime.'

When they had gone I felt tired and surlily pleased to be alone; all I wanted was to pour myself a brandy and get into bed and open the bundle of English papers I hadn't been able to look at since they had arrived the day before. I had a surfeit of the unfamiliar and unexpected; even the names of places that belonged to a known and predictable way of life would have been a respite. But I had, instead, to go looking through the suitcase on top of the bathroom cupboard where I kept a few clothes I didn't wear; for, the way plans one absently accedes to, thinking they will come to nothing anyway, suddenly materialize, the week-end in the bushveld with John Hamilton had caught up with me, and I was to be ready for him in the morning. He had told me what I must bring, but again, I hadn't listened very attentively, and so I had to throw into an old duffle-bag what my imagination suggested, and what the resources of the suitcase of apparently useless clothing could supply. It seemed to me to be idiotic to be going off on this jaunt, anyway; I was irritated, as I tried to find the things I supposed I should need, that I had let myself be drawn into it. I hadn't even remembered, when Steven had called back to me that he'd return my coat on Monday, that I wouldn't be in the office on Monday. Not that that mattered; Steven was an African and would understand. Perhaps I should take on myself the blessed prerogative of Africans, and simply not turn up for the shoot; but Hamilton, blast him, wouldn't understand, and was too likeable – in a curious way, too innocent a person – for one to be able to be rude to him. So I put in a couple of pairs of woollen socks, and a heavy pullover I had last worn at Zermatt, and a pair of brand-new khaki shorts I had bought in London for the outdoor life I had thought I was going to lead in South Africa, and went to bed, too tired to read and in an ugly mood. I didn't sleep well, either, but kept waking myself like an uneasy animal that is on guard, even in its sleep.

PART FOUR

Chapter 14

AT evening, the low horizon of bush ran together as the light left it, and seemed to sink over the edge of the world with the sun. And in the morning, it emerged again, a strangely even line of greyish trees, and, afar, was present all day. When we walked up to it, where it bordered the great mealie lands, it separated and thinned into growths of various characters; flat-topped, spreading trees, with mean and sparse foliage, waist- or shoulder-high bushes with short grass between them; low patches of briar; thickets of all three, trees, bush, and briar, through which not even the dog could crawl. And all these things were fanged with thorns. Everything that grew in this stunted forest had its particular weapon of thorn. The trees had long white spikes, clean and surgical-looking, like a doctor's instrument, giving off a powdery glitter in the sun. Some of the bushes had the same kind of thorn, but others had shorter, thicker ones, more like those of a rose-bush, and some had thorns like fish hooks from which clothing, flesh or fur could not easily be released. The aloes with their thick fleshy leaves were spiked with red thorns. But worst and cruellest were the black, shiny quills, so sharp and smooth that they slid into your skin as quickly as a hypodermic needle, that covered the trailing briars, ankle-high. As you tore through them you heard them clawing at your boots, and no matter how careful you tried to be, every now and then one would stab into your ankle or calf. If it did not break off in your flesh as you pulled free, it would tear a bloody groove through the skin, as if reluctant to let you go without a taste of your blood. If it broke off, it would fester in your flesh, just beyond the grasp of fingernails or tweezers, until the inflammation it had set up around itself softened and swelled the skin enough for you to press it out.

Walking through this landscape, so thinly green, so hostile with thorn that the living growth seemed a thing of steel rather than sap, I thought of old religious pictures, with their wildernesses and their bleeding, attenuated saints. This was a Gothic landscape, where the formalized pattern of interwoven thorns that often borders such pictures, was real; where one could imagine a martyrdom symbolized by the brutality of these clutching, inanimate yet live instruments of malice.

In some places, where the bush had been cleared but the ground had not been ploughed for crops, fields of tall dead grass made a hissing noise as you pushed through it. Here and there, there was a break, and you would come upon a clearing where the low, thorn briars spread over the earth, and no one, man or beast, could walk there. Bristling branches which had no foliage to stir in the currents of the breeze and give them an air of life, maintained grim guard.

Grass like wood-shavings, pinkish as if permanently touched with the light of sunset. Khaki-weed, the growth of neglect and desolation, standing dead and high. The seed-burrs, round and sharp as porcupines, of some weed that had been cleared away, that crippled the dog the moment she set foot among them.

And more thorns, thorns in your hair and your hands, catching at your clothes, pulling you this way and that. And in silence. Silence on the fringes of which the soothing *sotto voce* of the doves, settling into the trees in some part of the bush which you never seemed to reach, was like the slowed heart-beat of the heat of the day. Now and then, the cheep, or the imagined cheep, of guinea-fowl. Where, where, where?

And a shot, from one of the others. And silence.

Out of the bush, on the borders of the mealie acres, a shot sounded differently. There, it rang right round the sky, as if the sky were finite. It was like a message, beaten upon the four vast doors of the world, North, South, East, West.

We didn't get away early in the morning because when John Hamilton came to pick me up, not only did he still have some provisions to buy, but it was found that I didn't have the right clothing for the trip. He raced me briskly round the town, in and out Army and Navy stores and various other shops, hustling me into long khaki pants that didn't fit me (shorts, he said, were the one thing you could not be comfortable in in the bushveld), making me stamp up and down in bright yellow veldskoen, buckling me into anklets. In between, he collected the last urgent items on his list – salami and tinned soup, eggs, bread, matches, cigars, and lavatory paper. He did all this with the truant joy of a business man on holiday among the buildings and streets where usually he is to be seen hurrying from appointment to office. And there *was* a certain pleasure in going about the city on a grimly busy Friday morning, fitting oneself out in clod-hopper clothing from dark deep shops – whose existence behind gilded hotels and cinemas was unsuspected – stocked, it seemed, with props from an old Trader Horn film.

We met the rest of the party at someone's house, and after scenes of confusion amid guns and yapping dogs and harassed servants, the great mound of stuff that was to be taken along was packed into and on top of a car and a station-wagon. Johannesburg dropped away and we were out on an open road where the winter morning lost its edge and the chromium rim of the car's window, on which I was resting my arm, warmed in the current of the sun. Past Pretoria, the winter was gone entirely; there was a fine, fragrant warmth, like the breath from a baker's shop.

I was in Hamilton's car with a man called Patterson who was some sort of senior official in Hamish Alexander's mining group; the car was one of those huge, blunt, swaying-motioned American ones that Johannesburg people like so much, and the three of us sat in front, with a space just big enough for John's setter bitch among the gear in the back. John and Patterson talked of the probable state of the birds, the height of the grass, and the possibility of persuading a farmer named Van Zyl to let them shoot over his land. It was happy, practical talk, the talk of good children occupied in a game, and it put me to sleep, reassuringly; I dozed and wakened, like a convalescent on a journey, looking out at the thin bush that marked no progress because in its sameness, it did not seem to pass. Suddenly there was a railway siding with a grain silo, a butcher-shop, and a shoddy modern hotel. We got out of our great, over-loaded barges of cars and had cold meat and pickles and beer in a dining-room that had one blue, one green, and one terra-cotta wall, and smelled deeply of a summer of insect-repellent. One of the men from the other car, a stocky, fair chap with a jeering schoolboy's face, leaned his elbows on the table and said in his grim South African voice, 'We've got it taped, boy. Jist you wait, this time. It'll be the biggest bag you ever seen.'

John was full of doubts, like a thoughtful general on the eve of a campaign. 'The trouble is, with so much rain this summer, a lot of chicks must've got drowned. I don't think we'll find the big flocks we had last year, Hughie.'

'There'll be plenty birds, don't you worry.' He looked as if he'd know the reason why, if there were not. 'We must get old Bester to get Van Zyl to let us go over to his dam, too. I'm telling you, it's lousy with duck.'

Patterson said in his amused Cambridge voice, 'Blast, I didn't bring my waders.'

'Is that so,' John said, in the excited way of one confirming a rumour. 'What's he got there, mallard, yellow-bill, or what?'

'Man, there's everything,' Hughie was both shrewd and expansive, putting another head on his beer. 'I know Willard – he's the brother-in-law of one of those big guys that run the duck-shoots for Anglo-American, and he goes down with this guy to the farm next door, old man by the name of Geck, old German, owns it. There's geese too.'

'Geese?'

'By God,' said John, 'have you ever tasted a spur-wing goose? Two years ago, a shoot out Ermelo way, I got one.'

'You can't compare geese with anything else. A turkey's got nothing on a young goose.'

'We could go over there to old Van Zyl with a couple of bottles of whisky.'

'Well, I don't know, waterfowl are damned tricky, once they've been shot over they're wild as hell. . . .'

'That time at Ermelo, up to the waist in freezing cold water. . . .'

'I got my waders,' Hughie said.

'I can see us all with frozen balls,' Patterson murmured gracefully. It was from him that John had borrowed a gun for me; he said, 'I hope you won't find that bloody thing too cumbersome. I wanted to give you my Purdie but the ejector keeps jamming, and I wouldn't trust it. I had to give it over to the gunsmith.' I told him I hadn't yet seen the gun he was lending me, and he explained that it was a Geyger, old as the hills, but still useful, and had belonged to his father. We discussed the personality of the gun; Patterson had the amused, objective, slightly Olympian manner of the ex-hero – as if he were not entirely there, but in some way remained still, like an actor on an empty stage, in the battle air from which, unlike most of his kind, he had not been shot down. I had met men like him before, in London, those men ten years or so older than myself who had survived their own glory; who, having looked their destiny in the face, did not expect, as young men like myself whose war was the tail-end of childhood expected that face, anywhere and everywhere. I knew him slightly from Alexanders'; he didn't actually talk much about his war; but you felt that in thirty years people would come simply to look at him, as, early in the century, you could still go and look at some old man who had fought in the Crimea.

The alert, anxious, feminine face of the dog was waiting for us at the window of John's car. The three Africans who had been packed in along with the rest of the gear, sat eating over paper packets in the station-wagon and did not even look up when we came out of the hotel. Hughie Kidd and his companion, Eilertsen, drew a trail of dust round us and went ahead with a curt wave.

The talk of guns and birds went on, mile after mile, an assessment of known hazards, calculable satisfactions, action within the order of limits that will never change, handicaps that will remain fixed for ever, for men cannot fly and birds cannot fire guns. It was all improbable: the elaborate instrument panel of the car before me, trembling with indicators and bright with knobs that didn't work, the talk that, with a few miles and a change of clothes, had slipped gear and gone, like a wandering mind, easily back to the old concept of man against nature, instead of man against man. Outside, the bush was endless. The car was a fat flea running through the pelt of a vast, dusty animal.

We came at last to great stretches of farmland, where the mealies stood in tattered armies, thousands strong, already stripped of their cobs of corn. Children waved from ugly little houses. From road to horizon, there was a stretch of black ploughed earth, and the smell of it, rousing you like the smell of a river. Then, in a dead straight line, exactly where the plough had cut its last furrow, the bush began again, from road to horizon. We drove through farm gates, and made a choice at ochre sand crossroads where the roads were indistinguishable as those of a maze. A plump, pastel-coloured bird – John said it was the lilac-breasted roller – sat at intervals on a telephone pole, looking over-dressed, like a foolish woman, in that landscape that had dispensed with detail.

At three o'clock in the afternoon we skirted a mound of mealie-chaff at which a few dirty sheep were nibbling, passed a house with a broken windmill, like a winged bird, behind it, roused a ferocious old yellow dog, and bumped off on a track through the mealies. After a short way, there were mealies on one side of us and bush on the other; we came to a shallow clearing where Hughie Kidd's car was already at rest. John backed up under a thin tree whose thorns screeched along the car's side, and with a flying open of doors and an immediate surge of voices and activity, camp was set up. John, Patterson, and Hughie rushed about like boys who have come back to an old hide-out; they appropriated their own low, shallow trees as hanging-places for their things and shelter for their blankets, and allotted places to Eilertsen and men, to whom this clearing on the fringe of the bush was simply a piece of ground. Hughie chivvied everyone, shouting at the Africans, pummelling at and joking with his friends with determined impatience; the idea was to get a shoot in that afternoon, and not wait until morning.

When I had done my share of lugging things from the cars, I thought I had better have a look at the gun Patterson had brought for me, and I walked out with it twenty yards or so into the field of dry mealie stalks to get the feel of it. It was bigger than anything I'd used before, but well-balanced. In my hand, in the sun, it had the peculiar weight that weapons have; even a stone, if you are going to throw it, feels heavy. At school, in cadet target practice, I had shown a cool eye and a steady hand; a minor distinction that my mother had found distressing. Hardly anyone can resist the opportunity to do the thing he happens to do well, and for a year or two, I had gone shooting whenever I had the opportunity, more because I wanted to show off a bit, than out of any particular enthusiasm for the sport. On the other hand, I've never shared my family's sentimental horror of killing what is to be eaten; I've always felt that so long as you eat meat, you cannot shudder at the idea of a man bringing home for the pot a rabbit or a bird which he himself has killed. Among the people I knew in England, my somewhat freakish ability as a shot was regarded as a sort of trick, like being double-jointed or being able to wiggle one's ears, only in rather poorer taste, and I had lost interest in my small skill and hadn't used a gun for at least a year before I came to South Africa. But, like most things you don't care about, the small skill stayed with me whether I used it or not, and when I felt the gun on the muscle of my shoulder and I looked, like a chicken hypnotized by a chalk mark on the ground, along the shine of the barrel, I knew that I could still bring something down out of the sky.

I was only twenty yards from the others, from the big, beached shiny cars twinkling under their dust, the patent camp table and gleaming metal chairs, the boxes of food, the oil-lamps, and the paper-back detective novels; I could see Hughie throwing things to one of the Africans with a rhythmical 'Here! Here!', Patterson filling up the ammunition clips on the belt that was hitched round under his bulging diaphragm, Eilertsen shaking out a blanket, and

John bending down to give his bitch a bowl of water. But they had all shrunk away in the enormous bush and mealie-land; their boisterous voices were tiny in the afternoon, and their movements were as erratic and feeble as those of insects lost in grass. I was suddenly aware of a vast, dry, natural silence around me, as if a noise in my ears that I hadn't been aware of, had ceased. The sun came out of everything; the earth, space, the pale dry mealie stalks. There was no beauty, nothing ugly; it was as I had always imagined it would be if you could get out and stand on a motionless aircraft in the middle of the sky.

John looked up, where he was squatting beside the dog, as I came up. 'Mind you, I was in two minds about bringing her,' he said. She licked her lips and wagged her long feather tail, and her heavy belly swung; I thought she was pregnant. 'No, it's a big tumour, in there, poor old girl. A tumour on her liver.' Feminine, downcast, she submitted while he turned back her lips and showed me her pallid gums. 'I'm keeping her going with big shots of vitamin, and feeding her raw liver. She's nearly ten and the vet doesn't think she'd pull through an operation.'

'Let her come, it's her life,' said Patterson. He had put on short gumboots, and the sort of sharkskin cap American golfers wear covered the lank, thinning hair on his sunburnt head.

'Come on, Gracie, up, up, my girl.' John coaxed the dog to jump into the back of the car. I saw the muscles flex under the smooth freckled coat as she made the effort to lift her burden, and landed with a thud on the seat.

'No loaded guns in the car,' said John, as everybody got in. But Hughie, grinning in the driver's seat, kept the muzzle of his gun pointing out the window. 'I don't want to waste time. – Get a shift on, Eilertsen, for Chris' sake.' Eilertsen was feeling about himself like a man checking up on his train ticket. 'Nearly ten past four,' said Patterson, screwing up his bright blue whisky-drinker's eyes against the mild sun. 'Just right. They ought to be feeding nicely. Where're we going? Down to the far boundary?'

'Bloody birds'll be going back into the bush by the time

we get out. Let's go down where the ground-nut field used to be, and then fan out through that little patch of bush and come out on the other side of the mealies.'

'Look at that!'

'Burned to blazes!'

'Damn, damn, damn,' John moaned softly as we jolted along the track, crushed against each other, with the guns hard against our shins and elbows. A stretch of bush lay reduced to ashes.

'Half our cover gone!'

A cry went up from Eilertsen: 'Stop! Over there, look –' The car stopped as if it had hit a wall.

'Where, where?'

'By that stump? See? Just to the left of that dead bush?'

The back of Hughie's neck, before me where I sat, became red with an excitement like rage. 'What was it?'

'Two pheasants, didn't you see?'

'Ach, man, we don't want to go haring off after a couple of pheasants, let's get on.'

'I think they've gone now, Eilertsen,' said Patterson, distant and kindly.

'What I like to do,' said John, 'when I see something like that, a couple of pheasant where the cover's not too thick, near the road, I like to let Gracie work it a bit. Just go quietly through the bush with her, let her see what she can find.'

The car bumped and swayed on; far away, the broken windmill appeared on our left. We went off the track and through a mealie-field, the tall stakes with their ragged beards and torn leaves staggering at the impact of the car and going down with a crack like breaking bone. On the edge of the field we left the car and spread in a wide sweep through the dead mealies. I could just see Patterson's cap, now and then, on my left, and hear, on the other side of me, John whistle softly to the dog. There was the water-sound of doves, a long way off. A whirr of finches, like insects, went up over my head. The sun had not begun to drop yet, but it seemed to hold off its warmth, in preparation for departure. My own footsteps, over the clods and the stubble, and the brush of my clothes against the mealie-stalks, seemed the noisy progress of some particularly clumsy animal. Once I heard a low, clear questioning chirrup, a peevish, purring call. After a pause, it came again, or the answer to it, much nearer to me. But we came out, all into each other's sight, at the end of the field, all expectant, all with nothing to relate. 'Did you hear them though?' said John. 'That's guinea-fowl, my boy.' 'That rather plaintive sort of call?' 'That's it,' said Patterson.

We piled into the car again and crashed back over the field in the path we had already flattened before us. Hughie did not speak and swung the car determinedly this way and that. We came out on to a soft red dust road and drove cautiously, in first gear, along the bush. The car stopped, just where the bush ended and the mealies began again. No one spoke; like a yearning, our gaze and our attention went out over the field. And – 'There!' said John hoarsely. 'Look at them, look at them.'

'Ah, there.'

'Where. . . .'

'Look, hundreds of them. And there.'

'I had a feeling they'd be here.' Hughie, both hands on his gun, spoke lovingly. 'It's funny, I had a feeling.'

In the middle of the field, among the clods that looked like broken chocolate, and the pale, untidy shafts of the mealies, I saw dark, small heads, jerky and yet serpentine, plump bodies with a downward sweep, stalking legs: guinea-fowl feeding. They reminded me of pea-hens, and their plumage was the blue-dark of certain plums.

We all got out of the car softly and swiftly. John made a plan of approach. Patterson would go up the centre of the field, making straight for them; John and I would swing out in a curve to the left, Hughie and Eilertsen would do the same on the right, so that when the flock was disturbed by Patterson, he would have his chance with them as they took to the air, and either John and I, if they flew West, or Hughie and Eilertsen, if they flew East, would have a chance with them as they made for cover. It was unlikely that they would fly directly away from Patterson, to the North, because there was a stretch of newly-ploughed ground there, and no cover.

Hughie, scowling with concentration, was off with Eilertsen behind him and an air of going his own way, almost before John had finished speaking. Patterson's big heavy shape went nimbly into the screen of mealies.

The dog wove in and out just ahead of John and me, but discreetly, held by the invisible check of obedience. The discomfort of her body was forgotten, she did not seem aware of it at all, but followed the map of smells spread under her pads like a crazy, enchanting dream, the dream that gun-dogs, twitching, dream all summer, and suddenly wake up to find themselves inhabiting, in the winter. We trudged without speaking, round the margin of the field; a barbed wire fence stood between the mealies and the beginning of the bush, on the left side, and we followed it for a hundred and fifty yards and then stopped and waited. John was unaware of himself, and me; he gave me an absent, flitting smile, and kept his white-haired, cockatoo head lifted. The dog panted with happiness, like an athlete who has just breasted the tape, and he put a hand down to quiet her. I opened the breech of my gun to look at the two cartridges lying ready. It did not seem likely that there was anyone else alive, in the multiplication of mealies not moving out there; I forgot what we were waiting for, as, I suppose, fishermen forget when they sit with the rod in their hands, and Patterson forgot the moment before he loosed fire among the Messerschmitts. I watched John, in the perfect moment of inaction that only comes in action, and wondered, after all this time, if this was what Stella Turgell had meant when she had said of her husband that Africa was for active and not contemplative natures.

The guinea-fowl came over, black and sudden, tossed up into the air by their own alarm, and cracks sounded, sharp and near and far and feeble. John gasped as if something had got him by the throat and swung up his gun wildly. A second flock came, rising steeply as they passed us. I felt the recoil against my shoulder, smelled the explosion-warmed grease of the gun. The black, plump shapes were lifting; nothing touched them. Then I saw them along the path of the barrel; a line drew taut in the bright air between my eye and a bird that hung, a split second, breasted on the air. The gun nudged me; the air toppled the bird and let it fall. I spilt the smoking cartridges, re-loaded, and shot another. Out of range over the bush, we saw the rest of the birds skim down into the trees.

My first bird was dead, the second lay in long grass on the other side of the fence. The dog found it at once, and John, who had gone through the wire to look for his own bird, picked it up by the neck and snapped the thread of life that remained in it as neatly as he would pluck a stalk of grass. The heads of the dead birds were ugly; they looked like the carved heads of old ladies' umbrellas.

I followed John through the fence into the bush, carrying the soft, plump weight of my birds. As we searched for his wounded bird, we heard the voices of the other men, excited as the cries of boys on a beach. We went deeper into the bush, talking and purposeful; I had seen John's bird come down, he had seen it flutter, half-rising again, once or twice. I looked all round the thorn-tree where I had seen it fall, but there was nothing, not a feather; was it that tree? Wherever you looked there were trees exactly like it; the moment I found myself five yards into the bush I knew myself to be in a place of uncertainty, and this was right – the beginning of the bush was like the middle, you did not go deeper into it in any sense but that of distance, for it was same, all the way. It reduced time and space to the measure of the sun's passing across the sky and the tiredness of your own feet; I could well imagine that if you walked through it for ten minutes or ten hours, whether you went round in a small circle or covered miles in a straight line, you would have covered the same ground and have the same lack of sense of achievement. It had the soothing monotony of snow. John poked about and grumbled. 'You see it's hopeless without a dog in this stuff. We'd've lost yours, ten to one, if there'd been no dog.' The setter swam steadily, head up, through a drift of thick grass, sniffed round thorny thickets as if they were about to explode. We didn't find the bird. 'Lying low somewhere, under our feet.' John reproached the dog, but she gave him a moment's absent flick of the ears and went off again, her course erratic and mysterious as a water-diviner's. The voices of the others were lost; alone again and in silence except for the clumsy passage of our bodies, we followed the dog through the indifference of the empty afternoon. I heard my own breathing and felt the prick of the thorns; they were thicker than leaves, on every bush and tree and bramble and, with scabby bark and crusted twig, gave everything the touch and feel of old men's horny fingers. The enormous air paled; the sun was so withdrawn you could look right up into it, but the little scratchings of shadow from the bush did not seem to grow longer, but only to disappear in soft shoals of shadow that the grasses threw upon themselves, as the sea often seems to darken from beneath rather than from the failure of the light above. We went on, and, suddenly, the spasm of a muscle in a dream, three pheasant blustered into the air right before us. I was foolishly startled, and missed, but John, with that gasping intake of breath, wheeled on them and got one.

Back at the car, Hughie and Eilertsen were already there. They waved and shouted as we came up; there was a dark heap on the roadside beside them. 'Where the hell'd you get to,' yelled Hughie, extraordinarily cheerful and friendly, swaggering with satisfaction. 'We heard you potting away in the bundu; what's the score? Jesus, that was some flock came your way, we only got the lousy stragglers, the few that panicked and went the other way.'

'He got four, I got three,' said Eilertsen, turning a bird over with his foot.

'Jesus!' Hughie looked at what we had in our hands. 'I don't believe it! Whatsa matter with you, John, you paralysed or something? I ruddy well don't believe it! And what's that, a pheasant – one of them's even a pheasant. Didn't you chaps *see* a few hundred or so guinea-fowl over your heads?'

'Hughie, man,' John said worriedly, 'I come up too fast. I know it. You remember, it was just the same last year. The first afternoon, I'm just too damned het up and excited.'

'Jesus,' said Hughie resentfully, 'only two.'

'I did get one blighter, but he came down in the bush and even Gracie couldn't find him.'

Hughie began to piece together the strategy of the first shoot: 'Why did Patterson have to make right for the middle of the birds, like that? He should've gone round, and driven them down a bit.'

'Who can tell?' Eilertsen had the look of a man for whom almost everything is a little beyond him. 'You never know what they'll do.'

'But that's fine,' John said eagerly. 'That means they're not wild at all, this year, eh? Did you see, Hughie? He went right up close, eh? We couldn't see a thing, where we were.'

'If I'd'a bin him, I'd'a gone round a bit, that's what I would'a done.'

Patterson came out of the mealies with the happy, calm roll of a man who is smiling to himself. A cluster of dark bodies hung from the hooks on his belt, bumping against his hip as he walked. As he drew nearer, I saw a feather, stuck in the band of the shark-skin cap. 'Not bad,' he said. A year of alcohol was beading, streaming, oozing out of his skin.

Hughie was counting. 'Three, and me and Eilie seven, that's ten, twelve –'

Eilertsen tossed the pheasant to him.

'Thirteen, could be worse. Patterson, why'd you go straight for them, man?'

'It was amazing,' Patterson was telling John, while he smeared at his face. He had taken off the cap and his hair was brilliantined with sweat. 'I felt as if they would have come up and eaten out of my hand. They simply ignored me. One old boy just gave me a wink and went on feeding. D'you remember the one-legged one? He's still here. He's with this lot.'

At the sight of the car, as if at a reminder, the dog had dropped into exhaustion. She lay in the back, almost as inert as her prey. We drove back to the camp talking, scarcely listening to each other, and huddled comfortably together, rank and uncaring as animals in the loose, unquestioning association of the pack.

While we were gone, the three Africans had collected

wood and fetched water from the farmhouse. Hughie shook himself out of the car and at once began to shout and berate in the meaningless convention of men who are brought up in a country where there are many menials; the Africans, in the same convention, heard only the sense, ignored the words, and did the minimum of what was required of them. Two of the men were John's servants, very black Nyasas with blank faces that looked worried the moment they took on any task. The other was Hughie's own servant, a little snivelling Basuto with a face the colour of fear. Hughie bellowed at him harmlessly, as if he were deaf. He sat down on a camp stool and shouted, 'Here! Come on, get my boots off!' Then he was all over the camp, looking into everything. 'These lazy bastards! How long d'you think this wood will last, eh? That's no good, all that small stuff. You get on out there and bring some big logs. *Makulu*, *Makulu*, eh? Plenty big logs.'

The darkness was cold. It came up around our legs and, as we stood around the fire, drinking the first whisky, the whole land became steeped in dark, while the sky took on the sheen of a wet shell. The shapes of the men changed clumsily as they put on pullovers and mufflers; I dragged out of the duffle-bag my souvenir of Zermatt. Meat had been brought from town for the first night's meal, and John prepared and grilled it. Hughie opened a tin of beans and asked for bacon, butter, and various utensils John hadn't got. 'You should have one of those heavy iron pots, John, that's the only way to do these things properly. Isn't there a spoon with a long handle? Here! Find me a spoon, big one, one with long handle! – Jesus, this bloody thing's burning me up.' The unlikely-looking food was delicious, and with it we drank mugsful of red wine. We sat like spectators round the dance of the flames and the stars came out sharply and the dark seeped up and up. It was night, and in the great dark room of the world, we were a scene in somebody's sleeping head, alight, alive, enclosed.

We sat drinking until late. Wine brought out an innocence, a schoolboy crudity, in Hughie. His swaying, bobbing face, smeared with the grease of chop-bones, hung above his mug in the licking light; he told old, long dirty jokes that one could listen to with the pleasant sense of recognition with which one follows the progression of a folk tale. He boasted about his dog; 'If he was here and you touched me, like that – just touched me – he'd go for you. He's not more than a year old yet, I reckon, but boy there's nothing he's not wise to. He never lets my kid out of his sight, I tell you, a Heinz fifty-seven varieties, and more sense than all your pedigrees.'

'Poor old Gracie, she enjoyed herself this afternoon.'

'Well, give me pointers any day. I wanted to get a pointer, but then my kid wanted a pup and we bought this pooch. You know, I wouldn't be surprised if you couldn't train him to be a gun-dog. Honestly, I wouldn't be surprised. That dog's so damned clever. And what a watchdog! You won't see a kaffir pass our gate without crossing the road first.'

While Hughie discoursed on the superiority of pointers over setters, Patterson and I dragged an ant-eaten trunk four or five feet long, on to the fire, and as the flame delicately explored it, and the heat of the fire penetrated it, the life to which it was still host abandoned it in panic. First came long refugee-columns of ants, and hurrying woodlice; and then that creature out of the zodiac, a scorpion. Eilertsen suddenly got giggling drunk, like a woman, and kept pouring himself more wine with an air of recklessness. 'First damn time I've got like this since V.E. day,' he tittered. 'Reckon it's time I had a few again.' Hughie went off on a long disquisition on the habits of stomach ulcers, which were the cause of Eilertsen's long sobriety. Hughie knew so many half-truths and fallacies about so many things that the self-sufficiency of his ignorance was awesome; it was impossible to be bored by him. To people who prided themselves on their sensibility, he would seem to be a person completely without imagination, yet the truth of it was that he lived in a fantasy, was possessed by the new witchcraft, the new darkness of the mind made up out of the garbled misconceptions of scientific, technological, and psychological discoveries he did not understand.

Before he went off to bed, John called the servants to give them some wine. 'Not too much, we don't want them half-dead in the morning.'

'Ach, give them brandy, man,' said Hughie. 'They don't like wine. Give them each a tot of brandy. Kaffirs don't really like wine.'

A little way from our hollowed-out interior in the dark, the three men sat round a small fire of their own. They had eaten; they talked so low among themselves that in our rowdiness, we had not been aware of this anteroom. It was true, they were pleased with the brandy. Each stood, watching it being poured into his mug; on the face of the elder Nyasa, Tanwell, a smile, sudden and soft as the flame that lit it, showed incongruously on the fierce squat blackness of his closed face. The Basuto clowned for his, while Hughie growled appreciatively and threatened to kick his backside. They went back to their fire with their consolation; it was plain that they didn't enjoy this atavistic game of sleeping out. We had elaborate protective clothing, ground sheets, rubber mattresses, and sleeping bags, they had the blankets they slept in at home in the town. There was the unexpressed suggestion that they were naturally closer to nature, to put them back in the veld was like loosing wild things. But the Nyasas were close enough to a state of nature to know that, for man, the state of nature is the nest; the musky closeness there must be in the grass and mud huts of the tribe. The Basuto was a bleary-faced town-sharp man of about my age; I supposed that he would rather be gone to ground in Alexandra township or the tin and hessian of Orlando shelters.

But in my blankets, dressed up for bed in all the clothing I could muster, I felt the comfort of the voices about me, the cosy, confident sound of voices that held no tone of doubt; voices for whom God was in his church, justice was in a court, and all the other questions of existence had equally glib answers. The warmth of the wine in my body and the cold of the night on my cheek gave me that sudden, intense sense of my own existence that is all I have ever known of a state of grace; and that, exaltation of self that it is, must be the very antithesis of what such a state really is.

Patterson was pulling a woman's stocking on to his head.

'What's that, a trophy?'

He grinned at me. 'My dear boy, it's the best way in the world to keep your head warm. But you've got plenty of hair.'

The others continued to stumble about the camp. 'First damn time I've been drunk since V.E. Day, I'm telling you. . . .' Giggles. 'Look out there, you silly bastard, you'll have the whole thing over.' 'Here, girlie, good Gracie, good girl. . . .'

I woke up to feel someone looking at me. It was the moon, staring straight down from a sky full of her great light without warmth, that weird contradiction of the associations of light. I pulled the blankets up over my head but I felt it, the eye that has no benison. The bundles of sleeping men were pale shrouds, the fire was silenced. Rolling out over the stillness there came a yowl from the entrails of desolation, the echo of a pack of nightmares. It stopped, and came again, and I did not think I heard it outside my own head. Suddenly, beside me, Eilertsen sat up whimpering in his blankets and fired three shots straight past my ear. The dead rose. 'Good Christ, what's the matter?' 'What the hell's he doing.' 'I could see their red eyes in the dark,' said Eilertsen, caught in the moonlight, 'Just over there, in the bush.' 'Nonsense.' When John was woken in the middle of the night he was not another self, like most people, but simply himself. 'Jackal wouldn't come that near.' But after that, there was silence.

Chapter 15

IN the mornings, the birds were frozen stiff where we left them on the roofs of the cars, and the bottles of beer that John put out specially were opaque with cold. Patterson lay helplessly in his blankets, waiting for coffee to come, but

Hughie, with his gingerish bristles sparkling on his chin and his hair fiercely tousled, stumped about in impatience. 'Let's go out and murder the bastards!'

And with hands aching with the hard cold of the gun, we would follow him through a morning wet and fresh and strange as something torn from a womb. A rent caul of webs glistened on the thorns and the grasses swagged together in wet brushes. We heard guinea-fowl. We did not hear the doves or the starlings or the plover or the quail; only the guinea-fowl, like the words of a language one recognizes in a close murmur of foreign tongues. It seemed that they knew we were coming for them; there was the compulsion of an appointment between us; the birds were there and the men had come, and they must meet. When we rested in the camp, we heard them, were aware of them and felt strongly that they were aware of us. The flux and tension of the pursuit were completely absorbing, so that, in the heat of the day, when there was time to read, we did not read. The old fear, that had been bred into me, of finding myself with nothing to read (what would one do, caught somewhere, someday, without a book) was suddenly made harmless. I did not need to read. The books lay stuffed down in the duffle-bag.

That was a wonderful hour of the day. The morning shoot ended at about half past ten, when we came back to camp after tramping through the bush and the mealies for nearly four hours. We had the sour, dissipated look of unshaven men who have not breakfasted, the look that is permanent with tramps. First we drank the beer which, carefully kept in the shade, held still the cold of the night. Then we cooked a meal without the customary limitations of meals; so long as you were hungry, John would produce another chop, more bacon, more kidneys. Then we took turns to use the tin basin for washing and shaving. Only Hughie did not shave; he went to lie in his tent – he was also the only one who slept in a tent, an inflatable thing that he put up with a bicycle pump.

A noon silence fell. The sun was a power in the bush; nothing moved; the thorns glittered; Patterson took his shirt off and put it over his face to keep off the flies. My blankets were under a thorn-tree, but the shade was nothing more than a net between me and the sun. The doves sounded regularly as breathing.

At some point when we were all asleep or seemingly asleep, Hughie would come quietly out of his tent with his gun and go off into the bush. Once he brought back a hare, a poor thing with ears full of bloated black ticks. 'The boys'll eat it,' he said. 'Here! Samuel!' Bleary-eyed and sweating he would wait for us to make ready for the afternoon shoot, wiping his mouth with the back of his hand after a long drink of water, and keeping his head cocked, listening. 'That crowd that feeds in the ground-nut field, they're there already. S'tru'asGod. They're not resting in any bush.' He watched us resentfully. And mostly, after the first day, when we were all out together he would leave us after the first few minutes, and disappear, with or without Eilertsen, for hours. We would find him at the car or back at the camp, counting his bag. He out-walked and out-shot everybody. 'Let's go and murder the bastards!'

John said, troubled, 'Kidd takes it all too seriously. You know what I mean? He doesn't get a kick out of just walking through the bush.'

'It's his way of talking.' Patterson was amused, as he might have been amused by an almost-human chimpanzee. He said to me later, 'That chap's the most inarticulate blighter I've ever met. South Africans are a pretty inarticulate lot, anyway, don't you think?'

'He's got plenty to say for himself about everything under the sun.'

'Oh he'd chat to Einstein about relativity. But he's only got a few words to get along with; they have to fit every conceivable situation. Makes him sound like a savage.'

'That's what *he* calls the two Nyasas.'

'Those two gentlemen. I must say, they're not more than one jump out of the trees; John really is unbelievably patient with them. I felt like giving that one careless little bastard a kick in the pants this morning – if he'd been my own boy. The way he gutted those birds, simply hacked them to bits.'

‘Well, it’s all relative, I suppose, this savage business.’

He looked at me with curiosity for a moment, as if he had just remembered something. ‘D’you believe these black chaps could ever be the same as us, Hood?’

I heard Steven’s voice, mimicking him perfectly. Yet Steven was not Patterson, was not even me; was not Tanwell and the other Nyasa, chopping wood ten yards away as if all tasks were one.

‘Never. The French are not the same, or the Germans or the Italians. They’ll do all the things we do, but they’ll be themselves.’

He laughed, from that private vantage point on which I sometimes felt he was caught, unable to get down. He waved me away, as if I had offered him an evasion. ‘Run their own show? I’d like to see it. I just don’t think the poor chaps have got the brain. They’re limited. It’s just not there.’ He put down the rag with which he had been cleaning his gun. ‘Come on, let’s get some of those papiermâché things from the whisky bottles and stick ’em up on the mealies. See if I can hit a target, if nothing else, today.’ Big, handsome ruin, paunched, pouched and veined; sauntering heavily over the clods he reminded me of one of those splendid houses, thrown open to the public at half-a-crown a time, that seem to regard the trippers amusedly, and are seen by the trippers amusedly, as something over-blown and gone to pot.

In the bush I usually walked with John. The eager face of the dog, turning suddenly, beckoned us; the tip of her tail bled from the thorns and her ears held the seeds of khakiweed like a magnet that has trailed through a box of pins; at night she was too exhausted to eat, and lay looking at us over the weight of the death growing in her belly, but in the bush during the day she seemed to outrun it. ‘I don’t think she can be as ill as you think,’ I said to John. ‘No,’ he said, ‘she’s finished. Like a good race-horse, she’ll go on till she drops.’

These were the clichés of the Alexanders’ world, the curiously dated world of the rich, with its Edwardian-sounding pleasures. They thought of courage in terms of gallantry, spirit in terms of gameness; in the long run, I supposed my mother’s and my father’s definitions were my own, I could really only think of these things in terms of political imprisonment and the revolt of the intellect.

But beneath John's social sophistication, his equipment for Johannesburg, there was a strongly appealing quality. He reduced life to the narrative; we trekked through the thorns and the grass and all our faculties were taken up with what we were doing and where we were going. His thin brown face, alert above a bobbing adam's apple, was a commonplace reassurance, like the image of some simple, not very powerful, household god who serves to hold back the impact of mystery from ordinary life.

On Monday evening, I lost the others and found myself alone in the darkening bush. I walked about a bit, but was defeated by the silent sameness and thought it more sensible to stay still awhile, and listen; I had discovered that if you forced your hearing capacity, you could very often part the silence of the bush and make out, far away, the sounds – like feeble bird-sounds muffled in the nest – of men talking. I smoked and listened; the ground was pink as warm stone and the thorn trees were wrought iron. Presently I separated from the furtive rustle of the bush, the faint panting of the dog. It seemed to reach me along the ground, on a rill of air. I called, and though there was no answer, in a little while, the dog, held on the leash by the younger Nyasa, appeared. Sometimes, when the dog saw a lot of guinea-fowl moving in a field, she lost her head and wanted to give chase. It was then that if the Africans had been taken along as beaters, John would give her to one of them to hold.

'I can't find the baas,' said the African.

'It's all right, I'm lost too,' I said. 'Let the dog lead.' We followed her half-hearted zig-zag for a few minutes. The thorn bushes were black splotches, like an attack of dizziness.

'I don't think we should just keep on walking, do you?'

He stood there with the dog and said nothing. I sat down and he settled a yard away. When I spoke to him he did not answer, unless what I said was a direct question. He wore broken sand-shoes, out of which the little toe stuck on each foot, and a torn dirty khaki shirt and a pair of brown striped trousers that must once have belonged to a man with a big belly – they were folded over in front, under a belt, like a dhoti – and he must have been cold; a kind of feverish chill ran over the ground the moment the sun dropped.

At last I did not try to talk any more, and we sat there, together. The dog was exhausted, and slept. He did not look at me or at anything; his isolation came to me silently; I was aware of it then, but it must have existed all the time, while we ate and we drank and we sang and we cursed, in our camp. I offered him a cigarette but he would not take it from the packet and he cupped his hands and I had to drop the cigarette into them. Loneliness gathered with the chill, a miasma of the ancient continent; he and I were in hand's reach of each other, like people standing close, and unaware of it, in a fog.

After about an hour, Patterson found us – or rather we heard him, and the three of us managed to find our way back through the bush to where, in the mealies, the lights of the car turned on by the others to guide us hung two banners of heavily moted orange light in the blackness. As we stumbled into the colour and brightness, we got an applause of shouts and jeers of welcome. That night was our last and John insisted that we finish the red wine before we went to bed. I did a couple of imitations I had once done in a student revue at Oxford, and spontaneously added a new one to my meagre repertoire – Miss Everard and the Italians on the boat. John, using Patterson as a victim, showed us how he once tried to learn Judo. Hughie sang army songs with Eilertsen, and gave us, with no bones about it, his assessment of what makes a woman worth the trouble. Over at their own fire, the Africans drank their brandy ration and talked in undertones that now and then surged into laughter, or exploded, like a cork out of a bottle, into sudden onomatopoeic exclamations.

We went out after birds once more, early in the morning, but without much luck; yet the final bag was impressive – fifty-eight birds, not counting those we'd eaten in camp. When we had breakfasted we packed up to go; there was no point in washing or shaving in a tin basin when we could bath at home in a few hours. The camp looked like a house the morning after a party – everything was distasteful and begrimed, the flies sat about on all that was half-clean, half-eaten, half-done with in four days of thoughtless living. When we had loaded the cars, the patch of bush where we had lived simply looked flattened, as if some animal had lain there. We drove away. My arm, on the rim of the car window, was teak-coloured with sun and dirt. Patterson's heavy face was seamed with white where he had screwed up his eyes against the sun. John had a poll of red hair, dyed with dust. There was an air about us both spent and refreshed; as we came back again among houses and shops, it seemed to me that I had been far away and a long time. The boot of the car was piled with the thick, soft bodies of birds, their plumage tousled and lying brushed against the grain, as it seems to become the moment life has gone. All the way the old setter lay on the back seat, asleep or dead, one hardly knew; both were drawn so close in her now, there was little difference. We stopped at Patterson's house first, to divide the bag, and the birds lay heaped on the grass while Hughie dealt them out. The dog did not come when John called to her to give her a dish of water. He said to me, 'Give old Grace a prod, will you.' But when I put my hand on her rump she felt like the birds I had just tumbled out of the boot.

PART FIVE

Chapter 16

AFTER I had bathed and shaved the dirt away, and fried myself a plateful of eggs for lunch – I still felt as hungry as I had been in the bushveld – I went to town. The kitchen of the flat was piled with guinea-fowl, there were feathers and the smell of wood-smoke filled the place; I didn't know quite what to do with the birds and thought I'd decide when I came back in the evening. In the meantime, it was simple to shut the door on it all.

Saturday's and Monday's mail lay on my desk at the office; nothing much, the usual publicity handouts and invoices from Aden Parrot, letters from booksellers who had under-ordered and were now clamouring for stocks of an unexpected best-seller, a note from my sister, on holiday in Spain. There was also a long, hand-written (too confidential even for Faunce's confidential secretary) letter from Uncle Faunce, telling me that it was possible that Arthur Hollward might ask to be relieved of the South African representation of Aden Parrot; he seemed to be getting old and to have a hankering to settle down in England. How would I feel about staying on, perhaps for a year or two. Nothing definite; merely a feeler, and so on. It was what Uncle Faunce called 'playing with the idea'. While I read it, I was thinking about my guinea-fowl – half for Marion Alexander, half for Cecil? Perhaps a couple for Sam and his wife, and, of course, Anna Louw. I put Faunce's letter away without thinking about it; first I hadn't known what to do with my birds, now I didn't seem to have enough to go round. I wrote down the names of the possible recipients on the back of my cigarette box.

I worked on at the papers around me until nearly five, when the typist, her coat on ready to go home, came in and said, 'Oh I forgot. There was a mysterious phone call from the police yesterday. Something about stolen property.'

'Stolen property? Whose?'

'Well, I told them that as far as I knew you hadn't lost anything. You haven't had a burglary or anything like that at the flat, have you?' She was a good one, this one; an earnest, rather greasy-haired little girl who was a graduate of the university in Johannesburg, and had taken the humble office job because she was passionately interested in publishing and hoped to get herself a job with Aden Parrot in London, eventually. 'I've got the number, anyway, so perhaps you'd better phone them.'

Before I left the office, I did. When I had given my name and address, and had been handed from voice to voice until I reached the right one, it said hoarsely, patiently, 'We got a coat here, sir. There was a card in the pocket with your name and address.'

I said, 'A grey coat with checked lining?'

'That's right. We got it here for you.'

'But I'd lent that coat to a friend.'

'Well, it must've been stolen from him. It was found on a native on Saturday night. You're lucky. All you got to do is come along and sign for it.'

I said, indignantly, triumphantly, with a laugh, 'But I lent it to him. He's Steven Sitole, he's the friend. Give it back to *him*.' The card in the pocket. 'Whatever you've left in the pockets is mine, eh, Toby.' How Steven must be laughing, over this.

The voice said, 'He's dead, sir. He was with a whole lot of other natives in a car that crashed on the Germiston road, and the coat was on his body. They were making a get-away from an Indian club the police was raiding.'

How can I explain the jolt of horror, the *knowing*, the recognition with which, at that instant, I felt, beneath my hand, the dog as I had discovered her on the back seat of the car. Dread passed a hand over my face, cold. I understood. To my bones, I understood.

I said, 'What was his name? What was the name of the man? Have you the names there?'

He had not; 'You must go and find out,' I said. 'You must go and fetch the report or whatever it is and read it to me.'

He protested, but I made him. I did not think while I waited, *I did not think.*

'Native called Steven Sitole and another one, Dan Ngobo, both dead. Two other natives and an Indian arrested. Three bottles of brandy in the car.'

I said, 'All right.'

'And the coat, sir, whad'ju want us to do with the coat?'

I went to the mortuary and got permission to see him. The man said, 'Did he work for you? You won't recognize him.' But I knew I must look at him because otherwise I would never be able to believe that he was gone. I would go away back to England one day and it would seem to me that he was merely left behind, he would begin to live again, forgotten by me. I wanted his death to come home to me, as his quickness had done.

He was broken, that was all. He was still himself. He looked as if he had been in a long and terrible fight, and had lost.

I said to the man, 'He had a ring, a cheap ring with a red stone in it, that he always wore on his little finger?'

But he knew nothing about it.

I drove out to Sam's house and found no one there; not even the crones in the yard could tell me where he and his wife might be. I drove back again, through the flare and dark of the night-time township, cries like streamers, smoke and the smells of food, drunken men, children, and chickens, the tsotsis hanging around the cinema – and I had to keep drumming it into myself, *he* is not there, *he* is not there. He was made up of all this; if it existed, how could he not? I had to keep explaining death to myself over and over again, as I met with each fresh piece of evidence against its possibility. Despite the war, despite the death of my father, I had never proved the fact of death in my own experience; since I was a man, I had never lost anything that meant more to me than a pet; I understood death only as a child, who has been told the facts of life, thinks he understands love.

In the city, the white powdered faces of women above fur

coats showed under the neon lights of the cinemas and theatres, immigrant youth from Naples and Rome stood about on their thick-soled shoes before an espresso bar, the cars urged slowly round and round the streets, looking for parking-places. I drove slowly through the city, slowly through the suburb that climbed the hill.

In the flat, there were the guinea-fowl, the smell of wood-smoke and the feathers, floating along the floor in a current of air stirred by the opening door. The sight of the place was like a confrontation with the smiling face of someone who did not know that anything had happened. The amputation of pain severed me from the moment when I had shut the door behind me, not by eight hours, but by the timeless extension of experience; I had moved so far from that moment, that I felt stupidly unable to understand that, relatively, time had stood still, in my flat.

I knew I could not stay there. I closed the door and went back down the stairs and sat in my car. A hideous sense of aimlessness took hold of me; I sat like a man in an empty, darkened theatre, watching the scene coming down, being taken apart, and carted away. Where were the walls of stone, houses that would stand, a place of worship where you would find God? What had I known of Steven, a stranger, living and dying a life I could at best only observe; my brother. A meaningless life, without hope, without dignity, the life of the spiritual eunuch, fixed by the white man, a life of which he had made, with a flick of the wrist, the only possible thing – a gesture. A gesture. I had recognized it, across a world and a lifetime of friends and faces more comprehensible to me. How could it be true, that which both of us knew – that he was me, and I was him? He was in the bond of his skin, and I was free; the world was open to me and closed to him; how could I recognize my situation in his?

He had not come into his own; and what I believed should have been my own was destroyed before I was born heir to it.

At last I went upstairs again and wrapped up the guinea-fowl in newspaper and took them to Cecil. Sam was out; I could not telephone, across the breach of the town between white man and black, to find out if he was home yet. I couldn't go to Anna Louw; it seemed to me that it would have been, in some curious way, a disloyalty to Steven to do so. I went to Cecil, with whom I could not discuss Steven's death at all. Not to talk of it, to ignore pity or moralizing about the short, violent life – that seemed the only thing. For with Steven it was not that he was this or was that; simply, he was.

I drove to Cecil's flat and found she was, as usual, in the bath. She spent so much of her time lying, smoking, in the bath. She called to me 'I'll be out in a minute,' and I went to the kitchen with my burden of birds. Eveline was washing up the dinner things; 'Master Toby!' the woman giggled. 'Where are we going to put them, we got the fridge full with those things already! Master Patterson he brought us six.' And she showed me. But I left them to her and went away to the living-room and got myself a drink. In a little while, Cecil came in wearing a dressing-gown, the ends of her hair damp with bathwater. 'Those birds are marvellous! You're an angel! They'll be fantastic eating.'

'Eveline says you've got more than you need, already.'

She looked embarrassed, but careless of being found out in social lies, at once said, 'Oh Guy Patterson brought them. Some nonsense. He begged a stocking of mine to keep his head warm and promised me birds in exchange. How was the trip?'

'Fine. What sort of weekend did you have?'

'You *do* need a haircut. Look at this frill on your collar. You look dead-beat.' She came and sat beside me and took my hand in her warm lap. I felt under my hand the cold body of the dog and took my hand away and put it behind her head and kissed her hard. She was pleased as she always was by the rough and unexpected advance, and she laughed and said, 'Don't tell me you've come back from the bush all randy,' with the faintest emphasis on the 'you' that might have implied an unspoken 'you too'; it crossed my mind that perhaps she was thinking of Patterson. Yet I turned to her and I kissed her and passion came like a miracle in my numbness, and there was compassion in the love-making. I caught her looking at me, as, in her untidy bedroom with the neck of the bedside lamp twisted to throw its light away from her, on to the wall, we went through the ancient ritual of oneness; gazing back at her paused face, I too, was sorry I had not done more for her, wanted or been able to take her in and make life real for her. Yet, in the end, she seemed to hold back on the brink of her own pleasure; she let me go ahead and then she lay back, her eyes open, smiling at herself in some private justification. I said to her, 'What's the matter?' But she shook her head and still smiling, touched my hair, that she had complained about earlier, with a queer little gesture of finality and tenderness, as a woman might adjust her husband's tie before they are to go out.

She said, softly, 'It'll soon be time for you to go back to England, won't it. Perhaps I shall come and see you there.'

'Are you really coming?'

She closed her eyes and drew her nostrils in, a child making a wish, 'I shall marry a rich man and have a suite at the Dorchester and come and see you.'

I said, 'Oh, I see.'

Later, she led me to make love to her again, and in the dark I thought triumphantly, desperately: I am alive. Yes, one of us is still alive.

Chapter 17

STEVEN had died like a criminal, but he was buried like a king. All the hangers-on, the admirers, the friends, and acquaintances of his gregarious life came, as one of them expressed it to me, to see him off. There was a band in the funeral procession, there was Betty Ntolo and a whole parade of other entertainers, there were orations in three languages, there were wreaths three feet high. And he was not a film star, or a politician, or anyone known at the distance of fame; all these people had known him as one of themselves.

Sam, when he saw me, held my arm and wept; but I could not cry, just as, in the midst of the joy of jazz at one of Steven's parties, I could not dance. We went home to Sam's house and sat drinking the tea that his wife Ella served us in silence. Later he and I walked to the top of the ash-heap that made a promontory near their house. Spring was coming; even up there, a stripling peach-tree that had found a hold of soil under the ash put out a few fragments of thin, brilliant leaf. Beneath us, the township smoked as if it had just been pillaged and destroyed. 'I've sold my car,' he said. 'That's where I was on Tuesday when you came. I'd promised to deliver it.'

I knew how proud he was of the little Morris, how to him it was part of the modest stake in civilized living which it was so hard for Africans to acquire. 'But why? What was wrong with it?'

'My brother had to have some money. Ella's got two sisters who want to go on at school. Oh, a dozen different reasons, all boiling down to the same thing – cash.'

'That's a damned shame.'

He smiled, to put me at ease. 'Toby, man, the black skin's not the thing. If you know anybody who wants to know what it's like to be a black man, this is it. No matter how much you manage to do for yourself, it's not enough. If you've got a decent job with decent money it can't do you much good, because it's got to spread so far. You're always a rich man compared with your sister or your brother, or your wife's cousins. You can't ever get out of debt while there's one member of the family who has to pay a fine or get sick and go to hospital. And so it goes on. If I get an increase, what'll it help me? Someone'll have to have it to pay tax or get a set of false teeth.'

'Suppose you don't?'

He shook his head at me, knowing better. 'You can't. You always know yourself what it's like not to be able to finish school.'

'Steven once said it wasn't worth the effort to live as you

and Ella do, to try and keep up some sort of standard against the odds.'

'It's always worth it, for me,' said Sam, grinding the heel of his shoe into the ash. A group of children wandered up on to the ash heap; they seemed to belong there, as seals belong on rocks – the dusty skin, the bare backsides, the yellowed eyes, the animal shrillness of their wanderers' voices. As we passed them, they called out at us. 'They only know how to curse,' Sam said, and turning on me in sorrow, shame, and anger, burst out, 'The way that he died! A man like him! Running away in a car with a bunch of gangsters! D'you think if he'd been a white man that's all there would have been for him?'

I began to spend a lot of time with Sam and his quiet wife. At first I felt awkward about going to their house so much more often than I used to when Steven was alive; but they accepted me in their shy, unremarking way as if this was inevitable for all of us. The life they led was very different from Steven's; except for occasional jazz sessions, to which Sam did not take Ella, and to which she did not expect to go, they spent most of their time working; especially Ella – even when Sam played the piano or listened to gramophone records in the evening, she would sit in a corner, bent painstakingly over her books. She wanted to read for a Social Science degree, and was preparing herself, by following correspondence courses, for the time when she might be able to give up her teaching job and go to a university. She was pregnant again, but neither she nor Sam seemed to think that the care of a second child would push her hope of continuing her studies still further into the uncertain future.

At their house, I met a different sort of people from those I had become familiar with through Steven. An old Congress leader from another part of the country came to sit and listen while young doctors and lawyers criticized what Congress was doing; an elderly professor – educated in America in the days when such freedoms were at least possible for those who could afford them – spoke with the slightly soured, weary air of one who has heard everything, experienced every emotion of the speakers, many times before. These ageing men, sitting heavily on upright chairs, their legs planted apart, looked almost, already, the statues they might become one day, when the memory of what they had been was restored after the thrusting aside by the younger and more aggressive which was inevitable for them now. The old men kept the habitual gravity that the unsophisticated associate with wisdom. The young men had the swift, deliberately unpompous manner that belongs to a more worldly conception of the knowledgeable man. They seemed to have an exaggerated respect for each other; I often thought how this would change if they found themselves in a parliament and took to the conventions of white party politics. But perhaps this excessive show of respect was already merely a sign of jealousy between them. All of them, the old and the young, were passionate men – the energy of passion was coiled steely and resilient, ready, in them.

I had moved from my old flat, and in the new one, undiscovered as yet by my neighbours or the caretaker, Peter and one or two others who had been the matrix of Steven's daily life, came to see me. Even Lucky Chaputra came once or twice, awkward, worried and eager to absolve Steven from his shadow. '*He* wasn't ever in on any of my deals, he just enjoyed knowing me and my crowd.' Peter sat and drank a couple of brandies with me and didn't talk much; we'd play some records and he would criticize the players, suddenly confident on his own ground. Wherever Steven's friends gathered, in shebeens or at parties, his health was drunk, as if his death were another, and the craziest of his exploits. He hadn't been cautious enough to survive; they admired him for it. Only by the exercise of constant caution, in word, deed, and most important, mind, could an African expect to survive. But he hadn't cared to live that way; he was their sort of hero. Something in their faces when they drank to him made me shudder inwardly; I had only loved him as a man.

I had not been to the Alexanders' for weeks. I couldn't go there any more, that was all. Steven's death had provided a check, a pause, when the strain of the kind of life I had been living for months broke in upon me. While I had kept going, simply carried along, I had not consciously been aware of the enormous strain of such a way of life, where one set of loyalties and interests made claims in direct conflict with another set, equally strong; where not only did I have to keep my friends physically apart, but could not even speak to one group about the others. I went to Sam's house because there I could sit in silence, the silence of my confusion, and they would not question me. Sam, looking up from the notes he was making on a sheet of music manuscript, withdrawn behind his big spectacles, then suddenly seeing me and giving me that incongruous black sambo smile of his; Ella, earnest and big-bellied at her Mumford and John Stuart Mill. Was I with them, or were they a refuge? Could I give them up? Surrender them and accept the whisky and the jokes round the swimming pool? Why was it not as simple as giving up The High House?

Within, I started up in panic. Suppose theirs – Sam's and Ella's faces – were to be the casual face of destiny that I had known would claim me some day, the innocent unsuspecting involvement to which I would find I had committed myself, nailed the tail on the donkey with my eyes shut, and from which my life would never get free again? Like a neurotic struggling against a cure, I hugged to myself the aimless freedom that had hung about my neck so long. Suppose, when I went back to England, I should find that, for me, reality was left behind in Johannesburg?

Faunce's letter lay in a drawer in my desk. I had not answered it. He had not mentioned not having received a reply; perhaps already he had discarded 'playing with the idea' of my staying on in Africa. One or two years, longer? If I went on living here, how should I live?

Across the heads intimately drawn together in the Stratford Bar, Cecil sat with the chair beside her piled with parcels. As I came in, and hesitated a moment to find her in the smoky, vaguely underground atmosphere that always reminded me of London pubs, I saw her regard the parcels familiarly, as if, sitting there in a chair, was a friend of whom she knew what to expect. Then she saw me and hastily stuffed away, as it were, this feminine reverie, and put up her hand in her usual imperious style of greeting. She was as attractive as ever, not really beautiful, as I had once thought her, but irresistible in her defects, which she, in her vanity, crossly despaired of.

'I don't know why we always have to come to this place,' she said gaily.

I must have looked surprised, or even hurt, which was what she wanted; she knew I could not suppose her to be ignorant of why two people go back to the place where they first began to be interested in each other.

'Shall we go somewhere else?'

'No. But there *are* other places, I mean. Look at the table, so sticky you can't touch it. The man must wipe it off.'

I had not made love to her again, but we had had dinner together and gone to the theatre; our affair was running out, or had fallen into one of those lulls from which it might ignite again, mysteriously as a thread of dry grass under a piece of sunlit bottle. With all our old reservations of distrust, each pretended it was assumed that we knew why we had not seen much of each other lately, and that the reasons were satisfactory.

'You never notice much where you are, though, do you?' she said indulgently.

After a few sips of her drink, she took off her coat, grumbling about the stuffiness of the place, and sat back in a loose, bloused dress that hung beautifully on her thin body, and just caught, with a change in the sculpture of its folds, on those small, loose breasts of hers. It was green, and made her look very blonde; her hair was kept a silvery colour, now.

'That's lovely.'

'It ought to be,' she said, impressed by what she had paid for the dress.

'What's all this loot? You seem to have been buying up the town.'

'Oh – things. I'm getting older and I need expensive clothes now.'

'Why don't you come to London and show them what a model ought to look like, and get your picture in *Vogue* and what-not?' I tried hard to believe in it; we would have a mews flat together, a place of gin-bottles and dressing-gowns, smelling of love.

She smiled, the challenging smile with the corners of her mouth down. 'I'd be petrified. You'd be the only person I'd know. I can't even speak French; you've always made me feel so ignorant. Sometimes I've wanted to hit you when you've gone on talking about something I didn't have the faintest idea about.'

I said, astonished, 'What, for heaven's sake?'

She was vague with remembered frustration: 'Oh, I don't know, some Greek who was cut up in bits or was turned into a bull or something.'

We had another drink and our talk warmed and became malleable, it was like it was at the beginning, when all our mannerisms of speech were new to each other, and seemed delightful and amusing.

Suddenly she leaned back and gave a deep sigh, content, musing, as if we *had* been recalling some conversation of the past. She said abruptly, 'Darling, I'm going to marry Guy Patterson.'

The voice of a woman who had sat down with the back of her chair touching mine, cut across us with the insistent interruption of a radio turned up '. . . that sort of thing never enters my mind as a rule. But all day last Saturday, I was writing fives for sevens and sevens for fives. . . .'

I said, 'So that's why he had your stocking.' And she laughed: 'Oh no! I mean it wasn't then, the whole thing blew up in about a week. . . .' She was watching me, pleading for something.

And the woman's voice gobbled on, 'I said to my boss all morning, I said, I can't do a thing right, fives for sevens and sevens for fives, all the time, it must mean something. . . .'

'I thought he was married already.'

'He's divorced. We're all divorced. I believe you're cross.'

I said sourly, 'Of course I'm cross. I don't suppose any

man likes any woman he's been at all in love with to get married.'

'. . . Steady Joe was number five and Ascona was seven, honest to God, he took the double. . . .'

She was looking at me fondly, with the reluctance with which I have noticed women are seized the moment they have given something up. It was as if we had the licence now to discuss ourselves, to give ourselves away without the fear of giving away some obscure advantage. We had always lacked confidence in each other, and now it didn't matter any more. 'You're like a clam. I told you, I feel you watching me and keeping yourself to yourself.' She studied me, looking for the answer. 'Like an enemy,' she pleaded. And then, 'You never wanted to marry me, did you?'

'Fives for sevens and sevens for fives, I mean, could you beat it?'

'But when I marry it'll be someone like you, that I know.' And how do you suppose you'll reconcile that with a preference for the company of people like Sam and Ella, I sneered at myself? I put the thought away with all the other irreconcilables in myself; for me, the exoticism of women still lay in beauty and self-absorbed femininity, I would choose an houri rather than a companion. No doubt what I had seen in the nasty woodshed of childhood was a serious-minded intellectual woman.

'You do think Patterson's charming, don't you, you do like him?' She used his surname as if to ensure that she could convince herself that she would get an objective answer; nothing less, in the need for reassurance that beset her, would do.

I said what was expected of me, and she assented, in confirmation, with little alert movements of her head; and when I had done, looked at me, as if perhaps I might say just one thing more, *the* thing that would make it certain once and for all that she was plumping down on the right side of the balance.

So she had chosen Patterson; in her greed and fear of life, surely and fatefully, her hand had closed on him. Patterson, the hero preserved in whisky. She would have to face no challenge of any kind with him; she got him ready-made, with the triumph of a woman at a bargain sale, his purpose already proven and his windmill tilted at before she had ever known him. Again I remembered the Sunday afternoon in the empty house, when I had suddenly become aware of what she needed, what one might be able to do for her if one loved her. And now, as then, I could not give her her salvation; in the end, I had not that final word.

We began to talk of Patterson and his position in Hamish's group, and of where he and Cecil would live. 'Guy insists that we get a white woman to look after Keith, then I can be quite free.' I could see that this was the ultimate abdication of her relationship with the little boy, she would let him go, slip the bond, loosed now – even in her conscience – because he was delegated to a white woman, as she could never entirely be while he was delegated to a black one. Now there was no need at all for her to be his mother; her eyes, that had drawn their usual immediate brilliance from a few drinks, shone on some imagined future of money, travel, enjoyment, headstrong in the determined turning away of reality. I pitied her, but again, not enough to oppose her with the loss she chose for herself. I said, 'How does he get on with Keith?' And she said, 'Oh he adores him' and went on to tell me that Patterson had to go to Canada on business in three months' time, and that they would probably make that the wedding trip. Hamish had been going to go himself, but since he hadn't been too well lately – but, of course I didn't know about Hamish's high blood-pressure, I hadn't been there for so long. 'Marion thought it was because of me that you haven't been coming to The High House,' she said, with a smile. 'Because of Guy.'

'Hamish and Marion are really wonderful people,' she added, as if in defence of some amorphous threat that had never been uttered, but was sensed, like thunder in the air. But later she returned to me, free of me, no longer afraid of what she would find out about me. 'Did you really have natives coming to see you in your flat?' she asked shyly. 'Guy says that that's why you had to leave the first flat.'

'Now, where did he get that from, I wonder?'

‘There’s a man called Derek Jackson. Well, he’s a friend of Guy and he was living with some woman who had a flat in the same building. She told him about it.’ She was frankly curious: ‘You mean you can actually sit down to dinner with them and it doesn’t seem any different to you?’

‘But they’re my friends. The man I’ve known best since I’ve been here was an African. He was killed in an accident in July.’

She looked at me, fascinated. ‘And they seem like other people to you? You were really fond of this chap?’

‘Yes,’ I said, embarrassed with myself because I was explaining my affection for Steven as if I were trying to make comprehensible a liking for the company of snakes, or chimpanzees, ‘I got on particularly well with him.’

She looked down at her hands, with the long, red, filbert nails. ‘You know, I can’t imagine it – I mean, a black man next to me at table, talking to me like anyone else. The idea of *touching* their hands –’ Her hand came out in the imaginary experiment and hesitated, waved back.

I said, ‘It’s no good talking about it. Let’s forget it.’

We smiled at each other, holding the ground of the smile, two people who embrace without words on the strip between their two camps. Like an enemy, she had said of me. Like an enemy, I had lounged and taken my ease at The High House. Like an enemy: the word took away my freedom, tore up the safe conduct of the open mind.

Chapter 18

AWAY down the platform, I saw the short, hurrying figure of Sam, coming toward me from the Africans’ end of the station. A dry, warm wind of spring, that took me back full circle to the days when I had arrived in Johannesburg a year ago, lifted the covers of the pulp magazines on the vendor’s stand, and the gritty benches, the rails below and the asphalt floor seemed dusted with shining mica. He came on briskly, waving once, grinning, and I saw him say something to a black child sitting on a bundle among squatting and lounging relatives. 'I've squeezed in on the corner of Plein Street' he said, holding up my car keys a moment before putting them in his pocket. He was going to use my car while I was away in Cape Town on Aden Parrot business for a month.

'Don't forget, you must always leave her in gear, the handbrake doesn't hold.'

He laughed, 'I won't let her get away. I'll even tighten that clutch pedal for you. Where's the train?'

'Late, I suppose. My name's on the reservation list, all right, I've just looked.'

At this end of the platform, where white people stood about with suitcases and jewel-boxes and golf clubs, a woman close by turned her head and stared to hear us talking like any other friends saying good-bye. In a country where the simplest impulses are likely to be highly unconventional, it's a little difficult at first to take such astonished, curious, and even hostile glances for what they are, and to learn to feel neither superior nor angry. I had by now succeeded in doing so. For Sam, of course, it was different; but perhaps long ago he had forged himself a grin for anger, and the Black Sambo smile was also the smile of a tiger.

While we talked, the hollow, bumbling voice of the public address system began, and although I could not make out the English announcement, Sam understood the one in Afrikaans that followed. The train was going to leave from platform eleven, not from platform fifteen. With the swiftly roused excitement of people who are about to go on any kind of journey, everyone was at once caught up in a stir of talk and activity, gathering together possessions, giving each other instructions and counter-instructions, saying good-byes with the tentative tone of an orchestra tuning up. Sam and I picked up my stuff and trudged off up the platform. He was talking about his wife. 'I don't suppose we'll get down to writing, but I'll send you a telegram when the child's born. If it's a boy we're going to call it after Steven. I wish you could have been the godfather, Ella says she doesn't know anyone else she wants ...' he was panting under the weight of a heavy case, and we were being buffetted together and apart by the press of people.

'Good God,' I said, twisting my head to him, 'you talk as if I'm going for good. I'll be back in a month. The baby'll be just about born. I'm not leaving the country.' In my pocket were two newspaper cuttings; and a letter. The cuttings came from the same week-old issue of the morning paper; the issue of the day on which the paper had broken suddenly out of its accepted place in the ritual of shaving and breakfast, for there, in it, was a list of black and white people arrested on a treason charge, and half-way down the list was Anna Louw's name. She was out on bail and I had been to see her; she had been arrested because of her connexion with an organization of African women for whom she acted privately as unofficial legal adviser. The police had searched the cottage when they came for her before dawn, and the presence of Urmila, who was spending a few days there, had been an added mark against Anna.

When I read the list on that morning I felt myself suddenly within the world of dispossession, where the prison record is a mark of honour, exile is home, and family a committee of protest – that world I had watched, from afar, a foreign country, since childhood. Hours later, when I picked up the scattered pages of the paper I had left – in my haste to get to the telephone, confirmation, explanation of what I had read – I saw, on one of the fallen pages, one of those smiles that stare out, daily, from social columns. There it was – the face of Cecil, with Patterson, at a charity cabaret in a nightclub. It was a good one of her; she wore one of those dresses that look like a bandage across the breasts, and her pretty collar-bones showed as she hunched her shoulders in laughter. So I cut that out, too. The two pieces of newspaper rested in my wallet in polarity. In a curious way, they set me at peace; the letter that lay with them was the long letter to Faunce, written at last, asking him if he was still serious about replacing Hollward, and if so, telling him that I would stay on indefinitely.

'What's that? I do what?' shouted Sam, grimacing in the effort to follow what I was saying.

'What's the fuss, I'll be back before the baby's born. You talk as if I'm going away for good.'

We stopped at the top of a flight of steps; he would have to use the other, for black men, further along. 'Oh damn, I forgot about this.' I tried to take the second case from him. But he was looking at me, a long look, oblivious of the people pushing past, a look to take me in, and he was smiling slowly, wryly, the pure, strange smile of one who is accustomed to the impossible promise that will be broken, the hand, so warm on the quay, that becomes a flutter across the gulf and soon disappears.

I said, ignoring the irritated eddy of the people whose way we were deflecting, 'Sam, I'll be back for the baby's christening. If it's born while I'm away, you let me know, and I'll come back in time.'

He looked at me as if he had forgiven me, already, for something I did not even know I would commit. 'Who knows,' he shouted, hitching up his hold on the case, as people pushed between us, 'Who knows with you people, Toby, man? Maybe you won't come back at all. Something will keep you away. Something will prevent you, and we won't –' the rest was lost as we disappeared from each other down our separate stairways. But at the bottom of the steps, where the train was waiting, he was there before me, laughing and gasping, and we held each other by the arms, too short of breath to speak, and laughing too much to catch our breath, while a young policeman with an innocent face, on which suspicion was like the serious frown wrinkling the brow of a puppy, watched us.

NO PLACE LIKE

Selected Stories

'A magnificent collection worthy of all homage' – Graham Greene in the *Observer* Books of the Year 1976.

With this collection of thirty-one stories Nadine Gordimer displays all her descriptive power and acute insight, pinning Africa to the page like a butterfly for our inspection.

'This dazzlingly rich, impressively solid selection . . . The scrupulous intensity of her regard shouts from the opening sentences' – Valentine Cunningham in the *New Statesman*.

'To read these stories in their chronological order is to absorb what has been happening in South Africa over the years . . . This volume is not one to be missed by anyone who cares for real writing' – Elizabeth Berridge in the *Daily Telegraph*.

SIX FEET OF THE COUNTRY

'Gordimer's setting is Africa . . .
but in her Africa
we find ourselves' – *Washington Post*

Seven stories from South Africa's finest living writer that distil the essence of what has been happening in that country in recent years, through people and landscapes so intensely and evocatively drawn that they seem to burn a hole in the page.

'Sensuous, witty, wise . . . her qualities need no inventory from me' – Christopher Wordsworth in the *Guardian*

'To read her is to discover Africa's realities' – Paul Theroux in the *New Statesman*

The stories included here have been selected from two previous collections, *No Place Like* and *A Soldier's Embrace*.

THE CONSERVATIONIST

'A triumph of style . . . this is a novel of enormous power' – Paul Theroux in the *New Statesman.*

Mehring is rich. He has all that white privilege in South Africa can give him. Isolated, at once cold and passionate, he challenges history in his determination that nothing shall change his way of life.

But Africa cannot be bought by the white man, now.

'One of those rare works of literature that command special respect reserved for artistic daring and fulfilled ambition' – Paul Bailey in the *Observer.*

'The sounds, smells and foliage, the weaving lights of the veld, are evoked in the passages of cool delicate prose that prove their author one of the ablest descriptive writers alive' – Peter Kerr-Jarrett in the *Sunday Telegraph.*

JULY'S PEOPLE

It is war.

For years the situation has been 'deteriorating'. Now all over South Africa the cities are battlegrounds, Bam and Maureen Smales – enlightened, liberal whites – are rescued from the terror by their servant, July, who leads them to refuge in his native village.

What happens to the Smales, and to July, mirrors the changes in the world – and gives us glimpses into a chasm of hatred and misunderstanding.

'A brave and imaginative book and should be read' – *Listener*

'Every sentence she writes has the special impress of a true novelist's imagination' – *Sunday Times*

'Adventurous, powerful and despairing' – *Financial Times*

'It is so flawlessly written that everyone of its events seems chillingly, ominously possible' – *The New York Times Book Review*

LIVINGSTONE'S COMPANIONS

In these sixteen stories Nadine Gordimer deftly evokes the Africa of today, where, up-country and in town, Livingstone's 'fatal impact' still reverberates.

'Nadine Gordimer's stories are poised over the dilemmas of Africa and its denizens of both shades . . . she is always more interested in people, and what makes them happy and unhappy, than in political moralities' – *Spectator*

'Its originality is timeless and to me this is her best work: her incomparably precise, witty, unwhiny observations are webbed here with genius' – *New Statesman*

A SOLDIER'S EMBRACE

'Nadine Gordimer is one of the finest practitioners of the short-story form.' – *Chicago Tribune Book World*

When Nadine Gordimer's *Selected Stories* was published in 1976, Graham Greene called it 'a magnificent collection worthy of all homage.' *A Soldier's Embrace* demonstrates once more that Gordimer is one of the most accomplished writers now working in English, 'extraordinary not only for her style but also for her moral concern.' In this masterful new group of stories she continues to explore the emotional and physical landscapes of South Africa, through powerful themes that know no geographic boundaries.

'Nadine Gordimer tells us of the strange and immensely moving peril of being a woman in South Africa, as well as the strange and immensely moving peril of the races.' – *The New York Review of Books*

'Like the great nineteenth-century novelists she unites vast scope with minute attention to the ordinary. Gordimer's setting is Africa . . . but in her Africa we find ourselves.' – *Washington Post Book World*

Nadine Gordimer in Penguin

A GUEST OF HONOUR

'A novel of total immersions – physical, moral, social, political. It teems with human life, with landscapes of the map and of the mind, with events and insights.' – *Guardian*

James Bray, an English colonial administrator who was expelled from a central African nation for siding with its black nationalist leaders, is invited back ten years later to join in the country's independence celebrations. As he witnesses the factionalism and violence that erupt as revolutionary ideals are subverted by ambition and greed, Bray is once again forced to choose sides, a choice that becomes both his triumph and his undoing.

BURGER'S DAUGHTER

In this brilliantly realized work Nadine Gordimer unfolds the story of a young woman's slowly evolving identity in the turbulent political environment of present-day South Africa. The prison death of her father, Lionel, leaves Rosa Burger alone to explore the intricacies of what it really means to be Burger's daughter. Moving through sensuously described landscapes in Europe and South Africa, through painful love affairs and an overwhelming flood of memories that will not release her, she arrives at last at an understanding of a life bounded on all sides by forces not of her own choosing. Nadine Gordimer's subtle, fastidiously crafted prose sweeps this engrossing narrative to a tragic and triumphant conclusion.

'A riveting history of South Africa and a penetrating portrait of a courageous woman' – *The New Yorker*

and

THE LATE BOURGEOIS WORLD